The best book of short stories I ever read.

Feeling absorbed instantly into deep cultural resonance, fascinating places, mixtures and connections, unexpected difficulties, but most especially, greatest tenderness for a precious, particular father and family, was a journey of a reader's lifetime as well as a writer's.

This exquisitely written and remembered book is a treasure of love and care.

—Naomi Shihab Nye, Young People's Poet Laureate, Poetry Foundation

This powerful and beautiful novel in stories recounts the interconnectedness of the immigrant experience on a global scale. The epic scope of the collection ranges from Hawai'i to Oklahoma to California to New York to New Zealand to India, to name just a few of the stops along the ride. And what a ride it is! Beginning with the first generation of the Park family, immigrants to Hawai'i during the Korean diaspora, *All the Love in the World* does not merely retrace the painful and familiar struggle by immigrants everywhere to preserve the connection to their cultural inheritance; the book goes deeper in parsing what is left to us when those bonds are broken or erased by the overwhelming pressures to acculturate by a dominant culture. Who do we become? What is to be done? Cathy Song's contemplation of these questions is, in the end, filled with light, untinged by easy despair.

—Sylvia Watanabe, author of *Talking to the Dead*

All the Love in the World

All the Love in the World

Cathy Song

Bamboo Ridge Press

ISBN 978-1-943756-03-2

This is issue #117 of *Bamboo Ridge, Journal of Hawai'i Literature and Arts*
(ISSN # 0733-0308).

Published by Bamboo Ridge Press
Printed in the United States of America

Bamboo Ridge Press is a member of the Community of Literary Magazines and Presses
(CLMP).

Typesetting and design: Jui-Lien Sanderson
Cover art: *Mount Ka'ala* by Douglas Davenport, oil on canvas, 18"h x 24"w
Author's photo by Samuel Davenport

Bamboo Ridge Press is a nonprofit, tax-exempt corporation formed in 1978 to foster the appreciation,
understanding, and creation of literary, visual, and performing arts by, for, or about Hawai'i's people.
The organization is funded by book sales and individual donors and supplemented in part by
support from the National Endowment for the Arts (NEA); the Hawai'i State Foundation on Culture
and the Arts (through appropriations from the Legislature of the State of Hawai'i and grants from
the NEA); and the Hawai'i Community Foundation. This publication was made possible with direct
support from the National Endowment for the Arts.

Bamboo Ridge is published twice a year. For orders, subscription information, and back issues contact:

Bamboo Ridge Press
P.O. Box 61781
Honolulu, Hawai'i 96839-1781

808.626.1481
brinfo@bambooridge.com
www.bambooridge.com

5 4 3 2 1 20 21 22 23 24

For Captain Andrew Song,
in loving memory

The summer's gone, and all the roses falling,
It's you, it's you must go and I must bide.
—Frederic Weatherly, "Danny Boy"(1913)

CONTENTS

The Moon Flower Bakery

The Moon Flower Bakery was Grandfather Park's last business venture before he retired after years of service to his family. His other businesses, the laundry and tailor shop, the grocery store, had also paid the bills, but they never made him rich. He worked hard, yet his businesses never seemed to flourish. He was just too kind-hearted, his wife used to say without regret in her voice, only pride.

The small grocery store on Cane Street in Wahiawā suffered from Grandfather Park's generous credit system and relaxed accounting method. His customers would find him puffing on Chesterfields, puttering among the shelves, and would seek assistance from the man whom they knew would not turn them away. The lone source of light in the store came through the front window, creating a hushed, dimly lit setting. There was something confessional about the way they would approach him, tracking him down by the smoky trail of his cigarette. He would know even before they asked by the way they held their caps in their hands, shuffling toward him, heads bowed slightly. He received their hard luck stories as though they were injured animals left for him to take care of. Leaving the store with tins of sardines, some luncheon meat, a bag of oranges for their children, they were already out the door before they could hear Grandfather Park say, "Next time, whenever you can."

Grandfather Park left the mountains of central Korea for the sugarcane fields of Oʻahu to work as a common laborer, sailing for two weeks across the Pacific Ocean on the *America Maru*. After his contract year was over, having proven to be a hard worker and a natural leader, probably due to his height and large frame, he stayed on at the plantation, leading crews to repair the water systems in the vast fields of the ʻEwa plain. After learning to drive a truck, he drove crews to the various work sites in progress around the plantation. Reliable, he was promoted to better paying jobs, first at the plantation warehouse where he was in charge of delivering and returning equipment to and from the fields, and later, transferring provisions to the company stores in ʻEwa and Waipahu from the piers in Honolulu. By the time he married, he had been a bachelor for eighteen years, working like a miner, spending most of his time underground, directing crews in excavating the deeper layers of rock beneath the softer volcanic surfaces which had to be broken into manageable sizes and then carted away before the land could be used. There was always the threat of collapse as the men worked in the tunnels they had dug long after the sun went down, working to exhaustion by the light of kerosene lamps.

Moving out of the shadows of thankless anonymity, he felt he had attained a level of respectability when he secured one of the concession rights to run a tailor shop and a laundry service at Schofield Barracks for the 13th Field Artillery Division. He never saw the job as menial. In fact, he felt as if he himself had joined the military, and having done so, attained a kind of promotion. To provide the soldiers of his adopted country with clean, neatly pressed uniforms was a thoroughly respectable business. Even at the beginning when he and his young wife were just starting out, he felt a deep sense of honor in the early mornings, scrubbing the clothes with a tub and washboard on the stream banks near the barracks.

They wrung the clothes by hand. The starch his wife had concocted was applied over the clothes, which were then wrung once more and spread on the surrounding bushes to dry. After lunch, whether or not the clothes were dry, they were taken to the shop to be pressed with coal-heated irons. Soon he was able to buy his wife a sewing machine, and with that she was able to increase their profits by sewing caps and ties for the soldiers and offering alteration services not only for the soldiers but for their wives as well. Grandfather Park's reputation grew for swift delivery of the impeccable creases and the brightest whites. At great cost to his wife's health, Grandfather Park was one of the first practitioners of 24-hour service.

Grandfather Park had a sweet tooth. All during the war, with sugar in short supply, his tooth ached. Tobacco could not squelch it. He tried to irrigate his tooth with sugar from the sweetest fruits. Mango, lychee, guava, mountain apple did not satisfy the craving. A dormant diabetic, he dreamed of the very poison his body craved.

By the time the Moon Flower Bakery was a reality, he could only eat the sweets with his eyes. He filled the shelves of his sweet shop with cream puffs, éclairs, Long Johns, custard pies, glazed donuts, and flaky buns filled with red bean paste, the one thing his wife let him borrow from the Japanese.

Enemy sweets.

He longed for.

How the Moon Flower Bakery got its name, according to family lore, was because of the lotus seeds Grandmother Park brought from her father's house near Pusan when she came to Hawai'i as a picture bride. The same wicker woven suitcase that carried the precious seeds across the Pacific Ocean also carried the photograph of Grandfather Park, dressed in a borrowed suit, hair greased with pomade. The man she had with her family's blessings and the assistance of an eager go-between consented to marry. Having seen the land of the morning calm occupied and ruled by the arrogant Japanese, the prospect of marrying a man so much older and so far away seemed a practical solution for a future that promised only degradation. The past and the future, wrapped in a silk drawstring pouch, lay folded in the dark of the present moment, an ocean passage of seasickness and uncertainty. The present moment remained closed to those early years like the dried seedpods she would unwrap in her misery as if their soft rattling could dispel the loneliness. At night, as her husband groped for her, she would stare at the newspapers plastered to the walls with rice paste, allowing an illusion of privacy to the rooms let to the laborers and their families. She would stare at the walls as if the strange alphabet had sprung like worms from the cocoons of paste stuck in the cracks.

Luckily, her husband had no physical defect, consoled some of the other immigrant wives at the camp. Some of the women had been cruelly deceived, holding photographs of husbands who never existed. Common was the use of handsome stand-ins or photographs taken twenty years earlier when the prospective grooms were young. Gimpy legs were a reality as well as bolo bolo heads, bad breath, rotten teeth, no teeth, puka puka faces with pockmarks the size of rice kernels, missing or non-working appendages—chagee too small, chagee broken, or worse, chagee too big! At this the wives slapped their thighs and howled, but they all agreed the very worst were the wife beaters who were always the drunkards. So what was she complaining about? To them, Grandmother Park had appeared to land right side up, with a very able-bodied husband.

Morning sickness replaced seasickness, the continual upheaval in her belly blurred the green tassels of cane. Sometimes blue. Sometimes tall as waves. She lurched from field to kerosene stove, bright noon light to humid termite-swarming nights, the earth rumbling, opening up beneath her as she passed soft bundles of flesh, water stone children, unnamed and unformed, into and out of this life.

She shook the seeds of the dried pod, the ghost rattle, and decided to give herself fully to her husband. It was easier by then. They had left Castner Camp. With the savings and experience he had gained from progressing through the plantation system, he rented a two-story dwelling on Cane Street in Wahiawā that could serve as both a business and a residence. On the first floor he opened a small grocery store. Concerned that life in the camp had been too hard on his young wife because of her inability to carry a child to term, he found a way to make life easier for her. Whatever she needed, she had only to go downstairs for it. Her husband's efforts to make things easier for her touched her. She blamed herself, thinking that her babies had not been conceived under the right conditions. Giving herself up to her husband was met with a tenderness that surprised her. No longer did they have to cover the walls with newspapers and rice paste to secure privacy from neighbors. After five miscarriages, a son was born. She named him Sung Mahn, Overwhelmingly Blessed.

Grandmother Park was in love with her beautiful baby boy. She could not hide her joy, even at the risk of a jealous ghost taking notice of her pride, her good fortune. Where other mothers might divert such unwanted attention by saying the opposite of what was true—*Such a homely baby! And what a whiner too!*—Grandmother Park exclaimed shamelessly, "He is by far the most beautiful boy! Look at his fair skin! The soft curls on his head! The light green eyes!" Indeed, his fair complexion, the wavy nature of his hair, and the light-colored eyes caused speculation among the other immigrant wives whose children came with features similar to their own. The murmurings continued when Olivia was born three years later. The same light coloring of skin, hair, and eyes. When the gossip reached

Grandmother Park's ears, she retorted, "They are just jealous." Among themselves the wives quipped, "Some rogue Russian must've sneaked across the border back in Korea."

Unlike the five other water stone babies, Sung Mahn had survived to be born into this life with a strong set of lungs and, even more important, a strong will to live. With such strength Grandmother Park was certain he would be carried through this life of suffering. The summer of his first year, the first lotus bloomed in the cool hours of the morning. Everyone was too busy to see the jewel in the opening hand, the fringe of pale lashes circling an ocean of pearls grasped in yellow light.

Into the marriage Eleanor Yee brought a single jewel of a dowry—her mother's mooncake recipe. Her mother had long passed through to the other side when Eleanor walked into the Moon Flower Bakery looking for employment. The day was blue and shining, the wind of the night before having swept through branches of eucalyptus, leaving the air pure and clarified. That was what Eleanor remembered, the blueness of the air. She stepped into the day, and it surrounded her, twirled her through the door of the sweets shop.

Grandmother Park got the first look. Thin and pale, the girl at the door had a heart-shaped face that floated on the stem of a delicate neck. Her white full-skirted dress with a scalloped hem seemed to billow in the stillness of the empty shop. Grandmother Park had the impression of a hybrid bird or flower, something she couldn't quite name except that it wasn't from around here. She thought the young woman was looking for work in the wrong place. She belonged in a dress shop.

Grandmother Park waited for the hard luck story, but it never came. No one looking like her would come looking for a job in a bakery, let alone one in a small red-dirt town. Grandmother Park waited for the injured bird to be placed in her work-worn hands for her to take care of, but it didn't happen. And she was ready to take it, lift the weight of the wings off the young girl's shoulder, take in the bird, let it rest. She knew all about the passing on of kindness. And because it didn't come, the more she wanted to help even though the girl had no point of reference for Grandmother Park to consult. She came alone without a history. Just her quietness and her mother's recipe folded in the pocket of her white dress with the scalloped hem. And a lovely heart-shaped face.

The day was blue and shining.

Into the Moon Flower Bakery walked the two granddaughters, Alexandria and Catherine, otherwise known as Alex and Kitty, respectively. After school the girls walked the short distance to the bakery. Their instructions were to come directly to the bakery, have a snack, and wait for their father, who had gone home to sleep after working the graveyard shift, to drive them home, while their mother stayed behind the counter for the rest of the afternoon. Around four o'clock Auntie O came to manage the shop until closing.

The girls knew their father worked the graveyard shift, which despite sounding spooky, explained—if he hadn't gone home for a nap and a shower—why they would find him dusted with flour, standing in the bakery white as a ghost. Rushing to greet him, clouds of pastry flour would puff like blooms of pollen on contact as they hugged him. "Moon flowers," he would say. "You two girls are my moon flowers." There was nothing scary about him.

In the early hours of the morning, their father would shower, pull on his white clothes, and drive back down California Avenue to face the mountain of flour. To be dusted all over again. Dust-blinding, mind-numbing, backbreaking work. For pebbles and peanuts.

Sometimes they imagined their white-dusted father as a miner who had spent the graveyard hours toiling at the impenetrable diamond-hard white rock which, despite his earnest efforts, yielded pebbles, barely edible. Cream puff or éclair were indistinguishable from day-old rolls. Scones crumbled into pieces of chalk. Croissants, rubbery as erasers, could not be torn in half. Look out for the toe if an oatmeal cookie fell. But for his wife's mooncakes, the Moon Flower Bakery would have long since gone under.

Kitty inherited her grandfather's sweet tooth. Every day after school while the sisters waited for their ride home along California Avenue in the red Studebaker, Kitty, under Alex's watchful eye, would linger over the trays of pastries knowing very well her feigned indecision stirred in her older sister pure agitation. Pure as cane sugar. And every day Alex would sigh, "You know you're allowed only one."

Alex took the fun out of things, like pulling too soon the plug on a still perfectly frothy bubble bath.

"Yeah, yeah," Kitty would mumble, mimicking with a rubbery mouth the words her sister always said next.

"And no more mooncakes!"

How predictable! As if Kitty didn't know that mooncakes, being the bakery's best seller, were off-limits. They sold out by the end of the day.

There was a tightness to the way Alex held her jaw. She felt afflicted with a sternness she couldn't control. She would have liked to be able to skip into the bakery like Kitty and see the same trays of pastries as though for the first time. To skip from one tired éclair to another as though the sweets were treasures from faraway lands, take delight in choosing the inevitable cream puff and spend fifteen minutes savoring it as Kitty did, while twirling on the cash register stool.

But instead she marched into the bakery behind her sister like a guard responsible for the conduct of a potential parole violator.

It didn't make her happy. And all Alex could do was get after her sister, who was so easy to please. All that sugar made her teeth ache. But her sister's sweet tooth was happy.

The girls had nothing on their mother. Eleanor was known to smoke an occasional cigarette out in the driveway away from the view of Grandmother Park's kitchen window. The girls didn't know why their mother had to hide when Grandmother Park rolled her own Bull Durham, limiting herself to one or two a day, in the afternoons when all her work was done. And so did the other mothers, Mrs. Matsuura, Mrs. Chang, and Mrs. Rebello, ladies of the neighborhood whose children ran between the mock orange hedges that separated the houses.

Their mother had never been married to anyone other than their father.

She never looked at other men in an uji way.

She didn't swear, except for the occasional "Gunfunnit."

She had never been caught in a lie.

She didn't take what wasn't hers.

She never went gallivanting around town, leaving the girls alone and, worse, without supper.

She never went out at night alone.

She loved their father Mahny.

She thought James Shigeta was almost as handsome as their father but only because he had gone to the same high school. And it was so nice to see a real Oriental in the movies, especially one so talented and good-looking.

Besides "Gunfunnit," she said "Jiminy Cricket!" a lot in the kitchen.

She got the girls into the circus free by saying they were both under six, and when Kitty made "number two" in her pants—*Good thing she was wearing ballet tights!*—and refused to sit down in the car, she made a preemptive strike by saying, "It must be a rat," before Mrs. Rebello, who was riding in the front seat, sniffed and asked in alarm, "What's that smell?" Rat, indeed. A very dead rat.

She once wondered out loud how in the world Mrs. Matsuura's husband had a geisha girlfriend in Guam, inadvertently giving herself a headache trying to answer her daughters' pestering questions.

She never went out alone at night.

Eleanor never spent money on herself. Every day she wore the same uniform, five or six combinations of sleeveless blouses and pedal pushers. After seeing the girls off to school, she headed for the bakery in a clean pair of pedal pushers, a floral or checkered-patterned sleeveless blouse labeled Bobbie Brooks or Ship'n Shore, and tennis shoes. She wore the same uniform to the market, the post office, and the library. With her shoulder length hair tied neatly in a high ponytail, she could have easily passed for a teen-aged babysitter when the girls were with her.

Her closet revealed no treasures when the girls, looking to play dress-up, searched inside. Finding nothing of use, they would run to the back house and raid Auntie O's room. Kitty, pleased with herself, found a solution, resorting to wearing her own crinoline. On her head. The elastic waistband fit snugly below the hairline like an enormous shower cap. Tossing back her head, she imagined the gathered nylon and rows of lace were long glamorous tresses. To Alex she looked like Geronimo.

There was a bottle of White Shoulders perfume set on the bedroom dresser, on a mirror tray. Something about that bottle made the sisters sad. The delicate beauty of it, with its glass stopper, seemed from some other world, especially when surrounded by jars of Vicks VapoRub and Pond's Cold Cream.

She wore all the jewelry she owned, a plain gold ring on her finger, a Timex wristwatch, and a gift from her in-laws—a gold-encased jade pendant with a ruby set in the middle that had been found unclaimed in the trouser pocket of a soldier once stationed at Schofield Barracks.

Before Eleanor came into the picture, Mahny Park dated white girls. He liked them and they liked him. Their fathers, mainly military men, weren't so keen. *Didn't we just bomb the hell out of people like him?* Skinny and tanned, he was muscular from having spent much of his youth helping his parents hoist bags of laundry, sacks of flour. He wasn't particularly athletic, having barely squeaked by to make third-string on Leilehua High School's football team. His thick wavy hair spelled trouble. *What the hell is he, anyway, Jap or Puerto Rican?* Not to mention the jaunty way he maneuvered his father's Ford through the high-class parts of town. If anything, he was brave. He had no problem ringing the doorbell and introducing himself to the fathers.

By the time he met Eleanor, he had honed his repertoire of romantic songs down to a whispered one line, "If I loved you . . . ." She had no fancy door to be knocked on, no door in fact, having been consigned to live in an unfinished room under the house of her half-brother and his wife. It was a long time before Mahny discovered that the invisible bell-shaped space that kept her remote and mysterious was a way of avoiding this uncomfortable fact. Once their half-brother brought home his new wife, Eleanor and her younger sister were banished to living under the house in a room that could hardly be called a basement. It was more like a concrete slab with lattice siding for walls. The three older sisters realized that the more or less happy arrangement of all of them living together in a house Sonny bought with the money their parents had left them was about to be disrupted. The three older sisters scattered to find better arrangements. Eve became a rich old lady's companion. Eileen went to the university on a scholarship. Edna got married. That left Eleanor and her younger sister, Ruth, both still in high school, to endure the degradation of being treated like servants in what had once been their home.

When Mahny came too close, something in the bell reverberated inward, and Eleanor became smaller, quieter, more infuriatingly mysterious. He couldn't get a word out of her. He would have given up—*Plenty fish in the sea!*—but when she looked at him, he felt she was asking him something about himself. He never figured it out. She remained as mysterious to him as he remained to himself.

Eleanor was hired to take over a few of the shifts Grandmother Park and Olivia shared, managing the bakery store. As with the founding father of the Moon Flower Bakery, both wife and daughter were finding fewer reasons to work there. Although Eleanor still had a year of high school to finish, the part-time hours fit her schedule. She had set out to find a job because it would mean less time spent hearing her sister-in-law's harangue as she filed her nails, only bothering to get down on her knees to appear as though she too had been scrubbing the floors moments before her husband Sonny came through the door.

Eleanor soon discovered that she had stepped into a business that no longer had direction. Mahny assumed greater responsibility as Grandfather Park slipped unannounced into retirement, slipping too soon to pass on to his son his secrets of the light touch, his natural handling of sugar and butter and pastry flour. Through the veils of sugar he was tossing across a primed pastry field, Eleanor had noticed him the day she had come looking for work.

"He really wants to be a pilot," Olivia told her one day, lingering after her shift was done. "He's applied to some school in Oklahoma for training. He just hasn't told our folks yet."

"Has he been accepted?" Eleanor ventured to ask.

Olivia was about to answer, but Mahny came through the swinging door from the kitchen and, catching the two girls laughing, reversed direction, forgetting what he was looking for. They were laughing as though they had been nibbling on something forbidden.

Olivia brought up the subject of Eleanor at the dinner table, baiting him.

"Eleanor's awfully good with the customers. Today she got Mrs. Choi to try a Long John even though Mrs. Choi said the last time she ate a Long John she got diarrhea—she thinks the custard was sour."

"Wasn't us," Grandfather Park said, reaching for a toothpick. "Must be Cakeland custard."

"How'd she do that?" Mahny said, running a barbecue rib across his teeth as though it were a harmonica.

"Get the runs? I told you, she ate a sour Long John, blamed it on us. But I say good for her, the mean old lady."

Grandmother Park shushed her daughter. She did not want anything bad said about their best customer.

"Oh, you mean how did Eleanor do it? Well, she told Mrs. Choi that the bakery used only the finest custard, whipped with the freshest eggs and the richest cream, made that very morning by the owner's son. The handsome one."

Mahny snorted.

"What do you think?" Olivia enjoyed teasing her brother.

His mother's brighter than usual greeting always alerted Mahny that Eleanor had arrived.

Ah, Eleanor!

Eleanor was the only person his mother greeted in such a way, with dramatic relief. Mahny wondered what it was about her that his mother felt she could count on.

Into the rain his mother went, now that Eleanor had arrived, running to the Ford when his father drove up. Lately, emboldened by the fact that no one had questioned his absence from the bakery, Grandfather Park didn't even bother to park the car—*What for?*—check on his son—*What for?*—discuss the pastry situation—*What for?* He had no idea how bad it was getting, his son unable to replicate the pastries that had given the Moon Flower Bakery loyal customers. Grandmother Park worried about its loss of reputation, reflected at the end of the day by too many sweets being sold at half price. But she was getting old. She had done her time. Her share of pitching in. More than her share of laundry. She wanted to relax in her recliner. Besides, the family had Eleanor now. Good Chinese girl. Intelligent people, the Chinese. Frugal, clever, hard-working, good at making money, and saving it too.

"Eleanor!" Mrs. Choi called, her chihuahua cradled in one arm, her high-quality leather purse clutched in the other. She was the kind of woman who entered a room in mid-sentence. "The Long Johns from yesterday did not give me diarrhea, but ho! the tough! The bakery is going downhill, I tell you. Used to be Wahiawā's best bakery. Careful! Cakeland is going to give you competition. Where's Mr. Park? Let me speak to him."

Mahny bumped into Eleanor as she turned to call him. She had no idea he had been standing right behind her. They jumped apart, two sparks flying across the room.

The chihuahua yelped. Mrs. Choi kissed the top of its bony head. "Where's your father, Mahny?"

"He's not here, Mrs. Choi. Can I help you?"

"Not here? No wonder the place is falling apart. Where's your mother?"

"She left for the day." Mahny envisioned her reclining, watching TV. "But she'll be here in the morning."

"Good. At least someone's minding the shop."

"Mrs. Choi, how about an éclair? On the house, of course." Eleanor slid open the glass case, a pair of tongs poised to pinch a pastry. It took Mrs. Choi a moment to answer.

"No, no. It'll be just as tough as the Long John." She waved her hand dismissively, setting off a flash of diamonds. The chihuahua yelped feebly.

"Come back tomorrow, Mrs. Choi, and try our mooncakes."

"Mooncake?" Mrs. Choi shuddered at the impossibility of such a suggestion. "Who makes mooncake these days? It's a lost art."

"We do." Eleanor straightened herself behind the counter.

"Yes," Mahny said, flashing Mrs. Choi a smile. "Please come again."

With more fluttering of her bejeweled fingers, Mrs. Choi left in mid-sentence, " . . . back tomorrow."

Eleanor arrived at six in the morning to make the first batch of mooncakes. She heard the sound of the bus as it pulled away from her and turned the corner, leaving her to walk the short distance to the bakery. She peered into the front window and saw no lights on in the kitchen. She waited, huddling in a light blue sweater, standing on the sidewalk of the mostly empty street. The few people who passed by wore their collars turned up against the remnants of the night's chill. She waited, confused. The ovens, which should have been firing through the early hours to bake the trays of pastries for the morning rush, would be cold. The fact that neither the master baker nor his son had started the day's production worried her. She began to think she would soon have to look for another job.

Mahny left the house in a hurry, as he had in recent weeks, once it became clear to him that his father would wake when he felt like it, that it was up to him to get the first trays baked. Halfway down the hill, he remembered his arrangement to meet Eleanor, who had agreed to show him how to make the mooncakes. He didn't know how long Eleanor had been waiting, alone on the sidewalk, outside the bakery. She greeted him with a quick nod. He didn't detect any disapproval for having made her wait, huddling to keep off the chill, shivering in a light blue sweater. Feeling guilty about a lot of things that morning, the thought of her walking in the dark from the bus stop and waiting for him in the chilly morning while he had arrived late in relative comfort, in a car, Mahny offered to pick her up the next time. She declined politely, wondering if there would be a next time, and went straight to work. She felt the weight of the impending mooncakes. She hoped they would be sweet and light, out of this world as promised.

Mrs. Choi was finishing the last morsel of mooncake. Her chihuahua, unusually alert, yelped in disappointment. Mrs. Choi always saved the last bite for him. Her eyes were closed, she was moaning. "Delicious," Mrs. Choi pronounced. "Heavenly!" She opened her eyes. "I'll take two dozen."

The two bakers smiled at each other. For the first time. Two sparks flew across the room. Then, as if stung, they looked away.

"No, no. I change my mind." There again went the flashing of diamonds. "I'll take all of them. Whatever you've got."

Those first mooncakes, four dozen of them, went all over Wahiawā town.

Mrs. Choi's first stop was her husband's office. She knew he was at rounds, but she came to give a box of six to his partner, Dr. Langley, and another six to their nurse, Miss Yoshimura. Miss Yoshimura shared the mooncakes with her mother, who took five to the Hongwanji. Three were placed at the altar. *Namo Amida Butsu.* And two were eaten by the ministers. Before going home, Mrs. Choi looked in on Reverend Lee at the Methodist Church. He ate one immediately and served the rest to the church ladies busy bottling kimchee for the church bazaar. Unchristian of them to resent Mrs. Choi for never volunteering, preferring to donate money and be duly acknowledged for it, they grudgingly paused to taste the treats. Speculating on the secrets of the cake, the kimchee production came to a halt. Heading home, Mrs. Choi visited her neighbor, Mrs. Kwan, who took three bites and declared the lotus paste surrounding the rich yolk honored her ancestors. With only two left, Mrs. Choi waited to enjoy them with her husband. Dr. Langley brought his box home to his wife. She gave all but one to her best friend who served them for dessert that night. Mrs. Campbell didn't think her young children would like the cakes, they looked so foreign, so she cut the five cakes into quarters. Nineteen pieces vanished from the Wedgwood plate.

When Alex was born, her father filled the bakery with white balloons and calla lilies, the closest approximation he could find to a moon flower.

Grandmother Park frowned on all that white. What had never been lost in translation was that white was the color of mourning.

Mahny loved taking care of Alex. He liked braiding her hair, buying her books and records. Small yellow records the size of teacup saucers. He bought her a phonograph player that opened like a suitcase. He bought her Little Golden Books, mostly fairy tales, which together they soon grew to know by heart. When he braided her hair at night, they recounted the tale of Rapunzel. When he tucked her into bed, he called her his Sleeping Beauty.

Since being laid off, taking care of his daughter had become a project he could throw himself into each day, turning everything into a lesson. He enjoyed the results of his efforts by her quickness. Whatever he had to teach his daughter, she eagerly lapped up. Being involved in every aspect of her care pushed away the worry that he might never be hired back by Trans-Pacific Airlines. That the company's initial estimates in hiring pilots, stewardesses, and mechanics would prove to be wrong. That there were simply not enough passengers wanting to fly between the islands to warrant the competition of two carriers. That he would suffocate under the mounds of pastry flour waiting to be rolled, pulled, and punched.

Secretly Irish, Mahny was born into a Korean body. The older he grew the more apparent to his daughters it became. Their father had been born into the wrong body.

Where did that leave them?

They clung to their mother's fragile Chinese-ness, fragile because both her parents had died when she was under the age of ten. What sense of being Chinese she had came from her three older sisters and their half-brother, who maintained the family of sisters he had inherited when he was barely out of high school. She did have her mother's mooncake recipe as a link to an ancestral place. Without history, Alex and Kitty came into contact with their mother's bell-shaped wall and met silence. They could go no further. What Eleanor knew or remembered, she would not verbalize. The only thing she could pass on to her daughters was the taste of mooncake. Sweet and round as the full moon.

It was Alex who felt truly and deeply Korean, and after the elder Parks had passed on, Alex tried to reconnect herself to herself. Her Korean self. When she approached her secretly Irish father, he would answer, "I don't know anything about them." Them being those "kimchee-eating yobos." It always made Alex cringe when he said that.

Who else but Mahny Park had made a cassette recording of every rendition of "Danny Boy" he could find? And he made copies of the master tape for his daughters when they went away to college lest they get homesick. Years later, Alex chuckled when fragments of the song "Chop Suey" came to mind, how she had tried to assign that song to Kitty during their lip-syncing routines, the record spinning over and over the soundtrack to *Flower Drum Song*, how she always gave herself the better numbers. In the end, Kitty had run away from it, as she had too. In the end it was like living with their father, which was a mixed-up concoction, a hybrid dish like chop suey.

On Sunday mornings, lifting the arm of the needle, he would place it back to the beginning so he could hear his favorite singer singing his favorite song one more time. "Elizabeth Schwarzkopf! Nobody sings 'Danny Boy' like her. A voice made in heaven! Breaks your heart, doesn't it, girls?"

Eleanor felt at home the day she stepped into the Moon Flower Bakery. The plain storefront was decorated with the only ornamentation it would ever need, the blue letters of its lovely name hand-painted on plywood. The humble execution of the sign touched her, as if someone had just gone next door and bought a piece of wood and a can of blue paint, unaware of the image unfolded by the name.

Inside, except for a clock, the white walls were devoid of decoration. There wasn't even a calendar to add a splash of scenery. The ordinariness made no apologies. It was a simplicity without style, as if one day someone had set up shop quickly, sweeping the floor, cleaning the shelves in the glass cases, wiping down the walls, and getting down to the business of making pastries.

That was before Eleanor arrived. Within a few weeks Eleanor understood that the Moon Flower Bakery had seen finer days. The attention spared in the surroundings she assumed had been poured into production. Slabs of butter, bags of flour, and lacy sprinklings of sugar rolled and flattened into flakey crusts or pounded and kneaded into doughy shapes had been done with a fluidity and grace by someone who had imagined such confectionery would be his last rewards after a life of hauling rocks, digging tunnels, slicing meat, ironing trouser pleats.

In the mornings, after the girls had gone to school, Eleanor went to work at the bakery. She achieved a sense of tidiness there that she couldn't at home. At home the work seemed relentless, the clutter of toys and paper, clothes and books, appearing spontaneously like mildew in places she had just inspected, wiped, cleared. Only to bloom in some other corner, some other room.

When she entered the bakery in the morning, before opening the store to the day's first customers, she experienced a clarity of that same blue air that did not shatter the bell-shaped space but allowed it to ring softly and breathe. At the sound of the shop's doorbell, Mahny would see her through the glass window from the kitchen and squint into the sunlight as if he were near-sighted or dust-blinded from the pastry flour that pollinated every surface of skin, hair, stainless steel, wood, and concrete. He would wipe his hands on his apron the way a mechanic cleans the grease off his hands. That's how she first remembered seeing him, when she saw him at the bakery for the first time, helping out his folks. Seeing him that way now, his hair white with flour, with all the disappointments that had happened since then, he looked old. There were mornings when Eleanor thought for a moment she was seeing his father.

She made sure they enjoyed a cup of coffee together, tasting between them something old, something new, before he went home, to shower and sleep, before he came back to pick up the girls, feed and bathe them, snatch a few more hours of sleep before he returned when it seemed the whole town was asleep to move the same mountain of flour, like a bricklayer turning out the same bricks, following the same plans to a house that never got finished.

After he left, she surveyed his efforts of those graveyard hours that had not only cooled but had hardened on trays, waiting to be slid into glass cases. She hated to admit it but the pastries were looking more and more like turds—small, hard, dried out. So unappetizing she shuddered. Not wanting to add to his defeat, she resolved to suggest they stick to mooncakes. Twenty-five dollars in bills and coins in the register did not need to be counted, but she did because she liked the certainty of it. Folding the day's supply of pastry boxes in the most economical number of moves pleased her. Even during the busiest hours, she found the work peaceful, the customers friendly, the exchange of greetings and small talk pleasant.

At noon Grandmother Park came to give Eleanor a break for lunch. She went home to eat a bologna sandwich, to start dinner, to tidy the clutter. Waiting for her was the sound of Mahny sleeping, dead to the world. The blue air turned murky, sullen as the rains that gathered every afternoon. Driving up the hill toward home where the clouds gathered darkest, she could feel herself clanging inside, but the bell had been hung so deep inside the forest, no one could hear it.

Grandmother Park was pouring salt into the bathtub for the white cabbage she planned to soak overnight. Long ago she had begun using the bathtub in preparation for the production of kimchee. There wasn't a pot big enough in her kitchen for the amount she made. Pouring salt liberally over the layers of cabbage, she could have been getting a bubble bath ready for her granddaughters.

"We eat the cleanest kimchee," Kitty prattled, "because we are the cleanest people in the world."

"Or are we the cleanest people in the world because we eat the cleanest kimchee?"

"But how do you bathe if your bathtub is full of kimchee?"

"And how clean is your bathtub after a night of soaking white cabbage in salt?"

She ran outside after Grandmother Park told her to go home and take a bath. And not worry about kimchee. "It's all clean," Grandmother Park mumbled. Sometimes she just couldn't make sense of what that little girl was talking about.

Several days later, jars of kimchee appeared on the steps of Grandmother Park's porch, jars of pickled white cabbage stained with chili peppers. "Enough to feed a lot of yobos," Mahny said. Grandmother Park's impressive production now needed time to ferment.

A week passed, when Grandmother Park, who rarely crossed over the yard to their side, peered into the screened door of the patio. She was carrying two jars of kimchee, fermented according to her calculations, for their father who, for all his teasing about yobos was himself a kimchee-eating one. It was late in the afternoon during a break in the rain. Mahny was running a bath for the girls. Grandmother Park sniffed noisily. Swiss steak or beef tomato she surmised. It bothered her that her son was left to do his wife's work— bathing, cooking, taking care of children. Woman's work. When she felt most protective of him, she lost sight of things, blaming Eleanor for her absence when Eleanor was only doing her part, working double shifts to keep the family afloat since Mahny had been laid off. "It's only temporary," her husband had assured her. She wondered how long before temporary became forever.

Alex and Kitty looked up from the dining table where they were doing homework, ran to slide open the door.

Grandmother Park bent slightly to receive a kiss on each cheek, four in all from her two granddaughters. No time for juicy ones. "Where's Daddy?"

"D-A-D-D-Y!" Kitty yelled. She could always be called upon to yell. Her father called her Old Yeller, to which she added Good Speller.

"Yeah?" They heard the water shut off.

"Hams is here!"

"Hey, Ma, come in, come in."

Grandmother Park shook her head, held out the jars of sustenance. She never liked to come completely into the house.

"Thanks, Ma! We were running low."

Grandmother Park eyed the girls who had slid back to the table. "Okay, girls. Time to take a bath." He clapped his hands whenever he wanted "to get the show on the road."

The girls dragged themselves away. They knew that when grown-ups wanted to be alone something important was going to be said. Grandmother Park wouldn't have made the crossing just to bring over the kimchee. She would have called on the telephone to have the girls come and pick the jars up. They shuffled like rag dolls into the bathroom. Once out of sight they stiffened, motioned shhhh to each other, and listened.

"Is she eating?" They heard Grandmother Park ask.

They knew they were talking about their mother. Hearing no answer from their father, they could have answered for him. Their mother was shrinking, getting thinner by the day.

"Is she talking?" Grandmother Park pressed on.

Again, the girls could have answered. Yes, they had been worried that their mother didn't talk to them anymore.

"She needs to go and see a doctor," Grandmother Park said.

The girls craned their heads toward the hallway to hear their father say, "She'll be okay. She'll be okay as soon as I get called back to work."

By the time he turned three, Mahny still had not had his first haircut. Grandmother Park could not bear to cut his soft wavy locks. To keep the curls under control, she fashioned a cap out of an old pair of nylon stockings, which she placed over his head at night. He slept this way through kindergarten and into the first grade. By the middle of the second grade, Mahny was being taunted at school. *Mama's Boy!* After enduring such taunts for several weeks, he burst one day into the kitchen, seized his mother's sewing scissors, and snipped at the curls. Grandmother Park, upon finding the heap of hair on the floor, swallowed her tears, scooped up the cuttings, and stuffed them into a pillow. A tiny pillow, not much bigger than a pincushion. She kept this in bed, tucked under her own pillow, leaving a small opening, secured with a button, which allowed her to finger the curls at night. In that way she kept the little baby boy alive, the one who, all that first year, would finger her free nipple, working it furiously until it stiffened, while he sucked on the other one.

His mother's devotion found other ways of expression. Every morning she sent him to school dressed in a clean white shirt, freshly laundered and starched, and every afternoon he returned, his shirt soiled and crumpled. Mrs. Collins, the second grade teacher, began to keep him in at recess, a situation he balked at, understanding he was being punished because his teacher wanted him to keep his shirt clean. He sat sullenly at his desk, digging his pencil into the soft wood.

How unfair to be held back from taking part in the boisterous warfare he could hear outside in the schoolyard just because of a stupid white shirt! He told his mother not to bother giving him a clean pressed shirt each morning because he was only going to get it dirty anyway. That's like saying not to brush your teeth because you're going to eat anyway, was his mother's reply, heating water in a large galvanized tub. His sulking began to affect his schoolwork to the point where Mrs. Collins decided one day to walk him home after school. She wanted to meet his mother. Hesitating over the unusual request—his friends would see him being walked home by the teacher!—he complied. Mrs. Collins found Grandmother Park at the side of the house, soaping a pile of laundry with a bar of soap, preparing to boil all the whites first before washing the darker clothes. Grandmother Park straightened up and quickly wiped her hands on her apron. She thought something bad must have happened for a teacher to escort her son home. Mrs. Collins quickly reassured her that she just wanted to meet such a devoted mother, one who sent her son to school every day in a clean white shirt. *So immaculate!* She shook Grandmother Park's hand, and though Mahny remained in the classroom during recess for the rest of the school year, he sulked less, secretly relieved not to have to pretend to enjoy the rowdiness of his classmates.

Immaculate, the word the haole teacher had used, had a profound effect on Grandmother Park. Now she had a word for how she had always tried to live. Clean, starched, immaculate.

Mahny had a mother who told him he was loved every day. By contrast, Eleanor, who had lost both parents before she was ten, had a sister-in-law who told her how grateful she should be and what chore to do next. She became a boarder in her own house, the house her half-brother had been able to purchase with what little his father and stepmother had left them. Too busy to mourn the loss,

Sonny and his five half-sisters managed to stay together, the older ones pulling together resources from part-time jobs and seeing that the younger ones, Eleanor and Ruth, continued with school. There was also help from the Baptists. Although their mother had been a devout Buddhist, once she was widowed, her health diminished and soon after she died. The eldest of the five sisters, Eve, had eventually found herself among the Baptists who were happy to give Sunday school lessons along with light housekeeping work. When they heard about the plight of the family, they offered further assistance in spiritual and practical terms. Eleanor always felt that the Baptists had saved them from a life of degradation. The five sisters were given a place to go after school, food to warm the cold stone of hunger from eating leftovers Sonny brought home in tin pails from the Chinese restaurant where he worked, scaling fish, cleaning frogs, skewering squabs.

Eleanor felt she had been taken care of by a multitude of angels working tirelessly to help her along. So many efficient hands she couldn't remember. She couldn't remember to thank them all. So many prayers and dreamless nights. They blurred into an impersonal generosity she could never repay until Sonny married Stella. The older sisters—Eve, Eileen, and Edna—lit out like horses sensing an approaching storm. As the new lady of the house, Stella assigned Eleanor and Ruth a list of chores, which she kept in the ledger of her sour plum heart, crossing off debts to be paid, adjustments to be made as though the sisters were boarders. She moved in, and moved them out, down below, under the house, in a lattice-sided room on a slab of concrete. According to Eleanor's calculations, she would never be free of debt as long as she and Ruth were at the mercy of their sister-in-law. More than anything else, neither the untimely death of her parents nor the fleeing of her sisters, it was this that made Eleanor feel abandoned.

She was the daughter of a warlord whose favorite concubine had died in labor. Her infant's life merely magnified a lover's death so the warlord, in his grief, ordered the child to be thrown into the river, where she was rescued and taken to another country.

She was the child asleep in the hammock when the missionaries found her. The hammock was still swaying by the efforts of a mother who, with her last breath, gave her daughter a gentle push before she turned to the tenement wall and entered the gates of heaven.

She was the girl catching crabs in the stream that ran along River Street when her parents, unable to find her, hopped on a boat and went back to China without her.

Without her.

Left behind.

The stories she told herself helped ease the nights when the feelings of having been abandoned overcame her. The wind would whip up in the dark hours, and without the protection of secure walls and a door that could be locked, she lay awake, listening to the sounds of Sonny and Stella upstairs, the clinking of chopsticks against blue porcelain rice bowls, eating a late night dinner, a feast of meat, while she and Ruth had been fed boiled cabbage. It would be a long time before she could eat white cabbage again, a vegetable transformed by Grandmother Park's patient fermentations.

The debt grew when Stella's brother came to live in the vacant room upstairs, the room that had been theirs before Stella moved them out, insisting that she needed a spare room in case a member of her large family in Waimea on the Big Island came to Oʻahu for work, or school, or a visit. She probably had in mind her younger brother, who came soon after Eleanor and Ruth were sent to live in the room under the house.

"I'll protect you," Eleanor told Ruth, the first night they heard his heavy footsteps shuffling across the floor of what had once been their room. They didn't like how in the days that followed he would walk down into the yard and, through the flimsy lattice walls, peer inside their pitiful room. They didn't like how he sat at the dining table and never moved his legs when they needed to get past him into the kitchen. How he looked at them slowly, a smile smeared across his face that seemed to reflect a private joke he had no intention of sharing.

"If he comes down here, I'll scream. I'll scream bloody murder," Eleanor told Ruth. She would never sleep well again, plagued by a lifetime of insomnia. She developed asthma from the red dirt blowing into the diamond-shaped spaces of the lattice walls, the red dirt swirling, soiling their belongings.

Eleanor felt left behind. And though she had been carried along by the workings of goodness and charity, she remained apart, aloof, keeping to herself. She extended the invisible boundaries, and the bell took shape around her. Her innate modesty had found its shape. She answered when spoken to. She was quiet and unassuming. She made herself small. She didn't want anyone to notice her.

In keeping to herself, a profound sense of trust opened up. She could get along. She would get by. She would not be left behind. She had just about all the good Christian charity she could carry the day she walked into the Moon Flower Bakery. The air, the bell, were blue and shining.

Alex watched closely as her mother scooped with an index finger the film of egg whites still clinging to a broken shell. Another lesson in not letting anything go to waste. According to Eleanor, being wasteful was the gravest of sins. From Alex's point of view her mother's very adroit finger scooped the last remnants of things, things out of cans, out of ears, out of noses—the last two thankfully not ending up in anyone's stew.

Alex felt the lesson in good-to-the-last-drop-of-egg-whites a waste of time. Whatever last bit was scooped out ended up on one's finger. And by the time that was scraped against the rim of a batter-filled bowl, nothing was really saved. Or gained. She pointed this out to her mother.

"Not true," Eleanor countered. "There's always that little bit extra that's worth saving."

Like empty bottles of ketchup and oyster sauce stashed unwashed for one last rinsing to enhance the flavor of a stew before being thrown away.

Like discarded bathroom wallpaper making a final appearance as gift wrapping around a birthday present.

Like plastic bags reused over and over, washed and pinned on the line so that on any given day the family's laundry line consisted of rows of tiny transparent clothes.

Like three pees to one flushing.

Like floral-printed curtains having one last life as elasticized shorts.

Like pounding thickened knuckles into less than top quality short ribs to tenderize what a husband craved, weekend barbecues, never knowing the sacrifice.

Kitty watched closely as her mother scoured the bathtub—*no kimchee in this one*—working the tile grout with cleansing powder and a damp rag. And a very determined finger to ferret out the stubborn spots of microscopic mildew. Another lesson in not being sloppy. Next to wastefulness, sloppiness was to be avoided. Even if it meant one's knuckles thickened, one's skin coarsened, one's fingernails chipped. So be it. It was worth the effort.

Sometimes Kitty wondered what exactly her mother was scrubbing out, so furiously did her hands work, hands expressive as her face was not. It was as though her hands communicated what other parts of her could not. Hands busy were hands singing. Hands singing were hands praying. Hands praying were hands worshipping. Hands worshipping were hands grateful. And grateful hands sang, scrubbed, mopped, wiped, dried, washed, rinsed, folded, pinned, ironed, dusted, polished, swept, wept, stirred, cleaned.

They were the first parts of Eleanor to age. Although still in her twenties, she bore the hands of someone very old.

Mahny Park liked white girls, and the whitest of them all, the one he liked best, was Pat Blondell, whose single mother ran a dress shop in town. Without a father to stand guard against the invasion of boys white, yellow, and brown, Pat had a reputation for being fun-loving. Her mother shared a similar reputation. They were fun-loving gals. They seemed more like sisters than mother and daughter, at times dating the same men, mostly military, and in the case of the mother, occasionally married. Mahny was none of the above, and not because he was Oriental. Arlene Blondell might have dated him herself had he been willing. As long as he wasn't a Jap, it was nice to have a well-mannered young man around.

The first time Pat threw off her clothes, Mahny wanted to dive into her whiteness, creamy like a river of milk. And she laughed good-naturedly as he splashed, slim dark body darting, nibbling. Outside her bedroom window she listened for the sound of her mother's car, but it was parked in someone else's driveway.

Mahny's afternoon skinny dippings left him shivering and feverish. He looked pale yet oddly bright, especially the eyes which could see nothing in front of him—his mother peering, concerned—except the pink bedroom of the next afternoon, aloft, pink as a cloud. Grandmother Park suspected a serious depletion of her son's life force. Closely attuned to her son's life force, through which channels it flowed, the fact that it was emptying itself was certain, but where she wasn't sure. It was a devouring thing, and every day her son was getting weaker because of it. She plied him with kimchee soup, served hot and fiery, which he gagged at and refused. Unable to hold back her anger, she grabbed a spoon one day and thrust it back and forth lewdly in and out of her fist.

She did not need to speak. Her rude pantomime was enough. It was a devouring thing.

Mahny kicked back the stool and slammed the door. Only when he had backed out of the driveway did he unleash a mixture of foul words that would have made his mother's kimchee taste bland.

He drove straight to Pat's pink bedroom. He could not wait for that next afternoon. Parked in his spot was an unfamiliar car. But the laughter, good-natured, rich and milky, was familiar. It came flowing out of the bedroom window. Even the sound of the rain could not drown it. Shivering, Mahny remained stuck in his father's car.

Two days later Pat Blondell walked into the Moon Flower Bakery, looking for Mahny. She was bold like that, and friendly. Her friendliness disarmed Grandmother Park who knew Pat and Arlene Blondell as Cream Puff and Long John respectively. She named every customer according to what they usually chose. Mother and Daughter were generous, generous in the boxes of pastries they bought, generous in the clouds of perfume they swirled in, generous in the colors they wore, generous in their conversations which they didn't mind others overhearing, and generous in the affection they showed each other, arms linked, fingers laced, powdered cheeks pressed as Mother and Daughter cooed over the same selection of pastries as if they just could not decide, as if such decision-making was burdensome. They would laugh at their own silliness, apologizing to Grandmother Park for wasting her time, saying in unison, "We'll just go for some cream puffs and Long Johns."

When Cream Puff arrived without Long John, Grandmother Park folded the newspaper and slid off the stool.

"Cream puff?" Grandmother smiled in greeting.

"Not today, Mrs. Park. I'm looking for Mahny. Is he in?" Grandmother Park noticed no cloud of perfume, no loud color, only pale skin, and bright eyes that became brighter as they glimpsed Mahny rolling out the last batch of the day's dough through the glass window of the kitchen.

Grandmother Park understood at once where her son's life force had gone. Into Cream Puff—white, sweet, filling, and deadly. No wonder he was getting weaker every day, like a diabetic craving the very thing, the very devouring thing, that was the body's poison.

His mother's moaning brought Mahny out of the kitchen. Pat's attention was also diverted by the hair-pulling moans of the usually dignified woman. The lovers were too distracted to greet each other as Mahny helped his mother into the kitchen, led her to the chair where his father sat and read the paper between batches of baking. He had already gone for the day. Mahny lifted his mother into it.

Her moaning subsided. She slumped into a dramatic position, her dress hitched immodestly. Pat reached down and pulled the hem over the straps of a worn garter tab clipped to shabby stockings. She brought the newspaper Grandmother Park had been reading, returned with it to fan the old woman.

"Ma, you okay?" Mahny kneeled beside her.

"Good boy," Grandmother Park moaned. "Good boy. You my good, good boy."

Fanning her, Pat said, "Your mother sounds delirious. You think she's having a stroke?"

"Good boy. Good, good boy."

"Ma," Mahny repeated, "you okay?"

Grandmother Park smiled at her son. She wanted to convey to him her understanding about Cream Puff, but the only thing that came out was "good boy."

"Why is she saying that?" Pat asked. "And by the way, where were you yesterday?"

"Good boy, yeah? You my good, good boy."

Mahny motioned with his eyes that they shouldn't be discussing such things in the presence of his mother.

Pat whispered back, "But she's delirious."

Mahny disagreed, again with his eyes he tried to shush her from saying anything revealing.

"Good boy, yeah? You my good, good boy."

"I waited for you."

"Good boy!"

"I saw the car." Mahny couldn't hold back.

"What car?"

"Good boy, yeah?"

Mahny snatched the newspaper from Pat and began to fan the air around his mother's face. Loud flapping currents of air.

"The Oldsmobile in the driveway."

"Good, good boy."

"It's not what you think." Pat's whispering had turned into a hiss. "And I'm sorry you even thought it."

"Whose my good boy?" Grandmother Park wasn't appreciating the draft. Nor the hissing.

"Whose car?" Mahny mouthed.

"My mother's new friend."

Mahny wanted to accept this explanation. Any explanation that would erase the image of his mother thrusting the spoon in and out of her clenched fist. And here was the friendliest of girls with the milky skin who wanted him to say that he was sorry for thinking badly about her, but he was unable to say anything.

Partly induced by his mother's unspeakable pantomime, when Mahny met Eleanor, he felt defiled, untrue to himself. It wasn't that he regretted the afternoons he spent in Pat's pink bedroom. He regretted diving into the milky waves of skin and hair to avoid thinking about the letter that waited on his desk. The letter from Spartan School of Aeronautics that began "We are pleased to inform you that your application has been accepted."

Mahny was caught off guard. He was used to, if not the unabashed adoration of his mother, at least some gesture, some quickening of the pulse from the girls he met. Eleanor appeared impervious to his charm. She just didn't seem interested. She went straight to work. She wanted to finish that day's mooncakes as promised before she went to school. Her seriousness made it clear he was to watch and learn.

Watch and learn.

In the mornings that followed that first batch of mooncakes, he served as her apprentice. Her hands showed him the proportions, the right ways of consistency and handling. The lightness of touch. Too much touching soured the dough, like over-stimulating a pet, over-caressing a child. He had the right ingredients. He just needed to go lightly.

Exert less pressure.

In everything he did.

Even his small talk was passionate. Eleanor absorbed the words that came out with an explosion of pressure rather than volume, as though he hadn't quite learned how to modulate his throat, let alone his feelings. In like manner, in his presence, the way he moved his body, made Eleanor feel his impatience like a race car revved up at some imaginary starting line, full throttled but stuck. Far from being clumsy or awkward or heavy, his movements radiated heat, the inside machinery, the inner mechanics working overtime, churning relentlessly, never resting. He hadn't quite learned to put his gears in neutral.

A shortage of life force, in addition to the long hours at the bakery now that his father had slipped further into retirement and further into his Naugahyde recliner, left Mahny weak, his immune system susceptible to the flu. Years later, Alex the Weisenheimer, the nickname he called his eldest daughter throughout his life, would ask her father why the flu always came from Hong Kong, why the flu never blew in, say, from England, Norway, or Peru. The Moon Flower Bakery, following Mrs. Choi's generous distribution of mooncakes and subsequent enthusiastic patronage, stepped up the production just as Mahny's health began to decline.

Mahny couldn't remember how he dragged himself away from the last trays of mooncakes, his ears ringing with static, how he drove himself home through the rain, the steam off the pavement combined with the gasoline fumes churning into nausea, a surge he managed to suppress for the short drive home. Only when he had flung his body across the living room sofa, his own bed at that moment too far away, did the ringing diminish, the urge to vomit subside. His white apron was still attached to his body.

His mother had gone to visit her lady friends at the Korean Christian Church, but his father, dozing in his chair, awoke in the middle of a beautiful dream, one in which he was a young man again, at the sound of his son's moaning.

Slowly, as if the moaning were his own, he came to his senses, came back disappointed into his own tired body. "Why you sad?"

"I'm sick," was the answer coming at the end of a loud exhalation.

"You get one fever?" Grandfather Park heaved himself out of his chair. He reached for his son's forehead, but Mahny blocked the gesture, putting his arm across his face.

"No."

"Get one stomachache?"

"No."

"What? Get one headache?"

"No."

"What then?" Grandfather Park went back to his chair. "Must be lovesick then. You be okay."

Mahny groaned. He pulled at the apron, but the ties were knotted. They felt as thick as ropes.

Grandfather Park settled back to a reclining position, but after a few minutes, realizing he couldn't relax with his son in obvious pain, the beautiful dream over, never to return, he pursued his seemingly feeble interrogation. "So why you sad?"

"You just don't understand, Pop," Mahny muttered.

"What for I don't get? You think I stupid? I see what's going on."

While he waited for an answer, he fumbled in his pants pocket for a toothpick. He continued to wait, administering to his teeth. He was about to put the toothpick back into his pocket when it dropped on the floor.

"No need be lovesick, just tell the girl."

Mahny moaned. He kept pulling at the apron, which caused puffs of pastry flour to bloom like dandelion floss. He coughed, choking as if on a sudden dusting of pollen. "I'm sick of working at the bakery. I'm sick of you and Ma always telling me what to do. You think I'm going to be here forever. Well, I'm sick of it. You never asked me." Carried by waves of nausea, the words gushed out.

Grandfather Park stretched an arm for the toothpick, but it was beyond his reach. After considering whether it was worth the trouble, he got out of his chair and retrieved it. Since he was up, he went into the bathroom. Mahny heard his father's prodigious stream emptying into the toilet. He waited to hear the sound of flushing but instead heard his father say, "She da haole girl? Be careful, son. Just be careful. And slow down."

Turning on his side, away from his father, Mahny decided that his father was deaf, had always been deaf, and it was only going to get worse. That gave him a morsel of satisfaction.

Olivia took Eleanor aside the next day and told her that her family had decided that for the time being, they would be selling only mooncakes, and that being the case, could she handle the production alone. It would only be the two of them running things. She herself would skip school, wait on customers, box the pastries, work the cash register.

Eleanor didn't press Olivia further. She agreed, somehow knowing it was the opportunity she had been waiting for. It meant time away from Stella's demanding schedule of chores. Since her employment at the bakery, the workload at home had not decreased. Between school and the bakery job, she had to squeeze the same amount of chores into less and less hours. With the extra money she would be earning, she could pay her sister-in-law for the privilege of boarding. She heard Stella complain to Sonny that his sisters needed to pay their fair share. Well, now she could pay rent for the lousy lattice-walled room swirling with red dirt. She could repay whatever debt she owed for the acts of generosity that had saved her from a life of degradation. The thought that she could now pay her way fully was a way out of charity.

After the second batch of mooncakes burned, Eleanor tossed them into the trash bin, tore off her apron, marched out of the kitchen, and said to Olivia, "That's it. I want to see him." Maintaining a respectful distance with the elder Parks, she knew she could be direct with Olivia, the two of them being close in age. Without a word, Olivia locked the bakery, flipped the sign on the door from "Open" to "Closed." They drove up the hill in silence.

It was the first time Eleanor had been to her employers' home. What she saw, she had already imagined. The acceptance of her presence became even warmer when the Parks, leading her to his room, saw their son's response.

Eleanor held her breath as she gently inserted a spoon into his mouth, held her breath as though any disturbance of air would break the yolk of orange juice, brim it over the way even the slightest wind ruffles the surface of a pond. The metabolic rush that such patient feeding triggered made him shiver. Alarmed, she asked for someone to bring another quilt.

The fevered dreams swallowed his tongue. They swallowed the spoon that tipped drops of water, drops of broth into his mouth. They spit out chills from his pores, needles of ice, which his radiant core emitted like a distress signal. Too weak to thrash, he turned his mind ever so slowly outward with all the brilliance he could shine. He struggled to hold that beam as if it were a flashlight in which he could fix her in that moment so that when she left, she was still there.

Mist in the mirror, like a delicate mold appearing and disappearing at regular intervals, proved to be a dream he brought back with him when he opened his eyes and then shut them lest the vision of the girl holding a tiny mirror to his mouth to retrieve a sampling of breath which she brought to her own face vanish.

Unsettling to think she might not always be there waiting in the dark, in her light blue sweater, nodding hello without a trace of a smile, ducking past him as he held open the door for her. The one who entered a room utterly herself in her homemade clothes, as if she had been raised in a cave or a nunnery, who never said anything to advance herself, who remained encased in a bell-shaped sphere of solitude.

Unsettling to think he might have to be alone in the dark not quite knowing how to begin.

He began to thaw, moving day by day toward recovery. When he tried to speak she quieted him. He received each single green grape she placed like a tiny egg on his tongue. In half-waking light, he wanted nothing but the cool pendulums of breath above him. He had made up his mind. Eleanor sat on the edge of his bed, breathing, simply breathing.

Eleanor remembered those days as the happiest in her life. For someone without a history, her history began there. The mornings of the blue shining air, circulating, breathing, the bell not glass but skin. When she made and sold the first batch of mooncakes. When Mahny, standing next to her, made her feel she was a part of something.

Kitty arrived on Alex's fourth birthday. Mahny called from Wahiawā General with the news. Alex was just about to blow out the candles on the cake when Auntie O shrieked, "A new baby sister!" It was nearing the end of August. She would be starting school soon. It made Alex sad. Something about the end of summer. Something about endings.

The day her son was born Grandmother Park planted the seeds in a bucket of mud and water. By early summer the first lotus bloomed pink and fragrant like the hand of Buddha opening his mind to the world. The scent was pure, unearthly, unlike anything of this world except for the undiminished sweetness of her baby son's breath.

How the Moon Flower Bakery got its name, according to one of many appended versions of family lore, came by way of a young woman who got off the bus in a red-dirt town, carrying the wisdom of ancestors folded in her dress like a packet of precious seeds, and decided to stay.

Theories of Flight

Mahny Park was a long way from home when he arrived in
Tulsa early in the morning in early spring. He had tried to stay awake
for the final landing into Tulsa but had fallen asleep after the last
stopover. Revived by the cold air that greeted him, he felt alive to a
strange disorientation he had never experienced, and at the same
time woozy and lightheaded as if he had had too much to drink. It was
more than fatigue after the hours it had taken to fly from Honolulu
to Los Angeles, followed by three stops in San Diego, Tucson, and
Oklahoma City. It was being transported in reasonably pressurized
comfort while one slept, ate, read, and, hours later, was plunked down
in another place and time. He was in Tulsa, but at the same time
he was watching his family wave to him in the small window of the
DC-6 before the clouds hid all of them from each other. He too was
waving, hoping Eleanor knew that he was looking at her as she stood
alongside his mother and father and sister. He hoped she knew that
she was a part of them now.

Before boarding the United Airlines flight, he had never left
Oʻahu. He had never actually left the ground, the red-dirt soil of
Wahiawā until the day he took off from the airstrip near Haleʻiwa
in the Stearman biplane trainer. The exhilaration of that first flight
lesson that lifted him however briefly above the earth remained an

experience he sought to repeat. As often as he could he would drive out to the airstrip and pay Red, a crusty veteran of the recent war, for flight time, hours he racked up often without Red, who preferred a nap in his rusty hanger.

He boarded the downtown bus from the Municipal Airport, trying to hold steady to the plan he had made to stay one night at a hotel before he registered the next day at the school. He didn't comprehend what the bus driver was saying as he searched his pocket for change and, picking up his suitcase, headed toward the back of the bus. Something about the back of the bus being for coloreds. The few people on the bus were seated in the front. He didn't know why he shouldn't sit where there was more room. The bus driver waited, not leaving the curb. He was watching Mahny in the rear view mirror. Again, the driver repeated something about not sitting at the back of the bus. Mahny sat down quickly, somewhere in the middle. The bus lurched into traffic.

The drab color of the buildings, the drab color of the ground and sky, the leafless trees made him wonder if he had made a big mistake, coming to Tulsa to go to Spartan. If it doesn't get any greener than this, Mahny told himself, I'm going to California. But Spartan was the school that had accepted his application for the Airline Service Mechanics course. It would be a good way to get started, see if he liked it, at least get some kind of certification under his belt. He had told his parents it would only be for a year. He had no intention of returning to work at the bakery, but he didn't tell them that. Just give me a year was what he had told them. He had saved enough money; at least he didn't have to ask them for that. His absence would force them to sell the bakery, once they realized he had other plans, and retire, as they had been wanting to do. Eleanor had finished school, and so had Olivia. He had encouraged both of them to get an office job, something more promising than working at the bakery. There was nothing there for any of them.

He had no idea where he would spend the night. Once the bus reached downtown, he figured he would get off at the first hotel he saw. More people started getting on the bus the closer they got to downtown. Mahny watched the white people board and sit in the front and the Negroes board and head to the back. He held his small suitcase on his lap so that he didn't occupy more than one seat. As the front of the bus began to fill, the white people remained in the front, standing, even though there were seats toward the back. What constituted the back, he wasn't sure. It seemed that three-fourths of the bus was considered the front. What was left was considered the back. The Negro passengers boarded and seemed to understand just where that line began.

He had been in Tulsa a little more than an hour and he hadn't spoken a word to anyone and no one had spoken to him except the bus driver. So when he entered the Wells Hotel, he had to clear his throat several times before he inquired about a room for the night. The bus ride had made him suddenly worry that perhaps there were more rules and invisible lines he didn't know about. But the man at the reception desk made no indication that Mahny was breaking any rules. The man took the three dollars and handed Mahny a large key. It was the first time he had ever spent a night in a hotel.

All Mahny wanted was a shower and some sleep. He could have used a hearty breakfast of bacon and eggs and toast, but he didn't want to wander the streets looking for a diner. The fear that he would once again encounter that invisible line kept him from going outside. He wondered whether the diners in the area would also have rules he was too tired to negotiate. It would take him time to get the feel of the place. After taking a shower, and before getting into bed, he took out the two suits he had in his suitcase and hung them in the closet. For the trip he had worn his leather jacket, a white long-sleeved shirt, and a pair of jeans. He hung these items too, wondering how he was going to keep warm.

Mahny Park was born the year Charles Lindbergh flew his monoplane the *Spirit of St. Louis* across the Atlantic from New York to Paris. The solo journey took thirty-three and a half hours, but the extensive preparations before the flight added almost another day he would spend without sleep. Resisting the pull of sleep and the possibility of pitching the plane into the sea, Lindbergh would skim his plane lightly across the water like a mechanical dragonfly dipping its wings into the cold Atlantic, feeling revived by the ocean splashing against his face. That, and the stories of Lindbergh's roaming days as a flying daredevil in flat places like Nebraska took hold in Mahny's imagination. It seemed those flat places with so much sky compelled a person to want to fly. Walking along the wings high above the ground or exchanging planes in mid-flight as well as specialty maneuvers like spiraling in loops and spins and shutting off the engine at 3,000 feet in order to land gently as a feather to the roar of the awestruck crowds filled Mahny's mind as he glued pieces of balsa wood in his bedroom, gliders to be thrown like arrows into the air.

He was seven when he read the front-page news to his parents about Amelia Earhart becoming the first pilot to fly solo from Honolulu to Oakland. The fact that she had taken off in a Lockheed Vega from Wheeler Field, so close to home, made it seem that much more real. And just as real was her first attempt to fly around the world which, after the first leg from Oakland to Hawai'i, due to mechanical problems, she had to abort her plans at Ford Island, again so close to home. Two years later, he and his parents heard on the radio that she had disappeared over the Pacific.

The Pacific Ocean, the waters his parents sailed across from Korea, the waters he swam in off the shores at Mokulē'ia and Hale'iwa, the waters surrounding O'ahu, the tiny island where he was born, among a string of tiny islands in the center of all that water. The ocean Japanese aircraft carriers crossed when they struck Pearl Harbor.

Slipping undetected through Kolekole Pass, an auxiliary fleet of bombers and fighters fanned out on their way to disable U.S. Army fighter planes parked like sitting ducks at Wheeler Field. Returning eastward to carriers waiting out at sea, the Japanese pilots strafed Schofield Barracks. In the ensuing ground fire one of the fighters crashed near Wahiawā.

It was an early Sunday morning in early December when Mahny walked from home to meet some friends. They planned to spend the day swimming and fishing at the reservoir. Arriving before them, Mahny stopped on the bridge leading into town. He liked to look down into the water where, from that height, he could see the sky and his reflection in it. Torrents of black smoke gushing like dirty water from the direction of Schofield and explosions ricocheting across the cool air like strings of firecrackers broke his reverie. He remained transfixed, confused by what was happening, when a Mitsubishi Zero sputtered into view, flying so low he could see the pilot in the cockpit, looking down at him. On that Sunday, the Pacific Ocean had brought the war home.

Mahny had heard people say that the Japanese couldn't make airplanes, let alone fly them. He had seen cartoons in the newspaper depicting Japanese with buck teeth and slanted eyes behind thick glasses, riding planes that were as flimsy as the balsa wood ones he made. The morning Mahny saw the Mistubishi Zero slowly flying past him, the pilot having flipped back his goggles to get a better look at Mahny, a kid not much younger than himself, the war raging in other places in the world had come home. By the time the enemy pilot was dragged from the wreckage and taken to the fire station, it seemed the whole town of Wahiawā had rushed to stand in line to view the body. Mahny, crowding over the shoulders of his friends, was certain the dead pilot had been the one he had seen earlier that morning. When the pilot had pulled back his goggles as he flew slowly past, having strayed from his target or worse, perhaps having even been lost, in that singular exchange of looks, upon seeing Mahny, a boy who could have been someone from his own village, it was as if the pilot had wanted to call out to him. Mahny had been so close to home that morning when everything changed. Although the Japanese were the enemy now, Mahny carried a secret pride that a tiny country in the Far East could give the West such a beating. He had seen the Zero flying so close he could have jumped up and touched its wings.

Mahny got the breakfast he had been looking forward to the next morning. Across the street from the Wells Hotel was a diner with a large picture window. It gave him the advantage of seeing what he was getting himself into before he entered the place. There were only white people sitting at the counter and at several of the booths along the opposite wall. He opened the door, having already decided that he would take a booth. Safer that way. The counter formation seemed too conducive for the regulation of those invisible lines. If the diner wanted to separate people then the booth design was perfect. He could slide into one and, without disturbing anyone, quickly eat his meal.

A waitress came to the table, handed him a menu. And a smile. Mahny felt relieved. He had made the right choice. Always choose a booth.

"Coffee?" The waitress was an attractive middle-aged woman, her blonde hair curled and her lipstick red. Her peach-colored uniform and ruffled apron looked pretty enough to be a dress. She reminded him of Pat Blondell's mother. Even in a housecoat, Pat's mother always looked like she was going to a party. Was it Cream Puff or Long John that his mother used to call her? He couldn't remember, and not remembering made him miss home.

"Coffee?" The waitress asked again. She was still standing above him, still smiling.

Mahny managed a nod. He glanced at the menu, wanting to be ready with his order when the waitress came back.

She put down a cup and saucer. "Cream and sugar over there," she tilted her chin to the tray of condiments at the end of the table against the wall beside the napkin dispenser, while she flipped through the pages of her small notepad.

"Bacon, three eggs over easy, hash browns, toast, and coffee," Mahny recited, delivering the most words he had said since arriving in Tulsa, as if he were saying the first seven letters of the alphabet as fast as he could.

The waitress laughed. "Sure sounds like you've been holding that in! Now sip your coffee slowly, hon."

Spartan School of Aeronautics was on East Apache Street, across from the Tulsa Municipal Airport. Mahny found himself on a bus going in the opposite direction of the same route he had taken yesterday. Was it a little more than twenty-four hours ago? A good long sleep and a good hearty breakfast, well negotiated, left him feeling anxious to get the show on the road. He had no name for the same drab color of the surroundings which he had noticed yesterday. But he wasn't thinking about California. He had made it to Tulsa and he would do his best to make it work.

When Mahny got off the bus, he could see that Spartan had seen better days. He had heard about the school during the war, when he read whatever he could find about the U. S. Army Air Corps and the facilities that were taken over to provide advanced civilian pilot training to supplement the few flight training schools the Air Corps already had. The war had come so close to home the morning he saw the Zero fighter flying low above him. He watched the military maneuvers from the tailor and laundry concession his parents ran at Schofield Barracks, pressing the pleats of the soldiers' uniforms while he heard the rumbling of P-40s taking off and landing at nearby Wheeler Field.

The war was over when Mahny entered Spartan School of Aeronautics. The fact that the millionaire J. Paul Getty had once controlled and managed the school and the aircraft manufacturing division was not lost to him. Even more impressive to Mahny was knowing that young pilots from the British Royal Air Force had trained there at the beginning of the war, training with Fairchild PT-19s, PT-17 Stearmans, and P-40 Warhawks. Looking at the nondescript buildings for the first time, it was hard to imagine the place bustling with wartime activity. The war was over, and so were all the programs that had once made Spartan a lively place. By the time Mahny got off the bus on East Apache Street, Spartan was no longer an aircraft manufacturer but a maker of trailers. Instruction continued in a College of Aeronautical Engineering, School of Flight, School of Mechanics, School of Meteorology, School of Communications, and School of Instruments. He believed his chances of getting started on a career in aviation were good when he learned that Spartan had been selected by the Department of State and the Civil Aeronautics Administration to run a facility for the Inter-American Aviation Mechanic Training program. He figured being from Hawai'i was just as faraway as some of the places those Latin American students came from. He figured he would have a shot at one of the spots.

Mahny spent most of Saturday catching up on his sleep and reading old issues of *Popular Mechanics*. He stayed indoors, keeping close to the electric fan which had been twirling all day, trying to keep cool through the hottest August Tulsa had experienced in four years. By late afternoon, he was bored, and readily agreed to go to Dawson to see a movie with his roommate, Mohan Mahatra. The movie, *Ma and Pa Kettle*, was silly, and as the two friends walked to Mohan's car, they agreed that at least it had been cool in the theater and the movie had provided them with a few laughs, a diversion from the weekends that seemed so monotonous. There wasn't much to do in Tulsa if you were a long way from home. The two friends looked forward to going to school on Monday.

Sunday seemed no different to Mahny than Saturday. He spent the morning reading the newspaper by the electric fan, his most expensive purchase during his time at Spartan. He didn't regret it. The fan had been worth every penny. The days were chilly when he first arrived, but by the time May rolled around, the temperatures rose to degrees he had never experienced in the cool elevations of central O'ahu.

Mahatra seemed able to handle the heat better. "I'm from Delhi, man," he reminded Mahny. "You think Tulsa's hot? It's nothing compared to Delhi. When I go home, the first thing that hits me when the plane door opens is the smell! The hot stink smell of my hometown. It just hits you, man, like a bucket of steaming garbage."

Mahny offered the use of the fan to his friend, noticing that Mahatra never sat near the fan even when the two were in the living room together. With sweat dripping down his temples, he sat away from the circling blades, as if he didn't want to steal any of the breeze that belonged to Mahny.

Mahny wondered how he could afford a car and not a cheap electric fan. He offered this observation to his friend.

"I told you, my friend, I'm from Delhi. I'm used to sweat dripping down my face. And about the car, I have the use of it while I'm here, but I will sell it when I go back to Delhi. And when I do, I will make a profit, which will cover the expense of my flight home. It's all about planning, my friend."

The times when Mahny went out, left the apartment, he suspected that even then Mahatra didn't use the fan. He was that kind of a guy.

Mahny got up from the sofa. He would have liked a cold beer but that was beyond his budget. He opened the freezer and twisted some ice cubes from the tray. Standing at the sink, he gulped down two glasses of iced water, opened the refrigerator and surveyed the all but barren shelves. A carton of milk, half a dozen eggs, two limp carrots, and a head of lettuce that was starting to turn. He missed the short ribs his mother made on Sundays, crouching over the small charcoal grill in the yard, tending to the meat she had marinated overnight. If she could, he knew she would send him jars of kimchee, if she knew how he was eating, mostly canned goods and bologna sandwiches.

He missed Eleanor. Almost six months had passed since he left her waving at the gate as the plane took off. During their separation he had written a letter once a week, usually late on a Sunday night. He couldn't afford any more stamps than that. At the beginning, there was so much to tell. He described his courses, the new friends like Mahatra he had made, the movies he had seen. He wrote to her about the nice people of Tulsa. He hadn't expected them to be so nice, especially after that first morning of his arrival when he encountered the invisible line. When he went to Dawson to see movies with Mahatra, who was as dark as any Negro, no one made them sit in the back. The two friends made quite a pair, Mahatra, the plump and swarthy gentleman from Delhi, and he, the skinny Korean kid from Wahiawā, two friends who, for all practical purposes, were just as colored as any Negro if colored meant anything other than white. He didn't write about this to Eleanor. Some things were just too complicated to write about. As he fell into the routine of school and Tulsa became less strange to him, he began to have more time to think about Eleanor. She was a good letter writer. She kept him up to date on all that was happening back home. She had found a job as a typist at Pearl Harbor, a very coveted position she assured him, and had become friendly with the many other office girls. She had moved to Stillman Lane to share an apartment with her sisters. As glad as he was that all the sisters were together again, he was sad to learn that his parents had kept the bakery and that Olivia had not been able to leave.

By ten o'clock Mahny was at the kitchen table, musing over the letter he wanted to write to Eleanor. He found himself writing about the job possibilities he had investigated, how through a classmate's fiancée's father who was a lawyer he had heard about temporary typist positions becoming available shortly through the Oklahoma Civil Service. At one hundred eighty to two hundred dollars a month, the pay was considered good. The job consisted of filling out forms for new autos and licenses, he wrote, as if he was trying to convince her about something, and he realized that that something hadn't yet been named. Turning over the page, he found himself carried by currents of emotion, expressing his feelings for her in ways he never had before. Taking stock of what he had written, he wrote in the end that his desires had not obscured his judgment.

Eight days later, on a Monday night, he wrote to Eleanor, and asked her to marry him. While he waited for her reply, he thought about how he was going to fly her to Tulsa. He knew she had some savings, but money was tight. He worried about her flying all that distance alone. It was hard to keep his mind on his projects. Working late at dusk, he slipped one day from the wing he was riveting, taking the ladder down with him as he fell.

Eleanor had never been in a plane before the day Mahny took her up in one. He thought if he took her up for a ride, within moments after the straining of the engine and a bumpy take off, she would feel the surge, then the breaking into silence that had everything to do with leaving the dust and the noise behind. The sensation of flight was like being part of an ever-expanding circle of rings, on the clouds, in the sky that made him drive out to Haleʻiwa on the weekends and spend what little extra money and time he had on flight lessons and rental fees. If he could take her up for a ride, she would understand why he was leaving to go to Spartan. The wind blew her scarf off even before Red's workhorse of a biplane left the ground. Once airborne he banked so she could see the green sugarcane fields that seemed to splash against the dry slopes of the Waiʻanae range and banked to the other side so she could see the white foam of waves breaking at Haleʻiwa. When they flew over Wahiawā he circled his family's house. He had done it before and, at the sound of the engine above their roof, as if on cue, his parents came out to stand in the yard, squint up at the sky, and wave. He looked back at Eleanor. She was waving at them, waving and, at the same time, trying to keep her hair, whipping wildly, out of her eyes.

Mahny crushed the last of a cigarette into the dirt with his shoe heel and sighed. He took in the surrounding stands of loblolly pine, the Chinese pistache turning color. From the picnic table he had in recent weeks adopted as his own, he took in the scenery as if there was something here he needed to inhale. Some of the guys at Spartan, the ones from the area, had brought him and Mahatra to Mohawk at the beginning of summer, thinking the two foreigners could use an outing. Despite their dark complexions, the two of them were looking a little pale. The classmates mostly sat around the picnic tables, smoking and drinking sodas—sometimes they even brought beer— and grumbling about their instructors. A hearty few usually left the casual circle to explore the lakes and trails of Mohawk Park. Mahny and Mahatra never felt quite as hearty.

After the heat wave of August, the cooler weather had a calming effect on him. Thinking back to the madness he had felt in August when all his thoughts had turned to Eleanor, the schemes he had dreamed up to get her here, he had to shake his head and laugh. She didn't need to be told not to fly alone, not to spend any money during her overnight stay in San Francisco, not to buy a winter coat until she got to Tulsa. She didn't need to be lured with the prospects of a job, a good paying one, a position she was sure to get. She didn't need to be told any of those things. When she replied, she wrote that although she knew things would not be smooth for them, she would quit her job at Pearl Harbor, visit his folks, and, by the way, yes. Yes.

"That over there is a Chinese pistache."

Mahny turned to see who was speaking to him. A white man in his thirties wearing a plaid quilted jacket approached him. Stopping a few feet from the picnic table, the man extended his hand.

Mahny shook it.

Still standing, the man looked around. "Lots of trees from your part of the world here. Besides that Chinese pistache, we've got the sawtooth oak, and the Chinese elm, although we call it the lacebark elm too." He sat down at the edge of the bench, across from Mahny as if the offering of that information gave him permission to sit. "Olaf Hansen, pastor at the Methodist Church on Sheridan."

Sheridan Avenue was the road that ran perpendicular to East 36th Street where Mahny entered the park. He knew of the church and, once or twice, had been tempted to go inside. It was close to Spartan and some of the guys at school went there, the married ones.

Mahny introduced himself. He felt like lighting another cigarette but decided against it.

Reverend Olaf Hansen continued to admire the trees. Mahny, not knowing what else to say, pretended to admire them too. After a while, the Reverend spoke. "You one of the boys at Spartan? You must be a long way from home." He turned his kind eyes to Mahny, who at that moment felt very homesick.

He nodded. "I'm from Hawai'i," he said, wanting to correct the Reverend. "I came to Spartan six months ago."

The wide smile that appeared on the Reverend's face seemed to say "I knew it!"

"What school? Flight? Mechanics?"

"A.S.M."

"Ah, Airline Service Mechanics." The Reverend seemed to know it well. "Married?"

"No, but I'm about to be." Other than Mahatra, no one at school knew.

The Reverend's smile grew even wider. "That's wonderful. And may I ask where and when the wedding is to be?"

Mahny couldn't resist any longer. He lit another cigarette. "In a few weeks. It depends when she can get here."

"And where is she?"

"Back home in Hawai'i. She's going to quit her job after the first week in October. Then she's got to pack her things and fly here. So I'm estimating she'll be here by the middle of next month." Telling the Reverend his plans that had seemed so complicated made them suddenly seem simple.

"Do you have a church for the wedding?"

"No." Mahny didn't want to tell the Reverend that he was planning to use a judge to perform a simple ceremony. He reminded himself to find one.

"Well, son, I think you should consider marrying in a church. Are you a Christian?"

A picture of the ladies making kimchee on the lanai of the Korean Christian Church on Lehua Street in Wahiawā flashed in Mahny's mind. He saw his mother among them. He nodded.

"Then may I suggest to you and your lovely bride that you plan on getting married at our church on Sheridan. Does that sound good to you?"

Mahny nodded. The Reverend was making it easy for him.

"Now where will the lovely bride be staying until the wedding?"

Reverend Olaf Hansen and his wife addressed the congregation the following Sunday, telling the good members of their church about the plight of the young Hawaiian couple. Foremost on the Reverend's mind was finding a place for the bride-to-be to stay before the wedding date. He grew concerned when he learned that the young man had plans to have his bride-to-be stay with him, in an apartment he had just rented on East Seminole Place. Reverend Olaf Hansen didn't have to tell the good members of the church that that wasn't ever going to happen. All he had to do was explain that the young bride-to-be needed a place to stay. A hand immediately shot up. A volunteer! Mrs. Dale said she would be more than happy to have the young lady stay as long as was necessary.

Flying the biplane over the sugarcane fields where his father had worked driving plantation trucks, digging tunnels, laying dynamite, Mahny felt released from that physical labor, the knowledge of his father's early years as an immigrant laborer complicating the burdensome weight of obligation. Once airborne, the years of laundry service his parents performed at Schofield Barracks blew off from his mind, leaving him weightless as the lightness of passing clouds. In the air, he wasn't bound to anything. He didn't have to inherit his father's labor.

While working in the shop late one night, wanting to complete his project assignments before the wedding, an old memory visited him, one he had not thought about in years. He was accompanying his father on an errand that took them through the nearby town of Waipahu, closer to sea level, "hotter than hell," his father used to say, glad he had settled the family in Wahiawā, up in the cooler elevations. Passing a row of low buildings, his father pointed out one that seemed more dilapidated than the others. "That's where Shigeru Serikaku built and flew the first plane." He said it so casually that between trying to connect what his father was saying to the old storefronts along the road, Mahny turned to look at the one his father had pointed out, receding despite his father's slow speed. "You got it wrong, Pop. It was the Wright Brothers at Kitty Hawk." Mahny wore the mantle as the family's aviation historian. "Built and flew the first plane in Hawai'i," his father said, chuckling. "Nobody talk about Shigeru Serikaku. He was one car mechanic. I was here, working on the plantation when he took one French engine and made one airplane. Can you believe that? He actually took the thing off the ground. People like give the haoles all the glory. But I tell you, Shigeru Serikaku was the Okinawan guy who built and flew the first airplane here."

Mahny put down the drill. He looked out from the hangar open to the night sky. He could hear his father's voice so close, telling him the story as if his father were perched on the wings of the BT-15 he and his fellow classmates were working on. His father never mentioned Shigeru Serikaku again, but at that moment, he felt his father's clear admiration for the humble mechanic, and at the same time, felt the same admiration for his father, who remained on the ground, destined to move physical matter—cane stalks, rocks, canned goods, sacks of laundry, mountains of sugar—until he could barely move his own body.

Eleanor arrived at Tulsa Municipal Airport on an American Airlines DC-6 early in the morning in early fall. She had an overnight layover in San Francisco, and using her own common sense, did not buy herself a coat. She did, however, buy herself a new outfit for the trip, a pearl-gray gabardine suit with a belted tie. She adjusted her navy-blue beret as the plane taxied to a stop at the unloading ramp. She did a lot of adjusting of her hat and suit in the few minutes before the door opened. Gathering her purse and a large satchel as well as the plastic bag holding two carnation lei, one for the kind Reverend and one for his kind wife, she took a deep breath, caught the sweet humid whiff of flowers, and walked into a Tulsa morning.

Homestead

Closing time at New Canton meant the owners Joe and Aggie Chin could finally sit down for a meal at one of the large round tables. They invited their employees, all five of them, to join them for a meal that Joe cooked up, usually stir-fried noodles and vegetables and a succulent fish, steamed to tender translucency, selections that weren't on the menu. Known in the area for its one dollar and thirty-five cent seven-course dinner, American or Chinese, New Canton had hit upon a winning combination. The seven-course menu was the culmination of the several years Joe and Aggie Chin had spent in the business observing what white people liked to eat—fluffy omelettes stuffed with bean sprouts and green onions, spare ribs glazed with cornstarch and honey, fried chicken doused in a syrupy lemon sauce, and deep-fried dumplings filled with pork and shrimp. The sweeter the better. The thicker the better.

Joe and Aggie Chin treated their employees as though they were family. Some of them were—Tommy, the cook, was a distant cousin; Jimmy, the assistant cook, was a son; and Deedee, the go-to-girl, was a daughter. She wasn't on the books as an employee, being twelve years old, but she got paid in cash, under the table. The three other employees were from the neighborhood—Cicero, the dishwasher, from nearby Hialeah, and the two waitresses, Miriam and

Eleanor, from Coral Gables. Miriam was a former Chinese beauty contestant and her presence was a bonus for New Canton. Aggie Chin knew she had maneuvered a coup on their rival Fu Manchu Restaurant by hiring Miriam. Fu Manchu's motto was "A New Thrill in Chinese Food." Aggie Chin heard from a few defectors that the thrill was gone for some of the lonely bachelors when Miriam went to New Canton.

"Let's eat!" Joe called as he carried the fish on a platter, spilling sauce as he bumped into the swinging doors of the kitchen. He didn't wait for everyone to gather. He set the fish on the center turntable and started to serve rice into bowls. Tommy followed with a plate of noodles.

Aggie Chin finished counting the cash in the register and stuffing the bills and coins into her alligator purse, which she kept on her lap throughout the meal, the gold tone clasp snapped shut.

Deedee waited to see where Eleanor was going to sit. She liked sitting next to her, switching her alliance from Miriam, who had more seniority than Eleanor, who was still a novelty. This wasn't lost on Miriam. She took it in good stride. It helped that she liked Eleanor. Everyone did. Eleanor was just so pleasant. And pretty.

Too good to be true, Aggie Chin had thought at first, thinking she would keep Eleanor on a trial basis, but as the months passed, she had nothing to complain about. Dependable and hardworking, Eleanor also got along with everyone. As she looked around at the full table—Joe and Tommy sitting back lighting cigarettes, Jimmy shoveling the last remnants of his rice bowl into his mouth, Cicero working a toothpick in the bottom row of teeth, Miriam reapplying lipstick with the aid of a small mirror which she kept handy in her apron pocket, and Deedee and Eleanor doodling on the back of some old receipts—Aggie Chin had to count her good fortune. With more vacationers coming to the area and so many ex-military personnel staying after the war, Miami was growing and so too would her business.

Aggie Chin made sure there was always a leftover plate for Eleanor's young husband, ever since that first night when he came for her, his clothes reeking of fuel fumes and cigarette smoke. Now it was just unspoken. A plate of leftovers was set aside for him, one he could take with him if he came late, or if he was early enough to join the table, he was invited to sit and serve himself along with the others. Aggie Chin knew this was another bonus to Eleanor's hiring. Mahny Park added something to the table, driving in after a long day at Homestead, where he was training to be a pilot. He brought excitement to the table, tales that the bleary-eyed restaurant crew enjoyed. Besides, Joe and Aggie Chin had never seen an Oriental pilot actually fly in the states. The ones they knew back home in Sacramento had to go to China before the war, volunteering with Chiang Kai-shek's Flying Tigers if they wanted to get up into the skies. The Chins couldn't help but appreciate the young man's optimism about flying one day with a commercial airline and they hoped he was right. Times were changing and, as Joe liked to say, "That was be-four, this is be-five." Feeding the young pilot was the least they could do.

Seeing Mahny standing outside, peering into the restaurant, Deedee skipped to open the door for him. He pulled at her pigtail, offering funny nonsensical rhymes to her name—"How's Deedee, my little chickadee?" and "Sweetie, Sweetie, where in the world is Deedee?"—which she knew were for her, and her alone. He got the restaurant news from her first before he had a chance to greet the others—Cicero's wife just had another baby girl, Jimmy and his girlfriend just had a fight, Miriam and her boyfriend had just made up. Whatever the news, he gave Deedee his full attention, exclaiming "Wow? Really? Well, how do you like that!" as she reported to him the breaking news at New Canton. He never kissed his wife in front of them, but Deedee, thinking she was the only one to notice, saw the light fingertip pat he placed on Eleanor's shoulder as if he were placing a blossom there, a hibiscus or a gardenia he might have picked off a night-blooming shrub before he left the airfield and got into his car.

Mahny and Eleanor drove home in the Crosley, Mahatra's old car, which he sold to them before flying back to Delhi. Although Mahatra had boasted of his scheme to sell the car at a profit, in the end, he gave Mahny the Crosley for less than he had paid for it. He didn't feel right making money off his old roommate. Old Faithful, Eleanor nicknamed the car that took them from Tulsa to Miami. They had planned to reach Memphis on the first leg of their journey when the Crosley overheated three hours outside of Tulsa. The unexpected cost of an additional night in a motel as well as a new radiator sent Eleanor into a fit of tears. More than anything it was Mrs. Dale's red velvet cake on her lap that she didn't know what to do with. They ended up eating half the cake in the shabby room of the roadside motel and sharing the other half with the elderly mechanic who patted the hood of the car the next morning and told the young couple not to worry.

They dropped Miriam off at her family's house, taking the slight detour in recent weeks since her breakup with Bob Murray. Miriam's traditional Chinese parents did not approve of their daughter going with a white man, even though he was a lawyer, and their disapproval had put a strain on the courtship. Bob continued to court their daughter by way of her parents, appearing at their front door with gifts. A bouquet of flowers would have offended them—*such a waste of money!*—and so, at the advice of their daughter, he brought them edibles. He started off with fruit, bags of oranges and avocados, then worked his way up with all manner of meat: shrimp, fish, chicken, pork. His sincerity cost him a pretty penny, but it was worth it. The Moys relented and, as Deedee had broke the news, Miriam and Bob were together again. Before Miriam got out of the car, she told them that Bob would start giving her a ride again. She added that if Mahny were held up for some reason, Bob could always give Eleanor a ride home.

Eleanor squeezed her friend's hand as if to say thank you. She didn't know what she would do without Miriam. Miriam had become like a sister to her. She knew Mahny worried about her during the long days at Homestead, thirty-five miles away. She didn't want him to worry. He had enough on his mind. She tried to make the best of the situation. Everyone she knew was trying to do the best they could.

The scent of gardenias drifted through the open window. The flower-scented nights warm enough to sleep with the windows open brought her closer to a feeling of home, the streetlight illuminating the waxy petals of the shrubs in the front yard. She had been in Tulsa through the fall and winter, and when spring came, she felt buoyed by the blossoming fruit trees and the pink and white colors of dogwood along the roads, thinking the scraggly bushes in their own front yard on Seminole Street would too cough up more than a few roses, but she was mistaken. It wasn't until the end of August when they reached Florida that she realized all the colors she had been missing. Coral Gables lived up to its pretty name. When she saw the cottage they had rented hidden behind what seemed to be an orchard of fruit trees— lime, papaya, avocado, mango, and grapefruit—she knew she was closer to coming home.

How Mrs. Hansen, Reverend Olaf's wife, managed to acquire sprigs of carnation, orchid, and fern for her and her maid of honor's bouquets for a last-minute late October wedding, Eleanor would never know. Unprepared for the generosity that greeted her, Eleanor went through that first week after her arrival and leading up to the wedding in a daze. The newspaper reporter from the *Tulsa Tribune*, who had been given a tip for a personal interest story about the upcoming reunion of a young Hawaiian couple, staked out Mahny as the ardent lover in the crowd at the airport. The reporter had rushed at them as Mahny shouted, "There she is!" and had snapped a picture that would appear the next day in the paper, much to Eleanor's embarrassment—the photo of the two of them embracing on the tarmac before they could have a private moment, a word alone. Mahny answered the reporter's questions with a confidence that made her feel in that moment estranged from the man she had flown thousands of miles to marry, as if during the long months of separation he had become a person she didn't really know. She heard him speaking on their behalf, wondering how he could know what she was feeling about Tulsa and its people when she hadn't even left the unloading ramp. "We plan to go back to Honolulu," he told the reporter, "but our hearts will be back here with these grand Tulsans. I'll never forget how grand they've been to us!" Lost in the confusion of being introduced to Reverend Olaf Hansen and Mrs. Hansen, she remembered the lei she had brought for each of them. Later, reading the article, she didn't even remember placing the lei around their necks and giving them each a kiss and a hug. Going over the events of that morning with what the reporter wrote, only then did "the tears of happiness in her eyes" seem real.

During the night, when Mahny was asleep, Eleanor felt her mind tending toward worry the way a houseplant on a windowsill inclines toward the light. Unable to sleep, Eleanor found the old habit of her mind revisiting her, the nights when worrying kept her awake beside her sleeping sister, who felt safe enough to let herself fall into sleep knowing Eleanor was there as promised to protect her. She lay awake waiting for Stella's brother to sneak down into the yard and break loose the feeble chain lock on the plywood door of their lattice-sided room under the house. The fear that kept her awake in that squalid room and continued to keep her awake was more palpable to her than the night he forced his way in. The sound of Eleanor choking woke Ruth up, and together she and Eleanor assailed him with everything but their voices—biting teeth, scratching fingers, flying fists and elbows, kicking legs. They never screamed. They never used their voices. They never spoke of it, not after, not even to each other.

Eleanor worried that her mind was starting to worry again. She tried to keep the worry to herself, but sometimes it became just too much for her. Whenever she found herself worrying about their future, Mahny always said that things would work out. Before drifting off to sleep, he would caress her, mumbling, "Remember how it worked out for us in Tulsa?"

Mahny was right when he told the reporter that they would never forget the grand people of Tulsa. She would never forget Mrs. Dale for welcoming her into her home and treating her like a member of the family. By the eve of the wedding, Mrs. Dale and her daughter, Susan, had outfitted the bride and maid of honor in long satin dresses with short butterfly sleeves to be worn with three-quarter length gloves and white veils that sprouted a fountain of tulle from feathered headbands. The mother and daughter would have supplied the maid of honor themselves if Mahny hadn't already secured the wife of one of his classmates to serve as one. Dolores Johnson had married Lao Tzu Rodriquez in his hometown of Caracas, so she knew what it was like to have a wedding far from home. At precisely five o'clock the bride and her maid of honor stood on the cement sidewalk in front of the church on Sheridan Avenue beside a gravel driveway and a vacant lot. Beyond, a row of telephone poles looked like leafless trees. There was no one to give the bride away. At the sound of the organ, Dolores squeezed Eleanor's hand and, not wanting to leave lipstick on the bride's cheek, blew her a kiss. Inside the church, Reverend Hansen waited with the groom who, in a dove gray double-breasted suit, a carnation pinned to his left lapel, was barely able to contain himself, and the best man, Mohan Mahatra who had already decided to sell his car to the newlyweds at a very good price.

Mahny checked the tire pressure, the radiator, the spark plugs, the oil gauge and, satisfied, shut the hood of the Crosley. The gas tank was full, and they were ready to go. "Some people just get in the car and drive," he said to Bob, who had been watching Mahny's meticulous preparation for the trip. Shaking his head, wiping his hands on a rag he kept handy in the trunk along with cables, rope, a jack, a lug wrench, and a spare tire, Mahny said, "Yeah, but me, I like to make sure everything is tip-top shape. Only a fool would drive off on a long trip without first making sure everything was in order." Bob was thinking about asking Mahny to check under the hood of his Plymouth but decided against it.

Eleanor and Miriam came out of the house, carrying baskets of chicken salad sandwiches and soda, laughing. They were dressed for the outing, in shorts and strapless bandeaus. "Don't want more freckles!" Miriam shouted before the men could say anything about the wide-brimmed hats that kept the sun off their faces.

The women smiled and waved to each other as they parted, each one getting into the car alongside her man. Eleanor wished they could all drive down to Key West in one car, but they had a passenger to pick up, one of Mahny's pilot friends. True Blood lived near Homestead. "It's on the way," Mahny told Eleanor. "Just a short detour. He'll just hop in."

At Spartan, many of Mahny's closest friends had been foreigners, like Mahatra and Lao Tzu. She still couldn't get over Lao Tzu's name, the fact that his parents in Venezuela had named their son after the Chinese philosopher. Mentioning her amazement at the time to Mahny, he simply shrugged. "And why not? People name their kids Aristotle or Jesus, right?" She had to agree with her husband. He always had a point. She was slowly learning that his points had a way of making her look at things differently as though he were pointing her in directions she hadn't even bothered to turn her head to see. That he felt like a foreigner himself in Tulsa probably made him feel more comfortable with Mahatra and Lao Tzu.

She should have known to expect the unexpected with Mahny. Hearing about Lao Tzu through his letters, she had expected to meet a Chinese man. And Lao Tzu had turned out to be Venezuelan. So she wasn't surprised when True Blood stepped out of a lopsided bungalow with a screened-in porch and hopped into the car. She was expecting a Muskogee or a Seminole but True Blood was white. A bald and burly white man. Whatever hair he lacked on his head was compensated tenfold by the curly blonde pelts on his forearms.

Following her glance, True Blood introduced himself. "I've got true Mayaimi blood in my veins, all that sweet water of the Everglades. Got some alligator blood too." He winked at Eleanor as though she were a girl of fourteen.

Eleanor tucked a weak smile into her shoulder and looked out the window. She hadn't meant to be rude. It was like learning how to swim, being with Mahny, learning how to swim in deeper water, ever stronger currents. At times she felt not quite up to the task.

"You know the big companies will start hiring soon," True Blood said, settling comfortably in the back seat. "They're all expanding now and looking for pilots, mechanics, flight engineers. I heard Pan American Airways is expanding routes to South America,

Africa, and even the Orient. Can you believe it? Headquarters right
here in Miami and they want to fly to all those places. That would be
my first choice, but I'll take Eastern or Delta. Even National. Once we
get our foot in the door, why, we'll be set, being there at the beginning.
It's a new dawn of aviation, I tell you. A new dawn." True Blood lit a
cigarette, flicked the match out the window. There was nothing out
there to spark and catch fire, only miles and miles of sandy coral. They
crossed the first of the long bridges.

"They better be recruiting," Mahny said, his eyes squinting at
the bright flat road ahead. The noon sun bleached the surrounding
strips of coral shoreline, with nothing to cast the barest shadow.
"That's the whole reason why I came to Homestead. Get my flight
training here, where there's so much potential given the location and
all. I can be an airline mechanic anywhere, but if I want to fly, I figure
here is the place to be. If I can get hired by one of the big companies,
maybe eventually I can get a route from the West Coast to Hawai'i. If
they're expanding routes along the Atlantic and the Gulf of Mexico,
they'll be doing the same on the other side."

Eleanor sensed True Blood was nodding in agreement. "Yeah,
sounds like a plan, a good plan."

She was familiar with the plan, the plan that kept changing.
Although she wanted to join the conversation, she remained silent.
She could barely express herself to Mahny, how did she hope to jump
in with this stranger True Blood taking up the entire back seat of the
car? Each time Mahny changed the plan on her, she would hold back
tears, nod her head, and lie awake as he snored beside her, trying to
sort out her feelings. He had a way of easing the changes he knew
would upset her, hugging her and telling her it was for the best, for
the future. When he asked her to marry him, she agreed and came to
Tulsa thinking it would be only for several months, until he got his
airline mechanic license, and then they would return home. Once she

was there, situated in the typing job he had secured for her, knowing she was happiest when she was earning money, he changed the plan, telling her he needed to get his flight engineer's license, which would make him more hirable. She kept typing, saving money, writing letters home to her sisters. And then he changed the plan again. They would be moving to Florida. She suspected he had known the plan all along and was just slowly easing her into it. She didn't speak to him for a week.

Between Key Largo and Key West, they pulled over near Big Pine Key. The wide stretch of sandy beach was ideal for a picnic, and the sandy ocean bottom pleasant for swimming. Bob and Miriam, following close behind, stopped and waved their approval.

Mahny introduced True Blood to the other couple. After meeting Miriam, True Blood whispered to Mahny, "You think she's got a sister?"

Mahny shook his friend off with a laugh. "She does, but I wouldn't let you near her."

Eleanor rolled her eyes at her husband. She had to believe True Blood was a decent sort of fellow, but she kept her distance as she and Miriam spread the picnic blanket and began to unpack the lunch baskets. True Blood wasted no time in tearing off his shirt, stripping down to bathing shorts and racing into the water. Bob popped the tops off of several soda bottles, handed them around. After three long gulps, he came up for air.

The girlfriends adjusted their sunglasses under the wide straw brims of the sun hats. Mahny didn't need to ask them to pose. At the sight of his Baby Brownie, Miriam and Eleanor crossed their bare legs and leaned back as if to laugh at the sky.

Mahny sneaked behind Eleanor while she and Miriam, sandwiches consumed, flipped through the latest issues of *Movieland* and

Screen World, and scooped his wife up. As he lifted her off the blanket, she began kicking, struggling to get out of his grip. She didn't want to go in the water, she hadn't brought her swimsuit, and she was worried about losing her hat and sunglasses in the waves. Somehow Mahny, running toward the white foamy tide, managed to get her into the water. Carrying her in his arms, he waded beyond the shore break and dunked below the surface, holding her while he squatted underwater. The cold shock of the temperature hit her. When he brought her back up he thought she was teasing him, going limp. But when he loosened his arms to look at her, he could tell she was mad. He wondered if it meant another week of her not speaking to him. He didn't know what he had done to make her so mad. He was just having fun. She still had her hat on, and her sunglasses too. And he never let go of her.

True Blood watched them from the beach. He had been strolling along the shoreline, after lunch, gathering sand dollars. He found so many that he had to use his shirt as a carrier for the fragile disks. He watched Mahny try to cajole his wife back into humor, but, boy, she was mad. She stormed up the beach, wringing her hat like she could just strangle him. True Blood had never been married, but he knew never to throw a lady in the water, especially if she was reading a magazine and looking all pretty in a hat and sunglasses.

Miriam patted a place on the blanket for her friend to sit. She didn't have a towel, but the sun was so hot Eleanor would dry off quickly. She and Bob had watched Mahny carry her into the water. They were laughing at the way Mahny ran, exaggerating his heavy load by running with bent knees, making himself appear bow-legged. All they could see was this cartoonish pantomime and a peek of Eleanor's feet wriggling at his elbows. When they reached the water, Bob turned to Miriam and grinned. "Don't you get any ideas," she warned, lowering her sunglasses. He leaned closer and began kissing her. The kisses would have lasted longer if Miriam, peering over his shoulder, hadn't seen Eleanor stomping up the beach, Mahny at her heels.

Eleanor plopped down on the blanket, wetting the pages of the magazine Miriam quickly tossed aside. Mahny sat directly on the sand, next to her. The other couple knew it wasn't Mahny's first apology since coming out of the water. "I'm sorry," he said. "I didn't mean to upset you."

Eleanor stared at the ocean. She seemed at that moment unreachable.

Bob stood up. He took his time stretching, not knowing what else to do in the uncomfortable silence. True Blood at the water's edge was a welcome sight. He walked down the beach toward him. Miriam looked at Mahny. He looked so miserable, she felt sorry for him. She had never seen Eleanor mad before, but somehow she wasn't surprised. There was a lot she held in. There were times at the restaurant when she felt Eleanor had something she wanted to say. Miriam paused to indicate to her friend that she was listening, but Eleanor retreated, backed down, clammed up.

Miriam didn't want the day that had been so lovely to be ruined. She had to say something. "Well, I'd be mad too if Bob picked me up like that without my asking, ruining my hat and hair, giving me indigestion. Don't you know you're not supposed to go into the water until you wait at least half an hour? You can get severe cramping. People drown that way."

Taking the nudge from Miriam, Mahny continued to apologize to Eleanor. "I'm sorry. I didn't mean to mess your hair, or give you stomach cramps." Mahny pitched handfuls of sand as if he wanted to bury more than just his feet.

Eleanor wrung her hat once more, wrung it as though she were wringing a chicken's neck, plopped the dripping hat on her head and, knowing she looked ridiculous, like a wet scrawny chicken herself, she laughed. Everyone was trying to do the best they could. She knew that. She just didn't know what had gotten into her.

True Blood left her a bucket of sand dollars, which she placed around the house when they got home. She placed them on the windowsills, the bookshelf, the kitchen table, placing the fragile white disks solemnly as though she were placing into the hands of silent children at an orphanage cookies that crumbled so easily. Mahny and Eleanor retained long after the smell of the sea—the waters of the Gulf of Mexico, the Florida Strait, the Atlantic—the waters surrounding them as they drove to Key West and back on the Overseas Highway, reaching the southern tip that needed just one more bridge to link them to the horizon streaked with the last feathery plumes of sunset. Night seeped its blue-black ink into the porous clouds and coral as they turned toward home. They, like the sand dollars, retained the warmth of the sand, the bleached stretches of shore, the smoothness of moonlight on the water they crossed, crossing the same long bridges, one bridge and another, crossing the moonlit water, the moon shining the way out of the desert of sand and sea and sky and into groves of cypress and pine, dropping True Blood off at his dilapidated bungalow, shining the way along the road of coconut palms, fruit trees, flowering bushes and into Coral Gables. Mahny had been right when he chose Coral Gables on the map. "It's just got to be pretty, hon. What with a name like that."

Under Aggie Chin's supervision, New Canton closed its doors early in preparation for a private party. Eleanor had protested politely against making too much of Mahny's receiving his airline pilot's certification, but Aggie Chin waved her aside, saying, "It's his graduation, of course we have to celebrate! And who knows," she paused, giving Eleanor a pointed look, "we might have something else to celebrate." Eleanor squirmed. For several weeks Aggie Chin had been dropping hints that a pregnancy was long overdue.

To Eleanor's relief, Aggie Chin's hinting at another cause for celebration was revealed by Deedee, who kept pestering her mother, asking when she could put out the party favors.

"Party favors?" Eleanor had to hand it to Aggie Chin, she thought of everything. By making it so easy for Eleanor, she made it hard at the same time. Eleanor wondered how that was possible.

Deedee carried a box from the kitchen, having been given the go-ahead by her mother.

Eleanor watched as Deedee put a fortune cookie beside each plate. "Isn't it bad luck not to let people choose their own cookie?"

Continuing her task, Deedee shrugged, saying, "Not these ones. They're special. But we can't open them until after the meal."

Eleanor took a step closer to Deedee. The deliberateness of the movement made Deedee stop. "The cookies don't say something about a boy or a girl, do they?"

Deedee scrunched her face. "What are you talking about? Mom says she got the cookie factory to put in pieces of paper that will reveal our future."

Eleanor wanted to be there to see Mahny receive the certification he had worked so hard for, but he insisted that there really was no need to bring her all the way down to Homestead for what would be a very perfunctory ceremony, held in one of the hangars, essentially a meeting and a handshake. It wasn't like the high school graduations back home in Hawai'i where relatives came with cameras, armloads of lei, and envelopes of money. When Eleanor told him that Bob and Miriam were willing to drive her down, he again told her it really would be a waste of time. Her final pitch to him was how much Joe and Aggie and Deedee wanted to attend. They could all drive down in a caravan of cars together. And if he wouldn't accept a lei from her, maybe True Blood would. With so many flowers in the yard and those spilling over the fences of their neighbors, she knew she could string a few. He remained silent. He had said enough. At that point Eleanor had backed down.

He isn't going to like this, she thought, looking around at the swags of crepe paper at the window and the cardboard letters spelling congratulations that Deedee had cut and taped on the wall, even though he had reluctantly agreed to come as soon as he could.

The black bean sauce congealed into a molasses-like Jell-O. The thick strands of egg noodle hardened into cakes. The steamed fish shrank as it grew cold, releasing one of the cloudy eyeballs from a socket. Eleanor watched it roll and plop into the clear sauce that an hour ago had arrived from the kitchen fragrant with slivers of ginger and green onion.

She sat at the table, unable to get up. One by one the men left the table after Cicero said that he really needed to get home to his wife and babies, and Bob excused himself to return to the office for a late night at his desk. Joe followed Tommy to stand outside by the dumpster and smoke a second cigarette and Jimmy, without his mother's permission, sat on the stool behind the cash register to talk on the phone to his girlfriend. Only the women stayed in their seats, staring at the uneaten platters of food.

"Can I eat a fortune cookie?" Deedee asked her mother. Aggie Chin silenced her with a stern look.

"But I'm so hungry!" Deedee complained.

"Let her have one," Miriam said. She was hungry too.

"Why don't we just eat," Eleanor sighed. "I really don't know what's keeping him. I'm really sorry," she said to Aggie Chin, her voice faltering. "I'm really sorry that he's so late. I hope nothing bad has happened to him."

Aggie Chin softened at this last remark. "You're right. Let's just eat, although it's all gone cold."

"We could heat it up," Miriam suggested. "The fish we can't, but the rest can be put back on the stove."

"I'm really sorry," Eleanor said again, "after all the work everyone has done. I hope he hasn't had an accident."

Aggie Chin couldn't sit at the table any longer with Eleanor feeling so bad. She picked up the platter of egg noodles and headed for the kitchen. The noodles nearly flew off the platter as she swerved to miss the swinging doors.

"Look who we found?" Smiling, Joe stepped aside like a host on a variety show stage. Mahny walked through the doors, looking flushed.

Eleanor rushed forward, grabbed his arm, and pulled him closer to look carefully at his face. She caught a whiff of alcohol.

Mahny straightened himself, pushed away his wife as though he were dusting off the sleeve of his jacket. He lurched to the table like a man walking the deck of a ship in heavy seas. Making it safely, he plunked down in chair, ran his fingers through his hair, and smiled at everyone. "Sorry I'm late."

"Let's see it!" Joe said, standing above Mahny. "Let's see the diploma!"

"It's in the car," Mahny said, and then as if trying to change the subject, he added too cheerfully, "Hey, folks, again, my apologies, I am really sorry, but I am really hungry!" Listening to the almost imperceptible tremor in her husband's voice, Eleanor knew that wasn't true.

"Yes, yes." Aggie Chin seemed startled into action. "Let's eat. Too bad if it's cold. Let's just eat."

Miriam began serving large spoonfuls of food. Luckily, the cover of the rice pot had not been lifted. That was important. That the rice was still warm.

Everyone began to eat. The sound of chopsticks clicking against the porcelain bowls and the inadvertent groans arising from the consumption of savory dishes seemed to have a calming effect on everyone except Eleanor. She picked at her plate, anger at the embarrassment of her husband's drunken tardiness turning her stomach into a gaseous balloon. It was bad enough that Mahny was so late, but that he was drunk as well made her seethe with fury. She was so mad, she could hardly see the plate in front of her.

Deedee ate with great speed so she could get to the fortune cookie. Her mother was in no mood to tell her to slow down and eat like a lady. She cracked open the cookie like an egg and wormed her finger into the shell as if to pull at the viscous yolk, the thread of fortune. She read for everyone to hear. "You will be a pilot for Pan American Airways." She turned to her mother as if to say, "Huh?"

Mahny put down his rice bowl. He picked up the fortune cookie beside his glass of water. He cracked it open. "You will be a pilot for Pan American Airways." He laughed, but his laugh sounded like a partial bark, something else cut in half. He threw the pieces of the cookie onto the table, crushed the tiny white strip of fortune as if it were a gum wrapper, pitched it at the table, aiming for Deedee's teacup. He missed.

The others began to crack apart their fortunes, pulling out the white strip and reading out loud the same fortune as though they were reading the same ticker tape: "You will be a pilot for Pan American Airways." They looked up and met the same expressions of puzzlement.

"Okay, okay," Aggie Chin confessed. "I just thought it would be good luck if we all had the same fortune. The fortune we want Mahny to have. The more of us have the same fortune, brings more good luck."

Miriam murmured, "Mmm. Interesting."

Tommy shook his head, scratched the side of his neck. He felt as though he were back in his village, being asked to sit on a jury. "Not how we do things in China."

Joe decided to stay out of it. He had thought it wasn't a good idea in the first place, but his wife had ignored him.

Jimmy had nothing to say.

"But I want to be a stewardess!" Deedee pouted, and ate the cookie anyway.

All Eleanor could do was wait. Wait for Mahny to say something.

The night air blowing in the open windows of the car seemed to revive Mahny. After dropping Miriam off, he grew more sober the closer they got to home. He stopped the car in front of the house, turned off the engine, but made no move to get out of the car. Eleanor was ready to listen. Mahny had redeemed them both by the end of the evening, turning what could have been a disaster into a gracious parting. He thanked them all for their friendship, for the kindness they had extended not only to Eleanor but to him. Dabbing away tears, at the end of his speech, Aggie Chin leaned over and hugged him. "Pan American Airways, is it?" Mahny had managed to joke. Believing her own good fortune, she nodded. "Why of course!"

Eleanor waited. A ruffle of breeze brushed across her cheek, a whispered scent she couldn't quite name.

"They hired everyone but me," Mahny said, staring into the dark road ahead, rooted behind the steering wheel. "I just don't get it. I had one of the highest marks."

Only then did it sink in. The hiring had already begun. "What will you do?"

"Wait, I guess. There's supposed to be more recruiting in the weeks to come. I'll just wait, try again."

"And True Blood?"

"He got picked up by Pan Am, just like he wanted. He told me not to worry, that he was sure I'd be hired soon."

"But what will we do?" Eleanor felt the panic rising in her throat.

Sensing it, he reached for her. She sank into his arms. "Don't worry, things will work out. Haven't they always worked out for us? Haven't we been lucky?"

Muffling her tears in the curve of his shoulder, Eleanor nodded. Lotus, she thought. It's the scent of lotus.

Eleanor unpinned the sheets from the line, catching the sun-warmed smell of detergent in the folds. She had learned the hard way to bring in the laundry as soon as possible before the ants started crawling from the lime tree to the grapefruit tree, using the line like a suspension bridge to get from one source of sweetness to another. She was too late. The ants had begun their migration in earnest. She brushed them off with her hands. They kept appearing spontaneously out of the woven thread. Now she would have to pick them off, one by one, in the house.

She didn't hear the car drive up. She was preoccupied with shaking off the ants, muttering her dismay.

"Hello?" A voice called from the road.

Eleanor looked through a pair of pillowcases, pulling them aside like curtains. True Blood was walking past the fence, coming across the yard, carrying a bucket.

"Brought you some crayfish." He set the bucket down and began helping her take down the laundry. "Got to get to them before the ants do. Same problem at my place. I call my clothesline the Over Pine Highway."

Eleanor laughed as True Blood flapped the sheets in the air with such force she could almost hear the ants screaming as they flew off. The more she laughed, the more he flapped. Grabbing the last pillowcase, he whipped it like a matador with a cape.

He carried the laundry and the bucket of crayfish into the house. Eleanor hurried ahead to start a pot of coffee. She knew there was a quarter of a pound cake left from breakfast. She didn't have time to wonder why True Blood had shown up so unexpectedly.

When he came into the kitchen, Eleanor felt herself shrink as if she wanted to flatten herself against the counter. It wasn't that he was a large-framed man with a wide girth. His presence filled the space because however ordinary his individual physical attributes seemed, put all together they seemed excessive. The baldness was too bald, the hair was too hairy, the body odor too odiferous. And all of it at odds with the almost shy personality. Mahny referred to him as the Gentle Giant.

The Gentle Giant sat down at the Formica table. In their full extension his legs took up most of the kitchen floor. She glanced to see if he noticed the sand dollars displayed along the windowsill.

Eleanor hurried to get the coffee served, the cake cut. She didn't like standing in full view while he sat with nothing to do but watch her. She stepped over his feet, sat down quickly, after pouring herself a cup of coffee which she had no intention of drinking. She already had the one cup she allowed herself. Any more would keep her up at night. She wanted to keep her hands busy as she sat across from him.

"Remember all the sand dollars you found? I've put them all around the house." Eleanor indicated the ones at the window. True Blood seemed to be in no hurry. Miriam would be coming soon to give her a permanent wave.

"Oh, and congratulations, by the way. Mahny told me you've been hired by Pan American. That's great news. When do you start?" It was long overdue, but she hadn't seen True Blood since the day they had driven down to Key West.

True Blood seemed uncomfortable. He took a sip of coffee, set the cup gingerly onto the saucer, and cleared his throat. "Training starts next week. Lucky I won't have to move." The mere mention of luck made him regret its usage. He looked at Eleanor. He hadn't come here to talk about himself. "God damn it, they just don't know what they're missing, not hiring your husband."

Eleanor sat back as if bracing herself for a meaty fist to pound the table. "He's waiting, someone will hire him," she said, hearing the feebleness in her sentence.

"Yeah, the two-bit cargo operation that has him flying from Miami to San Juan to pick up flowers to haul to Newark and then fly back to Miami, all on one of them old reconditioned C-54s. He deserves better."

"It's just temporary, until he gets hired on the next round." She was feeling less sure of what she was saying, what Mahny had been telling her. Ferrying cargo during the last month had taken him away on overnight trips. She had to admit it hadn't been easy, but it helped pay the bills. During the months of training what she earned at the restaurant had made them scrimp to the point where the one good meal of the day had been the one served at New Canton at closing time. Flying cargo brought in money, gave him more flight hours, and kept him around Homestead. She imagined he had put his name down on some list, and in the event his name was called, he would be there to sign right up. He had made it sound so simple. The other alternative was to find work at the airfield as a mechanic. She knew Mahny. He would if he had to, but that hadn't happened yet. He was still hopeful.

True Blood realized that she hadn't been told. After the initial recruitment, there had been two more rounds of hiring. He reached for a sand dollar, flipped the flat sea urchin in his palm as though he were about to do a trick with a coin. "Sea cookies.

That's what they call them in New Zealand." Eleanor didn't know where that was.

The potent fumes of the permanent solution stung her eyes. Miriam handed her a damp washcloth. "Breathe into it," she advised.

Eleanor didn't know whether it was the fumes or the tightness of the rollers lifting her scalp from her skull that made her eyes sting. She regretted agreeing to the procedure. Her hair was thick and naturally wavy, but Miriam said it was as unruly as a wild raspberry bush. She convinced Eleanor that a permanent wave would condition the hair, soften the wiry strands.

"Really?"

"Trust me."

Miriam squeezed the last drop of solution from the plastic bottle, moving the tip in and out of the rows of rollers as though she were putting mustard on a tray of hot dogs. "There," she said. "Now we sit and wait for the solution to set. Want a magazine?"

Giving herself over to Miriam's expertise in all matters concerning beauty, Eleanor relaxed and let her friend reign over her kitchen as though it were her own personal beauty parlor. She mentioned True Blood's visit.

"Oh, yeah? Funny he should come around when Mahny's out of town."

"Oh, I didn't get that feeling. He brought crayfish. You can take some home. I'll take the rest to Joe and Aggie. Joe will know what to do with them."

"Oh, yeah? He's always giving you things. Remember all the sand dollars?"

Whatever Miriam was driving at, she was wrong. Eleanor ignored her. "He seemed really upset that Mahny hasn't been hired yet."

"Want your eyebrows plucked while you wait?"

Eleanor removed the washcloth from her face. "Sure, why not." She held her breath while Miriam hovered over her, her friend's face so close she could see the light dusting of powder across the smooth skin.

"Give it time, that's what Bob says. He'll get hired. Just give it time."

"But what if he doesn't? He can't keep flying cargo routes."

The job of plucking the errant eyebrow hairs accomplished, Miriam stood back to examine her work. She lunged forward once more to seize upon a particularly stubborn one. "Maybe the army pilots get the jobs first. So many of them flew during the war and now that they are civilians, they all want to fly commercial. That's what Bob says. There's too many of them now, fly boys he calls them. He's glad he went into law."

Mahny carried into the house an armload of limp flowers, stalks of birds-of-paradise, sprays of orchids, and anthuriums that had been rejected by the wholesalers in Newark because they had been bruised or broken during transport. Always that risk of spoilage with perishable cargo, these represented the permissible percentage of loss. Mahny brought them home to Eleanor. He knew Eleanor would know how to revive them. They reminded him of his parents' house on California Avenue, the front yard fenced by a row of golden-beaked flowers, the pots of heart-shaped, satiny flames set on the porch, the tendrils of purple and white blossoms curling from baskets hanging under the eaves. He wished he could buy her a real bouquet, a dozen red roses, but even if he could afford such an extravagance, she would be mad at him for wasting money. She probably wouldn't speak to him. He was beginning to gauge what offense determined what punishment—the length of her silent treatments. A dozen roses? Two days worth of silence, perhaps? Freely given away by the wholesalers or considered debris and retrieved from the cargo hold, nothing about these tropical flowers could make her mad.

He heard a car drive up along the road in front of the house, stop, and drive off after the closing of the door and Eleanor's voice saying, "Thanks, again. Goodnight!"

Before she reached the door, he opened it, holding out the flowers. The sharp edges of the tropical flowers prevented them from hugging properly. He tossed them on the floor and picked her up in the middle of the living room. He swirled her around. She kissed him, but when he wanted to kiss her more, she withdrew, pushed him away, and sat down on the sofa.

"How are you, hon? Did you miss me? I sure missed you."

Eleanor pulled off her kerchief. He noticed the tight curls. He didn't think they suited her, but he said, "I like it. It suits you. Now you look like Susan Hayward."

Eleanor crinkled her face. "I don't like it. I don't know why I let Miriam talk me into it. She's always talking me into things, like this lipstick. She says Calypso Coral is just the shade I need, but I think it makes me look cheap."

Mahny sat down beside her. Putting his arms around her, he said, "Hey, did you see the flowers I got?"

She glanced at the birds-of-paradise lying on the floor. They looked like dead parrots.

"I know they're a bit bruised having been to San Juan and Newark and back to Miami, but you can put them in water, can't you? You can make them come alive again."

She nodded, trying to be agreeable. He was trying so hard, she didn't know why she couldn't try too. "True Blood came by yesterday. He brought us some crayfish."

"That was nice of him but didn't he know I was out of town? I thought he knew my schedule. How long did he stay?"

She tried to manage the flow of her words. "Not long. I gave him some cake and coffee."

"Did he talk about Pan Am?"

She nodded. She saw True Blood sitting at the kitchen table, the slice of cake untouched, turning the sand dollar over and over in his large hand as though he didn't know what to do with his own good fortune as long as his friend had none. By the time he left, she had wanted to hug him. "He seemed very upset that you haven't been hired. He said that it was a shame you're having to fly a crummy cargo route. He said you deserve better. I know, I know. Everyone is telling me to wait, just like you're telling me we have to wait. Wait for what, Mahny? Wait for what? What if you never get hired by one of those airlines you always talk about? What if you're not what they're looking for?" She stopped herself.

Mahny pulled away to the far end of the sofa. "Is that what True Blood said?"

"What? No. No, of course not. He's the one that says you deserve better. Oh, Mahny, why don't we just go home?"

"I'm not what they're looking for. You're right. That's what they told me. Three different recruiters told me that. I'm not what they're looking for."

Eleanor moved closer. "What did they mean?"

"I didn't know what they meant, until Frank Conroy took me aside and offered me a job as a flight instructor. Would you believe, me, a flight instructor, and I can't even get hired as a commercial airline pilot? I'd be training all these guys on planes the big carriers are flying now."

"What did you tell him?" Eleanor had never met Frank Conroy, but she knew he ran things at Homestead. He had hired Mahny in the interim to work the cargo service.

"I told him no, of course. I didn't come to Homestead to be an instructor. I came to fly."

"But Mahny, wouldn't that be a good job? Wouldn't it pay pretty well?"

Mahny's retelling of the exchange seemed to be for his benefit as if he hadn't yet believed it. "He said to forget it. He said they're never going to hire you, Mahny, no matter how long you hang around. Might as well be an instructor. You'd be a damn fine one, he said. He said, they're never going to hire you because what would the passengers think, seeing an Oriental in the cockpit? Hell, they just got through fighting guys like you. They're never going to let that happen."

"They're never going to let that happen." Frank Conroy had finally said it. For weeks he had been watching Mahny Park show up for interviews and come out despondent. He would have preferred being involved in another Operation Vittles, supplying pilots to man the C-54 Skymasters in the Berlin airlifts after the Soviet Blockade than watch Mahny submit unknowingly to covert forms of humiliation. He had personally taken the time to put in a good word for the young pilot. The recruiting officers interviewed Mahny for a position they were never going to let him have, nodding their heads, pretending to listen as he politely pleaded his case. Frank Conroy had worked alongside the young pilot enough to know swaggering and self-inflation were not in his nature. He found himself saying what he had hoped to avoid. The young man from Hawai'i was never going to give up. Frank Conroy had to put a stop to the humiliation.

Mahny thought about the invisible line he had encountered on that first bus ride in Tulsa. He saw it now, how it moved, depending upon the circumstances. He could be invited into the front rows of a church and treated warmly as he entered, cap in hand, deferential as a refugee. He and his young bride-to-be could be featured prominently in the town paper, the picture of the exotic couple reunited on the tarmac of the municipal airport providing a human interest story. He saw it now, the line that allowed him to sit somewhere in the middle, just as he was housed with the foreign-born students at Spartan, the brown ones with funny names like Mahatra and Lao Tzu. And now that he was a full-fledged commercial aviation pilot with hard-earned wings, he could fly in the night, in the dark, without any passengers to offend, hauling shipments of tropical flowers in long boxes that reminded him of coffins.

Aggie Chin once asked Eleanor if her mother had been the one who taught her how to fold such delicate wontons. She couldn't remember what Eleanor had said. As she observed Eleanor wrap the wontons, folding the dumplings into tiny roses to be deep-fried the American way or boiled in broth the Chinese way, it bothered her that she couldn't remember what Eleanor had said. So as not to disturb the spell of seeing the tiny roses appear one after another in Eleanor's hands, she refrained from asking again. Eleanor worked silently, knowing she was no longer being judged. Aggie Chin approved of her light quick touch, the uniformity of her dumplings.

When she first assigned the task to Eleanor, she had demonstrated the steps by placing a dollop of the pork and shrimp mixture into the middle of the flour skin and using a fingertip's worth of egg white to seal the edges. Then came the tricky part of twisting and flipping the triangle into a rose. Eleanor watched, waiting for the demonstration to be done before she produced a wonton more perfect than her boss's. Then seeing that she had rendered her boss speechless, did another one, lumpy and poorly sealed so that some of the filling oozed out. Aggie Chin was certain she had done it purposely, not wanting to outshine the boss.

Aggie Chin was glad Eleanor had a chance to get off her feet, tending to the task before the restaurant opened for dinner. Eleanor was carrying her pregnancy well, the slight swelling of her abdomen hidden by the flounce of apron. Aggie Chin suspected Eleanor was carrying a girl. She was carrying high and pointed, not low-slung and wide. What with Miriam handing in her two-week notice after Bob's proposal and Eleanor soon to be out of commission once the baby was born, Aggie Chin had placed a sign in the window as well as an ad in the paper for more help. Jimmy was apprenticing at a car repair shop, which forced Joe to take more responsibility in the kitchen. Adjusting to the demotion, Tommy, who had been used to barking orders as head cook, made noises about going back to China. Gone were the savory meals served after the doors closed. The muted mood at the table had turned as cold as the leftovers from the seven-course buffet. It was starting to occur to Aggie Chin that maybe it was time to start over again. Get out of the restaurant business. Head back to Sacramento. Make better plans for Deedee than she'd had for Jimmy.

As Eleanor wrapped the wontons into roses, she thought of the tiny rosebud fists of the baby growing and stretching, making its presence known with increasing urgency. The first flutterings felt as though she had swallowed a butterfly. Now the sensation of a fist or a foot pushing against the tight drum of her abdomen was a knocking she not only felt and saw but heard. The baby wanted out. And so did she. She wanted to go home.

Eleanor wondered if going to New York had been a mistake. She was sure that was when she conceived, the weekend Mahny decided to take her on a trip. He sweet-talked me into it, she thought. After voicing her concern about expenditures, he had reminded her that they'd never had a honeymoon. They stayed at the Hotel Statler, across the street from Pennsylvania Station. They ate at an automat, for the affordability as well as the novelty of sliding their trays past wax-papered sandwiches and pies behind little glass doors. They rode to the top of the Empire State Building, admired the window displays at Macy's, strolled hand in hand down Fifth Avenue and, following the warm smell of chestnuts to a street corner, found a vendor who shoveled the roasted half-opened shells into brown paper bags. For two glorious days they forgot about the future, weaving in and out of Central Park, walking through ankle-deep tides of fallen leaves.

Mahny had a new plan. Eleanor could tell he was up to something, unable to sit still, walking back and forth across the living room. Eleanor prepared herself to listen, massaging her swollen ankles, wondering how much longer she could keep working. The long days of summer conspired to make a mirage of her due date.

He sat down on the sofa and took her feet onto his lap. He took over the massage, randomly rubbing her feet as he spoke. "Remember I told you about Ruddy Tongg, the man who started Trans-Pacific Airlines several years ago?" He waited, making sure Eleanor was listening.

She nodded as if to say yes, vaguely.

"That he started TPA because he was fed up with always having to board last on Inter-Island Airlines because he was Chinese. Can you believe that? Having so much money that you can start your own airline? He started with just three DC-3s, the C-47 military surplus planes like the ones we fly at Homestead."

Her eyes glazed over whenever he talked about airplanes. He couldn't help himself. He wanted her to get the whole picture. "Can you believe that? Having so much money that you can start your own airline? Well, I heard he's expanding the company and looking to hire more employees."

"More pilots?"

"More everybody!" Mahny squeezed her feet for emphasis.

Eleanor withdrew her feet from his lap. His massage, absentmindedly administered, was tickling her.

"Hey, hon, don't you know what terrific news this is?"

Eleanor knew she should be happy, but all she could think about was how she was going to pack up and move not only their belongings but her heavy body one step closer to home.

Mahny left her and went into the kitchen. She heard the refrigerator door open, the clink of a soda cap bouncing on the counter, the fizz of carbonation. She heard her husband swill down the contents of the entire bottle. She heard him burp. "You know," he said, rummaging in the refrigerator for something to eat, "Ruddy Tongg's going to give guys like me a chance." He stood in the kitchen, peeling a banana and talking to himself.

It took several trips to True Blood's bungalow before Mahny finally found his friend at home. They sat in the screened-in porch, sipping beers, breaking pistachios, catching up. Mahny was eager to tell his friend about the application he had recently mailed to Trans-Pacific Airlines. He had a good feeling about it. In a few months, he was certain of it, he would be returning home with his wife and new baby.

When he explained to True Blood about the routes he would be flying, from one island to another in the Hawaiian chain, the longest distance being about two hundred miles, from Honolulu to Hilo, he felt embarrassed. He had dreamed of flying for a carrier like Pan American World Airways that flew a DC-4 around the world, taking off from San Francisco to Calcutta with stops in Honolulu, Midway, Wake, Guam, Manila, and Bangkok. The second leg of the journey left Calcutta to La Guardia with stops in Karachi, Istanbul, London, Shannon, and Gander. It took one week to fly around the world.

To True Blood, listening to his friend rattling off the names of the islands he would soon return to, islands linked by flights, he heard the sound of birds in those names, the birds his Mayaimi ancestors might have known, flying across the lake they called Big Water.

The Book of Enchantments

The day Alex turned four, her sister Kitty was born, squealing like a piglet stuck under a wire, her arrival relayed by telephone from proud father at Labor and Delivery to his sister at cake-and-ice-cream duty just as Alex, about to make a well-earned wish, sucked in the hugest ever four-plus-one-for-good-luck-candled birthday breath, and wished for—lungs stretched to capacity—*shiny black patent-leather Mary Jane shoes!*—red grouper cheeks quivering like a balloon about to fart and fly—*and white lace-edged socks, three pairs in a package, folded like dainty underwear*. And wished for . . .

"A new baby sister!" Auntie O cried, receiver extended so that those on the other end at Wahiawā General such as Mommy Delirious—*Give me the gas!*—and Squealing-Pig-in-a-Blanket—*half-baked pink and two weeks early*—and Too-Bad-Daddy-It's-Another-Girl—*close but no cigar*—could share Alex's joy. And crash in on her party—*Reallocate the candles! Cut the cake!*—and seal forever the sisters' fate.

Alex was turning blue. The story of the Chinese brother flashed before her mind, the one who swallowed the sea for the benefit of others—the greedy, the whiny, the downright lazy—bringing extreme discomfort upon himself. Alex, most accommodating Alex, who held so much in, gave way, burst forth.

I hate her already was a thought that flickered as Alex blew out the candles. *Goodbye beautiful shiny shoes*, she said to herself as she made the switch. Drowning her own wish to embrace all wishes, rising to a wish that would make everyone happy. She turned blue, extinguishing her true wish, made room to share her birthday with the new arrival.

A magician made Kitty disappear on her fourth birthday, and Alex, who was her sister's guardian, became frantic looking for her. She should have gone first when Mr. Mike, his electrical services that day not required, called for the birthday twins—"guinea pigs" his eyebrows jiggled suggestively—to step up.

"Not pigs!" Kitty giggled.

"Not twins!" Alex corrected, wondering if Mr. Mike, when not moonlighting as a magician, had fried one too many brain cells via his cut-rate rewiring.

Alex knew all about brain cells. She had been told by every teacher since kindergarten that she, Alexandria Park, possessed more than the normal amount. Exceeded, in fact, the average-recommended-to-sustain-life requirement. To those with low-level amounts, Alex knew the teachers were referring to the town delinquents who huddled at bus stops to inhale the brain-killing toxic fumes. Shining beneath their beams of praise, Alex didn't have to be told that being highly intelligent came with certain responsibilities and expectations. To waste one's brain was a sin. Thus, as the family record holder of the longest breath since the day she had switched her wish for a baby sister—a capacity that was to come in handy whenever a bus roared past—despite an abundant supply of brain cells, Alex remained cautious. That very morning, remembering the teachers discussing the glue-sniffing epidemic at the high school, she held her breath as she squeezed glue onto the birthday card she was constructing for Kitty.

Alex should have gone first but as usual, gave in to Kitty's whining. "I want to go! I want to go!"

Alex, most accommodating Alex, had stepped aside, out of the limelight, to let Kitty climb into the box.

Whiners had their uses.

Relieved to be let off the hook without being made to look bad, Alex sat back on the folding chair, content to be a part of the audience, six school chums sitting on folding chairs.

Another reason for holding one's breath, the cardboard box, which only last week held a refrigerator humming now in all its avocado-green splendor in a Wahiawā kitchen, was spray-painted black. The box, laid lengthwise, was slit to flap open and shut like a lid. It looked just like a coffin. Into which the Whiner, the one without regret, climbed in, without looking back.

Six school chums stopped licking their cones as Mr. Mike twirled what looked like a baton. It sprinkled glitter like salt from a shaker. Another reason for holding one's breath—who knew what destruction such free-falling particles of glitter could do to one's brain?

In what appeared to be the securing of invisible locks and the mumbling of secret spells, Mr. Mike kneeled close to the left side of the box. In matador fashion he lifted an arm so that his cape draped like a curtain. The hem of the cape pooled black like tar on the patio floor.

He abruptly stood up and, in another matador pose, he strutted around the box as though the box, immense and black, was a bull he had maimed and mastered. As he strutted, he dragged the baton like a sword.

Alex remained unimpressed. She had read about real matadors in *National Geographic*, and they did not resemble in any shape or form Mr. Mike. But then, Alex shrugged, he was from the Azores.

By now six school chums were getting a little restless with all the strutting. Had they been supplied with popcorn, they would have pelted the magician with the snack.

Mr. Mike, sensing scorn from the Other One—the bigger twin—stiffened his cape in one dramatic swoop, drew his baton in a line across his chest, and then began swirling his cape over the box.

Not gifted in the verbal department, Mr. Mike's act relied on crude pantomime. Between the suggestive eyebrows—*So uji!*—he managed a string of elaborate abracadabras, but no one minded (except the bigger twin), mesmerized as they were by the black waves fluttering over the box, rippling and receding like the wings of a prehistoric bat.

Ice cream cones by now consumed, the six school chums started clapping and stamping their slippered feet.

Slapslap against the cold concrete.

"Voilá!" Mr. Mike pronounced, pulling back his cape, yanking it, snapping it whiplike à la lion-tamer style.

Alex remained unmoved. In addition to an overabundant supply of brain cells, she had good manners, more than enough to keep the smirk from fully forming across her face. A lethal combination—intelligence and manners, fused with an ever-present desire to please—created inner turmoil. It was this that Mr. Mike dimly perceived, interpreting it as tough-nut-to-crack. *What a pill!*

Slapslap went the slippers against the cold concrete.

Mr. Mike, cut-rate electrician/magician cried "Tada!" as if "Voilá!" weren't enough, and lifted the lid of the box.

Seven torsos torpedoed forward.

Alex couldn't help herself. Even she was lost in the moment. A rare experience.

Seven gasps clung to form one gigantic mass of expectant air.

From inside the black space, Kitty heard her mother mutter, "Oh dear."

From inside the black space, Kitty heard the collective gasp. A flimsy soap bubble, flecked with particles, wobbled, barely aloft. It collapsed, broke like an egg over the box. She caught a whiff of hot dogs and ice cream. Things she was suddenly missing. She felt the crush of seven bodies pressing forward, released from folding chairs.

Pleased with his contraption, for now he was sure he could patent it, Mr. Mike invited the audience to examine its contents.

Empty as a showroom coffin.

Gasp!

Vacant as a model home closet.

Gasp!

Truly the magician, Mr. Mike, the electrician, once again transformed himself. The matador became a used car salesman.

The audience crushed forward.

"Hey-hey! Careful with the merchandise!" He fiddled with the lid as though it were a car hood. A long black car. A hearse.

Where did the body go?

The eighth body pressed forward. Eleanor Park gently pushed aside one daughter and six school chums. She put her arm around Alex, who was entering a mild state of shock. Alex held herself responsible.

Eleanor was tired. Tired of the kids, the soggy paper plates and cups, the ice cream droppings. Most of all, she was tired of Mr. Mike. She had endured his burlesque long enough. She smiled a little tighter as if to say, *Bravo Mr. Mike, now will you please produce my daughter.*

She wanted them all to disappear. Go home. Clean up. Start the bath. Move her daughters along.

Kitty, having made herself smaller, made herself smaller still. On the other side of the cardboard, she sensed her mother's discomfort as her own, squished so tight she couldn't possibly become even smaller. When the lid had shut, she saw black and no way out except to make herself smaller. In that way she could lessen the impact of the dark, like curling bean-shaped in bed at night. In doing so, she had rolled into a corner, like a marble in a game of Labyrinth, and, in rolling, had slipped through a well-disguised flap to another compartment, a nesting box within the box.

Even before Alex and Kitty saw *Flower Drum Song*, a movie they would each absorb into their personal histories, they were told that their father looked like James Shigeta. Good-looking for an Oriental. This remark was made by none other than another Oriental, Olivia Park, their father's younger sister.

Auntie O happened to mention the resemblance one evening as the girls sprawled on her white chenille-covered bed, a Friday night ritual that promised and delivered Coke floats, new hairdos, a manicure, and gossip. All the things the girls' mother didnotcouldnotwouldnot do. But she didn't prevent the girls from running across the backyard to the original house where Auntie O lived with the elder Parks. The night would end with the two girls and their young aunt snoring softly, teeth unbrushed, the sweet sugar-laced breath of their breathing fluttering the hem of the bedroom curtain.

The original house, positioned far back on the skinny rectangular property, was dwarfed by the length of the front lawn, dwarfed further by the proximity of eucalyptus growing in the gulch behind. The original house, white-shingled and porch-graced, appeared grand in style but miniature in size when the front lawn had undulated in well-mown splendor toward California Avenue. Birds-of-paradise lined the sidewalks. Mock orange hedges were trimmed with geometric precision. With Grandpa Park's pampered Ford parked in the driveway, the original house gave the impression of hard-earned respectability. The house their son built for his young family blocked the original one from the road, blocked the breeze the elder Parks waited for as they sat on the porch, fanning themselves with the newspaper, watching a slab of concrete cover what had been their front yard. He erected a chimney and walls of red brick that nothing could blow down.

The house blocked the elder Parks' view of California Avenue. Now there were other things to watch, other changes, other signs of progress. From the porch where Grandpa Park sat and swatted at mosquitoes, he saw right into his son's patio. Alex and Kitty would wave to him from the sandbox. Pedaling around on tricycles, he was their point of reference. Sometimes China. Sometimes the Statue of Liberty. In actuality, his stoic face loomed immovable as one of the presidents carved into Mt. Rushmore. From the kitchen window Grandma Park watched her daughter-in-law smoke cigarettes in the driveway, grind them one after another into the gravel with the heel of her slippers. Eleanor was careful not to leave any stubs behind, burying them in discarded coffee grinds.

Auntie O looked forward to indulging her nieces, enjoyed Friday nights, the sound of the girls running across the yard, sometimes with flashlights, although the porch light was always left on. On her side, Eleanor kept the light on in the patio. There was a spot in the yard that remained completely dark, where the lights of the two houses did not touch. The girls always jumped over this spot as though it were a puddle of mud.

"Hi Hops!"
"Hi Hams!"
The girls swept into the elder Parks' living room, swarmed over their grandparents, who were watching TV in semi-horizontal positions like dental patients in twin recliners. Over the years so much

had been lost in translation that being reduced to "Hops" and "Hams" rather than the more respectful terms, "Halaboji" and "Halmoni," was okay with them. As long as the affectionate nicknames came with kisses. Slug lips and saliva trails. Big Fat Juicy Ones.

"Okay, nuf nuf, already!" Grandma Park laughed, signaling the two to move along, let her and Hops get back to their TV show.

"So what's Oriental?" Kitty wanted to know. She was walking around the chenille-covered bed like a zombie sleepwalking, arms stretched out to let ten pink fingernails dry.

"An expensive vase," Alex answered in an English accent. Auntie O yanked her niece's head back in a ponytail so tight Alex's vision blurred.

"Ouch!"

"Vase," Auntie O corrected so that it rhymed with lace. Race and face.

"So Daddy has a good-looking vase?" Kitty looked doubtful.

"Face," Auntie O enunciated the "f" so slowly she looked like a beaver with her front teeth exposed.

Alex burst out laughing, imitated her aunt, and soon they were both making beaver faces in the mirror, adding crossed eyes, dead man eyes, and other ghoulish features.

Kitty let her arms drop. The zombie was waking up. She squirmed between her aunt and sister, and in the dresser mirror, joined in, sticking her fingers into the sides of her mouth, into her nostrils, and pulling back the corners of her eyes.

Auntie O and Alex stopped making faces. In unison they spoke to Kitty through the mirror. "Never do that!"

Kitty turned to them, her fingers still stretching back her eyes. She was smiling. She thought they were too until Alex said, "You're making fun of yourself."

Auntie O grimaced as she twisted Alex's thick hair through a rubber band. "Okay, you owe me. Your turn."

Kitty didn't hear her aunt. She felt the familiar tightness in her chest, a sensation only her sister could produce. "You're making fun of me!"

"Hey, let's have fun, girls. Who wants a Coke float?"

"I'm not making fun of you. You're making fun of yourself."

"But you were making faces too!" Kitty said, choking with confusion.

"Yes, but not that one!"

Alex turned to her sister and slowly, with a finger at each corner, pulled back her eyes until she couldn't see her sister staring back at her. "This one." And slowly Alex began to rock her head back and forth and chant "Ching Chong Chinaman." The zombie had awakened. Anger in the shape of a bat flew out of Alex and clung to the window screen.

Auntie O picked Alex up, threw her on the bed, and began tickling her.

"Will you stop it?"

"Okay, okay!"

"Promise?"

"Okay, okay!"

"Never again!"

"Okay, okay!"

When Auntie O finally left the room to get the Coke floats, Kitty, curious enough to brave her sister, asked, "So what's an Oriental?"

Alex was staring at the ceiling. "A vase," she said limply.

"So why's Daddy a good-looking vase?"

Alex let out a dramatic sigh. It always made Kitty feel bad when she did it. "It's like if you say Koreans stink or Korean stinks.

If you say Koreans stink, that's bad. And if you say Korean stinks, that's okay."

"I don't get it."

"Forget it," Alex said. "It's just words."

They had sucked their Coke floats until there was nothing left, not even the stiff sticky foam on the insides of the glass.

"Auntie O?"

"Yes?"

"Do Koreans stink?"

"No, Kitty dear. We're the cleanest people in the world, on the inside, where it counts the most."

"Why?"

"Because Mr. Ogata, the mortician, told me that out of all the bodies he embalms, Korean bodies are the cleanest. No smell, he said. And do you know why?"

Kitty shook her head in the dark.

"Because we eat kimchee, and all that garlic wipes out all the bacteria."

Sometimes Kitty wished Auntie O had been their mother. But Alex said it was against the law for a brother and a sister to marry because then their children would be freaks. Siamese twins. Connected at the head. Watermelon heads so heavy they couldn't stand up. They had to sleep in a special crib, share the same dream, think each other's thoughts.

When the lights went out at Waikīkī Theatre Kitty thought the palm trees were real and the ceiling was the evening sky, the stars so perfectly spaced. She wondered what the audience did when it rained. Rows of umbrellas opening like tropical flowers. Families huddling together under all those flowers.

When James Shigeta appeared on the screen as Wang Ta, it was like the word made flesh. Kitty leaned over to whisper to Alex, "There's Uncle." Absorbing that talk of vase, face, Oriental, and race she had somehow arrived at the conclusion that James Shigeta looked like Daddy because they were clean-smelling, garlic-eating Koreans. That made him a relative. An uncle.

"Shhh!" Alex hushed. She had memorized the lyrics from the album of the Broadway show, listening to the record, side one more than side two, dozens of times. Pat Suzuki and Ed Kenney played the roles Nancy Kwan and James Shigeta were later given in the movie version because Auntie O said "they were tall and better looking." For Orientals. And in the movies looks were more important than strong voices. In the movies they didn't have to project their voices as they did on stage. And in the movies they could always dub in another person's voice as they did for Nancy Kwan. Looks always won over talent. But Auntie O had assured them, since she had seen *Flower Drum Song* first, that James Shigeta sang his own songs.

Kitty turned to her mother. "There's Uncle."

Without taking her eyes off James Shigeta, Eleanor sighed, "To think he was my classmate!"

Mahny Park sat on the other side of Alex. He wasn't watching the movie. He was having more fun watching his daughters experience what had been recently recreated in their own living room.

It was his idea to position the swivel-headed reading lamp like a spotlight on Alex, the self-proclaimed director and obvious star of the show. She gave herself all the fun numbers, the Nancy Kwan showgirl numbers such as "I Enjoy Being a Girl" and "Grant Avenue," snazzy routines that gave her the opportunity to show off fancy Radio-City-Music-Hall leg-kicks and twirls.

Not fair! Kitty whined, knowing in her heart of hearts that Miyoshi Umeki's part was a dud. No fun at all being stuck playing

Mei Li whose numbers never broke out with the brass-blaring-show-stopping zing of "Grant Avenue."

As a consolation Kitty was allowed to bang on a drum, an empty oatmeal container Alex was willing to sacrifice, emptying her colored pencils in a hurry, even wrapping aluminum foil around it, convincing her sister that it was a special Chinese drum.

A hundred million miracles!

Dumdadadumdum, Alex instructed, trying to sell her suspicious sister on the homemade instrument.

A hundred million miracles!

Dumdadadumdum

Dum

Kitty whacked on it, sometimes a bit too vigorously.

Alex interjected, "Cut! Cut! Softer! Lighter! Remember you just got off the boat from China! You're supposed to be shy!"

Dumdadadumdum

Sometimes too limply.

"Cut! Cut! You're supposed to be happy! You're in America now!"

For Miyoshi Umeki's other dud of a solo, "I Am Going To Like It Here," Kitty insisted on wearing her crinoline as a headpiece. Alex argued that it looked ridiculous, first of all because it was a crinoline and not a wig, and second, Mei Li came from China and Chinese women wore long braids! They didn't go around in public shaking their hair back like Miss America. And if anybody got to do that it was Linda Low, Nancy Kwan's character, who was American-born and free to shake her hair as well as other body parts at Celestial Gardens in numbers such as "I Enjoy Being a Girl" and "Fan Tan Fannie."

Alex cringed and conceded, allowing Kitty to wear the crinoline only because, according to Alex's own logic, as Linda Low then she herself should be wearing it.

Alex could barely maintain her impatience at Kitty's interpretation, standing in the small spotlight of their father's steady beam, crinoline shrouding her face like a veil. She looked like a child bride. She didn't want to lip-sync as instructed by her sister, she wanted to sing, and sing she did.

"I am going to Waikīkī . . ."

Alex jumped up, ready to say "Cut! Cut! I am going to *like it here*, *like it here*, not Waikīkī", but she was held back by their father. He was aware of the preciousness of it. The sincerity of innocence. How soon it would be over.

Neither sister wanted to play Helen, her part was too sad. Although they both agreed that the one song she sang, "Love, Look Away," was by far the most beautiful, in the end, Wang Ta leaves her and all she's left with is a tiny room in Chinatown, with a fire escape that doesn't really lead to a dreamy dance sequence in a landscape of silk paintings, only a tiny seamstress life with traffic noise and fish smells. And all the beautifully embroidered cheongsams hanging in her closet are made for somebody else.

For Kitty, Wang Ta abandoning Helen was something she couldn't bear to think about. It was so pitiful the way Helen lured Wang Ta to stay at her little Chinatown walk up, mending his jacket, fixing his breakfast. Why, he didn't even eat his toast or finish his coffee! And Helen had woken early to get it all ready for him. The rejection felt unbearably personal, James Shigeta being family and all.

One day Kitty refused to play Mei Li anymore. It stumped Alex, who had refined the role of Linda Low down to high heels (Auntie O's), towel (only panties underneath), and a fan (pleated-construction paper), each vigorous performance requiring a new replacement. Alex wasn't about to give up being a girl. A fun girl. A good time girl, according to their mother.

"I know!" She was talking fast. "You can be Wang Ta's auntie. And you can sing 'Chop Suey'!"

"No."

Alex broke into a desperate routine, enticing Kitty into cooperating by substituting jin dui, the heavenly fried donut, for the pedestrian noodle dish. Breathless, Alex surprised herself by not recalling any of the song.

"No." Kitty was adamant.

"C'mon. It's fun." Alex was already thinking that if Kitty wore a pillow under her nightgown, she would be big bosomed like Wang Ta's auntie, played by Juanita Hall, who was, according to Auntie O, not really Oriental.

"And besides, I don't even know what the song is about. Sounds stupid to me."

"Oh, but it's not! It's really fun . . ." Alex tried to remember the words to the song she had never really bothered to learn. Like the ABC song, in order to find her way though the letters of the alphabet, she had to start at the very beginning, humming the tune until her own words tumbled in. "Jin dui! Jin dui!" she improvised, "crisp and sweet and oily too . . ." For good measure, she threw in a phrase she vaguely remembered, something about Maidenform brassieres and the cha-cha-cha.

"You be Wang Ta's auntie!" Kitty cried. "You be that fat old lady who sings about food and underwear! I quit!"

Alex opened her mouth, then shut it. Sometimes there was no way to reach her sister.

O pretty Polly don't you cry
You'll be happy by and by
When he comes he'll dress in blue
That's the sign he'll marry you

Eleanor ground out a cigarette in the gravel driveway, reentered the house through the kitchen door, and exited by way of the patio. She didn't want to be seen coming directly from smoking. She knew Grandma Park was watching.

The others were in the backyard. Kitty was singing, skipping around Auntie O, who sat on a chair in the sun. Prone to freckles, she wore a hat to protect her face and a pair of cat-eyed sunglasses. Her shorts were very short and she wore a sleeveless blouse, but stylishly, with the last three buttons undone so that the hem could be knotted at the waist.

They were all wearing sunglasses, aunt and nieces. Alex and Kitty wore pink plastic-rimmed ones, one of the many presents resulting from one of many outings to the five-and-dime with Auntie O. Eleanor didn't wear sunglasses. She didn't feel they suited her anymore.

Kitty was singing, skipping around her pretty aunt, pretty polly of an aunt. Her hair, pinned in the latest poodle cut à la Audrey Hepburn in *Sabrina*, belied the fact that only a week ago Auntie O had stayed in bed for a week with an illness no one could explain.

Eleanor wanted to know the secret of her miraculous recovery.

Eleanor wanted to know. Was it the sunglasses? The poodle cut? The pampering mother? The adoring nieces? The kind, benign father? The kind, solicitous brother? The uncomplaining sister-in-law?

Eleanor wanted to know.

"Oh Pretty Polly don't you cry"

Eleanor had a headache that promised to get worse.

"You'll be happy by and by"

Alex, under an umbrella, felt out of sorts and didn't know why.

"When he comes he'll dress in blue"

Auntie O grabbed her sprite little niece.

"That's the sign he'll marry you"

And tickled and tickled her until she fell on the dark spot of the yard laughing.

Kitty even believed she had magical powers the day Mr. Mike Texeira, the magician, turned up one afternoon dressed in blue. It was the sign. The sign she had been waiting for. Never mind the blue he wore was his electrician's overalls and that as a favor to their father, he had come to take a look at the refrigerator. "Yeah, it's making funny sounds, alright."

Since the day they had overheard Grandma Park announce the antidote for Auntie O's ailment—a suitor—the girls had tried to conjure up prospects.

And came up empty.

Mr. Ogata, the mortician, was a widower. Do you think he embalmed his own wife? The likelihood made him instantly an unlikely candidate.

Dr. Choi's son, Vincent, was going to be a doctor, a "good catch," or so his mother bragged every time she stepped into the bakery, but wasn't he somewhere on the mainland? Cross him off the list. The mainland meant another time zone.

How about Henry Six Toes? He worked in the hardware store and came to the bakery for a bear claw whenever Auntie O happened to be working. Even though he was unmarried, he always looked cheerful. Maybe he liked being a bachelor. And he always had something nice to say to Auntie O. "Too nice," Auntie O said. But the sixth toe was problematic. They couldn't figure out if his name meant that he had six on one foot and four on the other, or if he had, indeed, only six toes altogether—3-3, 4-2, 5-1, 6-0?—or six toes on each foot. A total of twelve toes? They shuddered. Cross him off the list! Wait a minute! Not so fast! Kitty, having a vision, declared the feet of Henry the Sixth had four on one, six on the other—which gave him a total of ten perfectly normal, perfectly acceptable toes. She theorized that one of the hazards of working in a hardware store was getting one's toe chopped off by falling objects such as a machete or a saw. "That's stupid! " Alex corrected in scorn. "Then he had eleven toes to begin with? I don't think so!"

One day while singing along to the little yellow record, fooling with the speed on the phonograph, 78 rpm now fast, 33 1/3 rpm now slow, Kitty, old yeller, fortune teller, mystical speller, conjurer of magicians and electricians, stretched her mouth as if she were singing with a chorus of ghosts, sang the wobbly notes as big and heavy as soap bubbles—Oh Pretty Polly Don't You Cry You'll Be Happy By And By—and again, later, faster and faster, she sang that pink hot day in the sun, circling round and round her pretty pink aunt, pink-skinned, prone to freckles, green-eyed, red-tinged hair auntie. And only her sister knew what a spell she was casting.

Mr. Mike Texeira never saw Olivia Park that afternoon when he appeared dressed in blue, his electrician's coveralls. He never saw anything but a lot of dust, dust in the refrigerator coils and what looked like a turkey carcass plump with dust. And a pesky little girl.

He wanted to make Kitty disappear (again). He had to admit, he owed the little girl one. The kid had done a good job of not giving away his trick, but now she was driving him nuts, pleading for him to take a look at her grandma's refrigerator in the house at the back. The dusty carcass didn't even scare her off.

"Can't, kid." He had found himself in a tight situation, squeezed behind the refrigerator, realizing that he was stuck. He should've pushed the damn thing further from the wall.

"Pass me the wrench." A brown and hairy hand shot out from the side.

Kitty picked up a wrench-looking tool. The hairy hand took it.

"Nope." The hairy hand returned it. "Wrench. Looks like a hook."

The hairy hand was grasping blindly. It made Kitty think of *The Crawling Hands*, the spooky show they had watched once on TV. The crawling hands played the piano and strangled people in their beds at night. The crawling hands were always together. Like twins.

Kitty picked up a tool in the shape of a claw.

"That's it." Realizing he needed the kid's assistance now that he was stuck, he conceded. "So what's wrong with your grandma's refrigerator?"

"It's sick." If she could lure him to her grandmother's house, he was bound to bump into Auntie O, sunbathing in the backyard. Her plan didn't go beyond that. She just needed to make the contact happen, like rubbing two sticks together.

"Okay. How sick?" Mr. Mike softened, reminded himself of his magic touch with kids.

"Very sick."

"Okay."

"Funny noises."

"Okay."

Kitty felt he wasn't really hearing her. "Don't you want to fix it?"

A hairy word exploded, and it wasn't "Jiminy Cricket."

"Mr. Mike, are you okay back there?" It suddenly occurred to Kitty that he should use some magic.

"Gimme the thing," he growled.

"What thing?"

"The thing! The thing!"

Only to Kitty it sounded like "ting." She grabbed the first-looking tool that could possibly be the wrench "ting," passed it along the side, and dropped it. She didn't wait for the crawling hand. "So will you fix it?" she persisted.

"What?" The way Mr. Mike said it, it sounded like "fut."

"My grandma's sick refrigerator. You can use your magic stick."

"That's it! Get outta here!" Mr. Mike roared and the force of his voice almost toppled the refrigerator but for the viselike grip of his hairy hands.

He never saw Auntie O that day (only dust balls, a turkey carcass, and one pesky kid). What Kitty didn't know was that he had seen her out in the backyard, sitting in the sun, the day he and Mahny had returned from fishing at Mokulēʻia. He remembered seeing a hell of a lot of pink. Maybe it was his own sunburn, which only cold beer could relieve. It was his day off from electricity and magic tricks and, as far as he was concerned, it looked too much like a birthday party from the driveway where he and Mahny polished off a couple of beers. All that skipping and singing, no way was he going to go near it. He didn't know how Mahny did it, being surrounded by all those girls.

Kitty lay in bed crying that night. She couldn't understand how it had all gone wrong. How her magical powers had failed her. She hadn't conjured up a suitor dressed in blue but a hairy monster. With crawling hands. She began to doubt the abilities she had believed she possessed since the day she disappeared into Magic Mike's box. Maybe Auntie O was destined to be an old maid, like Helen the lonely seamstress. And like Wang Ta, maybe Mr. Mike was simply in love with someone else. His ex-wife, her mother would have told her had she known what Kitty was up to.

There were a lot of things Kitty realized she lacked the power to control. Her own feelings, the frustration when things didn't go her way. The sadness she felt when she waved to Grandpa Park as he sat on the porch watching her step into the sand box or go round and round on her tricycle, and he waved back, fly swatter in hand, each confined to a language the other didn't know, the backyard like an ocean of grass between them. The wild feeling of pumping her legs so hard that she almost flew off a swing when she thought she had made Mr. Mike appear dressed in blue. *A sign he would marry you, Auntie O.*

Alex, immovable Alex, snored softly in the next bed.

Kitty turned and faced the wall.

"Infinity," Alex began, startling her sister. Kitty felt even more deflated; she hadn't even been able to tell that her sister wasn't asleep after all. "Infinity," Alex repeated, voicing what seemed to have come to her in a dream, "means nothing. Nothing at all."

Her sister's pronouncement seemed to enlarge the shadows brought into the room from the nightlight's soft glow.

"Sounds scary," Kitty whispered.

"It is. It's nothing because no one can hold it. It just goes on forever."

"I don't think I like that." Under her nightgown, Kitty's legs retracted to her chest.

"Going on forever and ever, no end, no end in sight," Alex murmured as if in a trance.

"Tell me more," Kitty whispered, hoping her sister was sleep talking, that her words were coming from the world of dreams and magic. At the same time, she didn't want Alex to be asleep. She didn't want to be left alone, awake.

"Nothing to tell. Nothing at all but black black space. Where shadows come from and where shadows go. Nobody knows. Infinity grows and grows."

Hearing the rhymes, Kitty became suspicious. It sounded like one of the golden yellow records, played at the wrong wobbly speed. Alex was trying to scare her. Still, it didn't take away from the mystery of what she was saying. "Can I see it?" Kitty swallowed, wide-eyed, staring at the shadows that began to shape themselves into animal form.

"Nobody can see it. Yet it's all around."

"Like God."

"Infinity is God."

"Then there's nothing to be afraid of, right?"

"Nothing at all."

After Alex fell back to sleep, Kitty stared at the shadows that remained large and menacing. Thinking about infinity made Kitty feel lonely, lonely as the time she was caught in the grips of a great anxiety, when her name was pulled from her body, and she was left formless, without boundaries of bone and skin.

"That's thinking outside yourself," Alex explained later, matter-of-factly. Kitty wondered how her sister could be so sure. "It happens sometimes."

Kitty remembered the exact moment when her name was pulled from her body. She was lying on the living room floor, poring over "The Book of Enchantments" from *The Enchanted Princess and Other Fairy Tales.* The book, the size of the family atlas, contained illustrations as richly detailed and opulent as Old World European paintings of landscapes with castles and twisted trees and pale mournful faces in fur hats and enormous jewels that hung in faraway museums, pictures their father brought back when he returned from the Brussels World's Fair. He also came home with a doll for each daughter, two dolls in calico print dresses with long blond braids and eyelids that closed when the dolls were put to bed. She was reading a story about a boy and his sister held captive by a sorcerer. Using their wits, the brother and sister escaped by stealing the spells from the sorcerer's encyclopedia of magic. At the same time that she was caught in the story, aware of the rain and the sound of her mother in the kitchen, she became acutely aware of her own body, lying in space, the itch of the sisal rug beneath her. It was almost dinnertime. The rain and the soft calling of her name receded, and then the floor dropped out from under her. She was no longer contained by her name. She remembered the page where it happened, the sentence she was reading when she was struck. "Sorcerers must think only of themselves, not about God, and that is how they stay so wicked, by thinking greedily about themselves all the time."

The soft breathing of her sleeping sister gently cradled Kitty, rocking her like a boat, carrying her to another memory, their birthday party when she was hiding in Mr. Mike's magic box. Even though she knew she was pretending to be invisible, she wanted to come out of that black space, show everyone that she was still here, alive, in her body, that it was all a trick. Mr. Mike had made her disappear by having her roll into the hidden compartment. The others couldn't see her, and they couldn't know how lonely she was as she waited for the trick to be over, to jump out and reveal herself. They couldn't hear her, but then she wasn't saying anything. She knew that day that she was part of the magic, that Mr. Mike needed her to be quiet as she huddled in the secret compartment of the long cardboard box. Mr. Mike never told her what to do. She just knew that that was what was required of her, to hide and keep quiet. The success of the birthday party depended on it.

How could she be lonely, if she was nothing? It was just like Alex to talk above her and leave her confused. If you're nothing, it shouldn't matter if you're lonely, or dead, or invisible. But it did matter. She had played along with the trick, pretending be invisible, and for a terrifying moment, in the hot black box, she had felt that she was invisible, that she had indeed disappeared. And it wasn't nothing. It was worse because she was still lonely, and she wasn't dead. All that time, waiting for Mr. Mike to call her out and reveal to the others that he had made her reappear, she had been thinking greedily about herself. How she wanted to join the others, eat ice cream and cake, tear open the pile of presents waiting on the card table.

She lost herself every day in a song, a book, a game. In losing herself in such ways, she was made aware of the greedy part of herself enjoying herself too much to the point of ignoring the others around her and being called by the tired voice of her mother, the irritated voice of her sister, the impatient voice of her father to attend to the things that needed tending to, like baths and mealtimes, homework and chores. The afternoon her name was pulled from her body, she hadn't been thinking about God. She hadn't been thinking about anyone but herself. The little boy had become a lake and the little girl a blue fish swimming in that lake, the children having enchanted themselves beyond the sorcerer's grasp. How comfortable the boy and his sister felt, safe from doing the sorcerer's tiresome deeds. Without her name to contain herself, she had become immense, formless as water. But far from feeling comfortable, she felt without definition, insecure. She thought about herself all the time, and if that was greedy, then she had yet to be swallowed by something bigger, like infinity, blue as the lake the boy had become, metamorphosing into a fish as the little girl had done. And just as her sister's soft breathing held her, she heard the rain. And the rain was still falling. The sound of it filled her. And her mother was still calling. The sound of it filled her, the sound of her mother calling her back into her body.

Alhambra

Captain Park maneuvered the yellow Opel GT, enjoying the way the car gripped the corners as he made the series of turns to get home after he exited the freeway. Right onto Kīlauea Avenue, left at Pueo, right at Farmers Road, and one more left at Kōloa Street before he came into the driveway and slipped into the garage. Eleanor's car was gone. He had expected her back from work by now. Much to his annoyance, he was greeted instead by the sorry sight of his daughter's boyfriend's brown VW bus parked in front of the house. He knew the shenanigans that went on in that van and, locking the Opel, went to peer inside. The makeshift curtains had been lifted. He was prepared to bang on the back door until the couple fell out. The van was empty.

He waited for the blood rushing to his head to subside. He stood on the sidewalk, his heavy leather flight satchel at his feet and, for a moment, felt powerless. All hell was breaking loose these days, and there was nothing he could do about it. Everyone seemed to have a mind of their own. Eleanor had taken a part-time job at the museum as assistant to the librarian, which kept her out most of the day. She lingered after clocking out, chatting over sandwiches and pastries with her co-workers, extending the afternoons to other errands she had to do. When he questioned her, she grew angry. With her gone, the kids had free reign. Aidan was spending too much time in the water, surfing instead of studying. The comings and goings of the kids and their friends left his head spinning. Worse were the boyfriends who kept hanging around, especially the one who looked like Tarzan with his long locks and habitual lack of clothing. When he referred to Alex's boyfriend as Dennis the Menace, he was amazed how quickly he was shot down with just a shaking of his daughter's head, not to mention the rolling of eyes. Then there was the boyfriend of Kitty's, owner of the beat-up van, who drove in from the North Shore on the weekends, parking the van in front of the house and, later, in the early morning hours, shifting to neutral to quietly sneak away, spending the night in some other part of the neighborhood, bringing the property value down there as well. He tried to share his annoyance with his wife, but she just shrugged, saying David was a nice boy. She could tell he was from a good family. He had good manners. Grudgingly, he had to agree with his wife, but did she always have to feed him?

The border of periwinkles along the wall caught his attention. He reminded himself to water them. The alternating scheme of pinks and blues against the white wall cheered him. He had made the right decision, moving his family from under the rain clouds of Wahiawā to the sunny South Shore at the eastern end of the island. Now whenever he came in for a landing, approaching the runway from the south, the rain-locked heights of Central Oʻahu in the distance reaffirmed this. He was glad to be released from the thought of Eleanor and the children huddled in the house battered by rain. Thinking of them limp, listless, spending dreary afternoons with board games and books had made him want to fly home faster as if he personally could bring in the sunshine when he opened the front door. In those days, the way they rushed to greet him made him feel that was indeed the case. The sight of the thirsty periwinkles tugged at him. Slowly, he was improving the least expensive house he had been able to afford in one of the better neighborhoods.

He opened the gate and entered the courtyard. Once behind the wall he had built brick by brick over several months and inside its enclosure, he felt a sense of accomplishment at his handiwork, never dreaming that his efforts could have such a prolonged and positive effect. By enclosing the front lawn, which had required weekly mowing to keep up appearances with all the other manicured lawns on the block, he began to envision an oasis. He sought to improve the unimaginative ranch-style house with its simple three-bedroom floor plan. After the completion of the first phase of renovation, adding a hobby room and a master bath and suite next to the kitchen, he experienced a sense of satisfaction he no longer got from work. After years of flying, shuttling planeloads of passengers from one island to another, he had begun to feel like a highly paid taxi driver. At the end of the day, he had nothing to show for the long hours of flight, his time and skill evaporating like spent fuel.

The courtyard gave the house privacy from the street and another living space for the family to enjoy. Within its walls, he had laid a red-brick floor and planted Russian olive trees, dracaenas, and roses, trying to recreate something vaguely Moorish after taking Eleanor and the kids on a trip through Andalusia to see the Alhambra, "the pearl set in emeralds." He remembered approaching the palace and hiding his disappointment. Spinning tales of the Alhambra in the months before the trip, encouraging them to hasten along a little faster as they withered under the hot Andalusian sun, he had led his family to expect to be blinded by opulently bejeweled walls. He tore through a maze of rooms and corridors, with Eleanor and the children in tow, as if he could find for them the inner heart of the place. Strolling the grounds, the others managing to detach themselves to wander on their own, he thought he understood what he was looking at, how the plainness of the outer walls provided the first layer of concealment, how everything turned inward— the mathematical precision of mosaics, the intricate carvings of poems, and the fountains of water cooling the air—so that the true adornment, all that was intimately cherished and difficult to obtain was for the benefit and well-being of the family alone. Standing in the Persian-inspired garden, he had experienced a revelation. When he began to lay the bricks for his own garden, neighbors walking by with their dogs would stop to admire the wall. He would wave them off with a good-natured laugh as they dropped the invariable comment, "Trying to keep the boys out, Captain Park? Better put cut glass along the top while you're at it!"

He heard splashing in the pool as he opened the front door. The toy fox terrier was barking, up to his old habit of dropping a tennis ball in the water for someone to throw it. The kids complained that they couldn't get a single lap in before Kim, having retrieved the ball from the far corner of the yard, raced back to the edge of the pool and dropped the ball in again, his barking outlasting even Kitty, the most determined swimmer. Through the shutters in the living room he saw Kitty and David swimming the short length of the pool, ignoring the dog. He was relieved. They were just swimming.

He missed the earlier years when the kids still had their innocence. He didn't know how else to explain that brief period of time when all that he was was enough for them, when all they wanted was to be with him. They were so malleable then. He could get them to pull weeds for a dollar a bucket and think it was fun. He could tell them about the harrowing time he flew over the Bermuda Triangle and have them convinced he was the finest storyteller— Alex questioning the accuracy of his tale, Aidan sitting on his lap, listening, and Kitty writing down everything. The trick was to conceal his true motives. It was all about training, giving love, gaining trust, and then gently guiding them. He only had one chance with these kids, and he wasn't going to blow it.

He instilled in Alex a sense of duty that, as the eldest child, she was a role model for the younger two, who would look up to her, follow her lead. He gave her permission to be the boss of the kids, convincing her that she was his co-pilot. Now when she rolled her eyes at him, he thought he had somehow failed. The willful one was Kitty. He had known that when she was still in grade school, the times the fighting between the two girls drove him crazy and he would remove his belt with a flourish, threatening them with it. While Alex ran out of the room screaming as the belt came down, purposely missing her but loud enough to make an impressive cracking sound as it hit the floor, Kitty refused to budge. She would stare him down, daring him to strike. He knew that he could keep hitting her, and she would sustain the blows, letting herself be whipped to shreds before she gave in. It was easier with Aidan. He could build things with his son, model airplanes and go-cart engines from lawn mower parts, projects that brought Aidan into his sphere of influence naturally. While Alex and Kitty went to a public school, Aidan was sent to a private one for boys. He had plans for his only son.

The kids refused to get out of the car, the cramped green SEAT Captain Park had rented in Madrid and had been driving since morning, heading toward Andalusia. They complained that the whole village was going to come out and stare at them as they did in Baeza, where they had stopped to stretch their legs and buy refreshments before Úbeda. The plan was to drive from Madrid to Málaga with overnight stops at the towns of Úbeda and Jaén on their way to the Alhambra. Captain Park had corresponded with the government-run paradors, waiting for weeks to receive the tissue-thin blue envelopes containing letters of confirmation of reservations for his family. The drive from Madrid to Úbeda had taken almost four hours with the stop in the town of Baeza.

"C'mon, kids," Captain Park said, stepping out of the car. He was irritated that he had to do everything. The drive had been long and hot, and he felt covered with dust. Instead of reading the map, Eleanor had spent most of the drive napping. "We're here." Warily the three children peered out the windows of the car at the plain square building that seemed to be made of the same stones as the street. "This is it?" Eleanor couldn't hide her discriminatory tone.

"C'mon, kids," their father urged, losing patience. He had brought them around the world and they were behaving like peons who had never left the pineapple fields.

He didn't want to show his own dismay at the sight of the building that had once been a sixteenth-century Renaissance palace. With its unassuming facade the palace-turned-parador resembled more his idea of a Spanish prison, but when they found themselves in a sumptuous interior courtyard with an extravagant staircase leading to the upper gallery of rooms, they shared looks as if to say they had found themselves a little-known jewel, far from the beaten path. Not knowing what to request in his letters, he had simply asked, if possible, for rooms with a view. He didn't have to worry about his children misbehaving as he signed the registration forms. They were well mannered, but sometimes their shyness revealed their lack of sophistication. Eleanor was no help. She always stood behind the wall her three kids made as if to claim her deserved place among them. Anyone could see she was the mother. He was just grateful that she let the bellboy take the bags up to the rooms. Not one to tip, Eleanor was living it up on this trip so far. She was prepared to lavish a few pesos on the bellboy.

The sun was still strong although it was late in the afternoon, plenty of time to walk around the town, visit the nearby church of

Santa María de los Reales, which the concierge had recommended. The kids refused. He couldn't get them to leave their room, one of the two they had been given with a view of the plaza below. It was different in Madrid. The city was cosmopolitan, the streets full of tourists from all over the world. But in this tiny Andalusian town, the kids said they would stick out like sore thumbs. He let them relax, and when they dressed for dinner, he didn't tell his daughters their skirts were too short. He didn't like the granny glasses Kitty insisted on wearing. He thought it was a thirteen-years-old's affectation. When they came down to the grand dining room, he tried to make the best of the evening special he had heartily agreed to, the cold garlic soup and pimentos rellenos de perdiz, telling the kids the partridge was just a bird, just a Spanish chicken, even though he himself couldn't drink enough wine to wash the meal down.

Changing out of his uniform and into khaki shorts and a T-shirt, he slid open the screen door and went outside. They were still swimming. The dog was still barking. He bent down to pick up the tennis ball, bobbing in the wake of the swimmers. He threw the ball across the yard. He had to admit Kitty had a good stroke, a far cry from the time when she fell into the pool. She couldn't have been more than seven. They had just moved in and one of the things he had promised himself to do was to teach the kids to swim. Knowing how tempting the pool looked, he forbade them to go in without him. Circling the pool on their tricycles made him nervous, but he let them pedal around the concrete edge as long as he was nearby. He was raking the plumeria leaves when Aidan shouted that Kitty and the tricycle had fallen into the pool. Rushing to dive in to retrieve her, he saw her coming to the surface at great speed, eyes round as the wheels of the tricycle she had ditched at the bottom, arms and legs working through the depth with the proficiency of a frog. He reached his hand across the water. She latched onto it, coughing, shivering not so much from the cold as from the sheer power of her own exertion. He vowed to teach the kids to swim in earnest the next day.

He loomed above the pool. Sensing a tremor in the sudden cessation of barking, Kitty and David stopped their laps. Hanging onto the pool's edge, they flipped up their goggles.

"Hi, Dad!" Kitty's innocuous greeting lifted his scowl. She waded to the shallow end and sat on the steps. He could see too much of his daughter in the skimpy bikini top. He felt the scowl returning.

"Where's your mother?" He couldn't think of anything else to say.

"At work, I guess. Speaking of work, how was your day?" Kitty got out of the pool. He winced at the sight of her skimpy bikini bottom. He wanted to tell her to put some clothes on, or grab a towel, but he refrained. She would just roll her eyes.

Floating lazily to the shallow end, David remained in the water. "Hi, Mr. Park," he said, smiling. Something about Kitty's father kept him from standing to his full height in three feet of water.

Captain Park managed a gruff hello. He turned from them and went to pull weeds. His annoyance mounted as the pair spread out towels on the grass and warmed themselves in the sun. It was getting near dinnertime, Eleanor still wasn't home, and his daughter and her boyfriend were relaxing, enjoying themselves too much. Home from college for the summer, his other daughter abused her newfound independence. She was probably cavorting with Tarzan. Flying in on the last approach of the day, he had noticed the waves rolling in long perfect formation along the South Shore. He imagined Aidan riding the swell until it got too dark to see.

Driving up Santa Clara hill's winding road to the parador above Jaén, the sun blinded them, a medallion of rays bursting through the fortress gate. The night spent in Úbeda had ended memorably, the subject of their chatter into the morning and at breakfast. It was moments like these that made all the burden of traveling that fell on him worthwhile. The kids drank hot cocoa, nibbled cobblestone rolls, hoping for another glimpse of the bullfighter before they drove off to the next town. After the mostly uneaten dinner of peppers stuffed with partridge had been replaced by a cart of cakes that needed no translation, the waiters, dropping their solicitous hovering around the foreign family had rushed across the otherwise empty dining room, shouting the name El Cordobés. Flanked by an entourage of portly men in business suits and several slender picadores, the tired matador entered, minus his heavy suit of lights, not to eat but to greet his fans, the three waiters, who practically kneeled at his feet. At the matador's urging, they rose, took out pens for him to autograph the menu, which he graciously signed. Quickly looking over the menu, he pointed to a few dishes he wanted brought to his room. Kitty swore he glanced at them and smiled as he turned to leave, turning as though spinning on the balls of his feet. Suddenly Andalusia didn't seem that dreary after all. She wanted to see a bullfight. She wanted to see El Cordobés in the ring.

They found themselves the only guests in the thirteenth-century Arab fortress. Offered the pick of any room, they chose the ones with balconies that seemed to vault above the dry Andalusian plains dotted with olive trees and, like a silver thread, the river shimmering through them. They never went down into the town, but remained on the hill, following the path to Saint Catherine's Castle, only because that was the name of his daughters, naming both girls after one saint, Catherine of Alexandria, splitting the name in half, a half of a name for each daughter. He knew nothing about the saint, but he loved the idea of forever linking his daughters by the same name, one for a saint, the other for an ancient city in Egypt.

He heard the rumbling of Eleanor's station wagon in the garage. He didn't like the sound of it. He added it to his list of things to attend to, turning in the '69 Rambler for something newer. She was recently hinting that since she was no longer the family chauffeur, she could use something smaller. She didn't want a VW bug like the one he got for the kids; that was too small, and besides, she didn't know how to drive a stick shift. He heard his wife entering the house. It occurred to him to see if she needed help carrying groceries from the car, but he remained rooted to the ground, pulling at the stubborn patch of weeds. Kitty and David had left their towels splayed on the grass, something else for him to pick up.

When he had cleared the area of weeds, he stood up, grimacing at the tightness in his lower back. He went around the side of the house to empty the bucket of weeds and ran into his wife. She was crouched at the kitchen door, leaning out to crumble a Gaines burger patty into Kim's dish. "How long have you been home?" she asked.

"Long enough to find Kitty and that boyfriend of hers in the pool."

Eleanor stood up, held the door open for him. Before entering the kitchen, he kissed her on the cheek. "Who knows what they were up to before I came home."

Eleanor ignored his remark. "I've invited him to stay for dinner. Poor thing, he's so skinny."

"Poor thing? We give him our daughter, our pool, our food . . . . Gee, what else do we have?"

David, fresh from the shower, had come into the kitchen. "Anything I can do to help?" Captain Park noticed David was wearing his blue aloha shirt that Eleanor had given him as a gift.

He impressed upon the kids that the Alhambra was built by the Moors on what were once Roman ruins. He wanted to convey to them that they stood on a perfect example of how over the inexorable march of time, history moved in waves of migration and fortification, flourishing then receding to near extinction where once even squatters lived among the ruins. The dominion of the Moors, whose fortunes too would wax and wane like the moon, or the tides, derived from a cross-pollination of cultures that absorbed and integrated the influences of other groups, the Jews and the Christians, to create the very palace they were walking through. Over battles won and lost, alliances formed and broken, the Alhambra came into being, a monument to a moment when all the conditions aligned to create something magnificent, something the world had never before imagined. The sound of water cascading from the fountains was as refreshing to their ears as it was to the Muslim emirs of the Nasrid dynasty and later, the Christian kings of Castile. Even Christopher Columbus had walked under these archways to receive permission to discover America. The two younger children followed their father as he waxed poetically about the palace, reading from the official pamphlet and adding his own interpretation. They didn't hear any nightingales because it was blazing noon, but they agreed with him that the sound of water did make them feel cooler. Alex lingered back, embarrassed by her father's enthusiasm. Her mother, noticing she was lagging behind, motioned for her to hurry along. Wistfully, she gazed at the reflecting pools, wishing she could drift off and wander alone.

"The more the merrier," Eleanor said when Kitty, whispering in her mother's ear, thanked her for letting David stay for dinner. She searched the cupboard for a serving platter, anticipating her mother's famous spareribs, doused with hoisin sauce, ginger, and sherry, ready to come out of the oven. "Besides," Eleanor whispered, "what else would he eat in that van of his, granola?"

Captain Park sat alone with David. Eleanor had sent them out with two cans of beer to sit at the table in the side patio they used for company. He had built the patio after completing the front courtyard as if he still needed to lay more bricks. Replacing the two bedroom walls that faced the back yard with French doors, he poured a cement floor over the grass and built a high brick wall with a screen roof to keep out the bugs. Leaving an unpaved trim of ground for plantings, he continued the theme of roses and Russian olive trees. A heavy door with wrought iron ornamentation connected the living room to the courtyard. It was how the Alhambra gradually expanded, he found himself explaining to David, the quadrangular plan of rooms opening to courtyards and courtyards serving as passageways. He liked bringing the outside in, the sun and the wind circulating throughout the house. Before going to sleep, the kids could see the moon and the clouds lit by it. During winter storms, the doors were latched in place, and the rain was kept out.

David listened, whether it was simply politeness, Captain Park wasn't sure. The boy looked so serious that Captain Park couldn't tell, but he found himself wanting to give advice. The boy seemed receptive, like an orphan who had found someone interested in his welfare. He knew the boy had dropped out of school and was living like a hippie on the North Shore. The relationship between Kitty and David seemed to have taken a serious turn. At all costs, he had to prevent his daughter from joining the hippie commune out there. He needed to take a strong stance with the boy, offer some other plan, in case his daughter started getting strange ideas in her head.

Kitty carried in the platter of spareribs. She heard her father telling David to think about a career in aviation. "All the pilots that were hired just after the war are going up for retirement soon. That means there'll be huge openings at all the major carriers. It's not a bad way to earn a living."

"Dad," Kitty implored gently. "David doesn't want to be a pilot. He's a potter, an artist. Stuck in a cockpit is not his idea of fun." She turned to her boyfriend. "Right?"

Before David could answer, feeling uncomfortable that Kitty had in some way diminished her father, Captain Park spoke. "He can always do pots on the side. Look at me, you think I like sitting in a cockpit all day long—back and forth, island hopping day after day, clear skies, same weather day after day, no variation—hell, anybody can fly these days, just push some buttons, put the plane on automatic pilot—why do you think I build all these rooms and walls? Everybody needs relief. But you have to start laying plans. The future will sneak up before you know it."

Eleanor heard most of the rant, pausing at the door before bringing into the patio more dishes. "C'mon, let's eat, gang, before it gets cold." She sat down and began to pass the food around. "Help yourselves." The spareribs were from a recipe she was given a long time ago in Miami, before she had any children, by a family who had made a place for her at their table.

Having just stepped out of the shower, Aidan was unaware of what he had missed. He kissed his mother on the cheek. She feigned annoyance at the water dripping from his wet hair. He slid into a chair, reached across the table, and gave David's hand a firm shake, saying, "Hey, the South Shore was cranking, man."

Captain Park watched the way the two young men clasped hands as if exchanging secret handshakes. There was nothing how-do-you-do about it. It seemed to involve two movements, one firm, the other relaxed, like the sequence of a wave, rising and falling. It was always accompanied by "hey" rather than "hello."

David's face brightened. "Yeah, where'd you go?"

"Rock Piles."

"Short board?"

"Totally shredded it. Ripped off a fin. You should've been there. Heard tomorrow's going to be just as gnarly."

As twilight descended, softening the faces around him, Captain Park regretted that the screened roof kept not only the bugs away but the birds as well. He had caged the olive trees, constantly trimming back the branches so they wouldn't tear the screen of the roof above. He thought of all the miles he had flown to bring him to this moment, the gathering at the table that would inevitably enlarge to include boys that took his daughters' hearts away from him. There was nothing he could do to stop the invasion. The faded roses, bending forward by the weight of their own flowering, seemed to nod off to sleep.

They never saw El Cordobés in the ring. They never saw him again. By morning, the matador and his entourage had left the tiny town of Úbeda to fight bulls in other towns that departed from the family's itinerary. He bought tickets for a bullfight in Málaga when they finally reached the coast, pointing in the direction of Gibraltar, the incredible fact that Africa was just across the water. Kitty couldn't be consoled, not because she wanted to see El Cordobés in the ring but because she hadn't been told that the ears of the fallen beast in the dirt would be cut off and flung into the roaring crowd.

No one heard Alex come in the front door. Hearing their voices, she came through the living room and stepped into the patio. Someone turned on the garden lights. Only then did her father notice that one of Alex's long dangling earrings was missing and her dress was turned inside out.

At one time the Alhambra was a self-contained palace, a city behind high walls the color of the red earth with springs fed by the River Darro that watered the orange groves and myrtles where nightingales lived among the sweet fruit and the star-shaped flowers, where roses, cascading in a waterfall of petals, gladdened the eye as the fountaining pools in the courtyards of the Generalife, the Garden of the Architect, did the mind.

Conservatory

He tied the laces of his wife's walking shoes and stood up. She looked at him helplessly, sitting at the edge of the bed, waiting for him to initiate the next move. Holding a pale blue wool pullover with an Icelandic-style trim in one hand and in the other, a canary-yellow wool cardigan with gold-tone buttons, he asked her which sweater she wanted to wear. She looked at the sweaters, vacantly. "Okay, then," he said with a forced cheerfulness. "Smart choice. The yellow one it is." He guided her arms through the sleeves. For good measure he did all the buttons. "Looks like it's going to be cold out there. Beautiful and crisp but cold. Ready?" He extended a hand to help her stand. He braced to hoist her onto her feet. She was getting heavier.

He led her from the bedroom into the high-ceilinged living room. By the foyer he lifted the jackets from the coat rack and helped her into her cream-colored parka and then put on his navy blue one, zipping them both up. "Oh, I almost forgot. Your mittens. Your hands always get so cold." He reached into one of her pockets and found a single mitten. He searched the other pocket, but didn't find its mate. They would have to buy her another pair. He had lost count the number of mittens she had lost in recent weeks. He wondered if there was some friendly neighborhood bureau of the lost and found between Cranmer Court and Hagley Park. He was sure that's where the losses occurred. He wistfully kept his eyes out in case some good Samaritan—New Zealand seemed to be full of them—had picked up one or more of the mittens and, on one of their daily walks, they would find them dangling from a shrub, a whole shrub tied with her mittens, decorated like a Christmas tree. It would give them something to do today, search for that mythical mitten bush or buy a dozen the way one bought socks.

"Which way shall we walk?" he asked, adjusting the hood of the parka over her head. He pretended to hear an answer. They could keep standing on the sidewalk in front of their building on Montreal Street if he didn't make the first step. "I agree. Let's try Armagh, then we can walk right into the park. But if you want to walk along the river, we could walk along Kilmore." He paused, again pretending to hear an answer. "Yeah, you're right. Let's try Armagh. We did Kilmore yesterday."

"Keep your hands in your pocket because we don't want you to get frostbite," he warned as she tried to hold his hand. There was no danger of that happening. He was just exaggerating, hoping to get a response from her as if she were a child. Although it was mid-September, early spring in the Southern Hemisphere, the wind, carrying the chill of Antarctica, brushed lightly across their faces. To reassure her, he hooked his arm through hers.

They set off for the park, their outing for the day, crossing a footbridge over parts of the Avon River that were as narrow as a stream. In another time she would have delighted in the profusion of daffodils, walking on paths that flowed beneath clouds of flowering cherry trees. She would have been the one to rise early, stepping out for some exercise, hurrying back to exhort him out of bed lest he miss most of the morning, the best hours of the day. She would have seen the blossoms earlier; she would have seen how soon they would be gone. Now she walked through the tunnel of blossoms without comment, walking woodenly, staring ahead. In another time, although she would have mourned the passing of the cherry blossoms, she would have looked forward to the approaching weeks when there would be rhododendrons and azaleas to admire.

They came upon the empty rose garden, the rambling rosebushes pruned and fed by experts to bloom the way fireworks are wired to go off in a timed sequence. He wondered if they would still be in Christchurch when the show of roses opened in a few months. To his untrained eye, the garden looked desolate, in contrast to the flowerings they had just seen. He led his wife to the large artificial rose at the entrance and, making an extravagant show of sniffing it, coaxed his wife. "C'mon, Eleanor, your turn."

Wordlessly, she leaned forward to inhale the cold metal of the sculpted rose.

To kill time, he led her through every path in the rose garden, leading her through a maze of his own making. It occurred to him that if he abandoned her there, she would be lost. He didn't want to think about how long it would take before she abandoned her post, realizing he was gone, and wandered, looking for him, unable to find her way home.

In another time she had been the one to show him the conservatory, the large Victorian greenhouse with its collection of tropical plants. She had discovered it first, on one of her early morning walks. Finding the door locked, she peered into the conservatory, wanting in, wanting to feel the humidity on the other side of the glass where large fan-shaped ferns pressed from inside, grazing the high ceilings, and touch the flowers that were grouped as exotic—orchids and anthuriums—commonplace where she was from. Later, when she brought him back, she couldn't explain to him how much she needed to breathe in the moist green air. It became a ritual with her, to step inside the greenhouse, even for a moment, whether with him or alone.

Having zigzagged through every configuration of pathways among the rosebushes, retracing and repeating their steps, he started toward the conservatory. She followed but when he opened the door, she refused to go inside. He pulled. She resisted. "Let's go in. This is your favorite place." Another couple, following close behind, waited politely for the tug-of-war to be resolved. They cleared their throats after awhile, and he moved himself and his wife aside. The very words he had sought to contain came flying out, "What the hell's wrong with you?" He didn't have to look at her dull face, her stooped posture, to regret saying them. More people were coming through the rose garden. Soon they would be wanting to come into the conservatory. He led her away.

In another time she would have suggested they go home for a sandwich rather than waste money at the tea shop, saving that treat for a late afternoon snack of scones and whipped cream. He missed those little annoyances over nickels and dimes. She let him lead her into the tea shop, let him sit her down near the window. He didn't bother asking her what she wanted. He ordered two servings of scones and whipped cream and two cups of coffee. He wanted his wife to scold him for ruining their appetites with something so sweet so close to lunch.

On the way home they left the path and crossed the grass toward an ancient shoreline where on a sand mound, maritime pines older than a hundred years grew as though on an island unto themselves. In another time, whether they had just entered the park or were on the way out, he would make a habit of hugging one half of the largest pine and she the other half, their arms circumnavigating the trunk, their hands reaching blindly for the other's. The first time it happened, he was measuring the tree, placing his arms around it when she followed, throwing her arms around the other side of it. They had laughed at the same time, realizing what a sight they made, an old couple such as themselves hugging a big old pine tree. And in the lightness of the moment, their hands touched playfully.

"C'mon, Eleanor," he said, placing her arms around their adopted pine, "let's give our favorite tree a big fat hug." Before her arms could fall limply, he jumped to the other side of the tree and grasped her hands, trying to look around the trunk at the same time. They were both looking around the tree without seeing each other.

"You're a sight for sore eyes," he said kissing his daughter's cheek. He clasped his son-in-law Ben's hand, giving him a few hearty pats on the back, which was his way of saying what a good sport he was for not only bringing the family all the way down to New Zealand but for marrying his daughter. Then, as if saving the best for last, he reached down to lift his granddaughters, both of them, one at a time. Kristin protested. At nine she was too old to be lifted that way even by her grandfather. Three-year-old Amelia didn't want to be put down. "Mom!" Alex cried, seeing her mother off to the side, standing where she had been left by her husband who had rushed ahead to greet them as they exited through customs. She hugged her mother and felt no response. Her father's exuberance covered her mother's flatness, her feeble smiles. Alex wanted her father to put Amelia down, but he insisted on carrying his granddaughter while holding his wife's hand. Leading the way to baggage claim, he never let go of that hand, not until everyone had settled into the rental van.

Alex and Ben soon discovered they had inadvertently signed up for a whirlwind tour. Their one week of spring vacation was going to be anything but leisurely. Alex waited for the chance to ask her father about her mother's withdrawn condition, but the moment never came. Her father's demanding schedule didn't permit any opportunity for Alex to catch him alone. They never stayed long enough in one spot to make the distances they traveled worthwhile. Disheartened, Alex couldn't help but feel her father wanted to keep moving. By keeping them all in perpetual motion he could minimize what he was hiding, the apparent lack of interaction between his wife and the others. His itinerary kept them captive in the van he had commandeered, ignoring Ben's offer to take over at the wheel, making conversation impossible as he filled their ears by playing and rewinding cassette tapes he had made of Kiri Te Kanawa. They crossed the South Island at breakneck speed. Barely had they changed into swimsuits to sit in the thermal waters at Hanmer Springs before they had to dry themselves and get into the van for Queenstown. Before the girls had a chance to play along the shores of Lake Wakatipu, they rushed off to see the fjords at Milford Sound. At night, they found themselves too exhausted to complain as they crawled into lumpy beds of whatever motel still had its vacant sign lit. Alex couldn't peel her mother away from her father's side. By the end of the trip, Alex's buried rage made her, too, stop speaking. She was angry with both her parents. Her father's refusal to admit what was happening. Her mother's almost willful silence.

The day Alex left with Ben and the girls, Eleanor withdrew further into despondency. Mahny experienced brief misgivings, thinking he should have packed their things, locked the apartment, and gone with the kids. He felt like calling it quits before he rallied, and as the days passed, they somehow got through winter, the months when it was summer at home. He still thought of Hawai'i as home, however much he had tried to make a go of it in New Zealand. Maybe, he figured, in an attempt to understand what was happening to his wife, the reversal of seasons had finally caught up with her, that the

workings of her internal clock had become confused in the move
so far below the equator. He knew that it took allergies months and
sometimes years to take hold before a person eventually succumbed
to the pollen and dust of a new place. Maybe in the beginning when
they first came to Christchurch, she was still resilient enough to
withstand the displacement. He held onto the idea of spring. Once the
weather warmed and the buds of new leaves and flowers appeared,
she would feel better. He rallied, before he got stuck in the tedium of
carrying the compliant but joyless weight of his wife. He wouldn't be
doing anyone any good if he too went blank.

    Trouble was he had found himself before he had reached
the age of fifty with too much time on his hands. At forty-seven he
suffered a heart attack while flying on the last of his scheduled flights
of the day, coming in from Kahului to Honolulu. He told the co-pilot
to take over the approach as a massive wave of what he thought was
indigestion prevented him from doing anything but wait out the cold
sweat dripping from his brow. He dismissed his co-pilot's show of
concern, saying he was fine, fine, not to worry, and remained in the
cockpit until the passengers and the rest of the crew deplaned. Before
the quick turnaround brought a new replacement crew on board, he
found his way to his car, and drove himself to the hospital. He had
suffered a myocardial infarction, relatively minor the cardiologist had
said and, as if to make him feel better, added that if he had to have a
heart attack, he had had a good one. Chances of survival and recovery
were excellent as long as he gave up smoking, changed his diet, and
exercised. But he wouldn't be able to fly anymore, not commercially,
not according to FAA regulations. A pilot with a heart condition was
dead in the water.
    Aloha Airlines had hired him under its former name, Trans-
Pacific Airlines. He grew with the company, working his way up

from co-pilot to captain, eventually becoming a check pilot in charge of passing or failing pilots when they came up for recertification, testing them in the air or in a simulator. At the risk of accumulating the ire of pilots with greater seniority, he had no qualms about failing those who got flustered at the various scenarios he threw at them, causing hypothetical engine fires and other events that could happen at anytime. It didn't help that he had taken up the habit of smoking cigars, blowing huge clouds of smoke as he watched how they panicked, those senior ones, often the most lazy and least competent, who made sure they were seen strutting out of the cockpit, the ones who flirted with the stewardesses. He had the power of dangling the humiliation of suspension over them. His status as a senior check pilot made him the chosen candidate to fly beyond the small chain of islands, breaking the monotony of routine takeoffs and landings in conditions invariably clear and sunny. When the four Vickers Viscounts in the company's fleet had to be remodified by the manufacturer, he ferried the planes to Cambridge, England, routes that included refueling stops on the West and East Coasts, Newfoundland, and the Azores. When the lease expired on one of the Viscounts, he flew through the Bermuda Triangle to deliver the plane to its new owners, Aeropesca Colombia in Bogotá, Colombia. When the company upgraded its fleet, he piloted home the new jets, returning from England to great company fanfare the sleek BAC-1-11s.

He never piloted an airplane again. And although he could name every type of aircraft flying in the sky, hearing a plane before it came out of the clouds and into view, he kept it to himself. He feared he would bore everyone by talking about his younger days the way old-timers did, those who refused to be sidelined, with something to prove. He had to think ahead; he couldn't look back. He had a daughter in graduate school, another in college, and a son about to

enter one. He had to think fast, make the necessary adjustments. He
began to look for places where the cost of living would allow him to
stretch his reduced income.

Somehow he managed to convince his wife of their
predicament, bargaining with her that if he made the changes
the doctors had advised—giving up smoking, eating a better diet,
exercising—they could live well even if that meant they would have
to sell the house, take what equity they could out of the sale, buy
something more modest in an affordable condominium, which they
could lock and leave for months at a time, and still have money in
the bank. The kids had left home. There was no sense in keeping
the house. He had to think ahead. Nostalgia will kill you, he told his
wife as she wept when they left the house with the courtyards and
the roses, after years of tending, finally mature, offering a generosity
of blossoms when no one was looking. Within a week of signing the
sale of the house, she heard the new owners were tearing down the
house for something grander. He told her not to think about it. They
had to look ahead.

He tried Costa Rica, plunking down five thousand dollars
for a coffee farm outside the town of Alajuela, but the promise of a
bountiful annual bean harvest to supplement his income fell short
the very first year. After expenses, the small profit went to support
the resident farmer and his family. He postponed uprooting his
wife so soon after she had settled into the rhythm of their new life
as pensioners. She had adapted happily as if rediscovering the
simplicity of the early years of their marriage when it had been just
the two of them. The third-floor apartment they rented in San José,
overlooking Avenida Central, reminded her of their tiny cottage in
Coral Gables when they had nothing but each other. Every morning
she walked to the mercado, making it her mission to feed her husband
well, spending the equivalent of a few dollars for an unimaginable

assortment of fresh fruits and vegetables. He sported a mustache and cut a striking figure in a leather jacket and jeans. Except for his idiosyncratic Spanish, adding an O to any English word that would take one, he could have passed for a Tico.

Accompanying a friend whose import business took him to New Zealand, he changed course. On his return, he made sure to contain his excitement, knowing Eleanor would resist any new plan, especially if she felt she was being talked into something. He had been looking for an alternative once he became disillusioned with Costa Rica. He had failed at being a gentleman farmer, albeit a modest one, driving a battered Corolla out of the city only to hear tales of woe from the young farmer he employed who week after week, after leading him through the muddy hillside, would show him a handful of shriveled beans. He sold the coffee farm at a loss. Not only was New Zealand one plane ride away from home, it was clean, and the people spoke English. They could still be pensioners but live even better in New Zealand. Costa Rica, however romantic, was a third world country, the houses poorly constructed compared to the ones in New Zealand, especially Christchurch, which, he stressed to Eleanor, was more like England than England. She turned away from him. She felt simpatico with the locals. She was just getting the hang of Spanish.

Ann Berensen welcomed the Parks into her apartment. She and her husband Jules had been one of the original owners at Cranmer Court after its conversion into condominiums. This often-mentioned fact did not endear her to the other residents, who made it a point to avoid her. Introducing herself to her new neighbors with a plate of oatmeal cookies, she didn't waste any time in telling them the history of the place. Built in 1876, Cranmer Court, retaining the Gothic Revival exterior of its illustrious past, had once been the Christchurch

Normal School. One of the city's significant buildings, it had recently been registered as a Historic Place. She wanted to make sure the newcomers appreciated the status of their new residence, an address to be proud of. Once the introduction had been made, she found many reasons to drop by, for a chat, a cup of tea, and reciprocated with invitations to dinner. Proud of her culinary experiments, this evening she was serving paella, substituting chicken for rabbit, white beans for green. She had also invited Dr. Heathcliff, another original, one of the few who still talked to her.

During the winter, Jules had taken a turn for the worse. A dinner with Dr. Heathcliff would provide free consultation; he could take a look at her husband in his prudent way and later ring her up with an assessment. She wondered if Jules hadn't had another minor stroke. His memory, foggy in the last ten years, seemed to be accelerating its decline. His energy level was such that he spent most of his time reading in his armchair. Pretending to read was more like it. He often held the same book upside down. But he was so obedient. She had to be thankful for that.

In planning tonight's dinner, she had included the Parks, realizing the months had sped by without her seeing them, if only from afar, in the mornings from her living room window, as they walked past on Montreal Street, going, she assumed, to the Botanic Gardens. Many times she had wanted to pop out and say hello but something held her back. The couple's initial exuberance had lifted her own spirits at the sight of them enjoying their new surroundings as they set out each day to explore the city. It was hard to explain. She could see a change as they walked past her window, walking stiffly, side-by-side, looking straight ahead, as if they had just had an argument.

Ann Berensen found the husband more approachable than the wife. Mahny Park was so easy to talk to. He lavished praise on

the decorative touches of her well-upholstered apartment as well
as the gracious manner in which she served her painstakingly
prepared meals. Ann Berensen wasn't sure how to interpret the
docility of the wife. Sweet and demure women made her feel like
a bull in a china shop. She was always a little wary of wives who
seemed to defer to their husbands to the point of losing all sense of
themselves. But in Mahny Park's presence, Ann Berensen forgot that
she laughed too loudly, forgot that she was a lonely sixty-five-year-
old grandmother saddled with a husband who was slipping further
away from her. During those first dinner invitations, the table
seemed balanced. Jules and Eleanor anchored the table like pewter
candlesticks, weighing down their end of the table with small talk
and good manners while the effusive ones chatted about the charms
of Christchurch. She felt Mahny was the only one listening to her as
she augmented the things he had seen with her own versions, noting
how seriously he took her recommendations regarding all that he
had yet to see.

"Welcome, welcome!" Upon hearing the doorbell, Ann,
anticipating the usual promptness of the Parks, had brought Jules
forward, out of his chair so he would be standing when the guests
arrived. "Come in, " Ann said, opening the door and hugging first the
wife and then the husband, who held up a bottle of Merlot. "Lovely!"
She glanced at the wine. Before she could take it, she was at Jules' side,
nudging him with the cue, "Say hello to the Parks, dear."

Jules did as he was told. "Hello," he said, smiling sweetly.

"Please make yourselves comfortable." She gestured her guests
to the sofa. Again, she was at Jules' side, leading him to his armchair.
There! she almost said aloud. She let out a sigh and, unsure why she
had paused, dusted her hands, and looked at her guests, seated as
directed on the sofa. The change she had sensed as the couple walked
past her window over the last few months was evident. The winter

had not been kind to them. She scolded herself. She should have been a better friend. "It's been too long," she said.

Mahny Park, confident that he had picked the right wine, presented the Merlot like a child offering a gift to an esteemed teacher.

"Oh, yes, lovely. Thank you. May I pour you a glass?"

The doorbell rang. "That must be Dr. Heathcliff. Excuse me." Flustered, she went into the foyer and greeted the doctor, who did not hand her a bottle of wine, only his hat and coat. Tonight she was willing to forgive his odd habit of putting on outerwear when he lived down the hallway. She shrugged it off. He would earn his dinner by observing her husband. She led the good doctor into the living room. Once again, she found herself coaching her husband. "Say hello to Dr. Heathcliff, dear."

Once again, her husband did as he was told. He offered the same sweet smile. "Hello."

"Good to see you, Jules." The doctor clasped Jules' hand. His eyes lingered on his old friend's face and, almost reluctantly, pulled away to greet the other guests in the room.

Mahny Park was standing, waiting to shake the doctor's hand. Sitting on the edge of the sofa, Eleanor Park didn't look up when the doctor drew closer. "Good to see you both. It's been awhile. Glad we've gotten through the winter. Trust you two Hawaiians survived as best to be expected. I believe you skipped the last several winters—now that you've been through this one, one of the coldest we've had, do you really want to be Kiwis?" Behind Dr. Heathcliff's twinkling eyes was the true observer of the wise old practitioner.

"Good to see you, Dr. Heathcliff. You're looking well."

Dr. Heathcliff shook the husband's hand, but didn't take his eyes off the wife. He bent as close as his creaky back would allow and reached for her hand. "And what about you, Eleanor? How are you?"

Ann Berensen came out of the kitchen, a glass of wine in each hand, in time to see Mahny Park put his arm around his wife, to hear him gently coax her. "Say hello to Dr. Heathcliff, Eleanor. You remember Dr. Heathcliff, don't you?"

Rather than pretending that what was happening wasn't, that one partner in each couple was experiencing the same difficulties with their respective spouses, Dr. Heathcliff addressed the situation directly. He didn't think he would be offending the afflicted ones, probably only the suffering ones, suffering because they were the ones being left behind. He noticed Ann had to remove Jules' plate after the first serving or else, like a turkey, he would have continued eating, not knowing when to stop. He noticed Eleanor, who always had the most impeccable manners, now placed her bread directly on the table, and that she bent her head so far forward over the plate, if Mahny didn't gently nudge her back and hand her a spoon, like a dog she would have lapped at the paella. Whether Jules had suffered more little strokes resulting in a hastening of dementia or had developed Alzheimer's disease, he couldn't determine definitively. More tests had to be done. With Eleanor, it appeared to be clinical depression. Medication was in order. Dr. Heathcliff knew that Mahny Park would not have agreed to come to dinner if on some unconscious level he didn't want to hear the truth about his wife. Ann would not have invited him if she didn't want him to observe Jules close up. The ones suffering had brought their loved ones to the table for the good doctor to see.

Dr. Heathcliff went to bed with a heavy heart. Three hours later he was awakened by the phone. It was Mahny Park. Could he come right away, he apologized, but something had happened with Eleanor. The doctor put on his coat and hat, and walked down the hall to the Parks' apartment. He found Mahny cradling his wife. She appeared so small in his arms. She had seized to the point where every limb from her neck to her toes had contracted as if she were trying to fit herself into the smallest space possible. Jutting sharply out of her husband's arms, her elbows, oddly angled, made him think of broken wings. "Catatonia," Dr. Heathcliff said quietly. "We must get her to the hospital."

Mallards and leaves drifted in the lazy current flowing under the Armagh footbridge as he crossed the Avon River into the park. He supposed he was saying goodbye to Christchurch by walking through Hagley Park and the Botanic Gardens one last time. He had called to let his children know that he would be bringing their mother home. They would be coming home for Christmas. She was still in the hospital, but she would be released in a few days. He couldn't bring himself to tell them that she would be heavily medicated. He didn't know how to prepare them for that moment when they saw her again. The psychiatrists at Christchurch Hospital would not release her until the medications had taken effect. Slowly, as the weeks passed, she was beginning to thaw. She could walk with assistance, taking daily turns down the corridors to build up her strength. She could feed herself although her appetite was poor. He couldn't tell if it was due to her condition or the institutional food. Even the vegetables were steamed to soggy gray matter. Since her admission, he had spent every day at the hospital. It was as if, while they both were away, spring had turned into summer.

He avoided the tea shop and headed for the pine mound. On the promontory of the sand hill, he saw the old trees, distinctive against the sky. Departing from the path, he made a diagonal cut across the grass that surrounded the mound. Stepping from the grass onto the sandy soil, he had the sensation of leaving one element and entering another, and he was that kid again who, coming out of the blue waters at Mokulēʻia after tumbling in the waves for hours, had lost all track of time. Shaking himself dry, he lay on sand so hot it was barely tolerable. He felt the sun on his face, pressing him flat against the sand, withstood the burning. The sun, evaporating the droplets of ocean on his skin, prickled like a thousand needles. He lurched forward out of the memory and grasped the old pine as if hugging an old friend.

Someone had ignited the roses. As he came upon the Central Rose Garden, every rosebush seemed to be bursting their fireworks of petals as if all the pruning and fertilizing had been done for his benefit alone. He wished Eleanor were here to witness what she had been waiting so long to see. He couldn't leave until he had walked through the rose garden and the conservatory. Shortly after the day of Eleanor's puzzling refusal to go into the greenhouse, she had lapsed into a state of catatonia. He couldn't understand it—*catatonia*, the benign sounding word, almost floral and pretty, saying it was like rolling the names of Florida, or Alajuela, or Andalusia on the tongue, names that conjured places they had seen together. He couldn't reconcile the ruffled syllables with her sad state, hard and dry as a days-old biscuit. There had been signs, and he had ignored them all, thinking he could talk her out of her listlessness, her stupor, her stony silence as he had talked her out of and into so many things.

The contrast between the steamy interior and the bracing cold outside, so stark during the winter when pipes of hot water misted the air, mimicking the humidity of a tropical rainforest, wasn't as apparent now that it was summer. It still felt like a sauna. He closed the door behind him, unprepared for the assault on his senses, and his response. He wanted to reverse so much of it, to do it again but only better, to rewind at another beginning, and curl himself into the fist of an unfurled fern. Brushing against the umbrella leaves of the banana plants, breathing the damp green smell of dark fecundity, he looked up at the high glass ceiling, held by a structure of steel as intricate as lace. It was difficult to tell where the supports were as a second story of plants intertwined with the steel, those claiming the empty spaces, the climbing ones, the ones that loved the light.

The Art of Healing

Ching Ming, arriving like an old relative they had forgotten to invite to a party, surprised the two sisters every April as they made plans to visit their mother's grave on her birthday. This year was no exception. Her birthday fell in the middle of the Chinese days of remembrance, a time for families to honor the dead. Since their mother's death twelve years ago, the sisters had begun to do their own version. Bearing a simple bouquet on that first birthday without her, the sisters had noticed other families huddled around graves, performing elaborate rituals that produced plumes of smoke and loud, crackling noises. What they brought had seemed meager by comparison. Over the years their own version of Ching Ming grew haphazardly, mimicked from those around them or dimly reconstructed from the past. The two sisters were the elders now. They had no one but each other to rely on.

"Have you got the paper money?" Catherine inquired over the phone.

"Yes," Alexandria said, "plenty left from last year. We won't need to go to Chinatown. I've also got lots of incense."

"What about the whisky and the shot glasses?" Catherine realized she was having her sister supply everything. Quickly, she added, "I've got a lighter."

"Glasses, yes. Whisky, we'll get on the way as well as the oranges and flowers. Anything else? Oh! Do you have a coffee can we can burn the money in?"

"I'll find something," Catherine assured her sister. A coffee can was the least she could bring.

It was the same conversation every April ever since they had assumed the responsibility of taking care of the dead. It was the same way they put together family potlucks; somehow whatever they each brought to the table, it always worked out. There was never too much or too little of one food group. They preferred the spontaneous menu, the impromptu feast, as if they already knew what the other would bring. They couldn't bear the weight of planning anything too far in advance. They couldn't bear planning anything alone.

Alexandria, after discussing the matter over the phone with her younger sister, looked in the garage for the cardboard box, having not given it another thought after putting it away last year. The cheap floral vases and shot glasses had not been properly rinsed, and the candle stumps and bunches of incense were netted with cobwebs. However, she was glad to find the paper money—those heavenly notes for the dead to spend in the afterlife—still crisp as if newly minted in half-opened packages of cellophane, squares of gold and silver window-leafed on the thinnest paper.

Surveying the supplies and the stash of unspent notes, Alexandria felt dismayed. They should have been more generous. They should have burned the whole damn stash last year.

That was the problem. Alexandria and Catherine were the elders now, but they had not received proper instruction. They didn't know how many bundles of heavenly notes to burn, how many candles and sticks of incense to light, how many oranges to offer. They didn't know the sequence of such offerings, when and how to bow, which Daoist incantation to mumble, what kinds of flowers to choose, and if any of the things they thought to do or bring were meant to be done or brought at all. There was no one left in the family to consult.

"It's the intention," Catherine said, "that matters."

Alexandria agreed. "Our hearts are in the right place."

They were especially uneasy about the whisky. The first Ching Ming they did by themselves found them hesitant, doubtful. Maybe they were recalling the prodigious flow of whisky at weddings. They served the dead alcohol anyway, later, substituting sake instead. Would their grandparents be offended? Had their grandparents been alive to read about the Japanese Imperial Army killing, raping, and mutilating thousands of their Chinese brothers and sisters in the siege of Nanjing, they would have long since settled on a faraway island in the Pacific, and the Pearl River Delta would have receded into the distant shore of memory.

Catherine and Alexandria were the elders now and two heads were better than one. Piecing together what they remembered from the pilgrimages they had made as children accompanying their mother and her three sisters to the Chinese Cemetery in Mānoa to visit the grave of long dead parents, Alexandria and Catherine gave themselves high marks for intention. The rest they made up.

Even as a child Catherine had sensed that the circle of women who spent most of the visit telling each other what to do and arguing about where they would eat lunch afterwards—*Nothing too salty!*—were performing the ceremony half-heartedly. Many years later, during the one time she had witnessed as an adult her mother and her aunts go through the motions of being dutiful daughters, what she had long ago suspected was confirmed. The eldest aunt took Catherine aside and, in a hushed voice, confessed that lest Kitty had any doubts about the heathenish things they were about to do, she, Eve, child of God, had already taken it upon herself to receive clearance from above. The Lord had granted her special dispensation,

for their poor, ignorant parents had never had the chance to know
the Lord and to accept Jesus Christ as their savior. They remained in
the dark. He knew that as Christians they were not worshipping, God
forbid, their ancestors. He knew they worshipped only Him-Almighty-
through-His-Son-Jesus-Christ-Our-Lord-Amen. Catherine's head
spun as if suddenly struck by heatstroke. She was tired and hungry,
and in looking back, angry. It didn't help that her normally frail aunt
clutched her right forearm, squeezing it as she grew more agitated
at the utterance of His Name. At lunch—her mother and her aunts
had finally agreed upon Asia Mānoa for the Hong Kong-style shrimp
wonton mein—Catherine looked down at a trail of crescent moons
etched into her skin.

Awareness of the spirit realm came to the two sisters late,
well into middle age, the lifting of the veil coinciding during the time
of their mother's descent into dementia. It happened suddenly. It
happened slowly. It happened depending, they came to realize, on
how closely you were looking. One day she was shopping, eating,
laughing with her daughters. One day she was caught wandering
into traffic. Cries of distress from their usually self-reliant father
rallied Catherine and Alexandria to help him watch her. She could
no longer be left alone. They took turns during the day to free him to
run errands—it was too risky to take her along—but the nights were
his. When he appeared ragged and sleep-deprived having had to lock
her in the bedroom by installing a latch from the outside to prevent
her from cooking eggs at three in the morning only to slip out with the
stove ablaze to knock on the doors of strangers, his daughters gently
released their father's hold on her.

A barometer to her parents' well-being in happier times,
Alexandria being the eldest, prospered, having them all to herself for

four years until her sister's arrival. She witnessed the adoring look of her mother whenever her father, confident and jaunty, entered the room. She witnessed his ability to extract from her pretty mother a girlish self-consciousness. She was aware of her mother becoming aware the moment he stepped into their presence. It was his presence alone, Alexandria observed even as a young child, that could elicit such a flutter. Her mother betrayed herself at these times, her inability to hide her good fortune.

Over the years the look gave way to one of distraction, a blurring, a mixed crossing of signals that left Eleanor looking worried. The face fell, drooped, held in place by a mesh of lines. The eyelids seemed hooded, heavy. The burden of worrying about so much happiness had made her miss most of it.

Alexandria wanted assurances. Her own happiness depended upon the happiness of others. Such happiness depended upon her mother and father. If all was well and right with them, then all was well and right with the world.

Anxious about the recent palpitations clamoring inside her chest, Alex picked up the phone and dialed her sister's number. Catherine's answering machine clicked on. "Pick up the phone, Kitty," Alex muttered. Cold and forbidding—"Please leave a message!"—her sister's voice challenged the intrepid caller to leave one. Kitty was probably right there at the kitchen table, writing the morning away, making up stories about their deprived childhood, the perceived hurts, the disappointments.

Several hours later, the palpitations resumed. The anxiety would not be relieved until she had talked to her sister. Alex tried calling her again. This time Kitty picked up.

"I'm worried about Mom and Dad." Alex wasted no time in unburdening herself. She heard Kitty sigh on the other end of the line. "We need to do something. I think we should try some alternative healers, you know, maybe like massage or acupuncture. What do you think?" Sensing her sister's hesitation, she added, "We can't let them continue like this. They're killing themselves and each other."

What it was that she wanted from her sister, Alex couldn't say. Help sounded feeble, yet help was what she wanted. Help in the form of alleviating the pressure, the psychic weight of having to think about their parents. She wanted Kitty to think about them as much as she did. And since it was obvious Kitty didn't think about them as much as she did, she wanted to share her thoughts about them with her sister. Every day. Talking to Kitty helped to relieve some of the mental pressure building up, amassing like the clouds over the Koʻolau mountains every afternoon. Although Kitty listened with patience and sympathy, Alex suspected it was because of her sister's own form of convoluted guilt, guilt for not bearing her share of the burden.

Near School Street, on Lusitana, in a rundown block of old storefronts, they found Cal's place, a martial arts studio where he told them he also practiced his healing art. Just before their appointment he had turned on the air conditioner, a wall unit that seemed capable of blowing only hot air. The dark interior suggested a cool refuge from the afternoon glare, but within minutes after introducing themselves, Catherine felt claustrophobic. The room was stuffy and airless and the healer himself was glazed with sweat. He was wearing a tank top and swim shorts, minimal yardage that revealed a powerful, muscular body. Around his waist he wore a bulging fanny pack that held his special ointments.

Eleanor remained standing obediently between her two daughters. She waited to be told the next thing to do. She wanted to sit, but she remained standing. She wanted to go out the door, but she stood still.

Cal led her gently to the vinyl-padded table in the center of the room. He helped her to lie down. Eleanor obeyed, stiffly, wordlessly, her eyes conveying apprehension. He removed her sandals and began to talk to her, putting her at ease. Her daughters stood on either end of the table. She could see them. Still she looked worried.

"I'm Chinese, too," he said, trying to make her feel comfortable. "Your daughters tell me you're Chinese."

"You're Chinese?" Alex blurted. "You don't look Chinese."

Cal laughed. "I'm the Portuguese-kind Chinese. From Macao." Turning back to Eleanor, he asked, "And what about you? Where are your folks from?"

"Canton." Alex and Catherine were surprised by her response.

"Canton? You mean, Guangzhou," Cal corrected, good-naturedly. "Nobody says Canton anymore. Only the old futs, but you not one old fut, yeah?"

"Canton," Eleanor repeated, the word sounding more like a phlegm-filled cough.

"We're originally from Wahiawā," Catherine offered quickly. She could sense her mother was barely enduring the humiliation of being there.

"No Chinese in Wahiawā," Cal joked. "Only Filipinos, roosters, and a few Koreans."

"That's us," Alex said. "Our father is Korean."

"Oh, yeah?" Cal unzipped his fanny pack. He took out an unlabeled plastic squirt bottle and squeezed a generous amount of liquid into his palms. "Kimchee-temper kind?"

The sisters laughed.

"Except he thinks he's Irish," Alex added.

Cal was rubbing his hands together. "Oh-oh, what kind of mix-up confusion is that?"

"Maybe he should see you," Alex said, enjoying herself. Catherine gave her a look. She was afraid her sister was saying too much.

"Maybe," Cal said, taking a long look at Eleanor. "I'll straighten him out." He began to rub Eleanor's hands, examining each crooked finger, each knotted knuckle. "Isn't that right, Mrs. Park?"

The healer and the sisters fell silent after awhile. The healer, sitting on a stool, appeared to be in deep concentration as he worked his hands along Eleanor's right arm. He spent a long time at her elbow, bending it back and forth like a hinge.

Alexandria, uncomfortable with the silence, began talking again. "So, are you finding anything?"

Cal smiled and said softly, "Just a lot of goodies."

"Excuse me?" Alex felt caught off guard.

If he heard, Cal didn't answer. He brought his stool around to the other side to begin working on her left arm. "Yeah, you got a lot of goodies, Mrs. Park. You've been holding a lot of goodies for a long time now. Time to give them up. Open the drawer. Give them to me. No need hold them anymore."

Eleanor struggled to get off the table. Catherine and Alex watched her stoop to pick up her sandals. She sat down on a stool and started to buckle the straps.

"It's not time to go yet, Mom," Catherine said. "Cal's not finished working on you."

"I want to go," Eleanor mumbled. "Yes, it is. Time to go."

Cal took her hand and led her back to the table. Once again he removed her sandals, slipped them to the floor. "Almost done, Mrs. Park. Just a little bit more, okay? I'll take good care of you. Just relax. Your daughters are here." He held her feet with one hand while the other hand searched inside his fanny back. The plastic bottle came out again. He started to work her toes, examining each toe as he had each finger.

The sight of their mother's feet pained both daughters. The once beautiful high arches, narrow heels, and delicate bone structure had over the years become swollen and discolored. The toes sprang and curled in various directions, as if the joints were screaming in agony.

"Painful, yeah?" Cal said with complete understanding.

"Why are her feet like that?" Alex wanted to know.

"Goodies," Cal said, "all those goodies she won't let go."

"Can you fix it?" Alex wanted to know.

"Depends on your mother."

For a second time Eleanor struggled to get up. Before she could slide off the table, Cal gently guided her back. "See," he said, "she doesn't like it."

"Like what?" Again, it was Alex who wanted to know.

"Like being touched," her sister answered.

"That's right," Cal said, "and I'm hardly exerting any pressure."

"Too painful?" Alex asked.

"Too painful," Cal agreed.

Once again the healer and the sisters fell silent. The grumbling of the air conditioner and Eleanor's palpable agitation didn't seem to distract Cal, who had stopped the massage. He was no longer even touching Eleanor but seemed to be listening for something, a pulse or a vibration. His eyes were closed, his head hanging down. He could have been sleeping.

Alex wanted to know but waited.

Catherine was aware of being uncomfortable and hot. Eleanor was looking at her. Her eyes were saying *let me out of here.*

Then Cal woke up. "Quick! Get the incense in the can—over there—the can, in the corner on the desk—grab seven of them. Light them quick!"

Catherine responded first, fumbling for the bright pink sticks and a lighter.

"Light them—and walk around the room—now—quick! And you," he motioned to Alex, "grab the phone. Dial Walter in Kalihi. Walter Kunimura, the healer." Cal barked out the number.

Alex dialed and redialed, using the phone on Cal's desk, her fingers trying to match Cal's frantic tempo.

"Wait," Alex said. "Why am I calling him?"

"He can help," Cal said, visibly shaken. "I'm not at that level."

"What level?" Alex was starting to feel as uncomfortable as her mother and sister. The call was put through. "Hello? Hello? Is this Walter . . . "

"Kunimura," Cal filled in, holding Eleanor's hand. Eleanor looked as though she had had enough.

"Is this Walter Kunimura? Oh, hello. Yes. I'm with my mother. We're with Cal. And he wanted me to call you. Wait, just a minute." She handed the phone to Cal.

He refused to take the phone. "Ask him about your mother."

"Oh, hello. Yes, Cal wants me to ask you about my mother. She's here with Cal, and he wants you to tell him something about my mother."

Catherine, waving the bunch of incense around the table, paused by her sister. "This is weird. Never heard of a healer needing a consult during a session."

Alex shot her sister a look. "Yes, yes, okay, we'll bring her by. Okay. Cal knows where you live. Okay. Tomorrow. We'll come by tomorrow." The phone went dead. She placed the receiver into the cradle and looked at Cal for an explanation.

Eleanor sat up. No one stopped her as she started to put on her sandals. She was out the door and soon Catherine was too, still holding the pink sticks of incense like a decomposing bouquet. She wanted to know why Cal couldn't help their mother, why they had to seek another healer. This Walter what's-his-name in Kalihi.

Alex threw a wad of cash at Cal and, in exchange, she was given two addresses—Walter in Kalihi and Collin in Pālolo. And a thick bunch of incense to burn at home.

"I didn't like that man," Eleanor said in the car. "He gave me the creeps."

They strapped their mother in. The click of the seatbelt buckle sounded like a padlock. Alex took the driver's seat, and Catherine crept into the back, sitting behind Eleanor. She noticed her mother's hair, flat and matted, how much her mother needed a comb through it, some light fluffy teasing.

On the freeway heading east, Alexandria steered the Volvo expertly through the afternoon rush hour. They rode in silence. Catherine wished for a stick of chewing gum to dispel the odd pressure in her ears like a sudden drop in altitude.

"You're just going to have to accept it. This is the way I am. You're just going to have to accept it," Eleanor burst out.

"Like hell I will," Sung Mahn snorted at his daughters' request that according to Cal's instructions he was to light seven sticks of incense for the next seven days. Light them in the apartment, carry the burning sticks from room to room, preferably at twilight.

Sung Mahn had been downstairs in the lobby of the condominium, waiting for his girls to return his wife to him. He had taken the elevator down to the lobby entrance fifteen minutes early. He must have been nuts, he scolded himself, for allowing the girls to talk him into letting Eleanor go with them for the day.

At first the prospect of a break from caregiving sounded like a good idea, but as the hours dragged on, he found himself unable to concentrate on anything. He tried to watch television, something he couldn't do anymore with Eleanor roaming around the apartment, removing her clothes, turning on and off the lights. In no time he threw down the remote control, unaware that he himself was roaming from room to room, sprinkling each empty doorway with sighs, missing his wife. He tried scrubbing the shower, something else he had wanted to do but hadn't been able to as Eleanor's condition worsened. He couldn't leave her unattended. He was exhausted and yet he could not relax. He could not close his eyes and nap, not even for a few minutes. He made himself an early lunch, a tuna sandwich, which he ate without joy. No matter how many times Eleanor threw her napkin onto the floor, no matter how many times she stumbled to the toilet, pulling down her elastic shorts in the hallway as he lurched after her, calling her to come back, he missed her.

"Don't ask, just do it. Will you please?" Alex shouted out the car window. "And have Mom ready tomorrow at eight o'clock."

As they drove off, Catherine turned to wave. Their father stood looking long and hard at them, bewilderment flushing his face, astonished that he no longer had the last say. Eleanor, hunched toward the building, was already gone.

Through the revolving glass door of the condominium, Sung Mahn guided Eleanor into the elevator, into the apartment, and into the clean shower. He entered the shower with her, wearing swim trunks, and scrubbed her down. Careful lest she slip, he instructed her to hold on to him as he worked down her legs, calling out for her to lift one foot, then the other. She lifted, and shifted slowly. He soaped around the distended belly, the sagging breasts. He soaped her with the efficiency of a zookeeper in a stall with a docile beast.

Through it all, Eleanor remained mute, obedient. Once showered and changed into fresh underwear, T-shirt, and shorts, he guided her to the recliner, flicking on the television. He then had three minutes before she started to look for him. In that time he had pulled from the freezer two Lean Cuisine frozen meals and had zapped them in the microwave. When she wandered into the kitchen he was ready for her with a head of lettuce to tear. She liked tearing lettuce.

That night he remembered the incense. He lit the seven sticks as instructed and, holding Eleanor's hand, they went together into each room, sweeping passes of burning scent, like children waving sparklers at New Year's. He had an inkling that what they were doing was a kind of cleansing. Of what, he had not a clue. His crazy girls. But since he had come to a point where he had nothing to lose, he decided to make an effort. He wondered if he should be murmuring an incantation. He began to recite the only one that came to mind, "The Lord is my shepherd . . . " He recited over and over as they went from room to room, "The Lord is my shepherd . . . " Eleanor mumbled the four words she would say that night, "I shall not want."

Sung Mahn had Eleanor ready at ten minutes to eight the next morning. He could have had her ready the moment they dropped her off the afternoon before, so profound was her confusion that he could have turned her back around, called out to his daughters to wait, and strapped her into the car. She would have stared out the car window, giving him that look of helpless pleading.

They entered Pālolo valley and stopped at the Pālolo Higashi Hongwanji for directions to the Chinese Buddhist Temple, the one with the red door. Cal had been adamant about the red door, and a man named Collin who resided behind it.

The old ladies looked up from their quilting when Catherine entered the side hall of the temple. Alex waited in the car with their mother. Bright colored squares of material were being pinned in place for patchwork blankets the ladies were piecing together for the homeless.

"Getting real cold now," muttered one of the ladies. That was the answer to Catherine's second question, the first drawing no results. None of the ladies knew of any Chinese Buddhist Temple in the valley. Not even one with a red door. Try the Korean Temple, farther in, on the side of the mountain, the one with the big tiled roof, they suggested, or the Chinese Old Folks Home. "Get plenty Chinese over there. They might know what you looking for."

Catherine felt reluctant to leave them. They seemed content in the selfless task, enjoying what was being given them at that moment, the sound of mourning doves in the cool valley light, the opportunity to get together and make use of their still able hands.

They found their way to the nursing home, following the long driveway to the entrance. Once again Catherine ran out to inquire while Alex and Eleanor remained in the car. She found the common room where a dozen or so residents dozed in wheelchairs. Finding no one to help her, Catherine ran outside, shaking her head to her sister, who thrust her face forward over the dashboard, looking annoyed.

"May I help you?" A kitchen worker on a smoke break called out from the side of the building. She had heard about the temple with the red door. "Around this hill, take a right and another right into the road that leads to the back of the valley. It's there. A lot of people come driving up here looking for it. A lot of people need help."

Eleanor said nothing as her two daughters called out, "Turn here. Try this road. Shit. Turn around. Try the other road." When it seemed they had crisscrossed every street, they saw it. The red door at the end of the valley. They had been searching for a more substantial structure, a real temple with an ornate gate, a garden, banners, the drone of chanting monks, not an ordinary house. Disappointed, they entered the red door, flimsy as a curtain. Eleanor stumbled between them as they passed as if through a stage prop, into a carport that had been converted to a waiting room. Even the cloud of incense was an illusion, more like burning coils of mosquito repellent.

A couple, sitting very close, sat on one of the two benches. Catherine wondered what sort of help they sought—blessings for an imminent marriage, assurances for the birth of a healthy child, guidance for an elderly parent.

Before greetings could be exchanged, the couple stood up, called through a side doorway by someone who remained unseen on the other side. Bowing slightly, the couple went through the door.

Alexandria inched along the bench, craned her neck, and peered after them. "Must be him," she whispered.

"How much do you think we need to give?" Catherine reached into her purse.

"I don't know. Twenty? Thirty?"

Catherine fumbled for the envelope she had prepared earlier in the car. Inside was a crisp twenty-dollar bill. She suddenly felt insecure and plucked another twenty from her wallet.

Eleanor sat staring at the ground, the cement floor of the carport swept clean but stained with oil patches. Alex never saw the couple leave. It didn't occur to her to wonder if they had left by another door until, as in a doctor's waiting room, their turn was called.

A shadow passed through the doorway. "Okay?"

Catherine looked up, embarrassed to be caught putting more money into the envelope, like an afterthought. Bowing, she handed the envelope to the man whose shadow fell across their mother's feet.

The envelope disappeared into the folds of a gray robe.

Alexandria guided Eleanor by the elbow, and the three of them entered the next room, behind the man who had yet to introduce himself. He led them up three steps into another garage, one that had been converted into the main temple hall. Alex wasted no time in describing Eleanor's condition to the man who remained imposing in his physical height and emotionless expression, a neutrality Catherine interpreted as bored and, worse, condescending. He had heard it all before.

Catherine had to admire her sister's sincerity, saying too much too soon, as though this stranger were the family doctor and, if she could recount the story of their mother's descent into depression with enough conviction, he could make Eleanor well again.

Catherine regretted adding the extra twenty-dollar bill to the envelope, feeling shortchanged as they stood at the elaborate altar festooned with an assortment of Daoist gods and lavish offerings of sweets and fruits resembling a window display in a Chinatown gift shop. The gods from their great height looked down and scowled.

Opposite the altar was a view of the valley, the humble houses they had passed to find this place.

Alexandria rattled on about Eleanor's deterioration. The list of ailments seemed to move the man in the gray robe in no visible way. He almost seemed irritated, as if she were telling him the very things he was planning to reveal for a fee.

Moving his head in a succession of quick nods, which Catherine interpreted as *yes yes let's get on with it*, he held out a fan of fortune sticks to Eleanor. He could just as well have offered her a handful of cigarettes the way she stared at them dumbly.

Apologizing, Alex chose one for their mother. The man lifted his chin to indicate she should pick a few more. Catherine watched her sister's fingers pull at the long sticks the way they did when they were children playing pick-up sticks. So competitive were the games, the sisters dared not breathe on the other's turn. Chin to floor, they eyeballed the nest of sticks to make sure not a single quiver occurred as each stick was deftly extracted. The stakes were always high.

"Okay," the man said, meaning that's enough. He took the sticks from Alex and placed them in a bamboo container. He shook it like a bartender mixing drinks.

"What's your mother's name?"

Alex answered.

"Write it down." He thrust his jaw toward a notepad and pencil on a small table covered with a green cloth.

Alex wrote it down.

He added Eleanor's name to the cocktail and continued to shake the bamboo container. Great, Catherine thought, all we need are some tiki torches and paper umbrellas.

If he was praying to the gods behind him, he gave no indication. No spine-tingling mantra came tumbling out. After a few more rattles—was he actually counting, Catherine wondered—he threw the sticks onto a small table.

The sisters stepped closer.

With a quick glance, he studied the cryptic arrangement of sticks. "Okay," he pronounced, satisfied. Once again he thrust his jaw in the direction they should follow, toward a set of stools and a card table. Eleanor had already started to drift there.

They sat down. Eleanor looked miserable. She was probably hungry.

"Your mother," the man began.

Catherine felt herself retracting as Alexandria leaned closer to hear the reading. Her eagerness seemed to cause him to lose his train of thought.

"Yes?"

"Your mother," he began again, "has high blood pressure."

"Yes?" It was Alexandria's turn to indicate *tell me something I don't already know.*

"...and..."

"...and?"

"She's disappointed." The man's relief was evident at this last pronouncement.

"Disappointed?" The two sisters repeated in unison.

"Yes," Collin said, staring over their heads, at the view of the valley.

"I don't understand," Alex said, crushed.

Returning his gaze to the women at the table, he made his final assessment. "Yes, she's disappointed the way her life turned out. She's tried very hard and can't understand why things didn't work out the way she wanted." His eyes came to rest upon Eleanor.

"So..." Alex said as a cue for more.

"So, is there anything we can do?" Catherine pushed aside her sister's politeness.

"No," Collin said, standing to his feet, a sign that the session was now over.

Catherine had to control herself from demanding a full refund.

"No hope, no cure, nothing," Catherine ranted as they marched Eleanor to the car. "A big fat zero."

"What a waste of time," Alex agreed, opening the door for Eleanor, who looked miserable.

"And money!" Catherine snapped. "What was that all about?"

They sat in the car, fuming for a few minutes, before they drove away. Catherine wanted to shake her fist out the window, spit something vulgar at the man who was probably still watching them from his lofty carport. She didn't think he was capable of activating any spells, but the thought of the scowling gods made her control herself.

"I feel we've been had," she muttered glumly.

"We've still got Walter," Alex ventured.

"I don't know," Catherine said, discouraged. "It's just this silly wild goose chase. What do you think, Mom?" From time to time, they remembered to include their mother.

Eleanor didn't answer.

"Let's try Walter," Alex said, taking control. "Then we can have lunch."

"Mom looks tired and hungry. Are you hungry, Mom?"

Eleanor didn't answer. They decided to find Walter in Kalihi.

They found Walter easily enough in dilapidated, junk-filled squalor around the corner from Golden City Restaurant. They had the distinct feeling he had been expecting them, for when they arrived at the front door, he saw them first through the grimy picture window, smiled, and waved them in.

Barely.

They had to remain standing near the door in order to fit in Walter Kunimura's living room. Piled with chairs and tables and overflowing cardboard boxes, it seemed as if once upon a time he couldn't decide whether to move in or move out. Defeated by the two directional pulls, it was easier to live in the La-Z-Boy recliner and have the world come to him.

"I know you! I know you folks!" He grinned, his teeth as messy and dingy as the surroundings. "Come inside! Come inside!"

Catherine had the impression Walter spoke in repetitive couplets. She was going to make Alex pay this time.

Not for lack of manners did Walter not get up to greet them. There was simply no clear floor space for him to stand. Catherine shuddered at the image of the sprightly man coming toward them like a monkey, balancing on the precarious piles, lunging from table to box to chair.

"Excuse the mess! Excuse the mess!" He hadn't stopped waving since the moment he spotted their car.

Brave Alex began to speak. Catherine braced herself for the
litany of ailments.

"Never mind! Never mind! I know, I know . . . Cal told me. He
told me already. Your mama . . . it's your mama . . . Try wait, try wait.
Elsie! Elsie! Where you stay?"

From the dark airless kitchen, a woman of indeterminate age
hobbled out, stopping short at the boundary between the linoleum
floor of the kitchen and the mustard-colored carpet of the living room.
She stood waiting for instructions.

"Get the stone! Get the stone!"

She bowed once and disappeared.

Walter turned to his guests and offered them treats, dusty
pieces of peppermint in a koa bowl. Catherine unwrapped one for
Eleanor. Her mother grabbed it and stuck it quickly in her mouth as if
she was afraid it would be taken away from her.

"Take more! Take more! She look hungry! She look like one
hungry ghost!"

Catherine, having already decided they were on another wild
goose chase, chose to ignore what this third charlatan just said. She
gave her mother a second peppermint.

Elsie returned, weighed down with a rock. She stood at the
edge of the linoleum.

The sisters looked at each other. They wondered who was
going to retrieve the rock. It was obvious Elsie would go no further. To
their surprise, Walter jumped out of the recliner. Nimbly, he climbed
over several boxes and stood on top of a coffee table. As he reached
to take the rock from Elsie, he almost slipped on a mountain of
magazines.

"Watch out!" Alexandria cringed.

The weight taken off of her, Elsie retreated into the dark airless
kitchen.

"Sit down! Sit down! Anywhere alright. I go put the stone on your mama. I go put the stone on your mama's belly. Okay? Okay?"

Eleanor, upon receiving permission to sit down, promptly did so on the nearest cardboard box. Empty, the box collapsed. The swift downward pull extracted from her a loud cheerful fart.

Alexandria cringed. Catherine vowed once again that this time her sister would certainly pay.

"That's what I told Cal!" Walter hooted, standing like a mischievous monkey on the coffee table, the rock like a coconut he was about to hurl. "No need the stone! No need the stone! I already know what her problem! I already know!"

"Excuse me?" Alex and Catherine reached to help Eleanor to her feet.

"Your mama! She get gas! She get too much gas!"

The sisters swore off healers. They were all kooks, they agreed. They found a care home in the valley near the Chinese cemetery, which seemed like a good sign, that their mother would be close to her parents whom she had lost so early in life. They gently released their father's grip, telling him it was all right. He could rest now. The real professionals would take over and make sure she was safe and comfortable. He had done all that was humanly, husbandly possible.

When they brought their mother to the care home, it was the last time Eleanor walked unassisted, entering the gated garden sparkling with morning light and the sound of water trickling from a fountain surrounded by a grotto of ferns and orchids. The sisters knew their father's heart was breaking as he led his wife into the large room that served as a dining area for the residents, six of the seven seated at their own small round tables, waiting in wheelchairs for the noon meal. The smell of chicken and ginger simmering in a large pot filled the room. A few of the residents turned disinterestedly at the commotion of the new arrival shuffling toward an empty table. Their mother glanced at their father, turning her whole body the way an injured person would, stiffly, with a neck brace, looking it seemed for permission to sit down. One of the attendants went to get a wheelchair. It was as if she were his child and the three of them were dropping her off at a new school where a birthday party was taking place. The other guests scratched their heads, rubbed their eyes, each one brightly bibbed as though they were wearing party favors, the bibs—red, blue, and yellow—the color of balloons.

What disturbed Alexandria the most was the way her mother's face, once soft and tender, hardened. The effect for those who knew her when the life force coursed through her being was chilling. Eleanor stared at the ceiling, the bed an extension of her confinement, staring at nothing, staring at everything. There was no way to know. The swollen flesh around her eyes made her look mean; the bloated jowls dragged down the sides of her mouth into a scowl. "She was really a nice person," Alex felt compelled to tell the staff. "She was really the sweetest mother." The sweetest mother had stopped speaking the day she walked unassisted into her new home, sinking into the wheelchair that the attendant adjusted, strapping her securely with a Velcro belt. She never looked at her husband. She never looked at her two daughters. Once the meal was served, she fed herself that first meal, slurping the chicken soup with loud smacking sounds. It seemed to the three of them as they let her go, the gate shutting quietly behind them, that she could finally rest. She didn't have to be cheerful for any of them anymore.

Knowing that their mother was being well cared for and that their father could spend his days by her side—feeding her, combing her hair, holding her hand—and leave to return the next morning after a good night's sleep to repeat the loving attention brought Catherine and Alexandria a measure of relief.

That relief was short-lived. Not long after their mother entered the care home, whenever Catherine put on a T-shirt (paired with jeans, her uniform), she noticed an indentation would appear between her breasts as if an invisible finger were pressing down on the sternum. When it first appeared, she was unaware of it until her youngest child cried, "Eeew! Uji, Ma! What's that on your shirt?" She looked down, agreed that it was indeed uji, her children's go-to word for anything odd, amiss, inappropriate. She stepped in front of the bathroom mirror, shrugged, and changed into another one. The same thing happened. The indentation appeared, blooming right before her eyes. She thought it was a defect in the cotton fabric and went through her stack of standard-issue GAP Favorite T-shirts. She ended up trying on the entire collection of T-shirts. With each new T-shirt, the indentation appeared like a mysterious stain.

After the morning's upheaval of getting the residents bathed, medicated, fed by noon, and settled back into their rooms for the long siesta, Alexandria could hear the shuffling of papers as the nurse and the two attendants on duty retreated to their stations, portable desks tucked amid the warehousing of wheelchairs and crooked stacks of formula and diapers for the elderly. The endless minute-by-minute updating of medical files, reports that charted the fastidious progress of decline had the same effect on her as the sound of lids being peeled back from plastic lunch containers. The sound and the immediate burp-like smell of egg salad sandwiches made her feel sad. The nurse and the attendants on duty sat on stools, penciling in numbers, chewing soft tired bites, seeking nourishment from homemade sandwiches before the next deployment.

Staring at her mother as she lay in bed, asleep or awake, Alexandria was no longer sure, she had stopped feeling intrusive. Whether her eyes were opened or closed, her mother seemed unaware of her presence. She had left, she was gone, and no matter how hard Alex tried—reading to her, holding her hand, massaging her swollen legs—she could not call her mother back. Whatever that essence was that only recently and valiantly flickered recognition, amusement, weariness, and love had fled. Alex couldn't help but feel that her mother willed her own escape, that if she had wanted to stay she would have. There was something almost triumphant in the way she lay, solidifying right before their eyes, their tears hastening the process, resistant to the claims each of them made on her, beseeching her to come back, smothering her with attention.

Her feet, encased in skid-free, rubber-soled socks, were the last bony extremities left of her body. They fit into Alexandria's palms as she massaged them, the feel of a ballerina's high arches familiar; the toes, curled as though all her life her mother had worn shoes too small, still slender and pliable. Like a landscape altered by a lava flow, the rest of her mother's body had lost the finer undulations of hip and breast, clavicle and neck, hardening into an almost undistinguishable mass of flesh. It wasn't that she had gained weight since becoming bedridden, rather she was sinking under the weight of her own physical matter. She lay hard and frozen, the result of an internal collapse.

Her face, once so friendly in its openness, inviting others to approach without fear, seemed fixed in paralysis. Of all the expressions that had visited her face, Alexandria thought how unfortunate that the last one that remained would be one of fear, as though she had witnessed something dreadful. Whatever it was that she had seen, it stuck. It was hard to look at her mother.

It was hard to look at her, but Alexandria felt compelled to visit every day, during the brief hour when her father went home for lunch. She didn't need the added pain of watching him attend to her, stroking her arm, combing her hair, loving gestures he rarely exhibited when she was well. She felt she was coming closer to understanding that look on her mother's face. She had seen that face before. It wasn't until she was looking through old photographs that she discovered how much her mother in her present condition resembled her own father, their grandfather, in the last photograph taken shortly before his untimely death at the age of fifty-three. She felt she was coming closer to making sense of things that had happened in the past, things that no one had time to piece together in the rush of years and deaths, how her mother and her sisters had scattered after their parents had died within a short time of each other, scrambling to find other living arrangements in order to survive.

Alexandria called Catherine. She needed help.

The first thing Alexandria saw was the strange mark on her sister's shirt.

"I know," Catherine said. "It looks like an invisible finger is poking me. The kids say it's uji."

"I think it's someone trying to tell us something."

Catherine dismissed what she heard. "Oh, no. I refuse to seek the help of any more healers. There's nothing to uncover. No magic cure. Mom has dementia. End of story. Sad but true. At least we got Dad to agree to get her into a place where she's safe."

"But that look on her face, Kitty. It's not natural."

"It's what it is, Alex. We can't all look gorgeous at the end."

Alexandria took out the picture of their grandfather, the last one taken before his death.

Catherine took a long time with it, holding it up to the window. They were in Eleanor's room. Her eyes were closed, but that didn't mean she was sleeping. "I have to admit," she said, putting the photograph back into the album, "there is a weird resemblance."

"Resemblance? Kitty, it looks like his face has morphed into hers."

"What are you trying to get at? That our dear old grandfather's spirit has entered into Mom?"

Eleanor stirred in bed. The sisters lowered their voices. "No, but I was looking at all the photos, and figuring out the dates. Grandpa's first wife, Uncle Sonny's mother, died in China."

"And then he married our grandmother."

"Yes, but you see, after the three of them went back to China, and Grandpa's first wife died there, Uncle Sonny couldn't have been more than a few years old. We'll never know why they went back to China, but the thing is," Alex took a deep breath, she could feel her palpitations starting up again, "he married our grandmother so soon afterwards. Like he knew her while his first wife was still alive."

"They were probably from the same village. Maybe even family friends, distantly related. You know in those days everyone was related."

"I mean real soon after because when I looked at the date when Auntie Evie was born, it was the same year his first wife died."

Catherine seemed to need a moment to absorb her sister's detective work. "Still possible without being immoral. First wife could have died in January. Grandpa, already knowing our grandmother through village connections, marries her as early as the next month or so—still possible for Auntie to have been born that year."

"But Auntie Evie's birthday is in August," Alex said ominously.

All Catherine could say was "Oh."

They went to the Chinese cemetery after the hour with their mother. They left before their father returned to take up his usual position in a chair beside her bed. Although they knew it wasn't nice of them to leave without at least waiting to see him, they had too much on their minds. They drove separately, not wanting to leave either car behind should their father recognize one of them. It would get his hopes up. He would expect to find them with their mother. He would look forward to the company.

Under the ever-blossoming pink plumeria tree, the sisters sought the graves of the grandparents they had never known. A feeling of neglect pervaded the site, littered with soft petals and large brown leaves. No one had been there for a long time. Maybe not since the last time years ago when they had come with their mother and aunts to perform the ritual of Ching Ming. The time Auntie Evie had grabbed Catherine's arm, invoking the name of Jesus over and over as if that would dispel the superstitious practice of paying respect to one's ancestors.

Catherine decided that that wasn't such a bad thing to do. To pay respect to one's ancestors was a way of acknowledging the hardships they had endured. She knelt down to pray to her grandfather and grandmother. She was grateful they had left China seeking a better life for themselves and the grandchildren they would never know. If she had been born in China, she probably would be dead. She had read that those who came of age during the Cultural Revolution, if they survived, would be street sweepers and refuse collectors, having been denied years of schooling. She was grateful for all the years of school she had been given.

Alexandria knelt beside her sister. "Let's pray to Grandpa's first wife, Uncle Sonny's mother. I feel sad that she was left all alone in China. After all, she gave birth to Uncle, and he was a good brother to all his sisters. He was so young when he was left as head of the family, left to take care of his stepmother and all those sisters. Remember Auntie Evie said that after Grandpa had died, Uncle worked in the kitchen at a Chinese restaurant, how he would bring home the leftovers in a little tin for them?"

The two sisters fell silent as they sat under the plumeria tree that graced the grave of their grandparents with a never-ending shower of blossoms. They didn't need to tell each other what they prayed for. Although the valley was bright with sun, a light rain began to fall. They didn't need a healer to tell them it was a blessing.

Schedule

Sung Mahn opened his eyes, surprised to find he was still alive. He reached for the alarm clock before it went off, careful not to disturb the eight-by-ten-inch picture of his wife taken on her seventieth birthday, four years before she died.

Five minutes to seven. Right on schedule.

He pressed the button and returned the clock to its position beside the collection of pendants—silver-plated crosses he had received since moving to the retirement home from Christian charities thanking Mr. Sung Mahn Park in advance for his donation with a gift of appreciation.

He never sent a single contribution to any of them, discarding the pre-paid envelopes and pleas for help into the mailroom rubbish bin before stepping into his apartment, keeping the crosses, which he placed at the base of Eleanor's picture. She peered out from a cloud of flower lei as though she were wearing a ruffled turtleneck. She seemed baffled by all the attention.

If Sung Mahn had a shrine, this was it.

Five to seven. Right on schedule.

He lay still for a few moments, thinking about the day ahead. The weight of hours stacked like a wall of bricks around him, a confinement he found less unbearable since discovering the uses of buses. He knew the bus schedule pretty much by heart, better than he remembered the names of his granddaughters' boyfriends or the fact that his younger daughter had a cat. On his rare visits to Catherine's house, he was always surprised by the black shadow that appeared from behind the curtains, quiet as smoke. "Since when did you get a cat?" He stopped asking her, for her response silenced him— exasperation barely concealed in the slight shaking of her head— "Since about twelve years ago."

What surprised Sung Mahn the most was that he was still alive. Alive and well at eighty-four. Alive and well with no end in sight, just a wall of bricks moving closer each day. Alive without Eleanor.

It was crushing in the beginning, the weeks, the months following her death. But as a younger man of seventy-six, maintaining an intense vigil of daily visits to the nursing home, and, later, the months at hospice, he had had energy to spare. It was as if he had revved his internal combustion of will so high during the three years of his wife's confinement that when Eleanor at last died he found himself still focused and strong. Still poised for the emergency but without the object of his obsession.

He did what he always did, only this time without her. He went on trips. He revisited all the places they had been to together, without her. There wasn't a place he did not retrace. He purchased tickets to Hong Kong and Bali, Christchurch and Sydney. He ate at the same restaurants, rode the same ferries, signed up for the same city tours. The only difference his traveling made was that it killed time.

Another gorgeous day, Sung Mahn muttered to himself, unconvinced, like a man being forced to eat. The sun was already mounting its assault on the east end of the island where the retirement community sprawled across the slopes of the dry valley. Garden living was how the sales pitch went when he was taken on a tour of the place. Wherever one looked, whichever studio or

apartment one chose, whether ground, second, or third level, from
each lanai there was a view. Paths curved around well-maintained
lawns and hedges, flowerbeds aflame with tī and heliconia. Waterfalls
poured over a landscape of lava rock, oxygenating ponds for the
swirling koi. The immaculate swimming pool, where smoothies were
served at sunset, shimmered like a carpet woven with silver and ice
blue threads. Hidden under trees, a Jacuzzi simmered.

All lovely except for the fact that it was empty. Those who
lived independently kept up the illusion of living lives elsewhere,
driving off in cars they could still operate. Those who had moved
on to assisted living waited to be pushed in their wheelchairs. The
showcase amenities remained oddly a non-reality for the residents of
the retirement community.

Told of an apartment available immediately on the ground
level, Sung Mahn took it, not for the view—it faced the parking lot—
but for the convenience. Without having to walk through the grand
lobby and down a long corridor to enter the apartment by the front
door, he could slip in and out through the sliding screen, where from
the lanai his car was twenty feet away. He could pretend he still lived
in a condo.

He stretched in bed, both knees bent to chest, then a knee at
a time. He crisscrossed his arms over his head, finding resistance at
the shoulders. He sat up, slowly, and tried to reach for his toes. Then
slowly he got out of bed. He found resistance everywhere.

By eight the dining room bustled with the business of
serving breakfast to the residents who groped their way to tables
like passengers on a cruise ship, pausing to maintain balance while
the floor seemed to wobble and the horizon shift. The certainty of
mealtimes anchored the day, as did the self-assigned seating. Once a
comfortable arrangement was found, it solidified so that it could be

counted on, and the anxiety of trying to find a suitable situation could
be avoided. The horror of pulling up a chair at a table of strangers
only to be told the seat was being saved for someone else was
probably worse than eating alone.

Sung Mahn felt a ripple of anxiety as he entered, scanning
the room for his usual table. At the sight of Lorraine and Gertrude
hunched over their placemats, he felt better. They were the perfect
props—he didn't have to eat alone and they didn't talk. He could
appear to be congenial. He had been sitting with Lorraine almost
since the beginning; Gertrude had arrived some months later, relieved
just as he had been to join Lorraine who shook her head indifferently
when asked if the seat was taken.

When he first appeared upon the dining scene he had been
wooed by a rather aggressive woman named Beatrice. She presided
over a table at the back, away from the windows. Dark complexioned
and dressed in widow's black—T-shirt and shorts—she blended into
the dim corner where the gushing sunlight missed her. She invited
Sung Mahn to join her and two other gentlemen who laughed at her
comments about the other residents, put downs disguised as jokes.

Sung Mahn had wondered how it worked, how one joined a
table. For the lucky few with spouses, it was easy, they already had a
companion; as a pair they could shore themselves against rejection or
never find themselves eating alone. Standing at the periphery of the
dining room had placed him near Beatrice, who noticed his hesitation
as well as the fact that he was new, and attractive—he wasn't fat,
he had a head of hair, and he walked with an upright posture.
Her invitation rescued him from having to ask a table of strangers
whether he could sit with them. Had Beatrice not called out to him,
he probably would have considered eating alone, or at least, upon
finding himself an empty table he could be in a position to be the
one approached. Trouble was he didn't know which one of the empty

tables was available. In such a situation Eleanor's natural inclination of going up to strangers with friendliness and ease would have been an asset. She could ask for directions, offer an opinion to another shopper about the quality of fruit on special—"Picked too green"— inquire after someone's well being with sincere concern. She had no trouble humbling herself.

Sung Mahn remained indebted to Beatrice even after her negative remarks had begun to make him squirm. For several weeks he endured them, just as he suspected Harold and Roy, the other two gentlemen, did, both of whom he sensed shared an affliction similar to his, social anxiety and its attendant passivity. It was better to stay seated in a familiar situation rather than face finding a new one. In the chaos of the dining room the three men had landed at a table where they were held captive yet oddly grateful. Beatrice did all the talking. A noncommittal chuckle mimicking a weak assent to a disparaging remark was all that she seemed to require. She too dreaded eating alone. She too wanted to appear well-padded and congenial.

Beatrice had nothing good to say about anyone, and most of what she said was conjecture, blown out the side of her mouth with the force of an avid smoker.

"You see the guy over there?" she'd say, thrusting her formidable chin in the direction of some poor hapless soul shuffling to a table.

Harold and Roy, afraid to look, would turn in unison, peering over their shoulders.

"He so stink! The other day, I was stuck with him in the elevator and I almost went choke. I swear the guy never went take one bath in like a year." She'd laugh at her own joke, and Harold and Roy would nod, trying to remain neutral. In the case of a particularly mean remark, they'd glance at each other as if to say "your turn." By the time coffee was served, one of them would speak up as if trying to redeem himself from having participated in something foul. "Ho, hard for us makule to take one bath. Hard, you know, for get in and out!"

Beatrice, knowing she had gone a bit too far, would agree, but not before she had the last word. "Yeah, we so old, we all stink."

Sung Mahn, feeling at first indebted to the group, said little. The act of smiling tightly affected his appetite. He plowed his fork through the mashed potatoes, drank too much of the iced tea. In happier times, he would have steered clear of a woman like Beatrice. He found everything about her unpleasant—from eyebrows, saw-toothed and jagged, applied with a shaky hand, to wrinkles so heavily powdered it was as if her face had been crop-dusted, the flakes sprinkling onto her black T-shirt like dandruff. Her rough speech and manners exaggerated the unfortunate features, a face that appeared to have been smashed by a shovel. She relished the dirt on others as much as she did watching her table companions squirm. She enjoyed dropping the rotten remark, true or otherwise, but always at someone else's expense, into the middle of the meal. During the course of the meal—she was in top form at dinner—she'd take repeated stabs at her centerpiece, as if checking to see whether any maggots would come crawling out, flinging shredded portions onto the others' plates. She'd save the biggest bite for herself, gnawing and waiting for the men to take up theirs.

After several weeks of this, Sung Mahn had had enough. Beatrice had just flung a comment in his direction regarding Marianne, a recently arrived resident. Over three days, Marianne had been observed floating around the dining room, appearing at first to be lost. On closer observation, her wan presence, softly faded as the floral-patterned dress she wore, revealed a vague intention. She seemed to have devised a strategy as to how to approach the dining scene. She stopped and said hello at every table, or rather, she stopped at every table and waited for heads to glance up, conversation to pause, before she extended a trembling hand.

Marianne had tried it at their table, standing behind Sung Mahn. Beatrice's right eye lifted like a poised arrow. "May we help you?"

Marianne bowed apologetically, and murmured, "Just wanted to say hello."

"Well, hello," Beatrice retorted, straightening up in her chair.

Roy nodded a quick greeting. Harold waved a feeble hand. Sung Mahn turned and felt instantly sorry for her. To stand before them and initiate an introduction took courage beyond anyone's natural inclination. Sung Mahn knew. He stood up and offered her his chair. "Please," he motioned, "have a seat."

Beatrice began to make a noise that sounded rudely flatulent.

"No, no, no," Marianne murmured, backing away, almost tripping on herself. "Don't mean to bother. Just wanted to say hello."

"Well, hello," Beatrice repeated, dismissing her.

Marianne continued to back away, bumping into a parked walker, which startled her as well as the residents at the next table. "Sorry," she mumbled as if apologizing to the ambulatory implement. Her nervousness was contagious.

Sung Mahn sat down. He was angry with himself; he knew he could've taken Marianne by the hand and ushered her back, if not to his chair, at least he could've pulled up an extra one for her. Spare ones clustered in the corner.

He watched as she repeated the tentative process, watched her acceptance into a more gracious group.

"Get a load of her," Beatrice growled. "Think she can just walk around like one queen and say"—she assumed a stock gesture of haughtiness, nose in the air, hand extended for a kiss—"howdy-do."

"Be nice," Sung Mahn found himself saying.

"I beg your pardon?" Beatrice withdrew her hand, splayed her fingers across her chest in mock indignation.

"I said, be nice." Sung Mahn glared at her. Roy and Harold kicked each other under the table. They exchanged looks, which made it clear that it was Sung Mahn's turn.

All kidding aside, Beatrice puffed forward. "You got the nerve, telling me what to do."

"It's about time somebody did." Sung Mahn stood up and left the table.

The next day he drove to the mall two miles away, taking breakfast and lunch at Burger King, dinner at Panda Express. In between he had wandered the aisles of Costco, tasting the food samples—miniature quiches, tiny cups of Gatorade—watching the Golf Channel on big screen TVs and resting intermittently on the floor models of patio furniture. When he drove home, the dining room lights blazed as the workers cleaned up. He had gone straight into the shower, knowing he had to find another table.

The episode with Beatrice provided the opportunity Sung Mahn had been seeking. He had noticed Lorraine sitting alone at a table in the middle of the room, seemingly impervious to the murmurings and glances of others. The ill-defined shape of her body, slumped in the chair like a sagging pillow, added to the despondency of her expression, her vague features drawn and smudged as if by a child. There was something unconditional about her regard; when he sat down across the table from her, he could have been a complete stranger or a close relative joining her for dinner. His company made no perceivable impact upon her, and he settled into their first meal together with a sense of ease he had been searching for in the complexities of in-house dining. The few and functional words spoken between them served to pass nothing more than the salt.

His two daughters disrupted the agreeable silence he thought he had established with Lorraine when they had begun showing up for meals. The very friendliness he missed about his wife he couldn't appreciate in his daughters. He found them pushy and bossy. He was taken aback by the way they invited themselves for dinner—after all, each guest voucher cost him twelve dollars—the way they took over, talking in some secret language of sisters.

Catherine and Alexandria would complicate matters by adding and subtracting to the menu, one substituting brown rice for white, the other requesting fries instead of carrot sticks. He could never remember which one of them was vegetarian, just as he seemed to forget that they had somewhere, somehow become Buddhists. *Practicing Buddhists*, whatever that meant.

Complicating matters further was how they got Lorraine to talk. They found out more about her in one meal than he had after two weeks of eating with her. They found out more than he wanted to know.

"Let's keep it simple," he found himself saying more than once while he watched with exasperation the waiter take their order.

"Let's keep it simple," he repeated, as he would walk them to their cars, one of them telling him what they had just found out about Lorraine. "Dad, can you believe Lorraine used to be a librarian," Alexandria gushed as if it were breaking news. "And did you hear she has three children, too, and," here Catherine paused to deposit the winner, "she has the same birthday as Mom!" Both daughters would look at him for some kind of reaction, trying to make connections he had no interest in making.

"Let's keep it simple, girls," he'd say, kissing them goodbye.

He welcomed the weekly visits even though he knew they were simply discharging an obligation, checking off on their to-do lists one more thing: see Dad. He imagined them coordinating over

the phone, grappling with the ever-present concern: what to do with
Dad, as if they were responsible for his happiness, taking turns,
doubling up only when absolutely necessary. Alexandria, the older
one, kept constant tabs on his whereabouts. Accompanying him to
the doctor's with a lunch planned afterwards gave Catherine the day
off, and Catherine, aware of this, would be prepared to occupy him
later in the week—a walk around Kapiʻolani Park, a visit to Foster
Botanical Garden, an invitation to her house for dinner. It had become
increasingly difficult for his daughters to maintain such a schedule;
and Sung Mahn, trying to be less of a burden, began to ride the bus.
They all knew there was nothing they could do to make him happy.

At 9:40 a.m. Sung Mahn boarded the Number 55 bus that went
to the North Shore. The bus left the city and climbed along the Pali
Highway toward the twin tunnels carved into the Koʻolau mountain
range, the spine of the island fanning on the Leeward side into long
valleys and gentle slopes, and on the Windward side, starkly eroded
cliffs. Sung Mahn had taken a window seat on the left-hand side
of the bus so that when the bus burst out of the tunnel, he could
regard the view unimpeded all the way down the mountain. The
Koʻolau mountains, diminishing in the distance like a Chinese ink
brush painting, appeared more vivid and green in the clear winter
light. There was clarity to the air as though slowly moving Arctic
temperatures had at last reached the tropics, infusing the usually heat-
dazed island with a sparkling vitality. Winter in Hawaiʻi was triggered
for him by this rare kind of light. That, and the profusion of mock
orange in full bloom. The signal that the winter surf was churning
came on the clean subtle scent.

He enjoyed this route; it was in his mind the most scenic. Once
the bus passed through Kāneʻohe town with its banks and bakeries
and fast food chains, unrelieved by any definable aesthetic except for

a kind of haphazard utilitarianism, the bus took the road that hugged the coast. He could imagine he was somewhere else, where the ramshackle houses, the small farms, the banana groves, and roadside fruit stands in their rural simplicity reminded him of places he had once seen. He didn't realize that what he had once seen was being shown to him again and again.

Hardly anyone rode the bus anymore; when he was growing up, riding the bus had been perfectly respectable. He noticed how even the lower wage earners and recently arrived immigrants whizzed by in monster-sized vehicles, trucks loaded with kids holding kids. The bus nowadays carried those living on the periphery—life for one group about over, life for the other about to start—old folks like himself or sullen teenagers who boarded the bus yawning, slouching in hooded sweatshirts, no matter what the weather. They threw themselves onto seats the way they threw their backpacks onto the floor. He never saw a single one of them give up a seat for an elder when school let out and the bus began to fill. They stared into space, wired to tiny gadgets, bobbing up and down to something only they could hear. More often they seemed transfixed by their cell phones.

He looked around and saw mostly empty seats. After the bustle of people getting on and off in the stop and go traffic of Kāneʻohe, there were few riders left. Those who remained like him were seated for the long haul—a mentally ill gentleman carrying on an animated conversation with an invisible companion, an adventurous, budget-minded pair of tourists getting a tour of the island for two dollars apiece, and a teenaged couple sitting in the row in front of him. He wondered why they weren't in school.

The bus curved around the coast past Kahana Bay. He remembered being left there as a kid, all of fourteen, in the days following the bombing of Pearl Harbor. The civil defense had rounded up all available males, those too young to enlist but old enough to be posted at the backwater coastal roads in the event of another attack. Deposited by trucks, they were given armbands and orders to stand guard at intervals of every third telephone pole. They were instructed to make sure the residents in the area obeyed the blackout and curfew. He had stood alert and solemn during the first afternoon but as the sun set and darkness fell, he along with the other boys stationed nearby grew discouraged. They imagined the worst had happened as they drew closer to each other, leaving their assigned posts. They gathered driftwood for a bonfire they were not allowed to light, imagined the warmth of its flame. They huddled together until first light, when they reached into their pockets and pooled change. They were hungry. By jan ken po it was determined that he should walk to a store three miles down the road. He remembered bringing back a loaf of bread and a gallon of milk. He remembered the way they tore into the soft white bread.

Pulled from reverie by a bump in the road, Sung Mahn became aware of the teenaged couple making out shamelessly. After several miles of enduring the slobbery tongue licking, he tapped the boy on the shoulder. So engrossed in French kissing his girlfriend who looked to be about twelve, the boy didn't turn until Sung Mahn practically pummeled his back as though he were knocking on a door to a house that had music playing too loudly. When the boy extricated his tongue from the girl's mouth, he glanced at Sung Mahn.

"Yeah?"

Sung Mahn slowly enunciated three words. "Do you mind?"

The boy dismissed him with a shake of his head and muttered to the girl who peeked at Sung Mahn from behind her boyfriend's massive neck. "Fuckin' old fut."

He got off the bus in disgust at Lāʻie, where he wanted to get off anyway; still, he made a big show of it, glaring at the boy and girl.

They glared back. His hearing was bad but not that bad. The tourists got off too.

Sung Mahn waited at the light to cross the street to the strip mall, to Taco Bell, where he always had lunch. He had in his wallet a coupon—two beef burritos for the price of one—which he clipped every Sunday from the newspaper. He had half an hour before the next bus came to continue the journey through Kahuku, Sunset, Waimea, the towns along the North Shore. At Haleʻiwa the bus turned inland through fields once prosperous with pineapple and sugarcane.

Just as the signal changed, Sung Mahn was reeled back from the curb by a decidedly strong Australian accent. "Excuse me, " the man called out. "Do you know where Lāʻie Point is?"

Turning around perhaps too quickly, Sung Mahn felt dizzy.

"Lāʻie Point," the man repeated, realizing he was addressing an elderly person. "Do you know where it is?"

The man and the woman were squinting hard at him. He already felt annoyed by what had transpired on the bus and seeing the couple waiting for an answer he knew he knew but couldn't quite say, irritated him. He suddenly saw himself as others saw him. Just like the kid said, an old fut.

He felt the weight of the noon sun, the air heavy with salt churned by the waves at this time of year. The morning's clarity, its bright beginning, muddied.

The woman pressed closer. "Are you all right?" She gestured to the bench under the covered bus stop, inviting him to sit down. She seemed so solicitous; she could have been inviting him into her living room. She offered Sung Mahn a disposable bottle of water. "It hasn't been opened," she assured him. She had a kind face. Around her shoulders, draped like a scarf, she wore an orchid lei, what professional airport greeters gave to arriving visitors, shipped so inexpensively from Thailand they could be given away for free. The lei looked as though the woman had been wearing it for several days. It looked as thirsty as he felt.

"Lāʻie Point? Sure, I know where that is," Sung Mahn said, as if crawling out of a pause the length of one of the Pali tunnels. "It's up that road." He indicated the hill behind them. And he found himself offering to take them there.

It was decided that they would walk to the top. The hill was small; the climb would be short. It wasn't worth taking a taxi even if a taxi had been available. The McElroys—Ted and Shirley—seemed to hesitate given the intensity of the noon hour and the dubious age and condition of their guide. They were in their late sixties, and though they considered themselves fit, they had no idea where they were being led. "Over hill, over dale," Ted whispered in his wife's ear. "Of course, we could always hitchhike." She laughed off her husband's joke and hurried to be in step with their guide who had already started up the hill.

Sung Mahn hadn't been to the point in years. He hoped his recollection of how the road curved through a neighborhood of nice-looking houses was accurate. He regretted offering his services. Lunch at Taco Bell would be delayed, which meant he would have to take a later bus, and he would not be on schedule. He might even miss the five o'clock seating at dinner. There was no fixed rule that residents had to be seated at that time. If he wasn't able to be at his table the moment the servers brought out the refreshment carts, he felt anxious. He hated eating while those who had finished began to leave their places and the servers were starting to clean up. It made him feel rushed. It made him feel out of sync.

Grateful for the shade along the road, the three climbers did little talking. Used to sharing whatever popped into their heads, the

McElroys remained quiet; the angle of the road was steeper than they had been led to believe by Sung Mahn's initial enthusiasm. To their surprise, he was indefatigable. He kept a steady pace, a rather vigorous one for a man of his advanced age, pausing just twice to catch his breath. During these pauses, the three would give each other a smile that seemed to convey as well as acknowledge apologies from all—Sung Mahn for the climb turning out to be more extensive than he had thought, the McElroys for troubling him. They felt more conversation was in order, some general sharing of background information—where are you from, how long have you lived here— that sort of thing, but he seemed to be in a hurry. It was as if he wanted to deposit them as quickly as possible to their destination and excuse himself from a situation in which he had unhappily found himself. It was as if he had more important things to do.

Coming upon the last house, fenced in for privacy, they were briefly disappointed. Still below eye level of the point's summit, all they could see were concrete barriers and an overflowing trash can chained to a pole. The place looked desolate, like a picture torn from a desert outpost. The only thing missing were soldiers. They crossed the empty parking area, a flattened space filled in with gravel, and came to the top of the cliff.

Sung Mahn sighed. He remembered now bringing Eleanor to this place early on in their courtship, taking her for a drive in his father's old Ford. Back then the point wasn't crammed with houses; they had a sense of being all alone, perched far above the world.

The sigh Shirley McElroy heard was the sound of someone crumpling to the ground upon being told bad news. It wasn't the spontaneous sharp intake of breath she found herself making at the sight of the dramatic rock formations and the wild crashing waves.

For the second time since meeting him she asked Sung Mahn if he was all right.

Exposed to the wind now that they were on the crest of the point, she couldn't make out what he was saying. The wind acted as an invisible curtain flapping in her face, causing her to squint. "Aw geez," he seemed to repeat, shaking his head, as if he couldn't believe something was true.

Ted had stepped over the concrete barrier and was carefully balancing on the boulders jutting out over the waves. "Come on!" he yelled over the wind, extending his hand. "It's fantastic!"

"Shall we go?" she asked Sung Mahn, who in declining gave a weak smile like a man refusing dessert.

"You'll be alright then," Shirley said to assure herself, and gave Sung Mahn a light tap on the shoulder. She stepped over the barrier and caught hold of her husband's arm.

Sung Mahn sat on the concrete barrier. He couldn't move onto the rocks and join the McElroys who were taking pictures of each other, the dramatic rock formation rising out of the sea background for one shot, the Windward coastline for another. It wasn't that he didn't trust his footing; it was that he felt pinned by a feeling of separateness. He couldn't summon within himself sympathetic joy for their obvious delight in experiencing together an unexpected detour on their itinerary. In the short time he had been with them, he could tell they were close; their fondness for each other was painfully apparent. It made him feel like a third wheel.

He couldn't remember Eleanor's face that long ago day. People didn't take pictures of each other the way they did now; cameras and the rolls of film that went into them were rare, expensive. Now people took thousands of pictures of themselves and loaded them onto computers to send to friends around the world. He wished he had a picture of Eleanor the day he had brought her to Lāʻie Point. Although he couldn't quite piece together the exact features of her face, he remembered she had been wearing a kerchief tied around her head to keep her hair in place. She had looked at him with a softness he never recovered from, neither then when he knew she loved him, nor later when he had to spoon-feed her. The softness of her eyes when she looked at him made him then as now feel unworthy. Despite her shrieks and feigned protestations, he had managed to get her onto the rocks, just as Ted was coaxing Shirley to come closer, further, almost to the edge.

The Long White Cloud

The cruise seemed like a good idea at the time. Alexandria came up with the plan, as she always did, not because she was older by four years than her sister, but rather it was because she felt personally responsible for their father's well-being. And if he liked to travel but couldn't travel alone anymore, then someone—either herself or her sister—would have to accompany him. Catherine found herself usually agreeing, coerced by her own feelings of competitiveness; she didn't want Alexandria to appear to be the only good daughter. Aidan, their younger brother, was exempt from this struggle. Alexandria didn't have to remind Catherine that the year before she had gone on a tour with their father to Southeast Asia. Convincing David was easy; like his sister-in-law, he felt responsible for other people's happiness—the most important person being Catherine, his wife.

Alexandria, once given the green light, went into travel agent mode. Since their father had begun making noises about wanting to see New Zealand again and threatening to go there by himself, Alexandria found a perfect solution as long as Catherine was willing—a twelve-day cruise around his favorite country. The plan seemed to satisfy the pressure she had been experiencing lately—their father's restlessness. In this way he would get what he wanted. Confined to a boat he wouldn't have the opportunity to drive. He would save face, for his daughters wouldn't have to tell him he couldn't. And Alexandria herself could have a much-needed vacation, peace of mind knowing their father was safely occupied. As long as Catherine was willing.

Driving from Christchurch to Queenstown three years before, their father had missed a turn in the road. He had flipped the rental car, somehow managing to miss a group of schoolgirls waiting for a bus. Both daughters shuddered to think how close he had come to causing great suffering. One of the teenagers had a cell phone, and they stayed with him until assistance in the form of a lone police officer from Wanaka had answered their call. The events were pieced together by Catherine and Alexandria from the police officer's report, for their father continued to remain fuzzy about what had occurred that day. One moment he was driving through long stretches of open road and the next moment he was sitting on the side of the road surrounded by a group of girls fussing over him. One of them had placed a sweater around his shoulders. From the police officer's report it seemed he had careened off an embankment, unable to negotiate a severe turn in the road.

Alarmed by the fact that Mr. Park hadn't shown up at the hotel in Queenstown, Alex, the keeper of the itinerary, pressed further. The clerk at the hotel desk admitted to receiving a call from Mr. Sung Mahn Park saying he had been in a slight accident. He was in Dunedin, in the hospital, and his reservations would have to be postponed. The clerk's reluctance to give Alexandria this information was because he had given Mr. Park his word that he wouldn't tell anyone, especially not his children.

Recriminations never came from the three siblings once they had tracked their father down. Being a doctor, Aidan flew out first, from Honolulu to Dunedin, to assess the damage. For a week the sisters, suitcases packed, received daily reports from their brother about their father's condition. He had suffered a head injury requiring surgery to relieve the bleeding in his brain. To make matters worse, his left forearm had become seriously infected—Aidan described in detail the pus oozing out like cottage cheese—the tissue degraded to such a degree that a skin graft was necessary. Both procedures had gone well, but he had to remain in the hospital until the swelling in his brain subsided and the skin graft took hold. Aidan couldn't stay away from his practice indefinitely; the sisters switched places with him and came to be by their father's side.

Aidan gained a lot of points in his sisters' estimation by dealing swiftly and dutifully with the emergency. This almost made up for his perceived lack of participation during the months their mother had been in hospice care, and the years leading up to the inevitable decline. It was at that time that Alexandria and Catherine became used to a high level of vigilance regarding their parents as they tried to share some of their father's burden while he struggled to care for a wife with dementia. What they expected of their brother wasn't quite clear to either of them. Although they rationalized that after all he lived on Maui, another island, and he had a hectic family life and a busy practice, they wanted more from him; they wanted him to be as involved as they were when it came to the well-being of their father. They wanted their brother to fret and worry about their father as much as they did. It was all so emotional.

There was little they could do once they arrived in Dunedin. They had come to bring their father home, but until the doctors signed his release, there was little they could do while they waited for him to recover. He had been a most difficult patient. The longer he had to remain in bed, the more agitated he became. His agitation turned to stubbornness, and by the time his daughters arrived, rather than being apologetic for all the trouble he had caused, he fumed. Rather than being grateful for all the care he had received, he grumbled. The food was lousy, the nurses bossy, and the doctors too busy to give him the time of day. His daughters found him in the men's orthopedic ward, in a room he had to share with three strapping males recuperating from apparent work-related injuries, full of vitality despite being strung with pulleys and casts, flirting with the nurses, bantering amongst themselves about the All Blacks. They found their father in a bed next to the window, curtains pulled tight around his quarter of the room, sealed off from his ward mates. The nurses had tried to get him to agree to open the curtains so that not only could light be let in for all to enjoy but the view as well, the spectacular fall foliage turning the hills above Dunedin into gold.

The chilly reception that greeted them, inexplicable at first, became clearer soon enough as they too experienced their father's anti-social behavior. Aidan hadn't adequately prepared his sisters for the visual impact the initial sight of him would have. Alexandria burst into tears as both daughters rushed to embrace their father. He was glad to see them, but he didn't like all the tears. "What's the matter with you guys? Jiminy Cricket! You guys act like I'm about to die." He looked beat up like an old boxer too old to have sustained injuries from a legitimate ringside fight, which made it all the more pitiful as though he had been in a recent barroom brawl or the victim of a random assault. His swollen face swallowed up his eyes. One half of his head had been shaved, the side where the incision into his skull had left a patch of Frankenstein-sized stitches. The other half had been left untouched so that the effect was like a lawn that had been only partially mowed. That side badly needed trimming as whiffs of white hair, light as dandelion floss, blew across one side of his face. The growls emitted from the downturned mouth in chorus with the untended teeth were quite frightful. During the evening visitation hours, the children of visiting family members, intrigued by the noises coming from behind the curtain and, Alexandria and Catherine surmised, the fact that the curtain was always closed, would peer under the hem. "They've just seen the Elephant Man himself," Catherine whispered to Alexandria the first time the little faces popping under the curtain registered horror and then disappeared. They could hear the scurrying back to the bedsides of fathers, hear the fathers say, "There, there, don't bother the old grump."

He made it impossible for them to keep him company all day long. He seemed to grow tired easily, tired of having them sit on either side of the bed and stare at him with a forced cheerfulness. He kept sending them away. They would check in on him in the morning, bringing the newspaper, fresh squeezed orange juice, proper coffee, seeing if there was anything he needed. He kept sending them out to find the elusive orange glazed chicken, as if they were still children, sent on a scavenger hunt, searching for something they could never find. Lest they thought he had turned infirm overnight, he'd by evening come back in full form, lifting the lid off the dismal dinner tray to be yet again dismayed at the colorless shriveled sausages floating in a murky broth. "What the bloody hell is this?" he'd say, and his daughters, having come back empty-handed, sad to disappoint him, would say, "Shhh, Dad, shhh."

The ship sailed out of Sydney Harbour after dark. Tugboats sprayed oscillating fantails of water to which the ship replied by blasting its impressive horn. On board the mood was festive. Passengers settled into staterooms, gleefully familiarizing themselves with the location of all the amenities—spa, pool, Jacuzzi, gym, library, game rooms, theaters, bars, boutiques, dining rooms formal and informal—like gluttons surveying an all-you-can-eat menu. David and Catherine remained outside on the topmost deck at the stern, huddled together against a strong wind until the last solitary light was gone, and the ship entered the open water.

So far, smooth sailing, Dad's behaving himself, Catherine wrote in an email to her sister from Hobart, their first port. Behaving himself was the code Alexandria understood to mean that either their father was keeping his willfulness in check or that things were going his way. Without giving David and Catherine the chance to protest, Sung Mahn had jumped aboard a city bus with the assurance that he could find his way back to the ship. They decided not to follow; it was too soon into the voyage to chaperone. "Remember, pace ourselves," David cautioned wisely. Clearly visible from any point in the quaint town, the ship's presence loomed large.

Two nights crossing of the Tasman Sea made Catherine realize how big the earth was. The slow passage magnified the unrelieved hours with no land in sight. Keenly aware of the ship's plunging headway, the lumbering effort of oil and steel, she'd leave the ship's sealed environment to enter the buffeting wind and lean at the railing, feeling the immensity of water. So much water.

Taking into account the average passenger's short attention span as well as trying to anticipate those demanding their money's worth, the program planners ratcheted the entertainment for this part of the voyage. Talks by the in-house naturalist and the resident personal trainers were tucked in between the major events: variety shows headlined by talented staff and crew, and tours of the inner workings of the kitchen bustling to feed around the clock a veritable city.

Despite these distractions and the ongoing food, drink, and merriment, which struck Catherine as somehow forced, she resolved to make the best of it. While David found respite in plugging in the miles on the treadmill and meditative time in the sanctuary of the sauna, Catherine shepherded her father to the morning lecture. He had difficulty hearing the bearded naturalist discuss the flora and fauna of New Zealand, adjusting without success his hearing aids until in a fit of irritation he unplugged the damn things from his ears and stuffed them into his pocket. Watching the slide show brought him no enjoyment, and before abruptly leaving the theater, he announced rather loudly to Catherine that he would see her at dinner. "Knock on my door. Five minutes to six."

She saw him later, after lunch, at the talk on lower back pain held in the matted floor space of the exercise room. The two personal trainers, one male, one female, seemed annoyed at the unexpected crowd, perhaps because the overflow, including Catherine, piled precariously onto the treadmills and stationary bikes. The female trainer had the posture and figure of a former gymnast and her Eastern European-accented English aggravated her stern expression. She was not happy to see the machines being used as benches. Her assistant was less rigid. He came across as affable as he demonstrated what soon became evident, the point of the talk. Once the trainers had a show of hands by those who suffered from lower back pain—most of the people in the room—they proposed the cure: hard plastic shoe inserts, which they were selling at a not inexpensive price. The crowd began to lose interest. As people began to drift away, some slipping out the door, the female trainer grew strident, asking for volunteers to try the inserts, to see for themselves the relief the scientifically proven angle of the technologically advanced lifts provided.

In the reshuffling of the room, Catherine caught a glimpse of her father seated in the front row. Being one of the late arrivals she wondered why he hadn't seen her. She moved to a vacant seat in the back row to be closer to him. Observing him from a distance without his knowledge saddened her. She saw that he had on the slightly baffled smile of a lost child who doesn't know how to ask for help. It was an expression he wore to hide his isolation, presenting to the world a fragile mask, as if he believed he didn't count anymore. It was the same look he wore at family dinners when everyone around him was laughing.

Her attention turned to the demonstration. A volunteer had been found. A middle-aged man in a Yankees jersey was being a good sport. Following directions, he walked back and forth in front of everyone, a set-up for the trainers to disparage his poor posture and the deplorable condition of his loafers, the heels worn down unevenly—proof that he needed realignment. When Catherine looked for her father, he was gone.

Catherine knocked at her father's door at five to six. From inside his stateroom she heard the TV: CNN. She had heard it on the other side of the wall, from her and David's stateroom, inner ones without portholes or balconies. She didn't have to turn on their own set, so clearly could she hear the news, the skirmishes, and the bickering woes of the world while they sailed across the Tasman Sea. She kept knocking, pulled off balance by the sudden opening of the door.

At eighty-four, Sung Mahn was still a handsome man. Her mother used to say he looked like a Korean Elvis Presley. He had that kind of wild hair. "Right on time," he said, as if surprised by her promptness. "Where's David?"

"Oh, he's coming," she said, mildly annoyed that David wasn't quite ready. Dressed for dinner half an hour earlier, she had been sitting in their room watching David do yoga. The mirror-lined walls, giving the room an illusion of spaciousness, multiplied the figure of her husband. She had been watching too many Davids saluting the sun.

He saw her peer into his room. He moved aside, gesturing for her to come in. "We'll wait for him. Just don't want to be late."

Catherine hesitated. She wanted to run next door and hurry David. More than that, she felt awkward about entering her father's sacred space. In the retirement community where he lived, she was used to visiting the modest apartment, staying only in the living room, taken up mostly by his impressive TV, recliner, small sofa, and coffee table piled with travel magazines. She didn't want to see too closely how he really lived. Hearing the TV as she lay on the other side of the wall transmitted the loneliness of someone killing time.

Neat, she noted, nothing out of place. The room's only disturbance of human occupation was the indentation left on the bedspread where her father had been resting. It was the way he traveled, boarding planes with just a passport in his pocket, while she carried on board books, extra clothes, several shawls, toiletries, ointments, decongestants and inhalers for an unforeseen emergency.

"I saw you at the gym," Catherine said, as if making an accusation. She seated herself on the twin bed opposite his, the bedspread pulled taut by housekeeping.

"What about the gym?" Sung Mahn asked, confused. He sat down on his bed. He looked very formal in a navy blue blazer, his wavy hair shiny and freshly combed. Catherine could smell the familiar trace of Brylcreem. Father and daughter sat facing each other, the narrowness of the room, barely accommodating two beds, made their knees almost touch.

"At the talk on lower back pain."

"Oh, that. Lousy. Trying to sell those stupid things." Sung Mahn shook his head. Then, after a moment, he said, "Were you there? I didn't see you."

"Yes, I came late. I'm surprised you didn't see me."

"Lousy," he repeated. Catherine assumed he didn't hear her. Still shaking his head, he muttered, "Lousy."

To the relief of the three of them, they had a dinner table to themselves. Although it was near the entrance by a busy thoroughfare, they didn't have to walk deep into the crowded dining room. The location of one's assigned table corresponded to the level of one's stateroom. Those whose rooms had private balconies on the upper decks were seated near the windows. Having an inside stateroom on the same level as the lobby proved convenient if not exclusive.

"Steerage," David whispered jokingly to Catherine as they were led to a small round table, crammed into a space like an afterthought. Juan, their waiter, introduced himself, releasing the ornately folded napkins and laying them across their laps.

The sommelier avoided their table once Sung Mahn raised a hand, gesturing no thanks before the wine list could even be given. Rebuffed, the sommelier moved on.

"Drinks aren't included. They jack up the prices on these cruises," Sung Mahn said, leaning toward David. David glanced at Catherine. She shrugged. He was thinking a beer would have been nice right about now. She was remembering how her father used to tell the grandchildren "Sky's the limit, kids!" whenever he took them for a treat at Zippy's.

Juan hailed from the Dominican Republic. He had an engaging smile, exerting a natural kindness, which came across as attentive, not intrusive. Catherine disliked waiters when they were coldly solicitous. She felt they often stood in judgment as she indecisively contemplated a menu. Juan was patient with Sung Mahn, who had to be told several times the evening's special.

Juan recited the delectable entrees like a storyteller describing a beautiful woman. "Oh, this one, Madam, is very sweet. The duck glazed to perfection. The skin is light and crisp. Inside, very tender." Ever so slightly, he puckered his lips. Pen in hand, he pecked the air.

Catherine was reluctant to disappoint him. "My husband and I are vegetarians, but," she added lamely, "we'll eat seafood."

"Oh, in that case, Madam, we have the pasta primavera. But may I suggest the paella? The broth is a bubbling sea of juices."

Catherine condensed Juan's recitation for her father, who still seemed uncertain. She looked pointedly at David for help. On the verge of yelling, David gave his father-in-law an even more abridged version.

"Jiminy Cricket! You think I'm deaf or what?" he joked, winking at Juan. They all laughed. Catherine was happy to see a flash of her father's old humor.

After all that, Sung Mahn chose the prime rib, Catherine the primavera, and David, at his wife's urging, the paella. Juan had tried his best. He smiled at each selection, murmuring, "Excellent." The only disappointed ones would be the chefs who needed to move the duck.

Olga, introduced by Juan as his assistant, stood discreetly to the side, stepping forward once the order was taken to attend to the minor details of removing and replacing utensils. She worked with a quiet efficiency, her eyes downcast. The effect underscored a modesty borne of an Old World upbringing. The three of them were not surprised to learn she was from Yalta.

"I've been there. Beautiful place," Sung Mahn announced.

Olga demurred.

"Yalta, is it? Miss Yalta." He seemed tickled to be making another joke.

"No," Catherine interjected. "Her name is Olga."

"Yes," Olga murmured, embarrassed to be suddenly the center of attention. "My name is Olga."

"Miss Yalta," Sung Mahn said with finality, as if christening her.

The noise level in the dining room made it impossible for Catherine and David to have a conversation that included Sung Mahn. What could be said between them had to be saved for later, in privacy. They had to choose carefully what they said, or rather shouted, to Sung Mahn, for it would be heard within the radius of nearby tables. "So Dad, are you enjoying the cruise so far?" "How's the prime rib?" Catherine addressed her husband in the same simplistic manner, as though he too were a child; she didn't want her father to feel left out. "How was the sauna? Was it crowded?" David's one-word answers needed elaboration, which Catherine took upon herself to make. "Dad, David went into the sauna today. He said it was crowded." By the end of the meal she was exhausted. Her father looked stuffed before he even got started, while her husband ate tirelessly, never coming up for air. Throughout the meal, Olga resupplied the breadbasket, wiping the crumbs away with a small scraper. The three of them watched the invisible markings she made on the tablecloth.

After dinner David suggested they walk outside. Being early summer in that hemisphere, there was still light. They pushed open the heavy glass doors and entered the elements. Catherine felt immediately refreshed, doused by the cold wind. Sung Mahn peered perfunctorily over the railing at the churning white caps five floors beneath them and in all directions.

"Fantastic," he said. Never one to linger, he kissed his daughter goodnight, shook his son-in-law's hand. "Okay, you two. See you at breakfast. Knock on my door. Five to eight. Don't be late." In a moment he was gone.

David stood behind Catherine, wrapping his arms around her. "Let's play some ping-pong," he grinned.

Catherine opened her eyes. Wrapped in darkness, she was aware of a pervading stillness, expanding outwards and, as she continued to concentrate on the sensation of spaciousness, it was as if she were at the heart of it. The ship's rocking, which she had at first resisted and then grown to like, had ceased. They had reached Milford Sound. Without waking David, she threw on a jacket and slipped out. She rode the elevator to the eleventh floor to the open decks where those who had risen before her stood at the railings. No one was talking. No one was taking pictures. On every face there was a soft expression of reverence.

The sun had yet to rise above the mountains. The sound, still deep in shadow, held the cold silence of night. A spectrum of blue and green surrounded them—the water flat and shiny as a field of steel, the mist rising like smoke into the trees, and the trees, slowly coming into light, revealed their dazzling leaves. It was as if they were in an arena of unimaginable beauty and, as the sun rose, the sky poured in.

Catherine saw her father first. She was glad she did. Ever mindful of the time whenever she was with him, she would have knocked on his door at five to eight as he requested and finding no answer, she would have worried. Seeing him on deck eliminated that scenario. He was taking a picture for a couple. They leaned into each other like newlyweds. Catherine recognized the man as the hapless volunteer whose unevenly worn loafers had been disparaged by the trainers.

"Oh, Kitty," her father chuckled as she came up to hug him. He handed the camera to the couple, who waved their thanks and turned back to the view, arms around each other.

Her father's hearty greeting warmed Catherine. And she liked it when he called her by her pet name. He always chuckled, as if to say what a coincidence if she saw him out of context, in a circumstance different from the designated place and time. He was a man who let the little coincidences of life surprise him, while the great mysteries went unnoticed.

"What are you doing here?" he asked, kissing her cheek.

"Same as you."

"Where's David?"

"Sleeping."

"Well, wake him up. He can't miss this." Her father made a grand gesture, his arms sweeping the view.

David found them later, eating breakfast in the sunshine on the terrace deck. "Good job," he told Catherine, acknowledging the feat it took to find a vacant table in the coveted spot. The wild crossing of the Tasman Sea had left the terrace damp, and although the workers had tried to keep the tables and chairs dry, it had been too cold and windy but for the stalwart.

When David went for seconds, Sung Mahn sighed. It felt like a sigh he had been saving for a long time. "Oh, Kitty, I sure wish your mother were here."

"I know," Catherine said, her mouth tightening. "I know you do."

He sighed again, shaking his head. She never knew what to make of it, whether he shook his head in disbelief that his wife was dead, or regret. Catherine supposed it was both. A part of her wanted to cry out "Then why were you so mean to her?" He had been truly cruel: the unrelenting control, the merciless teasing at her penny-pinching—"You're gonna nickel-and-dime me to death!" Catherine remembered her father shouting as her mother pursued him around the house for an accounting of expenditures, criticizing her increasingly more boisterous laughter at gatherings, wanting at his side the once demure wife. Later, when she stumbled and fell, the insidious disease that would damage the pathways in her brain silently at work, he was unable to grasp what was happening and could only poke fun at her clumsiness. In the end it was fear that made him mean. Her mother lay mute, the dementia solidifying what had once been a supple and lithe person into a carcass that was no longer recognizable. He had wrung the very last bit from her, and still she wanted to please him. Her mother had wanted to please him, struggling to swallow one more spoonful because he couldn't stop feeding her. He couldn't help himself.

The day in the sound was the last sunny day. After that glorious day they encountered dreary weather. In Dunedin they took the shuttle into the town center. In a strange way it was like coming home for Catherine. She and Alexandria had spent so much time wandering the streets. She expected her father to feel the same way, but as usual, whenever she expected him to respond the way she thought he should, he disappointed her. David wanted to see the art museum, steps away from where the shuttle dropped them off. Sung Mahn complied, growing bored quickly. He walked through the museum as if he were walking through an airport corridor, seeing nothing on the walls. Although he had been to Dunedin with her mother many times, he had never taken her to see the museum. Some flickering recognition, Catherine knew, would have lit up within her mother had she been allowed to stand as long as she wanted at each painting. Each painting, a window opening to a view—landscape or face—rendered by someone who had really looked. To really look required love.

Her mother never had the chance, for it was always only what he wanted to see, and what he wanted to see could be seen from the window of a car or a bus, to pleasantly pass through scenes that required minimal interaction on his part. Catherine could hear her mother's voice suggesting a visit to the museum, a hopeful hinting, all she could muster against her father's rigid itinerary.

Sung Mahn was anxious to catch the city bus. Catherine had already decided they would first visit the hospital. He looked at his daughter, as if she were joking. "Really? Must we?"

"C'mon, Dad," Catherine said brightly. She was thinking of the hours until they had to return to the ship. She didn't know what else to do with him. "Don't you want to see the hospital?"

"No." He spat out the word. It made her feel small.

"But you spent a month there." Catherine felt squeezed between trying to convince her father to see the hospital and trying to recall where exactly it was. "You always talk about how nice they were to you."

"The food was lousy." Sung Mahn was starting to shut down.

Catherine knew she had cornered him. If she didn't find the hospital soon, he would flee. He would hop on a passing bus. "And it cost you nothing. You spent a month in that hospital, and they didn't charge you a cent." She wanted some kind of admission from him. She could feel herself poised for a confrontation. David glanced at his wife. He had seen that determined expression before.

Sung Mahn grumbled. "Jiminy Cricket. Is she always like this," he asked David, clearly wanting his daughter to hear, "so one-track minded?"

"The nut doesn't fall far from the tree," David said without a trace of humor.

Catherine slowed down, and then stopped. The hospital was a block farther than she had thought.

Her father seized upon her hesitation. "Boy, this sure looks familiar," he said facetiously, pointing to a sushi restaurant. "Just like your mother, no sense of direction."

David saw his wife's face crumple. "How can you say that?" she cried. People on the sidewalk turned to stare. Thrusting his face at her, she felt he was mocking her. His face suddenly looked ugly. As ugly as my own, she thought, stepping back. Lowering her voice just enough so there would be no mistaking, she said, "Mom was right. She always told me you killed her fight."

"No!" Sung Mahn covered his ears. That, and the way he said "Kitty," sadly, made her feel ashamed.

David grabbed Catherine by the elbow. "C'mon. Quit it. Is this the way?"

She nodded, tears of frustration began spilling down her cheeks. "He makes me so fucking mad," she muttered.

"I know," David said, "but you just have to let him be. You're not going to change him. Not now." He turned to make sure his father-in-law was following them. He was, although he had slowed his pace considerably.

"Is that it?" David asked, pointing to an institutional building occupying an entire block. Catherine nodded, and David, taking the lead, walked into the lobby. Sung Mahn followed, passing his daughter, as if nothing had happened. Catherine reminded herself to be very nice to her husband. Her father looked around at the vinyl-covered chairs, the reception desk, the donut-slash-gift shop, and pronounced, "Okay. I've seen enough."

They decided to go their separate ways, reminding one another that the last shuttle to the ship left the town center at four. David headed back to the museum, Sung Mahn caught the city bus, and Catherine just wanted to be alone. She mumbled something about going shopping.

She walked along George Street, but nothing interested her. She thought about buying a present for her sister, but when she went into a gift shop, she found the selection of sheep skin rugs, shell pendants, T-shirts, and jars of honey and lanolin cream overwhelming. She thought about going back to the ship, peeling off her wet clothes, and crawling into bed. How in the dark sealed chamber she would be gently rocked.

She left the shop, heading in the direction of the town center. As she came to a crosswalk, she noticed a group of young men waiting for the light signal to change. They were joking and laughing and, as one of them reached to playfully punch another, she recognized Juan, the waiter. Out of uniform, in a plaid hoodie, jeans, and sneakers, he passed for a teenager. She didn't want to be seen by him. Abruptly, she turned around and started walking.

The last time she was in Dunedin, it was April, the leaves were turning, and she was with Alexandria. They had walked up and down George Street, stepping into every shop, buying presents for the family, as though they were on holiday. They sat in coffee shops, spent time in the museums, returning to the motel with cartons of take-away food. She realized now they were being nice to themselves, fortifying themselves for the next hospital visit. Their father had no idea of the effect he had on his daughters.

On Easter morning, while cathedral bells rang throughout the city, the sisters had climbed a hill to the Dhargyey Buddhist Centre, having seen a flyer advertising a talk on Three Principal Aspects of the Path to be given by the young resident lama. On Royal Terrace among a row of old mansions, they had found it, the porch draped with a garland of prayer flags. There were roses in the garden, magnificent ones—coral-colored and lavender-hued—each the size of a child's small face.

In the great hall that was once a wealthy family's formal sitting room, the sisters had listened to the young lama. He couldn't have been more than twenty-four. He looked like an overgrown boy with his soft body and soft face. He spoke in long Tibetan passages while an interpreter, a professor from the University of Otago, waited to translate for the group of mostly angular, gray-haired women. Between the two of them, the deliverance was seamless—with her eyes closed, Catherine could barely tell where the Tibetan ended and the English began. So much of it had gone over her.

For four hours she had sat on a cushion, eyes closed, letting the two languages dissolve into one sound, humming a blue color in her mind. It could have been the sky in the high window above the lama's seat she saw just before closing her eyes, but as long as she offered no resistance, the blue remained constant, shimmering through her. She had the feeling of being suspended in that great hall, its walls and ceiling shifting, curving into a globe, round and perfect as a single compassionate tear.

Standing in the rose garden in the rain, Catherine buried her face in a fragrance of petals. She never thought she'd return to Dunedin once she and Alexandria had ferried their father home. How unlikely, she thought, to have returned, to be standing in this garden, in the rain, alone. She spun the heavy prayer wheel beside the front door. She supposed if she knocked someone would let her in. She remembered a young woman serving tea and cookies on the porch after the lama's discourse. She remembered feeling happy and rested, as if she had woken from a long nap. She remembered the lama's smiling eyes, the garden sparkling in the noon light, the prayer flags fluttering above them.

Her thoughts turned to her mother who had traveled the world with her father, visiting towns like Dunedin more times than she had probably wanted. Her mother never saw the Dhargyey Buddhist Centre. Traveling with her father, her mother had seen only what he had wanted to see, a blurred view from a city bus. Her mother never got to eat a region's authentic cuisine. She had eaten only what he had wanted to eat, finding herself invariably at a food court in a mall in a country she finally couldn't name, as if the only way to endure his persuasion was to collapse. In the end she simply went numb, for nothing she said or felt or thought counted.

It was a curious thing, her father's need to travel. It was never about discovery but rather a balm for a deep affliction. Of the many obstacles to liberation, restlessness looms large. Her mother had seen it coming, long before he retired. At his insistence her mother quit her part-time job at the museum library, a job she enjoyed, to keep him company. She kept him company for the next twenty years until she got sick. During her confinement, until her death, he stayed put. After she died, her father's restlessness grew worse.

It began to rain in earnest. Standing among the drenched roses, Catherine knew the rain would destroy the petals by morning, after they had left Dunedin, heading up the coast toward Christchurch. She thought of her father traveling alone on the city bus, the rain-streaked windows blurring the streets, the shops, the houses on the hillside—how much he missed her mother—traveling the land of the long white cloud, looking for her. He would ride to the end of the line, wait, never leaving his seat, wait to return back the way he came, while the bus driver changed the sign.

All the Love in the World

Sunday was the one day of the week Sung Mahn Park looked forward to. He met what remained of the old gang—Harriet, Janet, and Molly—at seven-thirty in the morning for breakfast at Zippy's on Piʻikoi. Molly's son, Warren, in recent years had joined the group, bringing his mother when she could no longer drive. They sat at their customary table, waiting for Thelma, the Filipina waitress, to bring "the usual"—chilled halves of papaya and cornbread. Only the men ordered coffee as the women, who had given up coffee, were brought mugs of hot water. They shunned even tea. They had been meeting together like this for so long, there was nothing left to say to each other. It was enough to show up every Sunday, as if by making the effort, they kept each other going.

By eight o'clock Sung Mahn was off to Home Depot's garden shop to buy flowers for the graves at Nuʻuanu. By nine-thirty he was at the first of the seven graves he would visit, the grave of his wife. He always bought Eleanor the biggest pot of flowers. Catherine, his daughter, would find him there, just as he was finishing replacing last week's flowers with fresh ones. Catherine accompanied him as he made the rounds to the other graves, those of his parents, his grandsons who had died in infancy, his nephew, his brother, and Jimmy, his co-pilot of many years. Sung Mahn had a way of greeting his daughter that let her know he was pleased to see her, chuckling as he uttered her pet name Kitty and lifting the brim of her hat to give her a kiss on the cheek. At the same time, he let her know that she was "too much," "crazy," as if she didn't have better things to do than leave her husband on a Sunday morning and show up at the cemetery. The times she didn't appear, he made light of her absence and completed the mission alone. Every week the distances between the graves seemed to grow longer.

Duties done, he drove back to the retirement community in time for lunch, which was served at noon. He would have an hour to rest before he boarded the Sunday afternoon shuttle bus ride, a treat offered to the residents. The routes varied according to the driver's whim, but Sung Mahn didn't care where they were taken—up the mountain, around the coast, through the tunnels. He suspected the others dozing on the bus didn't care either. It was better than sitting alone watching the TV.

The phone was ringing in the holster he wore attached to his belt. The phone had been ringing quite a while before Sung Mahn heard it, or rather felt it, the insistent vibration at his side. Paul and Ann, his two mealtime companions at the retirement home, both of them spouseless like himself, heard it, but excusing his lack of hearing, went on eating. They excused each other for a lot of things. The lack of conversation, mainly. They were just grateful to sit beside a familiar face at mealtimes.

"Hello?" He opened the flip top phone, covering his mouth with his free hand so as not to disturb the other two at the table.

"Dad?"

"Hello?"

"Dad!"

"Alex?"

"No, it's Kitty."

"Who?"

"Kitty!"

"Why hello, my dear. What's up?"

Catherine sounded irritated. "Where are you? I've been trying to reach you all morning."

"Why, I'm having breakfast."

"At Zippy's?"

"What?"

"Are you at Zippy's?"

"Please? Please, what?"

Catherine increased the volume of her voice and enunciated with exaggeration. He hated when she did that. "Dad, are you at Zippy's?"

"Why?"

"Why?" She began to speak fast again. She sounded breathless as if she had been running, searching for him. "Because it's raining, and I don't want you to drive in the rain. Don't go to Home Depot. Forget the flowers. Don't go to the grave. We'll go later, when it stops raining, okay?"

"Okay," he said. Lately, he knew it was better to just say okay to his two daughters even when he didn't know what he was agreeing to.

Catherine didn't seem satisfied. "Dad," she said with a finality that seemed to dislodge the plug that kept him from hearing, "where are you?"

"Why, I'm at Hawai'i Kai having breakfast."

"So you're not at Zippy's?"

"No."

Father and daughter, linked by the wonders of technology, came to the same realization. He had forgotten to meet the gang at Zippy's. He had forgotten it was Sunday.

Harriet sat alone at the table waiting for Mahny. Janet and Molly had called the night before to let her know they wouldn't be at breakfast. They both weren't feeling well. Mahny was usually good about calling if he wasn't coming. Since he hadn't called, Harriet figured it would be just the two of them at breakfast.

It had happened before when it was just the two of them. At such times Mahny became more present to the moment, a glimmer of the old vitality apparent. Sitting across the table from her, he could see her sadness, which made him forget his. He would mention her late husband Nigel and say what he always said to make her feel better, what a great friend Nigel had been, and, if it hadn't been for Nigel, he would never have experienced New Zealand. "God's country," he would say to Harriet, reminding her that it was Nigel who had first taken him there. Having heard it before, Harriet still liked hearing it. She had lost Nigel several years before Mahny lost Eleanor, but she found it endearing the way Mahny kept her husband's memory alive.

After Eleanor died, Mahny made pilgrimages to the places he and Eleanor had enjoyed—New Zealand, Australia, Southeast Asia. Harriet, sitting alone at Zippy's, remembered how Mahny, returning from his travels, would bear gifts for the breakfast widows, emptying the contents of plastic sacks like an Old World merchant. Pashmina shawls from Vietnam, beaded drawstring purses and fashion wristwatches from Hong Kong's Ladies Market would come spilling out, a pile of silk and jewels from which, at his urging, the widows would pick and choose.

Harriet glanced at her wristwatch as she had been doing throughout the hour, nibbling at the square of cornbread, now cold and congealed. With its wide shocking-pink vinyl band and rim of rhinestones encircling the round face, it was more a fashion accessory than a serious timepiece, meant to be worn by a young girl, not an old

lady like herself. She had worn it every day since Mahny had given it
to her. At her age it wasn't often that someone remembered her.

Five minutes into the breakfast hour, Harriet knew Mahny
wasn't coming. He was usually so prompt, in fact, early, securing for
the gang the customary table, making sure to tell Thelma ahead of
time to give him the bill even though he told her the same thing every
week. He had the good manners of so many of the old-timers, like
her husband, who were slowly dying off, the children of laborers who
had come to the islands long ago. Well-groomed, clean shaven, his
silvery hair slick and shiny with Brylcreem, Mahny would rise to kiss
the ladies in greeting. Such attention still managed to fluster them. In
his cotton blue zippered jacket, striped polo shirt, belted cargo shorts,
socks and Velcro-strapped walking shoes, he looked at eighty-eight
every bit the distinguished gentleman that he was.

I'm too old to be disappointed, she scolded herself. Just like I'm
too old to be wearing such a silly watch.

"Gang not coming?" Thelma stopped by to refill Harriet's mug
with hot water.

"I guess it's just me today." she said, glancing once more at
her watch.

The rest of the day Sung Mahn dozed in the recliner with the
TV on. He missed lunch and slept through dinner. His daughters tried
calling him, but he never heard the ringing. He roused himself as the
evening news was ending, managed to shower and brush his teeth.
He sat at the edge of the bed and mumbled the long passages of his
prayer, mostly a list of naming those dearest to him—his wife, his three
children, his seven grandchildren, his great-granddaughter, and all
the close friends and other extended members of the family who were
ill, asking that they get better, that they be kept safe and protected.
The prayer he had carved into memory had never been updated.

Once named, those who appeared on his list were never forgotten, their names never removed, even though most of them had died in the intervening years, succumbing to the illnesses that had originally brought them to his attention. He turned on the air conditioner, its white noise and blast of chilled air signaled the moment he looked forward to, when he didn't have to remember anything. Eagerly slipping between the cool sheets, he could at last go to sleep.

He felt more alive asleep than awake. There was nothing to forget. Every dream he encountered he could react to with the same ease he had possessed as a boy swimming in the ocean at Mokulēʻia, his mind and body fully immersed in negotiating the wild convergence of elements. Diving into the waves, he was pummeled by the crushing walls of water, rising to meet repeatedly the surging impact of unpredictability until he dragged himself to shore.

Awake, Sung Mahn held on to what he could remember, the essential routine that kept him out of trouble. The last thing he wanted was to have the police call his children to tell them that their father was found wandering along some lonely stretch of highway without a clue as to how he got there. He noticed with concern his increasing unsteadiness, which required all the concentration he could muster to keep himself from falling. It was as if the lapses of mind had infiltrated his legs, leaving him with a wobbly gait. He was aware of lurching from one routine to another in order to get through each day. He resisted taking the walker his children had bought for him on his outings. He satisfied their insistence that he use it by taking it down the long corridor to the dining hall. He had to admit it got him to where he needed to go quickly. He was never late for a meal. But as long as he could drive to Ala Moana, park as close as he could to the bus stop—repeating the section and stall number to himself like the phone numbers of his children so he could upon returning find his car again—the walker stayed home.

He would catch the city bus that would take him around the island and so take up the hours until dinner. Once on the bus he could rest. He didn't have to worry about getting lost. He could rest for a few hours. The graying of his mind he supposed was similar to what his friends used to tell him about macular degeneration, the view kept getting dimmer. Once on the bus, he remained on it until the route was completed. It was too risky to get off for lunch anymore, stopping at Taco Bell in Lāʻie, no longer confident of his ability to make it back to the bus stop in time to catch the next one and continue on his way. To ease his hunger he had begun to bring along a snack. Only when the bus passed Kahana Bay heading north would he remember to unwrap from his jacket pocket a napkin of cookies. While the crumbs fell, he watched the passing scenery outside the ever-diminishing window.

The corridor from his apartment to the dining hall seemed to have doubled in length the next morning when Sung Mahn, glad for the stability provided by the four-wheeled walker, headed for breakfast. The state of being perpetually tired was compounded by a lightheadedness, which he attributed to the fluorescent lights flickering overhead, a sign one of the bulbs was about to quit. It used to annoy him when simple things didn't work properly, when a quick adjustment, regular attentive maintenance, could make all the difference. He had other things to be annoyed about now, primarily his own mind and body not working properly. He thought he had slept well. He assumed, even though he couldn't recall, that he had dreamed. His slow progress down the corridor was further hampered by the swirling designs on the carpet wavering until the entire ground seemed to be in motion. He stopped, and gripping down on the handle bar, he squeezed his eyes shut. He thought with a sinking sense of inevitability that he was experiencing the beginning of entering a new phase of growing old.

Somehow he made it upstairs, the elevator door opening to a room full of elderly people, the same collection of residents who met every day for meals, buttering toast, sipping coffee, moving mouths in conversations he couldn't hear. The lightheadedness had the effect of making him feel lifted off the ground, as though he could float right through the middle of each table, pass into the heart of each person, and no one would feel him passing through.

He was weaving toward his usual table where he spotted Paul and Ann already seated. He was afraid they would be done with breakfast before he could reach them because he didn't know what to do with his walker. He couldn't let go of it until he knew what to do. He was afraid he could keep pushing the walker past his table, past Paul and Ann, that he would be unstoppable, pushing past the last table and walking straight into the swinging doors to the kitchen. Maybe only then would someone tell him what to do.

"Dad," a voice called at his side. It was Alexandria, his older daughter. Gently, she prized loose his tight grip on the handle and led him to a table where his other daughter, Catherine, rose to greet him. He received a simultaneous kiss on the cheek from each of them as they settled him into a chair.

He watched Alex wheel the walker next to the window, out of the way, where a row of others was parked.

"That's right," he said when she returned to the table. "That's where it goes." He said it with authority as if he knew it all along. He looked from one daughter to the other, and said, "My two girls," shaking his head, as if they were ages eight and twelve. "My two girls," he repeated, as if their unexpected appearance was a wonderful surprise.

He felt uncomfortable when they didn't say anything. They were leaning too close, peering at him. He frowned, protruding his lower lip, mimicking the expressions on their faces. This made them frown even more. He could feel the squeeze coming. Whenever his daughters leaned forward in unison, with such serious faces, he knew he was about to be scolded or told bad news. To deflect whatever it was they were going to say, he resorted to an old trick. He wiggled his eyebrows.

"C'mon, Dad," Alex said. "This isn't funny. We've been so worried. We were calling all day yesterday, but you never picked up. You didn't hear the phone. If only you'd wear the hearing aids."

Alex was speaking much too fast for him to catch anything she was saying. Catherine, meanwhile, was silently stroking his arm. He didn't like the look on her face.

"C'mon, girls. Let's get started." He turned around, ready to call one of the servers. It was as if in the force of twisting his torso something shook loose. He slumped in the chair, the muscles of his face suddenly slack.

"Oh, my God," Alex cried. "Dad? Dad? Are you okay?"

"I think he's having a stroke," Catherine said, unable to stop stroking his arm.

Sung Mahn tried to speak. Unable to coordinate the muscles of speech to thought, he was aware of a miserable spool of dribble at the corner of his mouth. It broke off like a melting icicle and splattered the front of his T-shirt. Someone wiped his mouth. Someone was stroking his arm.

He felt as helpless as he did the night the Viscount he was ferrying across the Atlantic lost radio contact with the controller in the Azores, a scheduled stop to refuel before heading to Cambridge, England, to deliver the plane to the manufacturer for a modification to the wing spars. The plane's instrument panel went cold, like the hands of many clocks falling limp at six-thirty. Held in a suspended web of time, they had flown into a dead zone. Carrying barrels of fuel calibrated for the long crossing, there was no one on board except for himself, Jimmy his co-pilot, and the flight engineer. The plane had suddenly become a flying missile of metal they couldn't control. Without the ability to land with the aid of instruments, they would most likely fly past the Azores, run out of fuel, and eventually pitch into the sea. He had prepared the crew for this scenario when the lights flickered, the instruments resumed their positions, and an urgent voice crackled through a storm of static guiding them to the tiny island.

He felt the lights flicker back on in his body, the instrument panel of his brain connecting the fundamental coordinates as the paramedics were securing him onto a gurney.

"I can walk," Sung Mahn said. "Please," he insisted, sensing the commotion around him was causing a disturbance for those still left in the dining hall. He had witnessed this too many times—the odd fascination and the averting of eyes, the pull and tug of what was to come.

"Please, let me walk out of here." He searched the faces around him, and settled on the two he recognized, but even they didn't hear him.

Strapped down onto the gurney that slipped inside the ambulance with the precision of custom-fitted shelving used by delivery trucks to make their rounds, he felt an easing of resistance. He was being delivered, he mused, to cold storage. Having never been one to contemplate beyond the random, fleeting thoughts of what it would be like at the end, he had to admit as the metal doors locked into place and he was ferried down the freeway, it didn't look good.

Flying in the dark, estimating into his frantic calculations the factors needed to locate the Azores, a sprinkle of lights in a black churning sea, the hope of finding it without instruments as unlikely as catching a momentary phosphorous bloom on the tide—he had believed then that he would die. In the eternity before a foreign-accented English-speaking voice crackled over the radio, throwing with its urgent call a lifeline into the void, he saw Eleanor and their three small children sitting at the dinner table. He saw their heads bowed as they said grace. He heard them pray for his safe return.

His body felt chilled, achingly so, yet whenever he moved his left leg, a burst of heat shot through somewhere in the lower region of flank and hip as though a pistol had been fired deep inside the muscles. If he could reach to touch the site where the pressure was most intense, he was certain to find a gaping hole. But he was strapped in tight, and like a good pilot, he was going to go down with the ailing plane. He couldn't begin to untangle himself from all the tubes, more complicated than the wired circuitry in a fuselage—tubes inserted into his nostrils, tubes poking into his arm, ropes of tubing coiled around the bed for the phone, the TV remote control, the nurse's call button. There was even a tube, a wide one, looped around his ankles, which had set off an alarm and a flurry of activity to his bedside when he had tried to get to the toilet. "We got you, Mr. Park. You can't escape," one of the nurses said, easing him forward so she could put a bedpan in place. He was strapped in for good. There was nothing to do but wait for the water to start filling the cockpit and seep into his lungs. The sporadic beeping of the heart monitor screen kept him tethered to the dim thought of being rescued, that somehow in all that ocean his distress signal would be received. He couldn't understand why he wasn't being lifted by all who entered the wreckage. They came and went, entering the scene only to stare at the instrument panels. I told you, it went dead cold at six-thirty, he shouted at them. The way they stared, riveted at the information they were interpreting as though they were keeping score of a game or watching a disaster unfold on the evening news, convinced him of all he needed to know. He was going to fly past the Azores after all.

"I had a stroke, right?" The sound of his own voice startled him, pitched into the dim room with its grayish light. He had lost any sense of time.

Catherine, who had been dozing, sat up in the chair beside the bed. She shook her head. She looked tired and sad. He turned to the other side of the room, looking for his other daughter. He needed now more than ever the two coordinates, one daughter on each side of him. Alex, too, looked tired and sad.

"Why the long faces, girls?"

"You're very sick," Alex cleared her throat, dabbing her eyes with a clump of tissues.

He sighed. "Oh, c'mon, sweetie pie. Can't be that bad, right?"

"You have a bad leg infection," Alex sobbed, crumpling over. He couldn't see her beyond the bed railing. He wished to have the bed raised so he could see her. He wanted to be able to see his two daughters.

Catherine pressed the control by the bed, positioning him until he was upright, satisfied. She quietly handed him a note. She was always handing him notes, pieces of paper which explained in the simplest terms the answers to the same recurring questions. It was better than being shouted at. He would feel comforted by the slowly burgeoning comprehension as he read over and over her large childish handwriting. Sometimes she even drew for him diagrams of the family tree, or twisted stick figures engaged in the exercises he needed to do, or rudimentary maps that always made him laugh. Her proportions were always wrong, but at least she knew where north and south, east and west were. He kept the notes along with the city bus schedule on the coffee table, near his base of operations between the TV and the recliner. There was only so much information he could handle. She titled the notes, stapling them into little books, which he had begun to find more interesting to read than the newspaper.

Now it seemed she had anticipated the confusion that would arise once he had been settled into the ICU. What she handed him was the answer.

He read the note three times. Then he folded it carefully and told Catherine to put it with his other things—his clothes, belt, socks and shoes, wallet, cell phone, and keys—all the things he had thought he would need when he got out of bed in the morning.

"So," he paused, looking directly at Catherine, "they are not going to operate."

Catherine, nodded, her eyes never leaving his.

Alex broke into more sobbing.

"And I'm not going to walk out of this bed."

Again, Catherine nodded but with tears streaming down her face.

"Alex? Kitty?"

"Go to sleep, Dad. We're here," Alex said, rising from the chair she had been curled up in. She pressed her face against his. "Don't worry, we're here."

"Where? Where's Kitty?"

Alex moved aside to point to Catherine asleep on the two chairs she had joined to form a makeshift cot.

He relaxed, falling back into an open air marketplace where he was being swept against his will by a crowd pushing and yelling, going in the opposite direction. Sellers hawking wares, jugglers hurling balls, butchers running with knives, mimes gesturing toward the sky—everyone but him seemed to be in costume, carrying the implements of trade. Among the trinkets, wristwatches, cheap handbags, he saw the suitcase he was looking for, but he couldn't reach the stall. The strong current of the crowd turned into a river carrying him toward a narrow passage where he could feel the softness of moss against his head, where he could see every leaf sparkling in a tunnel of branches. He drifted, alone, into a great dispersion of silence. When he woke up, he told his sleeping daughters that their mother had come to bathe him.

He was exhausted, barely hanging on. The line of visitors kept coming to say goodbye. He wanted to be cheerful for each one of them. They deserved to be greeted with cheerfulness.

He didn't need any promptings from Catherine, who stood by ready to interpret in the event of confusion. He didn't need any more notes to tell him where he was, where he was going, who was who. He remembered every person who came to his bedside, some tearfully, some shyly, some collapsing in fits of grief. He clasped their hands and told them what he felt they needed to hear. He thanked them for stopping by, which they knew was his way of thanking them for everything. To his two grandsons, he told James the eldest to look after the others, and Luke the youngest to be a warrior. He told Kristin, Amelia, Frances, Anuhea, and Hoku, his five granddaughters, to be sweet and kind like their mothers.

He saw everything clearly—that his son Aidan had already become the patriarch of his wife Malia's family; that Catherine and David, having patched whatever had been broken between them, would find the fruits of forgiveness in becoming grandparents together; that Alexandria and Ben would settle companionably into the best kind of old age, an uneventful one. He had brought his family as far as he could in the twelve years since Eleanor had died, carrying them alone through the rough times of raising their own children. He had no more to give. He saw everything clearly, and it was done.

He was forgotten momentarily as the room emptied at the news that the pizzas had arrived in the lounge. Aidan stayed behind, and once he was alone, he embraced his father, and wept.

"When's the bus leaving, son?" Sung Mahn asked, beginning to drift back into the silence that was waiting for him, that peacefulness of drifting on a great body of water.

"Soon, Dad. Soon."

Before the family would let him go, they returned. He could smell garlic and pepperoni on their breaths as they continued one by one to cover his face with kisses.

"Let's get this show on the road," he said, which prompted a rearrangement of chairs.

"C'mon," he added, afraid he would miss it. "Time to board the bus. Which bus should we take?"

There was laughter. He wasn't trying to be funny. He heard laughter but mostly he heard crying.

The women started to dance hula to a song he didn't recognize. The music was coming out of someone's phone. He watched his daughters and granddaughters bump into one another, their circular arm motions scrambled, depicting waves or swaying palm trees or rain rushing down the mountains, he couldn't tell. It was his turn to laugh, because he knew they weren't trying to be funny.

When the hula ended, to his relief, his granddaughter Frances asked the family to gather themselves into a circle. His hands were held in that circle. Once he felt his hands being grasped, he didn't wait for the coughing and the shifting of feet to stop. He launched into the prayer he had said every night, thousands of recitations of that long list including so many who had entered into that dispersion beyond. Saying their names all these years had given him courage to face this very moment, the strength of his voice lifting him closer to the moment when all would be silent, a great body of silence drowning out the noise, the pain of striving, the ache of continuing. He ended with the only psalm he knew, "The Lord is my shepherd . . . " Those who knew the words joined in, their voices lifted by his. And when it was over, he looked around the circle of those he had carried for as long as he was able, and said, "I wish all of you all the love in the world." It was finished. It was done. And it was good.

Forty-Nine Days

Alexandria was the first one to dream about their father in the days following his passing. She was running in a train station when she saw him sitting on a bench with their mother, both of them dressed in the clothes they wore for travel—jeans, jackets, caps and sturdy shoes—heads bent close as they studied a map, which of course, Alex remembered noting in the dream, he would be the one holding. Their father appeared so vividly, Alex could see the lint on his corduroy collar, the stubble he had missed when shaving that morning. Their mother was out of focus, a soft silhouette, more particles of light than flesh. Alex called to them, but they couldn't hear her. They can't hear me, she remembered thinking in the dream. They can't hear me because they are in a different dimension, and the crying that ended the dream woke her up.

Catherine listened to her sister's recalling of the dream. They were sitting in their father's apartment on the carpet of the living room surrounded by boxes labeled with new destinations for his belongings. Those designated for charity filled quickly. Things of sentiment—the old globe their father had used to teach them geography, the hand-painted ceramic pair of clowns, the Van Gogh sunflowers enameled on square ashtrays—were pushed aside, to be dealt with later.

Their father didn't have much in the way of possessions. What he and their mother had chosen to take with them when they moved out of the family home after the three children had left had already been reduced to fit their new life in a condo. A second move to a smaller unit required another reduction of nonessentials. A year after their mother's death, their father moved to the apartment at the retirement community, which was to be his last place of residence. He had brought only the things that mattered to him, a movie projector, a slide projector, reels of family films, slides, photographs, letters, and the leather satchel filled with flight plans he had carried into the cockpit during the years he flew. In the twelve years of living alone, he had converted his library of home movies to the current state of the art, first VHS and later DVD. Every letter he received during those twelve years of being alone he saved.

Amelia, Alex's younger daughter, sat on her grandfather's bed in the next room, sorting through the photographs, making piles of pictures of the ones to keep. Her mother and aunt were grateful to her for the help. They couldn't bear facing that task.

He had died on Thursday. It was only Saturday. The sisters had already smoked too many cigarettes, had drunk too many Cokes from the stash of twelve-packs they had found in the closet along with jumbo-size rolls of paper towels, industrial-size buckets of laundry detergent, containers of disinfectant wipes. The refrigerator was jammed with packages of Chips Ahoy and Oreos cookies as well as half-eaten candy bars wrapped in napkins swiped from the refreshment table in the retirement home's dining hall.

As they slowly began to dismantle his life, their father had provided the necessary supplies—envelopes, pens, tape, scissors—all but the smokes. He would have been outraged to see his daughters smoking shamelessly on the lanai. In no uncertain terms, he would have told them so. According to Alex, Dad could see everything now. And that included hearing. Although he had lost most of his ability to hear in the last few years and had refused the aid of the multiple hearing devices they had outfitted him with, Catherine always suspected he heard what he needed to hear. He heard what was going on.

Catherine didn't care. She felt reckless, mean, ready to bark. She listened to Alex describe her dream, detecting within herself a hint of resentment as if her sister having been the first one to dream of their father was proof of a long-held suspicion, that Alex had been his favorite. She kept her own interpretation to herself, that a dream so intense, so soon after the passing, could only mean a message from the other side. It would make sense that their father would have chosen Alex to receive the first message, the message that he was well. He had crossed over safely with Mom there to greet him. It made sense. After all, Alex was the eldest, the go-to daughter.

Catherine looked out at the lanai through the sliding glass door. The view of the strip of lawn, the pink hibiscus hedge, and the parking lot beyond was obscured by the trash bags they had filled in the first day of purging. The stuff of daily living that couldn't be given away—newspapers, magazines, junk mail solicitations, shampoo, soap, razor—the very things he had used on the last morning he went to breakfast, pushing his walker forward along the carpeted corridor, feeling inexplicably lightheaded, never to return again.

"It's ridiculous," Catherine said. "Look at that pile of trash out there. You'd think they'd haul it all right away. Can't make the other residents feel good, seeing all that. A reminder that another one of them has kicked the bucket."

"Do you want me to ask them at the front desk, Auntie?" Amelia offered from the next room.

"No, sweetie," Catherine said, catching herself. "Let's just wait. Let's see how long it takes."

The next night Aidan received his dream. He called in the morning from Maui to tell his sisters about it, the telling of it more wistful than sad. He saw their parents in the early days of courtship walking through ironwoods. It was windy, the wind amplified by the ironwoods' long flimsy branches rustling tassels of soft green needles. Eleanor wore a kerchief that matched the dress she was wearing. Mahny was saying something that made Eleanor turn away, smiling. He reached to tickle her and managed to bring her closer, into his orbit of charm. She resisted, only a little, her head still turned away as if to avoid being kissed. It was the day of that great picture, the moments before or after it, when sitting at a picnic table somewhere in the mountains, someone had taken a snapshot. Mahny had come up from behind to place his hands on her shoulders, clearly looking at the camera with a mischievous gleam in his eyes. The camera caught her surprise, the pure mirth that took over her face. Demure in the pretty kerchief framing her delicate face, whatever he was about to tell her, she was willing to believe.

The mound of trash was still there on the lanai when the sisters drove to the apartment on Tuesday morning. Catherine steered the Corolla into their father's parking space and turned off the engine. She and Alex sat in the car, unable to move, to begin another round of dismantling the remnants of their father's life. The mound of trash had too visual an impact of what he had left behind.

When he first moved in twelve years ago, their father had tried to make the place his own. Alex remembered how he had brought from their mother's hospice room the fake orchid plant, setting it on a table in the sheltered corner of the lanai with two molded plastic lawn chairs as if he had expected to sit with a guest and enjoy the view of Koko Head in the distance. No one ever sat in those chairs, and years of sun and wind and rain had tattered the silk petals and leaves. It was the first thing Alex had thrown away. The contrast between their father's lanai and that of his neighbor, Mr. Hoopai, had always struck her. Mr. Hoopai's passion for plants overflowed the boundaries of his lanai, making their father's imitation orchid seem that much more forlorn.

Catherine decided it was time to speak to the manager. They had waited long enough for a courtesy call, some kind of acknowledgement that their father had died. "It's simply ridiculous," she said as she got out of the car.

Amelia looked from her aunt to her mother. She hesitated in the back seat, wondering if she should accompany her aunt.

Since Friday when they had left word with the front desk receptionist that their father had died, they had been waiting to hear from the manager. All they had been given were the instructions read indifferently as if straight from a handbook by the receptionist—how to go about closing his account, prepaid by automatic withdrawal through the end of the month. This was the same receptionist who had seen their father every morning as he went to breakfast, checked his mailbox, or purchased a food voucher for whichever family member was planning to join him for a meal. There would be no refund, the receptionist had told them, closely guarding the small change on the counter which she had been counting when they had interrupted her. Not even, she had added rather smugly, if they cleared the apartment early. In fact, there was a twenty-eight-day notice from the time of notification, which meant rent would still be owed in addition to the amount already automatically withdrawn. The sisters had asked to speak to the manager, who happened to be unavailable. Without a word of sympathy, the receptionist had assured them that the manager would be in touch.

Before Catherine could make a beeline toward the office, Alex cautioned, "Kitty, let's give it a bit more time."

Grudgingly, Catherine heeded her older sister. Instead, they each had a Coke and a cigarette on the lanai, the two of them smoking behind the barricade of trash like two sullen teenagers.

Her grandfather had kept all the letters he had received, mostly those sent to him in the last years of living alone, even the seemingly inconsequential ones, the Hallmark greeting cards his sister mailed every Christmas and birthday, dashed off in such haste it was as if she had signed it while jumping out of an airplane. With a tenderness Catherine found almost painful, Amelia went through each envelope, setting aside those she thought were "precious." She read out loud the funny ones, those she herself, her sister, and her cousins had written, the ones with the many references to the family joke about rule number one being the boss is always right and rule number two being that if the boss is wrong, see rule number one. The precious ones also included the many uses of the term "mipseng," a Korean word misappropriated by the grandchildren to describe their indescribable grandpa, code word for his stubbornness. The sad ones were preceded by a sigh and a long utterance of "Awww, listen to this one," at which her mother and her aunt paused, looked up from their unhappy tasks of shredding, sorting, and deciding which things were to be discarded, saved, or given away.

Sad by Amelia's definition—and her mother and her aunt, listening, agreed—were the ones that verified for them a certain aspect of the man they had loved and now missed, his kindness toward strangers whom he had touched. Sending them into a round of tears was the thank you note from Bea, the driver of the retirement home's shuttle bus, thanking him for the flowers he had brought to the hospital when she was sick.

After a lunch of tuna sandwiches made the way their father used to assemble them when they were young—thick with grated carrots and minced kimchee—Alex and Catherine smoked on the lanai. Amelia poked her head through the half-opened sliding glass door, waved away the fumes to make a point. She was giving them special dispensation under the stressful circumstances, allowing them their vice.

"I found this in one of the drawers," she said, dangling a small pendant of a device attached to a black nylon cord.

"Let's see?" Catherine examined it. "It's some kind of personal alarm to be worn by old people. I bet your grandpa never used it."

Before Amelia could warn her that it was probably indeed an alarm, her aunt had pressed it. Nothing happened. No sound came out of it. Nothing by remote control moved. Catherine shrugged, took a drag from her cigarette, and handed the device back to her niece.

Fifteen minutes later, Myles, the assistant dining room manager, came around the back, up the grassy slope to the lanai. They knew who he was. He had poured coffee for all of them at one time or another during their many meals in the dining hall. An employee of few words, he had at least attempted a feeble smile as he went from table to table offering servings of coffee.

"Did somebody press the alarm?" he asked, annoyed, choosing to ignore the pile of trash bags which he had to squeeze past in order to peer through the glass door.

Alex rose to slide open the door. Amelia started to giggle. She anticipated the expression on her aunt's face. Catherine rolled her eyes in mock disbelief, shaking her head, muttering "Daaaa . . . "

Myles showed no sign that he recognized them.

"Oh, sorry," Alex said. "I guess we pressed it by mistake."

"Ho, now I gotta reset the damn thing."

"Do you need it back?" Alex contained herself. She wanted to laugh with the others.

Amelia pointed to the device. She had put it on one of the bookcase shelves.

"Here," Catherine said, grabbing it and flinging it at him. He caught it like a punch to the stomach.

In the twelve years of living there, their father had never used the alarm. He had never once inconvenienced anyone in the office. Catherine felt an odd satisfaction for being the one to use it, now, when it was too late.

"By the way," she added, standing beside Alex as Myles turned to leave, almost tripping on the overflowing mound, "we're still waiting for the manager to call us. We're still waiting for the trash to be picked up."

Amelia, by this time, had also come forward so that the three of them, who loved Sung Mahn with the fierceness of women raised by a strong and loving man, stood firm, rooted at his door.

That night Frances, Catherine's daughter, had the third dream. She called her mother in the morning on her way to work.

"James and I were fighting about something. He was about twelve, I was nine—I was crying, mad that he was making me cry. And Grandpa came and instead of scolding us, he said, 'Shhh, it's okay, kids. It's alright.' I woke up Chris with my crying. What do you think it means, Mom?"

Usually an early riser, Catherine was having trouble getting out of bed. Like her sister, she enjoyed being consulted by her children, the chance to dispense advice on matters both practical and spiritual. Long ago she had convinced her three children that she could see things. She thought it would keep them from misbehaving. It didn't and despite maintaining the myth of the all-seeing-eye and her ability to read signs for mystical interventions, they had turned out rather normal. They were, in fact, good kids.

"Mom, are you there?"

Catherine heard the concern in her daughter's voice. Stuck in morning traffic, Frances often used the time to call her.

"Mom?"

"Just tired, sweetie."

"I know you and Auntie have been working hard."

"Amelia, too," Catherine inserted, knowing Frances would become defensive, but she couldn't help herself.

"Amelia's on break. You know I would come and help too if I didn't have to work."

"I know, I know," Catherine said, feeling now truly tired. "I know you would. And that was a nice dream you had. You're lucky. Grandpa's telling you everything is all right."

Frances arrived at the apartment on Saturday morning. She arrived with Kristin, Amelia's older sister. The two cousins came on their day off. They came in time for the final push. The husbands showed up soon after in their trucks. Aware of the fragile states of their wives, they came resolved to do whatever would be asked of them. Without resistance, Ben allowed Alex to convince him that he should take the vintage stereo equipment and tinker with it in his spare time. His daughters caught him wincing at the words "spare time," but forgave him instantly when he made the magnanimous gesture of concession. David agreed to haul the twin mattress, bedsprings, and nightstand to the Zen folks, relieved that Catherine didn't ask him to take it to their house. Frances' husband Chris happily accepted Grandpa's plump massage chair, shamelessly, as far as his young wife was concerned, admitting he had always had his eye on it. His mother-in-law seized the opportunity to add the dining table set and hand-painted Japanese wall screen as part of the deal.

The women watched as the men drove off. The five of them felt as if Sung Mahn were standing beside them on the curb of the parking lot, where he had stood so many times to see them off, standing as recently as two weeks ago, insisting on walking out despite the obvious effort, to see them to their cars, telling them to drive home safely. They would wave goodbye, catching one last glimpse of him growing smaller as they made the turn to the main road, the moment when he was framed by two palm trees. He would turn to go inside only when they were out of sight.

Alexandria had two more dreams two nights in a row. As Alexandria recounted them, Catherine, who had been feeling left out by the plethora of dreams everyone else was having, minimized the impact of these two most recent dreams by telling herself that Alex's latest duo seemed to be more of a working out of residual guilt and grief rather than direct visitations. Alex's first dream, coming so soon after their father's passing, like their brother's, had been unmistakably a sign from the other side. Those dreams had convinced the dreamers—and Catherine who had experienced them secondhand— that their father was telling his children he and their mother were well and happy.

In the first of the pair of dreams, Aidan was hovering over their father who had slumped unresponsive in his recliner the way he had at breakfast the day the ambulance was called for him. The shock of seeing the flesh erupting on his thigh shook Alex in the dream as it had that morning, but in the dream the infection was burning through one side of his face like flames through paper. Alex knew what she hadn't known that morning as she and Catherine prepared to follow the ambulance to the emergency room, that their father was very sick.

Feeling helpless, Alex told her sister that all she could do for him in the dream was convey her deep love and gratitude.

There was nothing more to do but lock the door and turn in the key to the front desk. They would never hear from the manager. The letter of complaint they had imagined writing would never be sent. Their work was done. In less than two weeks the daughters had cleared the apartment, dispersing their father's possessions one letter, one photograph, one article of clothing at a time to be scattered and repossessed until the next round of dispersion. They sat in the middle of the bare living room, stunned by what they had accomplished. They sat, confronted by the emptiness.

"One last cigarette?" Alex asked, reluctant to leave without some final act.

"Sure, why not." Catherine, the keeper of the pack, rummaged through her purse.

They moved outside to the lanai, found flattened cardboard boxes to sit on. They didn't care about the ashes dripping onto the cement floor. The wind would take care of it. Eventually, the trash bags would be removed.

They sat in silence, smoking, taking in the view their father saw every day. After a while, Alex said, "You appeared at the end of the dream like a little China doll, in a red dress with black satin trimming. You had bangs and your hair was in pigtails. When you entered the room the three of us, full of grief, bowed. We were able then to convey to him our deepest love."

"So I'm the little Chinese angel," Catherine said ruefully. She snuffed out her cigarette.

Alex went on. "In the other dream Dad and I were at the mall, and he fell. I was terrified. I tried to help him, but he said he was all right. He just wanted to see Sylvie. Just then Mia and Sylvie came around the corner. She wasn't a baby. She was walking. She and her mother waved at us."

Alex broke out of her reverie. "Strange, huh?"

"It's only strange that I haven't dreamed about him," Catherine said. She was feeling even more excluded by this last detail, that her granddaughter and daughter-in-law should appear in her sister's dream.

Alex heard the bitterness. "Maybe, unlike the rest of us, you don't need pictures."

Catherine lay in bed mumbling the Mettā Chant. She had made a pact with herself the night Sung Mahn died to chant every evening for forty-nine days, the length of time as she understood the Mahāyāna teaching for consciousness to transition to the next rebirth. Although the Mettā Chant is traditionally sung in Pali by the Theravāda school, which believes that the passage happens quickly, instantly, in one breath moment—the last breath of one life giving rise to the first breath of the next—Catherine dismissed the initial flickering doubt that perhaps the mixing of practices would nullify the intention. She intended to see her father through to the other side. She intended by a show of devotion to accompany him while he was still around.

She lay in bed, falling asleep during the interminable section that listed the myriad directions inhabited by beings—female, male, noble, worldling, celestial as well as those who have fallen from grace—sputtering awake to the chorus of wishing all to have no enmity and danger, no mental and physical suffering, wishing all to be able to take care of themselves joyfully, and be released from suffering and be not deprived of the happiness they had obtained.

The first nights of chanting were done with an intensity more of resolve than grief, the commitment to do well by him. To keep

her mind from straying she struck each word with the precision
of a metronome. She didn't miss a beat. Chanting wholeheartedly
resurrected an image of Sung Mahn as he appeared at the end of
one of the home movies, from the summer of 1964 when he and
Eleanor had taken the family on a sentimental journey. San Francisco;
Washington, D.C.; and the New York World's Fair were for Kitty, Alex,
and Aidan highlights of that trip, but the points in between, Tulsa and
Miami, where their parents had begun their life together, were the real
reasons for the pilgrimage. In Tulsa they had stopped to visit the flight
school their father attended, the church where their parents were
married, the little cottage they called home. In Miami, joined by a
nice couple named Bob and Miriam, they stopped to eat at a Chinese
restaurant that had once been where their mother and Miriam had
waitressed. A man with the funny name of True Blood took them to an
alligator farm. They wanted to see the people who had been so kind
to them as if, Catherine remembered thinking then, to see if it had all
been real.

    It was a rare glimpse of their father as he was so often the one
behind the camera, directing the movements of his wife and children.
He must have handed the camera to Alex, giving in to her repeated
requests. She could be trusted even then to hold steady, the footage
no more than a few seconds as he walked toward the camera, smiling,
handsome in his black suit, crossing one of the delicate bridges at the
Japanese Tea Garden in Golden Gate Park before the reel flapped to
an end, the last few seconds a swirl of flames.

    Over the nights of vigil Catherine lost count of the forty-nine
days. She lost her way through the long Pali passage, finding herself
lost, confused, like a child in a fairy tale returning to the same grove
of unknown trees. Her mind wandered. She dropped into deep
spontaneous moments of sleep. What had begun with clarity and
vigor—good intentions—disintegrated, fell apart. She skipped several

nights, simply too tired to chant. She had lost the momentum of the beginning. She had lost the will. As the end of the forty-nine days approached, she found the effort to sit and chant too difficult. She lay in bed and mumbled sprinklings of loving kindness, ending by wishing her father safe passage to his next rebirth. May your next life, she thought before falling asleep, be a happy one.

She confused disappointment with fatigue until, hurt by the continuing nights without a dream, without some sign from her father despite her vigil, she realized she was holding onto him. She wasn't letting him go. She was still waiting to hear from him. She wanted some words of praise. She wanted him to show himself to her and acknowledge her efforts—the cleaning, the packing, the chanting, all the acts of devotion.

She recalled reading the story about the monk who was asked by one of his students, "Master, what happens when we die?" "I don't know," the monk replied. "But you're a monk," the student, disappointed, insisted. "Yes, but I'm not a dead one."

"What does it mean?" Frances had asked. What did any of it mean, that one afternoon he would be buying batteries and Almond Joy candy bars at the drugstore and six days later he would be dead from necrotizing fasciitis, a fittingly gruesome-sounding name for the flesh-eating bacteria that first appeared as an innocuous bruise on his thigh. When told by the doctors what he had contracted, he had asked, perplexed, "But how can that be? I shower every day."

She had to trust that he was well and happy. Just as she had chosen to trust one set of ancient texts that expounded the belief of rebirth rather than another set proselytizing an eternal heaven, whether rebirth happened instantly in one breath moment or over the course of forty-nine days. It was all an uncertainty. She could keep waiting for a sign, wanting him to show himself to her in a dream as if such an appearance would assure her that she had not been forgotten.

Such an appearance would allow her to accept the fact that he was gone. She was bereft as the little girl who had waited for her father to return from a long trip. Everyone else who mattered to him had received their letter.

On the forty-ninth day Catherine did not lie down. She kneeled at the altar. She bowed three times. She rang the little bell. Lighting a candle and three sticks of incense, she would end the ritual of the vigil right. She would chant one last time properly, voice strong, mind steady. She would trust herself and not lose her way. She made it through, her voice as clear as her mind, the chanting coursing into the night like an unimpeded stream. Afterwards, she felt refreshed, alert. She knew she would chant again tomorrow on the fiftieth day. She would for the rest of this life make the effort. If not for her father, then for herself. A wish for peace and happiness. A wish to be free from longing.

The Road to Bodh Gaya

Mobin Ansari rode his bicycle to work. Depending on the assignment, he left home with enough time to ride the two kilometers to Mr. Gupta's car service, where he was employed as a driver. He didn't operate the long buses anymore, having left that company to work for Mr. Gupta, who had contracts with tour companies handling smaller groups. Sometimes he had only one passenger; at others a couple. Occasionally a family. He felt Mr. Gupta was beginning to like him, for lately, he had been assigned foreigners. Mr. Gupta was very stingy about giving out these assignments. Foreigners tipped handsomely, unlike the locals who wanted something for nothing. His entire life had been struggling with people who wanted something for nothing.

His assignment today was to pick up two passengers, foreigners, at the Hotel Clarks Varanasi in the Cantonment section of the city. He knew the program. The guide would meet him at the hotel. He would drive the guide and the guests as close as he could to the river, slipping the Ambassador past the long buses, and find a place to park. That was always a problem. He would wait in the car for the three hours it took for the guide to accompany the guests on a boat along the famous ghats of the Ganges, while the foreigners took pictures of the locals doing their morning rituals. Fall into late winter was peak season.

By spring, scared off by the threat of monsoons, the tourists stopped coming, and Mobin spent that time keeping his three children dry as they ran back and forth through the open courtyard to the kitchen and the toilet and the one room that served for everything else.

He had lived his entire life in Varanasi and never once had he been on the river. He thought the foreigners were crazy, traveling great distances—more than he had ever traveled, even when he drove the long buses to places like Mumbai and Kathmandu—to take pictures of people bathing and praying, washing their clothes, burning their dead. As a minority in a city of Hindus, he understood the holiness of the river to the locals. Still, he thought the river was filthy, and besides, he couldn't swim. The idea of revealing his skin to the world made him shudder.

It occurred to him while bicycling to work through the dark, mostly empty streets that although he was a driver, an excellent one at that, that he didn't own a car. All he had was his bicycle. To own a car for a man like him was inconceivable. He pedaled faster. Bodies, wrapped like mummies, slept in doorways; whatever crevices the city offered, a living body filled. A few ghostly shapes appeared upright in the cold November night, ready to begin a day of begging, of picking through the mounds of garbage heaped everywhere.

He wore a sweatshirt over his white long-sleeved shirt. He used to have a jacket, but it was stolen when he left it unattended in the car. He pedaled faster, clenching his teeth against the cold. It was imperative that he arrive with the car at the hotel before the sun rose. Mr. Gupta had made it quite clear to him that he not botch up this assignment. If he handled today well, he could take this small group for the next ten days around the Buddha's footprint, the major sites for Buddhist pilgrims, without an accompanying guide, using instead local ones at each point. Remember, the whole reason foreigners come to our city, the oldest city in the world, Mr. Gupta liked to say, with an uninterrupted history, is to see the sunrise on the water, to buy candles from children, to send these little lights floating on leaf boats down the river.

Mobin's heart sank when he turned the Ambassador into the curved driveway of the hotel to see Pradeep Singh waiting at the entrance. He disliked the man intensely. He hated the way Pradeep spoke one way to the foreigners and then another way to him. He hated his greased hair, the heavy gold watch he wore, the way he always carried the day's newspaper rolled like a stick, which he was now tapping as he conversed with the doorman. Soon a couple appeared. They looked Japanese, but Mobin, who had rolled down the window, heard them speaking a distinctly American-accented English.

Mobin, who understood more English than Pradeep gave him credit for, jumped out of the car to open the back door for the couple. He waited for Pradeep's usual slight, which came when Pradeep didn't bother to introduce him, hissing in Hindi to hurry up and get the car rolling. The woman looked at Mobin before she ducked her head, and smiled. Pradeep's superior attitude made him nervous. Mobin knew a man like Pradeep could get him fired. Men like Pradeep Singh were always looking for ways to humiliate the powerless. With his well-groomed appearance, his flawless English, and his smooth delivery of historical places and events, he couldn't be easily replaced. Mobin was just a driver. With Pradeep, it was best to remain silent and invisible. He wanted to, but didn't dare, look in the rearview mirror. Only when the couple returned from the morning's boat ride on the river did he get a good look at the couple. They were walking out from one of the alleys, the woman carrying packages. Mobin knew Pradeep had taken them to some of the tea and sari shops where he had prior arrangements with the owners. The woman probably purchased the same quality of tea he and his family drank but for ten times the price.

They were older than they seemed. Driving them earlier through the dark streets, he had listened to them laughing, their voices young, playful. He rarely heard people that age speak so freely and lightly to one another. They seemed more like a pair of friends than a married one. His own parents certainly never spoke to each other that way. Now when his mother spoke it was hard to understand what little she did say, covering her mouth to hide all the missing teeth. His father, long dead, died leaving a worn down wife, five daughters, and Mobin, his only son, at the mercy of his younger brother. Misery entered their lives when the uncle displaced the family and took title to the house. His sisters scattered into marriages. Eventually, Mobin and his young wife—she was just fifteen—settled into the one room with the open courtyard. His mother spent her days moving from one daughter's house to another, staying with Mobin's wife while he was away during the busy tourist season to help Bilkish as the babies started arriving. His uncle hid behind the second story window, but Mobin knew he and his children watched as Bilkish cooked in the doorless shack or bathed the babies, scooping water from a rain barrel.

Mobin saw the couple approach the car. Once again, he jumped out to open the door for them. Pradeep, looking pleased with himself, barked, "Back to the hotel," as he came into the front seat. Gray-haired with thick glasses, from a distance the man appeared older than the woman. On closer inspection, as the man brushed past him, Mobin noticed the man had no wrinkles. He had the soft face of a boy and the soft hands of a woman, a woman who never washed clothes in a dirty river or a rain barrel. Around his neck hung a gold chain with a green stone pendant. Mobin wanted to warn the man to hide the stone inside his shirt. Under his arm, he carried a small black purse, zippered without straps. The man checked inside it frequently, as though he was making sure of something. His leather shoes were of the highest quality.

The woman smiled at Mobin as she got into the car. Her smile was even more direct than the one she had given him at the hotel. He thought this was most unusual as well as the fact that the man got into the car first. Despite the floppy cloth hat and sunglasses, the morning on the river had disheveled her hair, which fell loose from a clasp. Compared to the neat and tidy man, the woman's clothes were wrinkled, her bulging nylon bag hanging lopsidedly off one shoulder, the long strap tangling with the prayer beads she had looped around a wrist. The extra burden of packages added to the overall rumpled effect. Yet, Mobin could tell that she had been pleasing to look at when she was younger. She was pale as though she had lived surrounded by snow, and when she removed her sunglasses to smile at him, he saw that her eyes were green.

After lunch Mobin met Pradeep back at the hotel to pick up the couple for the tour to the Deer Park of Sarnath, where the Lord Buddha gave his first sermon. He opened the car door for them, and as the man got in before the woman, he registered surprise for the woman was looking at him, amused. Once inside the driver's seat, the woman leaned over and asked him his name. Without waiting for him to answer, Pradeep said it for him. Mobin resented Pradeep uttering his name, not giving him the chance to speak for himself. Pradeep didn't bother to make any introduction. As if sensing this embarrassment, the woman said brightly, directly, offering her hand, "Hello, Mobin. I'm Catherine, and this," she turned to her companion, "is Norman."

"Hello," the man said quickly, as quickly as one could say that word.

Mobin shook the woman's hand, rather too vigorously. He regretted a moment later as she withdrew it. At the same time, although he was aware of Pradeep shifting uncomfortably beside him, he couldn't stop smiling. "Let's go," Pradeep ordered, frowning.

Pradeep's mood changed once they headed toward Sarnath and he regained center stage. The woman peppered him with questions, which he answered languidly, as if she were the lucky one to be in the presence of so much knowledge. Mobin concentrated on the road, dodging around pedestrians, cars, trucks, mopeds, bicycles, ox carts, all spinning in a pinwheel of directions. He liked this couple. He wanted to be their driver for the next ten days. He vowed to remain silent and invisible, as long as Pradeep was riding in the car.

It was hot outside, even hotter in the car. He felt drowsy, but didn't dare fall asleep. Through the fence he could see Pradeep sitting on the grass, in the shade, licking an ice cream cone. The man and the woman were sipping cold drinks with straws. He had driven passengers dozens of times to Sarnath, but he had never been inside the park or the museum, where he knew they were headed next to visit the famous Sarnath Buddha. His job was to drive and wait, hold open doors, and wait some more. He knew a few of the other drivers, and ordinarily he would get out of the car and join them for a cold drink from vendors selling refreshments under the trees. Always keeping an eye on the car, he would do this but not this time. He didn't want to give Pradeep the satisfaction of telling Mr. Gupta that he wasn't reliable. A man like Pradeep was always looking for any excuse to keep a man like Mobin down.

Daydreaming of a perfect world where he could tell Pradeep with impunity all the things he hated about him, Mobin was startled by the woman. Through the open window, she handed him a cold drink, in a can, unopened, and a straw. He hadn't seen them leave the park. How could that have happened? Had he fallen asleep? His eyes were burning from watching the gate. He jumped out of the car, causing the woman to step aside. Luckily, Pradeep was busy buying the museum tickets.

Mobin nearly grabbed the drink from her. He didn't want Pradeep to see her giving him the drink or, worse, taking it. "Thank you," he managed to say, placing the can under his seat.

"You must be thirsty," the woman said. "It's so hot here. You must be boiling in the car."

In a panic, Mobin looked around for her companion. The last thing he needed was to have Pradeep see him talking to the woman alone.

"Where's your husband, ma'm?" he asked, worried.

"Who, Norman?" She seemed confused, as if she had forgotten something. Mobin wondered whether the heat was affecting her. She fanned herself with a pamphlet. After a while, their gazes found the man named Norman across the quiet street, standing among the souvenir carts. He had removed his glasses and was peering intently at an object. Mobin started to laugh.

"He's checking to see if it's antique," the woman said. "You know 'antique'?"

"Yes, ma'm. Very, very old."

The woman laughed. Just then, Pradeep turned and saw them laughing. He frowned, waving the tickets impatiently.

In the morning they left for Bodh Gaya, Mr. Gupta had given Mobin the keys to the car and an envelope thick with rupees to cover the cost of petrol and the entrance fees to sites along the Buddha's trail. He warned Mobin to keep a strict account of expenditures. Included in the envelope was a small allowance for his meals. There was nothing for his lodging; it was understood that he was to sleep in the car. As for the foreigners, meal and hotel arrangements had been prepaid.

Mobin felt lightheaded as they drove out of Varanasi. Unaccustomed to such a feeling, he was giddy, stopping in the middle of the bridge—much to the annoyance of the other vehicles—to point out the Ganges shimmering beside the hazy outline of the city.

"Goodbye, Mama Ganges! Hello, Bodh Gaya!" he shouted, blasting the horn.

The man and the woman laughed, echoing his cheers.

No more Pradeep Singh watching his every move. No more Bilkish greeting him every day with a list of complaints—Nadim needs new shoes for school, Kushgu has a toothache. No more hiding his paan habit, the sweet buzz he needed to keep going. The road to Bodh Gaya promised ten unfettered days ahead. Of course, there were worries. He had been to Bodh Gaya many times, ferrying tourists to and from the Buddhist Mecca, but for the most part, since being employed by Mr. Gupta, his assignments had been confined to city tours of Varanasi. He had never been on the Buddhist trail beyond Sarnath and Bodh Gaya. He had a vague map in his head. Mostly, he would rely on asking for directions along the way. If all went well, Mr. Gupta would reward him with more foreign tours, and he could finally buy a television for his family. "I'm counting on you," were Mr. Gupta's last words as he handed the keys to the Ambassador and the envelope over to his young driver.

He drove fast, using the horn to communicate with the other drivers to let them know he was passing. He passed them all, the horn's language blending into one long sound. He wanted to arrive in Bodh Gaya before dark. The open road gave him the opportunity to show his skills as a driver. Seemingly reckless when behind the wheel, he never felt out of control. He negotiated the car with ease, weaving in and out of personalized, tinsel-decorated trucks, dodging past dilapidated buses loaded down by humanity. He regarded himself as the still point; everything else in his field of vision moved around him. Even the legless beggars.

Paan, the cheap synthetic version, helped his concentration. He needed some now. Tearing the foiled packet with his teeth, he tipped his head back, still keeping an eye on the road. He poured the perfumed crystals into his mouth and tossed the empty packet out the window. In the rear view mirror he caught the woman's look of dismay.

"It's India!" he grinned.

She shook her head disapprovingly, but somehow he knew she was joking. A few miles later, he spat a wad of paan out the window. The woman squealed as most of it landed in a bloody streak across her window.

"Good thing you had the window rolled up," the man said.

Mobin needed to relieve his bowels. There were no trees along this stretch of the road, and although they had passed several restaurants and chai shops, the next one was several miles away. He couldn't wait that long. He pulled to the side of the road, and turned off the engine. He didn't know how to excuse himself but managed to say, "Just one moment, please." He walked behind the car, squatted as close to it as he could, and in the shadow cast by the bumper, he left a dollop of turd as parched as the sunbaked road. Quickly buttoning his trousers, the thought came to him that even the shit he made was pitiful—no steamy piles coiled like snakes. When he came back into the car, the woman handed him a moist tissue. Too surprised to be embarrassed, he accepted it gratefully.

The couple intrigued him. They included him in ways he thought not possible even for foreigners. He had found foreigners to be friendlier than the locals, who wanted something for nothing, who bickered over the price of each kilometer. Foreigners seemed relaxed, as if they came from places where they didn't have to fight so hard for everything. This couple seemed even friendlier. He knew it when they wanted to know his name despite Pradeep neglecting to introduce him. He knew it when they smiled every time he held open the door. He knew it when the woman joked about her husband looking for antiques. And he knew it when she handed him, without comment, without judgment, the clean wet tissue. They acknowledged his presence, included him as an equal, a man who had just shat on the side of the road.

By late afternoon, they stopped at a roadside restaurant. Mobin was hungry. He hadn't eaten anything that day. The man and the woman just wanted chai. They sipped the hot milky tea while Mobin ate an omelet. They watched him eat off a tin plate, scooping mouthfuls with flat bread. The woman ordered a second cup and moved to a table outside. When she took out a cigarette and lit it, Mobin knew she would give him one. He settled into a hammock strung between two straggly trees, enjoying the American cigarette. A slight wind snatched the curling smoke.

Swaying in the hammock, the sun slanting behind the small rocky hills, he felt he had entered a dream where there was no sound and the people in it, moving in slow motion and seen as if from a great distance, had a significance he couldn't explain.

He watched three small children gather around the woman, approaching silently like stray animals. He thought of his own children at home. She smiled at them, reaching into her bag to give them pieces of chocolate wrapped in silver foil. They ate the chocolates quickly and waited for more. The woman laughed and reached again into her bag. She took out three colored sticks, which the children started to put into their mouths.

"No!" the woman exclaimed, putting her hands in front of the children, a signal to wait. "Norman? Do you have any paper?"

Mobin watched the man fumble into his small black purse. "How's this?" he asked, producing a folded paper with print on it.

She drew something with one of the colored sticks. The children gathered closer. Carefully, she tore the paper into thirds. "There," she said. "Now you draw a picture."

On the road to Bodh Gaya, she brought out other things from her bag. Besides the cigarettes, the tissue, the chocolates, and the crayons, there were small squares of seaweed—salted, dried, as thin as paper—chewing gum, and breath mints. And Mobin was the recipient, holding out his hand whenever she tapped him on the shoulder. Every few kilometers it seemed she surprised him with another unfamiliar yet not unpleasant experience. He was overwhelmed as much by the range of tastes—sweet, salty, bitter—as he was by her attention. He felt self-conscious at first, bowing his head and mumbling, "Thank you," but as she continued to lean forward, as if waiting to see his reaction, he would chew with care whatever had been offered, pronouncing, "Very good," which seemed to make her happy.

"Can you believe it, Norman?" she'd say to the man. "He likes it!"

He was being truthful. He liked everything he tasted except for the tiny white candy that she offered him out of a tin, which he swallowed like a pill, telling her it tasted like toothpaste. He was proud to make that comparison because he was proud that he and his family used toothpaste, unlike the very poor who used sticks to clean their teeth.

They arrived in Bodh Gaya as the sun was setting, turning off the main highway onto a tree-lined road, passing fields of mustard, the delicate flowers golden-tipped in the flooding light. Another turn and they were on the road straight into the heart of the town, the Mahabodhi Temple glowing like a column of rose quartz, an unearthly wonderment. One among the many—buyers, sellers, hawkers, beggars, pilgrims, monks, and nuns—travelers all, they entered Bodh Gaya.

At the hotel gate a guard waved them through. Driving around a circular garden designed like a fountain, spouting not water but a profusion of fat roses despite the scrawny, leafless stems, Mobin parked the car. He turned off the engine, exhausted.

A doorman greeted them, holding open the car door. Before following the man into the lobby, Mobin asked the woman for cigarettes. She gave him one but was surprised when he asked for three more. She hesitated, and he said, "For my friends."

"Friends?"

"Kitchen staff."

"Oh, of course," she said, offering him more. He tucked the four cigarettes into his shirt pocket. He could already anticipate the reactions of Anil the head waiter and the cooks shouting with delight when he brought out these American cigarettes. He expected there to be speculation and teasing as to how he had managed to procure such gifts. He planned to hand them out after he was fed. They always fed him whatever was left in the kitchen. They were his friends.

Getting out of the car, the woman paused, as if remembering something. "And where will you sleep?"

He didn't want to tell her he would be sleeping in the car. He had a feeling she would upset things, demanding the manager to give him a room. He didn't want to draw attention to himself, fearing somehow it would get back to Mr. Gupta. She gave him no choice but to lie.

"Where?" she persisted. He pointed vaguely in the direction of the guard's shack.

In the morning the man discovered that Mobin had slept in the car. The man had wandered into the garden before breakfast to take pictures of the roses when he saw Mobin shivering in the driver's seat. It distressed him to learn that Mobin had spent a fitful night trying to sleep through the cold. He had forgotten to bring a blanket.

The man insisted Mobin sleep in his room. Mobin refused, as politely as possible, shaking his head. He wanted the man to go away and not make a disturbance. It was his fault. He would be okay, he said. But the man refused to listen. "At least take a hot shower in my room. Otherwise, you'll be miserable. You'll get sick."

Mobin relented. The thought of becoming too sick to drive led him to leave the car reluctantly. Mr. Gupta had put his faith in him. He could not let him down.

Mobin followed the man into the lobby, past the disapproving looks of the manager and his assistant standing importantly behind the reception desk. He hoped the woman was in the dining room eating breakfast. He didn't want her to see him like this, in such a pitiful state. How stupid of him to forget a blanket!

The man led Mobin upstairs to his room. Unlocking the door, he said, "Take a hot shower. I'll be in the dining room." He made no mention of his wife.

Alone in the room, Mobin was overcome with emotion. The man trusted him. He looked around the room. There was nothing in the room to suggest anyone occupied it. The bed was made. All that the man had brought with him was in the suitcase, closed and zippered in the corner. There was no sign of the woman. He showered and shaved as quickly as he could. It occurred to him that the man and the woman slept in separate rooms.

The spider people he called them, those with maimed limbs, came crawling toward the car. The ones who couldn't crawl—legless torsos lashed to scraps of wood and wheels—hung back at the top of the steps, waiting to chase after tourists, propelling themselves with surprising speed. Mobin got out and shooed them away. Before he could open the door for the couple, the spider people had crept back. He raised his hand, threatening to strike, and barked at them. They crawled, scuttling into the shadows cast by the leafy trees in the dusty square.

Out of the same shadows, a middle-aged man in a gray suit appeared. Distant and formal, he introduced himself as Mr. Rishi, the local contact. The man and the woman placed palms together in greeting. Mr. Rishi reviewed the day's program, directing his crisp English to the couple. First they would tour the Mahabodhi Temple and the grounds, and after lunch, which would be taken at the hotel, they would visit the Sujatha Temple by the river. Stepping aside, Mr. Rishi spoke rapidly to Mobin, handing him an invoice for the day's program, which he had yet to conduct. "Cheater man," Mobin mumbled as Mr. Rishi gestured for the couple to please follow him up the steps to the plaza where a patchwork of vendors displayed their wares on blankets and tarps.

The woman hesitated. The spider people and the legless torsos, sensing their imminent departure away from the car, seemed agitated, ready to spring into action. Mobin raced up the steps, shooing them away.

"Useless, really," Mobin heard Mr. Rishi say as they passed. "It's like trying to hold back the tide. They'll just keep coming back." The woman smiled at Mobin. "The trick," Mr. Rishi advised, "is simply to ignore them."

Mobin waited and watched. He would wait and watch for the rest of his life, until his eyes bled, he thought, tearing open a packet of paan. It was his last one. He would have to get more from one of the stalls on the outskirts of town. He remembered driving past them, seeing the long strips of the foiled packets fluttering like the tails of kites in the wind.

He didn't recognize the other drivers, who too waited and watched, smoked and talked, drivers like himself of the smaller vehicles, cars and vans. They were allowed to park close to the temple. The long buses deposited their groups in the dusty square and parked elsewhere. Locking the car, he drifted over to a group of them, struck up the usual conversation—where are you from, where are you going, how many in your tour, are they foreign or local. Conversation helped pass the time. Mobin had a lot to brag about. Not only was his group a foreign one, the journey was long, and he had been given full responsibility. There was no guide along for the ride.

He wanted more than anything else to talk about the couple, as if their kindness was a reflection on him, that he was worthy of such acts as the man letting him shave and shower in his room, but he felt shy about mentioning such things. Anil and the cooks had as he predicted teased him about the American cigarettes once they heard it was the woman who had given them to him. When she got into the car that morning, they had stood outside the kitchen to get a closer look at her. They laughed as Mobin glared at them, backing the car in a hurry.

"Look! Your friends!" the woman had said, waving to them.

Mobin closed his eyes. The day was over, his services done until the morning when he would perform all over again the duties of driving, waiting, watching. He would sleep well tonight. Anil had made sure of that, loaning him a blanket and feeding him a meal of rice and chicken.

"Namaste," he heard a voice say to a worker hauling a wheelbarrow across the gravel. "Good evening, ma'm" was the polite reply. Mobin opened his eyes and saw the woman leaving the hotel, walking past the fountain of sleeping roses.

He fumbled for the door. "Hello! Ma'm!"

She stopped and turned. "Hello."

"Where are you going?" Mobin asked, coming closer. She was wearing a coat and a shawl wrapped around her head. She was carrying the round cushion she had purchased earlier in the day.

"I'm going to the temple."

"Where's your friend?"

"He's tired. He's going to turn in early."

"I'll drive you," Mobin said.

"No, no. I'll be fine. It's just a short walk. You rest. You did enough for us today."

"No, ma'm," Mobin said more firmly. "Very dangerous. I'll drive you."

She reassured him with a smile. "I'll be fine."

"Please. Get in the car."

"I might be long. I want to sit at the temple."

"Okay, okay. No problem. I'll wait. Please, now, get in the car."

She seemed to consider the offer and, either deciding she couldn't argue with him because he was after all responsible for her safety, or thinking of the dark stretch of road she'd have to walk, she agreed with reluctance.

She saw him remove the blanket from the back seat. "I've disturbed your sleep, haven't I?"

"No problem, ma'm. Okay?"

Mobin steered the car slowly out of the driveway, long and dark as a tunnel, bordered on one side by the museum walls and on the other the high fence of a park. At the end of it, a streetlight cast a pink feeble glow. The woman could have walked faster than the speed he was going, but he wanted to prolong the drive, as if to show her he was right—look how far it is, look how dark and empty. The roadside barbers had removed the mirrors nailed to trees, taken home their stools. The souvenir carts had been folded shut like magic boxes and padlocked. The tailor from whom she had bought the cushion had carried home his sewing machine. Backpackers, beggars, monks, and nuns remained, inhabiting the night, impervious to danger. Outside the Om Café, tourists sat at plastic tables, smoking, talking, paying no attention to the ash-colored children who crouched at their feet. They waited with the patience of stones, covered in dust, indistinguishable from the ground.

She wanted to buy him a soda from one of the stalls still open, but he said no. He only drank tea. She looked around. The chai sellers had closed up shop. A thin figure appeared at her side, an arm emerging like a stick out of the rags. "Mama, mama," a voice pleaded. Mobin tossed the beggar a coin. The woman glanced at her watch, promised she'd be back in an hour.

"Okay, ma'm," he agreed, unable to hide his weariness. He watched her climb the steps. No spiders or legless torsos chased after her. He returned to the car, rolled up the window, and without meaning to, he fell asleep.

The sound of the guard's whistle woke him. He sat up, alarmed. The whistle signaled the temple's closing. Locking the car, he hurried to the plaza, going against the exodus of pilgrims leaving the temple. There was no sign of the woman. He waited at the entrance with the few hawkers still trying to pitch CDs, face masks, prayer beads, packets of preserved bodhi leaves to the indifferent masses.

As the crowd parted, he saw the woman talking to a boy. The boy could pass for fifteen but was probably older. Despite the boy's neat appearance—shirt tucked in, trousers belted—Mobin knew his kind. Wherever there were foreigners, there was a network of professional thieves passing themselves off as struggling students who wanted to become doctors and teachers, to help their families, but being so poor they couldn't pay for books or tuition. They never directly asked for money. A donation perhaps for their school. Their polite manner, coached by a boss who directed them from a distance, picking and choosing among the multitudes the likely candidates, the unsuspecting ones. The fact that the woman had been chosen to be preyed upon offended Mobin. He flew at the boy, nearly knocking the boy off balance as he grabbed him by the arm and told him to go away.

"But Mobin . . . " the woman began, coming to the boy's defense. "He's all right. He's not bothering me."

The boy stepped closer to the woman and seemed to challenge Mobin with a steady gaze. Mobin glared at him. Nearby, a guard blew the whistle, herding the stragglers toward the gate.

The boy stayed close to the woman as she tried to keep pace with Mobin. He couldn't explain his rage, not to himself.

"Please, Mobin, stop," the woman said, visibly upset.

He kept walking, wanting to kick something. At the car, Mobin turned and looked at the woman, as if ready at last to hear her. Beside her, the boy stood firm. He stared at Mobin.

"Listen, Mobin," the woman said, catching her breath. "I've asked this boy to meet me tomorrow morning at the hotel. He'll walk me to the temple. I want to go very early, at sunrise, and I don't want to bother you. We have a very long drive tomorrow. I know you don't want me to go alone, so I've asked this boy to be my guide." At the mention of guide, she smiled at the boy. He beamed, pleased with all the attention.

Her explanation was too much for Mobin. Too many English words, too much confusion. He shoved the boy, and shoved him again, as if he could stuff the boy into the night and the boy would be swallowed up, never to return.

"Mobin!" the woman scolded, like a mother to a child.

He grabbed her by the elbow and pushed her into the car. He got in, and before starting the engine, he turned, his heart racing, and said, "When you go to temple, you go with me. Not him. Nobody but Mobin. You go with me." The boy was gone. Mobin had made sure of that, and the woman shrank away from him, as if she too had been swallowed up.

They left Bodh Gaya in the morning after breakfast. The man had risen early to hand out tips. For that act they had quite a sendoff. The day manager and the doorman bowed at the entrance. Anil and the cooks came out of the restaurant to wave goodbye. The gardener stood up from a bed of roses, and smiled. Even the guard, reaching to pluck the rupees the man held out the window, saluted them.

"They sure come out of the woodwork, don't they?" Mobin heard the man say.

"I bet you feel good," the woman replied.

"I feel rich," the man giggled.

The boy had not appeared. Before sunrise Mobin had been waiting, and he brought the car around the driveway the moment she came out of the hotel. She got in without a word. In the rear view mirror he watched her scan the slowly awakening street, as if searching for the boy. At the temple he waited while she went inside. When she came out an hour later, her mood had changed.

"Okay, ma'm?"

"Okay," she said, meeting his eyes in the mirror.

On the way to Rajgir, he began, because she asked, to talk about himself. He was self-conscious at first speaking about his life. It was like trying to weave cloth with broken thread. Living as he knew it was a struggle, yet the bare facts of his life couldn't convey the substance of it. He felt himself alive, if alive meant being in a constant state of exertion, speeding forward in time, the car gobbling up the rutted roads through his effort, the perpetual shifting of gears, the pressure of his foot on the accelerator, the demands on his eyes, ears, hands to avoid obstacles ahead. Hampered by his English, when he was finished, the story of his life looked as pitiful to him as his family's laundry hanging on a rope to dry.

When his father died, he was eight years old. As the only son, he went to work the looms after school, weaving until his vision blurred and his fingers locked by beating miles of thread in a room clogged with lint clouds. The clacking sound of the treadle and the beater pounding the thread into the fabric cracked his bones, piercing with exquisite precision his acoustic nerve. Better to have been born deaf, he thought, stuffing his ears with cotton, until, at eighteen, he became the driver of the long buses, and he met the deep silence of high mountain passes on the way to Kathmandu.

Mobin was hungry. He pulled the car over at a roadside restaurant and sat at a table in the sun. He tossed the keys onto the table, threw his head back as if he could pour the dust, the noise out of it. The proprietor came out from behind a wooden counter. He didn't seem anxious to serve customers although the place was empty. Mobin ordered an omelet for himself and chai all around. The man and the woman stretched their legs. The man needed a restroom, and Mobin shouted to the proprietor, who led the man to a door behind the counter. When the man returned to the table, he was laughing. He extended cupped hands to the woman who laughed, digging in her bag, bringing out a small plastic bottle. She squirted some of its contents into the man's hands, which he began to rub together vigorously. The scent of rubbing alcohol stung the dry air.

"Can you believe it?" the man began. "I open the door, and there's nothing there. Five feet off the ground, I almost fell out of the restaurant. I had to pee out the door." The man's re-enactment was amusing.

"Surprise, surprise," the woman said, lighting a cigarette. "A room with a view."

"A standing-room-only room with a view," the man corrected. Mobin laughed at the man's pantomime.

"I wish I'd taken a picture—oh, the inconveniences we must endure on the road to enlightenment . . . " Meal over, the woman seemed eager to return to Mobin's story. She slid the cigarettes and matches across the table, as if to fuel him. "And what about your wife? Was it an arranged marriage?"

"No, no, no," he shook his head emphatically. "Not arranged. It was a love marriage." In all his miserable life, this was one thing he could say with certainty, that he and his wife had fallen in love. He had seen enough movies to know that falling in love was a miracle. He had caught a glimpse of her radiant face in a classroom window when she was a schoolgirl, before she had to assume the weight of the veil. He waited two years after maneuvering an introduction, securing permission from her family to sit through stifling visits, heavily chaperoned by relatives, young and old, on both sides.

He possessed nothing, not the car he drove, nor the house that should have been his had his mother in her widow's distress not scratched her name on a piece of paper, signing over to her husband's younger brother what she had been led to believe would be his eternal protection. He was a driver without a car, owner of a rickety bicycle and a heap of ill-fitting clothes. Mobin wanted the woman to know that his was a love marriage. Telling her this was like showing her a treasure, that despite the years, the children, and Bilkish's sad disappointed face as she lit the stove in the morning, they had once loved each other.

The woman's attention drifted, as if she had heard enough. Chai glasses drained, cigarettes stamped into the ground, the three of them gazed at the fields across the quiet road, too far from any nameable town, washed out in the near noon light.

"Shall we go?" the man said, littering the table with rupees.

At Rajgir they found the hotel after Mobin stopped several times for directions, asking at the man's suggestion for the "Japanese" hotel. After checking in, they followed the porter, passing a circular red-bricked tower, which to Mobin resembled a water tank. The man and the woman stepped inside the structure, while Mobin and the porter waited. Housed on one side in a niche of its own sat a large Buddha. The two of them watched the man and the woman light incense and bow. The stillness inside the pristine space reminded Mobin of a mosque.

Curious to see the accommodations, to see if again they took separate rooms, Mobin followed as the porter led them across a treeless garden and up a flight of stairs. The single-loaded rooms allowed a view from the hallway of the dry hills and fields beyond. Pocketing a tip, the porter frowned when Mobin slipped past him, entering one of the rooms. The man had gone into the bathroom. The woman was next door.

Mobin breathed in the orderliness of the room. Noting the twin beds, the desk, two chairs, and a chest of drawers, he experienced a momentary tranquility standing in space so perfectly arranged. The window let in light and the distant mountain capped by a gleaming white stupa. A large mirror revealed his whole reflection. Startled by his appearance—his unruly hair, his bloodshot eyes, his teeth stained with the telltale red of his paan habit, his face coarse with stubble—it was like seeing a photograph of himself, just as he was. He needed a change of clothes. He thought of his family confined in a room without furniture. They ate on the floor. They slept on the floor, rolling and twisting in a heap of thin blankets. They hung what clothes could fit on nails stuck in the wall, and the rest spilled in corners. They never saw themselves completely; what fragment they did see was squeezed in the cracked handheld mirror they shared.

The young mothers standing in line for the gondola ride up the mountain were twirls of color in their electric blue and pink saris. The way they kept their children close made Mobin miss his wife. Cradling babies, smoothing brows, readjusting braids were familiar gestures of attention, transmitting patience as families waited in the hot sun. He recognized himself in the husbands calling gruffly to the errant ones climbing the maze of railings to control crowds. His wife and children would enjoy spending such a day set aside for pleasure—a gondola ride, ice treats later after they had visited the white stupa, feeding peanuts to the monkeys, listening as the wind carried a monk's solitary drumming down the mountain—to be far away from the heat and dust of their usual dwelling. He wondered how other families managed. After counting the crumpled rupees for food, water, gas, medicine, and tuition for school, there was little else left. Certainly never enough for a holiday. And Bilkish, shrouded in black, would be sweltering among the brightly clad women who made music wherever they went, their arms sleeved in bracelets, the wind lifting the thin gauzy fabric behind them like wings. Far from being invisible as intended, Bilkish would stand out like a moth among butterflies. After a morning at the market, she always entered the house, sighing and flinging off the cloth prison, as if cursing it.

The man and the woman came back to the car and found Mobin asleep. The walk up the mountain had taken longer than expected. Earlier, Mobin had secured a policeman to escort them to Vulture Peak. Seeing the long line they had decided not to take the gondola.

"Is it necessary?" the woman had asked as Mobin made arrangements with the policeman, who agreed to be of service. Mobin told the man to tip the policeman afterwards. The sight of the policeman would deter any thief, Mobin felt sure of it. In his uniform and erect posture, he cut an imposing figure. His tall frame cast the thinnest shadow.

Again the woman had asked if it was necessary. Mobin turned to her. "Yes! Very, very dangerous. This is Bihar!" A driver had told him a story about a busload of tourists from Korea. The bus was held up by bandits somewhere between Rajgir and Kushinagar. The tourists, having been warned about such dangers, had prepared packets of false money, which the bandits plucked gleefully at knifepoint. The discovery must have been made long after the bus had sped away, for the bandits never chased after them.

The sound of the two of them getting into the car woke him. He sat up straight, momentarily disoriented. "Everything okay?" he asked.

"Everything okay," the man said. "No thieves but plenty of beggars."

"Good, ma'm?" Mobin asked, turning around to look at her.

"Good, Mobin," she said. He liked hearing her say his name.

At Nalanda, in the late afternoon light, he watched the couple emerge from the ruins of the ancient Buddhist university, walking through a tunnel of trees. They paused, palms together, to speak to a group of young nuns. The light slanted in a way that seemed to burn the edges of their robes, dispersing the pink color into a cloud of blossoms. He didn't know history well but he knew centuries ago Muslims had done a terrible thing here. The less he knew the better, he thought; there was enough conflict in the world being blamed on Muslims. Far from being devout, he was born a Muslim and would die one, his body buried in a cemetery allotted for his kind, a plot of parched ground in a country that still considered people like him descendants of invaders. Maybe Buddhists were different. The couple certainly were—they treated him as though they were blind, entrusting themselves to him, and in return, he received only kindness and respect.

They left when it was dark, before the sun rose, the moon a jewel in the sky, the night manager asleep at his desk. They slipped away like guests who hadn't paid their final bill, giddy to be the only ones on the road. Wide awake and alert, the three of them leaned forward, as if lured by the headlights boring through the dark, flickering into illumination the startled apparitions streaming past, like mummies rising from the dead. Every few kilometers, those who waited for buses with bundled possessions resembled refugees fleeing famine and devastation.

They drove through the morning, the couple dozing in the back seat, the early departure throwing a sticky net of drowsiness over them. Mobin struggled to keep awake, turning on the radio, singing snatches of songs, honking, cursing, spitting. If the woman wanted to know his life, she could witness it now; being on the road encompassed it. He drove with urgency, pressing forward, as if he were trying to get out of this life and into another one as quickly as possible. If he could get through each day as fast as possible, he'd reach his destination sooner. Yet, his destination turned into the next day, and the next day brought another tedious stretch of road fraught with hazards. Slowing down at junctions bristling with commerce conducted on the side of the road and centers of small towns with names he didn't know, he rolled down the window, yelling for directions. The sound of his own voice flew back at him, coarse as the stubble on his unshaven face.

He reversed the car, avoiding a dead goat, nearly toppling a cart piled with pots and pans. The peddler picked up the scattered wares with resignation, and shrugged as Mobin yelled out an apology. He glanced in the rearview mirror. The man was sound asleep, but the woman was crying. He thought she might be feeling sorry for the peddler.

"He's okay, ma'm. No problem."

She dabbed her eyes, removing her sunglasses. Engine idling, foot on the brake, he waited for her to reassure him. "Ma'm?" he asked, uncertainly.

"I don't know what's got into me," she said.

"It's India, ma'm. Many, many problems."

She looked at him with a directness he found disconcerting, her eyes colorless, brimming with tears. The droplets pooled and streamed down her face. She did not wipe them away. He felt he was being given something, freely, not unlike spring water.

Mobin stopped behind a bus parked beside the road. He recognized the driver. "TCI!" he exclaimed happily. "My friend!" The bus belonged to the company he used to work for. The man and the woman were left to sit in the car while he hopped out for a chat. Well-dressed Korean ladies, some carrying umbrellas and designer handbags, filed out of the bus and made their way gingerly into a field of bushes. One by one they filed out, down into the bushes, disappearing. Umbrellas popped out of the field like enormous sunflowers. Then the men came out, crossing the opposite side of the road, to stand evenly apart, their backs to the road. As the women worked their way once again gingerly to the bus, the men, zipping up trousers and readjusting crotches, gathered in the shade between the car and the bus to smoke.

Mobin returned to the car, smiling. He would sleep well tonight, in the luxury of the long bus and its reclining seats. They followed the bus to Kushinagar, rolling into the dusty town with its scraggly eucalyptus trees, passing the stupa commemorating the site where the Buddha attained parinirvana. "Where Lord Buddha went to heaven," he said, slowly driving past. He was pleased to be able to impart that information. Outside the gate children hawked incense, candles, and water lilies to wealthy pilgrims, most of them having arrived in comfort. In the arms of children the last breath of flowers drooped in the late hour.

The man found Mobin wiping down the car. It was still early, but the bus was gone. There was a damp chill in the air, a heavy mist, which would burn off as the day progressed.

"Did you sleep well in your friend's bus?" the man asked, surprising him.

"Very well, sir. Good sleep." Mobin pitched the rag into the front seat. "And you, sir?"

"Very well, thank you. I sleep better when it's cold."

"And," Mobin paused, hesitating on the right word, "your friend?"

"She's not in her room. You haven't seen her, have you?"

"No, sir." Sensing the man's concern, Mobin walked over to the guard at the gate. He came back, reporting, "The guard says she went to the temple very early." Mobin pointed to the temple across the road.

"Oh, dear," the man muttered. Then remembering something, he handed Mobin a one thousand rupees note.

Mobin stared at the equivalent of a month's salary, a month of working for Mr. Gupta.

Noticing Mobin's hesitation, the man urged, "Please. I see the bus has left, and you'll need a place tonight. I've checked with the hotel manager, and he says there are rooms in town for drivers. Please, take it."

Aware of the guard watching intently from the gate, Mobin slipped the money into his shirt pocket. He didn't know what to say. He could only very softly nod his head.

They went to find the woman. They crossed the deserted road, narrow as a dry stream bed, and entered the temple compound, passing under a large sign advertising the temple of the future, like a coming attraction. On the other side of the wall, they came upon a construction site. The unfinished temple bore little resemblance to the artist's depiction of a temple's graceful roofline rising above

lotus ponds and bridges. Before them was a massive square edifice
of cement. At a right angle to the temple was a row of rooms, similar
but smaller, cement boxes. Wheelbarrows, buckets, and ladders were
strewn randomly, as if workers had vanished spontaneously. Across a
weed-fringed pond and a raggedy vegetable garden, they found her
at a table under the eaves of a temporary structure, sharing a bowl
of noodles with a monk. The monk called out a greeting, waving
chopsticks in the air.

Once the man had seen her, he seemed to be in no hurry.
Avoiding patches of mud, he paused to examine a small garden stupa
at the end of a shallow trench of turnips and radishes.

"Antique?" Mobin whispered.

"Not quite."

Mobin hung back, taking his cue from the man. He could hear
the woman laughing with the monk. Jealousy fluttered through him,
peripheral and subtle. "Norman, come join us," the woman said.
Mobin felt invisible again. He thought he should return to the car, but
the monk was striding toward them. He wore rubber boots and a down
jacket. Except for his shaved head, he didn't look like a monk. Not to
Mobin, who was always keen on ferreting out imposters. Cheater men.

"Welcome!" the monk said. Tall and robust, his exuberance
made Mobin shrink. The feeling dissipated as soon as it arose, as the
monk's friendliness included him. "Come, come. Sit down." He led
them to the table and ducked into the shack, bringing out a kettle. He
poured hot water into a teapot.

"This is the Venerable Sung Kwan," the woman said. Mobin
and the man remained standing. "He's been in India for twelve years,"
the woman went on. "He's building this temple to train Indians to
become monks."

"Slowly," the Venerable Sung Kwan demurred. "Slowly, very
slowly." He lifted the lid of the teapot and peered inside, assessing

something. The left side of his face as well as the left hand were scarred, as if from a fire. "Lotus tea," he pronounced, pouring the fragrant brew into four teacups. Mobin counted them.

"Lotus tea?" the man said, showing interest. "I've never tried it. I didn't know there was such a thing."

"Only white lotus for tea," the monk explained. "Leaves of white lotus roasted, slowly, slowly, chopped finely."

"This is how his temple in Korea supports itself, how he's able to raise funds for this project." She seemed to know so much about the monk. Mobin wondered how long she had been sitting with him. He was aware of the ease already established between them.

"Slowly, slowly, very slowly. In India everything slowly, slowly, very slowly—permits, workers, good workers, time—very slowly here."

Mobin felt a shift in alliance, as if he and the man were now pitted against this formidable monk, so impressed did the woman seem to be by him. She continued. "It's been a dream of his since he was a young man in Korea, to bring Buddhism back to India."

"Slowly, slowly, very slowly," the monk sighed, setting out two more bowls.

The man seemed distracted, unable to enjoy this unexpected divergence. "They're waiting for us at the hotel. They're waiting to serve us breakfast."

"But I'm having breakfast," the woman frowned. She acted as if she didn't know she had done anything wrong.

"We should eat back at the hotel," the man insisted. "It would be rude not to eat what they've prepared for us."

"Can't you eat without me?" the woman asked sweetly.

The man relented. He sat down. Mobin was left standing.

"Now walking, now working, now eating. Sit!" The monk pointed to a chair. Mobin sat down without pulling the chair close to the table.

"Our driver has to sleep in the car," the woman said, introducing a new subject now that Mobin had seated himself. "Evidently they make no accommodations for the drivers."

The monk pushed the teacups across the table. He nodded, unsurprised. "This is India. No workers' rights. When I first come to India, I cry every time over the suffering of people. Now slowly changing." Mobin felt uncomfortable hearing his situation discussed. The monk took a sip of tea, exhaling a deep sound of satisfaction. "He can sleep here. Plenty of room."

The woman pressed palms together. "That would be wonderful!" She looked at Mobin, beaming. Then raising her teacup, she exclaimed, "To workers' rights!"

The monk and the man raised their teacups. The three of them turned to Mobin, waiting for him to raise his. He brought the cup to his lips and, slowly, slowly, very slowly, he took a sip.

The mist had burned off, revealing a clear sky, like a blue door they walked through, leaving the garden of turnips and radishes, the fragrant tea, the companionable slurping of noodles, and the monk assured of their imminent return. They climbed aboard a pedi-cab waiting for a fare at the hotel gate. Mobin let the man and the woman settle in first, facing forward, before getting in, turning to tell the driver to go. Slowly they set off, the driver, staggering under the load, bearing the full weight with his body, as if hauling them out of a ditch. They were quiet, their bodies rocking slightly, knees touching knees to keep themselves steady. The soft branches of eucalyptus swept the air, a cool current rustling the woman's scarf. The interval of trees and sky, sunlight and shadow, veiled and unveiled her face. In a few days Mobin knew they would never see each other again. As if she sensed what he was thinking, she took his picture. He didn't pose. He didn't smile. He stared into the camera as he stared into the miles behind them, and the miles ahead, long after they were gone. He imagined they would return to a place much like this one, not the dusty town in Uttar Pradesh but this moment, silent without haggling and cheating, vibrant without squirming and grasping, this moment, immeasurable as the space between the trees. The heave and pull of the driver's exertion carried them forward to the Parinivana Stupa.

For one day he had nothing to worry about. There was no driving to do; the three scheduled sites to visit in the town could be reached by foot or by pedi-cab. The car was safe at the hotel, under the watchful eye of the guard, who had been tipped by Mobin, an unnecessary extravagance but Mobin, feeling expansive, knew the guard was a good man; he wasn't a cheater man. Besides, he had Mr. Gupta's envelope for expenses as well as the money the man had given him. He planned to save the one thousand rupees for the TV he had promised to bring home to his family. He wouldn't have to spend it on a room; he had a place waiting for him at the temple. All felt right with the world.

He, too, for one day could be like the couple, on holiday, moving at leisure, slowly, slowly, very slowly. He smiled to himself, recalling the monk's repetitious phrase. The woman caught him smiling.

"Slowly, ma'm," he began, "slowly, very slowly."

He thought she would laugh at his joke, but instead she seemed to slip into herself, which caused her to lose her balance on the narrow bench, pitching her forward almost, to Mobin's alarm, onto his lap.

"Are you alright?" The man asked, grabbing hold of her shoulder. Mobin heard concern in his voice, in contrast to the usual teasing, which at times seemed to Mobin to be slightly dismissive.

The two men waited for a response. Reverting to a familiar tone, the man turned to Mobin and winked, "She's getting old."

"Okay, ma'm?"

Her answer didn't seem to be for anyone but herself. "Why be sad?"

"Okay, ma'm?" Mobin again asked.

"Sung Kwan said I was being foolish. He told me that there was no need to be sad about my father's passing. Why be sad, he asked, your father, if what you tell me about him is true, that he was a good father, has upgraded his existence. He's in first class now. Why be sad?"

She bought water lilies from a little girl, placing the bouquet at the feet of the massive statue of the reclining Buddha. The man snapped his camera in rapid succession. Mobin, pushed into one corner of the temple by the kneeling, chanting, praying and circling masses, did not worry about being unfaithful to Allah by his proximity to the golden idol, strewn with marigolds. The Buddha's sleeping face transmitted serenity like the drifting clouds reflected in the smooth lakes he had seen driving the long buses to Kathmandu. He couldn't help but feel that the devotion he detected swirling around him was the same as those of any faith.

Glad to be out of the sun, growing more intense by the minute, they retreated into the dim rooms of the dilapidated museum. The man seemed to know what he was looking for, dismissing sculptures, architectural fragments, bronzes, clay seals, banners, and coins until he came upon a stucco statue of the Lord Buddha in meditation. "This represents the Gandhara school of art at its height," he said.

Mobin and the woman admired it politely, Mobin trying to see what they saw. It wasn't until he saw a torso draped in the thinnest veil, which the man pronounced as worth the price of admission, did Mobin appreciate the unknown sculptor's skill, conveying through stone the faintest suggestion of cloth. In the dark and musty museum, the broken statue shimmered with light and life.

Too shy to take possession of the room at the temple before nightfall, he rested in the car while the man and the woman ate lunch. He was hungry, but he didn't want to go back to the noise and dirt of the town. He didn't want to eat at the same food stall he had gone to with the other drivers, shoveling rice into mouths, tearing apart pieces of chicken, nibbling at bones. He saw his own unwashed hands grabbing at the chapatti, stacked like cakes of cow dung the women and children of his country shaped and slapped against the sides of huts and walls to dry for fuel. Last night none of it had bothered him. He was happy, laughing, joking, spitting, downing glass after glass of chai. He didn't want to break the spell, a reverie, which had descended upon him slowly, slowly, very slowly. The monk's words floated in his head.

The man stood outside the hotel entrance, waving at Mobin. Once he got his attention, Mobin hurried out of the car.

"Have something to eat with us, " the man invited. "You must be hungry."

"No, sir. I'm not hungry," he lied. He knew eating with guests in the hotel wasn't permitted. He could lose his job. Resenting the idea that low-level managers posted in the remote regions of Bihar and Uttar Pradesh could report him to Mr. Gupta, he decided to accept, slipping into the lobby and into the restaurant. He felt somehow protected by the man. He glanced around before taking a seat at the table where the woman had prepared a plate for him. He was relieved; his boldness only went so far as did the guest status of the man and the woman. The woman seemed to know this; helping himself to the buffet would be most unseemly. He kept his chair slightly back from the table, making sure he chatted with the waiters, letting them know he knew he was one of them. He minded his manners. He did not shovel food into his mouth. He picked up a fork. He had already handled chopsticks.

"This is where the body of the Buddha was cremated," she told him.

"Like Ganges, ma'm."

She thought for a while. "Yes. You're right. Buddhists cremate the bodies of the dead just like Hindus. What about Muslims?"

"No, ma'm. No cremation. Very, very bad burn body. We put in ground."

"Like Christians," she said.

He thought for a while. "Yes, like Christians," he said, reluctantly. "And you, ma'm, you burn when dead?"

She laughed. "I've been burned already. Many, many times. In this life and in all the others."

He didn't think it was funny. "Where, ma'm?" He pointed to her arms and legs for proof of scars. "Like Baba monk?"

"No, not like that. Buddhists believe we are born and we die and are born again and again. Many, many times. Many, many lives."

"No heaven?"

"There are heavenly places, but even those aren't permanent."

He was quiet. "Why be good?"

She laughed. "Because it's good to be good."

"Good?"

"Like not being greedy or mean."

"Not be cheater man."

"Exactly."

"No reward?"

"There is a reward. After many, many lifetimes, a person can eventually become free, never to return, never to have to come back to suffer and die. One becomes liberated."

"Free." He let the word drift like smoke out of his breath.

"Extinction. Like blowing out a candle."

"Like dinosaurs."

She smiled. "Yes, and like Buddha, never to return."

"Did it pain you, ma'm?"

"What?"

"Burning."

She took in the view of the stupa, from a distance, round and perfect as the moon. "I don't remember. Maybe that's why I keep returning."

The cloudy broth freckled with green onions, swirling with seaweed, warmed his belly. He dredged his bowl, bringing up spoonfuls of bean curd, square and white like gambler's dice. This was the kind of meal that turned into steamy piles of shit, rich manure for a garden of turnips and radishes. He understood now the woman's ease, for he felt it too. In the monk's presence the things that hounded him stayed away. The things that mattered in the heat and flies became still and silent. Into the light cast by a single bulb dangling from a beam, a dog came. It too was fed and petted.

He appeared at the temple in the early evening, bowing obsequiously to the monk who crouched among the turnips, an apology waiting to be given for troubling him, an expression of gratitude rehearsed in his mind. The monk, leading him to the table under the eaves, would have none of it.

After a simple meal and a cup of tea, the same fragrant tea, the monk, carrying a kerosene lantern, led him to one of the rooms in the row of rooms reserved for guests, laborers and pilgrims alike. In the room, sparse as a cell, the monk lit a candle. "Person of no rank, noblest person," the monk said, going out the door.

When he blew out the candle, he heard the woman's voice telling him about extinction, a flame snuffed out, never to be lit again. He wondered how she could live unafraid, preferring that to the prospect of repeated lives. His idea of heaven was formed long ago, and he could resurrect it in his mind, like a child playing with a dollhouse, adding and subtracting precious objects, moving angels around. Lying in the dark, he returned to the old habit of imagining such a heaven, but tonight the angels appeared grotesque as the cheap dolls he had bought at the bazaar for his daughters. In the absence of light he thought of Bilkish, extinguished by the thick black shroud, little by little, every time she crawled into it before going out the door. That couldn't be what the woman meant. He tossed under the heavy blanket, one moment cold, the next hot, his thoughts making him restless. And then he simply stopped. He stopped thrashing. He began to notice his breathing, that the more he watched it, the slower it became until a calmness floated up, and he found he had lost the edges of his body. He saw the late afternoon light at Nalanda blurring the outline of the nuns' pink robes, turning them into clouds of blossoms. And the veil carved into the hardness of stone, he saw that too.

He heard the monk chanting at the dark hour. He dismissed it as he did the call to prayer, falling back to sleep. When he awoke, it was to the noises of his world, the sound of his language, formed on the tongues of men, like him, who spoke roughly, between bursts of spitting and coughing. When he emerged out of the room, two workers, sitting on their haunches, stared at him. Then they questioned him. He didn't feel he had to explain himself. He was tired.

He heard the woman before he saw her, standing on the roof of the temple. "Hello!" he called out. Hearing himself, he felt no better than the two workers whom he had just ignored.

She came to the edge, saw him, and waved. The man came up behind her, peered, and pointed to the stairs. He climbed the stairs to the roof. Through the mist, the pearl gray light made the trees in the surrounding fields appear insubstantial, as unfinished as the temple itself. The temple of the future would one day be higher. The monk, magnificent in his priestly robes, posed for a photograph. The man circled around him. Showing the camera his unblemished side, he seemed to regard the trees, the fields, the rising sun with equanimity, all the work to be done, one monk at a time.

Leaving Kushinagar, they headed for the border. Behind schedule, Mobin sped, making up for lost time. The things that chased him came barking back. Traveling through forests, monkeys limped and shuffled out of the trees, gathering at the roadside to beg. Like their human cousins, young and old, they huddled and waited, groomed and scratched.

At Mobin's invitation, the woman sat beside him. He didn't know why he did that, just before they left, gesturing for her to join him up front. She stared wide-eyed, as if watching a movie, as the car pressed forward, veering to avoid the onslaught of obstacles rising out of nowhere. "It's like being in the *Millennium Falcon* up here," she joked to the man, "and we're being assailed by aliens and asteroids. You've got to try it."

"No, thank you," the man said, amused. "Unlike you, I don't need the stimulation."

Close to the Nepalese border, they merged into a congestion of commerce and filth. Lines of trucks waited to get the right documents to ferry cargo into Nepal. Miraculously, Mobin managed to park the car in front of the immigration office. Flies buzzed around the jostling foreigners trying to fill out departure forms. At the man's request, Mobin cornered a moneychanger after much haggling, but when the moneychanger wanted to take them to another place to do the transaction, Mobin had a bad feeling about it. He shut off the deal, motioned for the two of them to hurry back to the car. "Cheater man," he said. "Next place we go."

They inched slowly forward, one among many, all wanting the same thing, to get through to the other side. One among many exiting and entering, coming and going, funneling through archways erected by each side—one exit point indistinguishable from one entrance point—mirroring each other. The flies on the other side were the same, arising out of an open sewer bubbling with human excrement. Ten feet away families lived and raised their children. Again, on the other side, they repeated the same action, filling out more forms, entry forms indistinguishable from departure ones. Mobin went to get the car papers, and returned, grumbling. "Very cheater men. Everywhere very cheater men."

Papers in order, they disentangled themselves, Mobin honking and yelling at whatever was in the way. They passed shabby-looking hotels. The man and the woman read out loud the names on the hand painted signs—Buddha Hotel, Shakyamuni Guest House, Buddha Air. Stationed at intermittent roadblocks, Nepalese soldiers eyed the Ambassador suspiciously. Each time Mobin got out to talk their way through. Each time the soldiers strutted around the car, holding mirrors under it, and, as if disappointed to find nothing they were looking for, with a lazy flick of the hand, they were allowed to pass.

"What did you say to them?" the man asked, the first time they were stopped, and Mobin, visibly shaken, returned to the car. "I tell them Japanese Embassy car. Very, very important!"

They were the only guests when they arrived at the Hotel Hokke situated within the extensive temple park. On a flat glacial plain, among rows of evenly planted scrub trees fanning out in every direction, temples representing different Buddhist countries could be seen in various states of construction, abandonment, maintenance, and repair.

Mobin honked the horn at the gated entrance. They noticed the barbed wire along the top of the fence. The way Mobin said Hokke Hotel made the man and the woman laugh. He didn't know what was so funny, but he said it again to make them laugh. "Okay Hotel."

The manager and the staff had been expecting them. At the sound of the car turning into the gravel driveway, he rushed out, a portly gentleman in a dark gray suit. He seemed genuinely relieved to see that they had arrived safely, and told them so, ushering them into the quiet lobby. He didn't bark orders at the porter. Without having to ask, the manager said he also had a room—at no additional cost—for the driver, acknowledging Mobin with a nod, and although it was half past two, lunch would be soon be served. Since the staff had already eaten, the driver, again the manager nodded at Mobin, could join them in the dining room.

"Kind face," Mobin whispered to the woman.

"I agree," she whispered back.

On the terrace, while the porter led the two to their rooms along the covered walkway, Mobin sat down. A young woman brought him a glass of juice. He grinned at her. She averted her eyes, bowing as she backed away. Good face, he thought. He wanted to tell her she looked like his wife, but he didn't want to sound coarse. Already he liked the place. The simple lines of the single-story, red-bricked buildings suggested a design laid out by a thoughtful, clear mind. It had a feeling of orderliness, like the man's room at Rajgir, a place where one could do things properly, with one's fullest attention. Like the way the young woman served him the glass of juice. There was nothing else on the tray but the chilled glass of juice.

He sensed the orderliness at lunch. Lunch came in a large black box. Inside the box were smaller boxes dividing distinctly individual bits and pieces of food. It was like being served a picture to eat. He copied the man and the woman as they unrolled the warm washcloth and wiped their hands. Despite the manager having arranged for him to eat with the guests, he felt uncomfortable. He had to pull the chair close to the table in order to eat, so in order to create polite distance, he kept his eyes down. The young woman, after serving the trays, stood by the kitchen door. He tried a friendly banter with her, but her answers were monosyllabic, noncommittal. The woman noticed this, and said, "Nice Girl. Big Tip."

After lunch, the woman wanted to rest. The man invited him to his room to watch TV. Okay Hotel, the man joked, as if to say it would be all right. He watched cartoons while the man took a shower. Lying on the tightly woven matted floor, he ate the small crackers wrapped in seaweed from a package the man had left for him. He noticed the brand on the TV set: Panasonic. He vowed to get one just like it. Tomorrow he would look for one, in Gorakhpur, once he had dropped them at the airport. As the end of the trip drew near, he found himself missing his family. How happy they would be to see him. At the same time he dreaded the long lonely road back to Varanasi. How empty the car would feel. At lunch the woman had asked him again how many children he had, as if it was a way to begin to tell him something. He told her three. That's a good number, she had said. Life is very hard if you have too many children. Three is enough. No more. And then she had turned away, embarrassed, as if she had said too much.

He heard a mechanical whirring sound coming from the bathroom. When the man came out, he asked the man about it. The man looked puzzled. He imitated the sound of buzzing. Oh, this? The man showed him a device that blew out hot air. The man demonstrated, moving the device back and forth over his head. "It's a hair dryer." The man let it blow across Mobin's hair. He took it with him when he went to his own room, to try it, after he showered that night.

Unable to sleep, he left his room in the staff quarters, and went out to the terrace. He sat in the dark and smoked. A light turned on in her room. He felt reckless, as if he had nothing to lose. He cut across the wet grass, shivering. He heard water running, and then splashing. After a long silence, he knocked. She opened the door, her hair wrapped in a white towel. She was wearing glasses and a cotton robe patterned with small blue flowers. He offered no explanation, no apology. She stepped aside, and he came in.

He sat on the floor at a low table. She started to make tea, plugging in the electric pot. They said nothing while the water boiled. He watched her dip tea bags into cups. He watched her pour the hot water. A green smell like the wet grass outside rose up. Her glasses misted with steam. He wanted sugar and milk. She handed him packets of sugar and powdered cream. And then a spoon.

Only when he had finished stirring did he speak. He knew that she knew his life, he said. She had seen it on the road, somewhere after Rajgir, before Kushinagar, when she cried. He knew the tears were for him. He had no other way to say this to her, but to seek her out in this way. He never would do such a thing otherwise, to knock on her door, but he felt safe here, and there might not be another chance to tell her that he knew this. He had driven many people over many miles, and many of them had been kind. They had treated him well, some had been sympathetic, but no one had seen what she had seen—the hounds chasing him. "No work, no money. No money, no food." That was his life. No one had understood this. The repetition of his life.

He stopped, exhausted. He didn't realize he had been carrying these words, these words gathering force as they got closer to the end of the road.

I could have been your mother, she told him. Maybe not in this life but in another one.

His mother's face, withered as a dried fig, dropped like the tea bag into his mind. Instead of a green scent arising, he sensed the odor of something bitter. For as long as he could remember, he had been taking care of her. He was like her father, his mother the helpless one. How little she asked for, taking up the smallest space in the room. Unveiled now, she no longer needed to hide her face.

Even touching sleeves reveals a deep bond from another life, she told him. And we've touched more than sleeves, haven't we, she said, on this road together. We've done more than just brushed past each other.

At Kapilavastu he kept an eye on the car. He didn't follow the man and the woman into the ruins of the palace, where the Lord Buddha had lived as a prince, before he gave up everything. He was concerned when he dropped them off, thinking the palace was beyond the grassy field. "There wasn't much to see," the man said, returning to the car, "not even ruins."

At Lumbini, he wanted to see the birthplace of the Lord Buddha, but he had to guard the car. He wanted to be able to tell his children that he had seen the place where the Lord Buddha was born. It was important for them to know that their father had been to important places in his life. He could tell them he had seen the place where the Lord Buddha died and the place where his body was burned. He could tell them about a woman he once met who believed in extinction and something about the brushing of sleeves.

By three the sun was slanting low. They had two hours before the sun went down, two hours to visit some of the temples within the park. Mobin drove slowly, as if there was nowhere to go. We're already here, he thought. We have arrived. In the hours before dark, he didn't want to leave the serene grounds of the hotel, which they had enjoyed all to themselves, an atmosphere created by the kind-hearted manager. As with Baba monk's temple, he felt safe. Finally, he could rest.

Into the neglected garden of the Burmese Temple, he walked behind her. She was quiet as she had been since the morning when he came to her room, initiating nothing, speaking only when spoken to. She had stopped taking pictures. They walked into the small temple as though they were visiting a house belonging to friends. A dusty chandelier hung from the ceiling like a decoration forgotten long ago. The house needed sweeping, wind-blown leaves gathering in corners. She bowed at the shrine at the moment light was streaming into the western window. She looked sad. He didn't want to remember her that way.

Mobin drove slowly. There was nowhere to go. All the temples had been visited. He positioned the car along an open field so that the man, leaning out the window, could take a few more pictures. They had traveled hundreds of miles together, all the moments lived apart to meet at this junction, the man and the woman having traveled across the world to slip into the door he held open for them. The gradual accumulation of a look, a feeling, accelerating with each mile they burned through together, meeting on the road to Bodh Gaya, in the bracket of timeless space in Kushinagar, and now, the end of the road, the last stop, quiet, safe, expansive as the glacial field in the forest, in the garden that was Lumbini.

Acknowledgments

For expertise & insight, encouragement & friendship
and, above all else, kindness & generosity—
the Bamboo Ridge 'ohana, especially Joy Kobayashi-Cintrón, Juliet S.
Kono, Gail N. Harada, and Wing Tek Lum; Andrea Gelber and Alan
Song, together we rode the waves on *Catalange*; Douglas Davenport,
who steered us through some of these waves; Ellen Soo Sun Song
Kang, chronicler of family stories; David Chock, who cheerfully
responded to all questions aeronautical; Deborah Pope, who led me
through, among other places, the Alhambra; Deborah Buccigrossi,
who told me to write the story as we sat at a sidewalk cafe in Florence;
and Naomi Shihab Nye, who was there at the end and at the
beginning—

my love and gratitude

Cathy Song is the author of five books of poetry, including *Picture Bride*, which won the Yale Series of Younger Poets Award and was nominated for a National Book Critics Circle Award. A recipient of the Hawaiʻi Award for Literature, she divides her time between Honolulu and Volcano on Hawaiʻi Island.

Poetry collections by Cathy Song

Picture Bride
Frameless Windows, Squares of Light
School Figures
The Land of Bliss
Cloud Moving Hands